Last Chance Mill

# Last Chance Mill

Susan Iona Swan

Wright On books

## Dedication

Thanks to Kevin and Daisy for their humour and support and endless cups of tea.

And thanks to all those of you who live with the threat of flooding. You inspired this story.

# Chapter 1

Dawn couldn't decide whether moving from London to Devon was the best thing they'd ever done or the worst. She glanced across at her husband who was thrumming his hand on the steering wheel and singing along to his favourite Canned Heat track about leaving the city. No need to ask what he thought. Her reservations rose as they turned down a lane where grass was growing up the middle. The high hedges on either side made it seem more of a bobsleigh track than a road. Douglas had just admitted they were lost when she glimpsed a sign nailed to a tree: Last Chance Mill.

'This is it. Next left.'

He swung the car down a rutty track, scattering pheasants and splashing through puddles.

'I wish we'd found a place with a cheerier name,' she said with a sigh.

'Well Crouch End doesn't sound very cheery and you loved living there.' He turned off the radio. The silence was abrupt.

'So I did.' Her voice shook.

They parked in a gravelled area next to some willow trees and she stepped from the car and stretched while Douglas rummaged in the glove compartment.

'Well, we're here,' he said, holding up a large rusty key as if it unlocked the gate to paradise. 'A new start. A chance to achieve my ikigai.'

'Your icky-what?'

'My ikigai. Becky sent me the book after I lost my job. It's a Japanese principle where you identify what you love, what you're good at, how you can make money from it, and I've forgotten the other thing. Oh yes, I remember, what the

1

world needs. That's how I came up with the art holidays idea.'

So she had her daughter to thank for this uprooting. Dawn opened the boot and pulled out their suitcases.

The Mill was just visible through the trees: a pink stone building dotted with higgledy-piggledy windows, the little miller's cottage tacked onto one side. As they crossed the stone footbridge, the sound of water tripping over stones soothed her. She'd been concerned at how close it was to a river but Douglas had assured her that the flood search gave the all clear. It was more of a stream really; you could wade across it in wellies.

He took a deep breath. 'This is exactly the right place to relax and be creative.'

'Let's hope you're right.'

As they neared the Mill her spirits sank further. They'd viewed it last October, months ago, but she hadn't remembered it looking this bad. Mind you, she hadn't bothered to look at it properly as she hadn't considered it a serious contender. It was the sort of place an estate agent showed you so the next ghastly place seemed ideal. She'd seen enough TV property shows to know that. And she'd had other things on her mind back then. The outcome of the hearing had been around that time. But she looked now.

The place hadn't wintered well. Sunlight glinted off broken window panes. On the roof, a blue tarpaulin was flapping in the breeze and a tree sprouted from a chimney. Brambles had smothered the cottage walls and a length of guttering hung down like a broken arm. Regret struck her like a blow to the chest.

'Oh my God. What have we done?'

'It's nothing that a coat of paint won't fix.'

He'd been full of such mindless optimism since they first viewed. Despite her concerns, he'd steamrollered the purchase through. She'd heard the note of incredulity in the estate agent's voice when they'd phoned with what Douglas described as a 'cheeky offer'. The agent hadn't even needed

2

to check with the Pooks family who owned it, but had accepted it immediately. Dawn had been in no state to argue.

'It's a way to move on,' he'd said in an effort to convince her. 'Since the…the incident you've been saying the thought of going into a school makes you panic. Well, now you don't have to.'

It was blatant manipulation but you had to hand it to Douglas, once he set his mind on something he wouldn't be swayed. She sniffed loudly. 'What's that funny smell?'

'That, my darling, is what the world smells like without exhaust fumes.'

She didn't reply because at that moment, a shaft of sunlight slipped between the clouds and illuminated an upstairs window. Was that a boy's face? The eyes locked with hers like two pale magnets. He had the same red hair, the same high forehead. A cloud must have blocked the sun and the face faded. Dawn's grip on reality loosened. She must have imagined it. Her therapist had warned that moving house was high on the list of stress inducers, above job loss. If they divorced, or a close family member died, they'd have the stress hat trick.

'Luckily, the Pooks brothers start the renovation tomorrow.'

'We'll need magicians to get this place ready by the summer,' she remarked stepping in a puddle and splashing mud on her jeans. She set down her suitcase, whipped a tissue from her bag and rubbed it.

'Dawn, try to be more positive.'

'Let's go inside. I can't remember it that well but I'm sure it's straight out of House & Garden.' If he'd noticed the irony he was ignoring it.

She followed him up the path towards the door, unsnagging bramble briars from her coat sleeve, and thought of the way the stained glass sun above the door at home had beamed sunshine even on a cloudy day. When they'd moved in Douglas had carried her over the threshold, Becky toddling and Chris in a carrycot. A life of possibilities had lain ahead, like a tree with branches sprouting in all directions, an endless cycle of growing, blossoming and bearing fruit. She glanced up at the stunted tree on the roof where a crow perched, cawing out its ownership. Wasn't that some horrible omen?

Fingers of ivy had snaked across the stone walls and bitten into the heavy wooden door as if to seal it from intruders. Dawn clawed at the strands while Douglas fumbled with the key. When it turned in the lock, they looked at each other in surprise as if neither of them had expected it to work and now it had, they weren't sure whether to go in, like characters in a fairy-tale. Dawn heard the witchy voice in her head, 'come on in, children, and taste the gingerbread.'

He pushed the door against a barrier of mail and they ducked their heads under the stone arch. The dark interior had an earthy, animal smell. The door creaked shut and Dawn yelped when a flap of peeling wallpaper stroked her neck.

Douglas looked down at the suitcases. 'Where would you like these?'

Her head prickled with heat and she ripped open her coat, yanking the collar away from her neck. 'At the nearest hotel?'

'Well, we could stay at the pub –'

'I was joking. We don't have the money. We're going to need every penny we've got to get this place sorted.' She didn't care if she sounded snappy. He needed to come down to earth and stop pretending everything was fine. She bent down to unzip her boots but the mushrooms sprouting from the carpet changed her mind. The boots stayed on. Ahead, a staircase led up to darkness. Down a passage to her right, dust swirled.

'Needs a bit of an airing,' he said, wrestling with a window catch that snapped off in his hand. 'I thought we could sleep in here.' He opened a door off the hall. It led to a white-painted room which had French windows overlooking the meadow behind the mill. 'Tony Pooks told me he built this room for his mum when she couldn't manage the stairs.'

4

Dawn noticed a dark stain on the carpet and wondered about Mrs Pooks's last days. Douglas covered it with their suitcases and tried to hug her but she stepped away. She opened a door into a shower room, turned on a tap in the basin but snatched her hands back when brown water spat out. After finding an antiseptic wipe in her bag, she rubbed everything that might have been touched: the taps and shower controls, the light switches, the door handles.

She caught sight of herself in the mirror. Beneath her amber eyes, usually her best feature, dark circles were winning the battle with concealer. Her frown lines had deepened; hardly surprising as frowning was her default expression. Strange, how you could go for years and not age much and then, all of a sudden, lines would spring up overnight like cracks in a drought. She pushed back her shoulder length hair. The roots looked grey where the auburn tint was growing out; she should have had her hair done before they left civilisation, god knows what they'd do to it down here, but her hair had not been a priority. In a heartbeat, everything that had once mattered became trivial. She'd hoped moving away would help her to move on but what if she couldn't?

Her heart beat in her ears, heralding an anxiety attack. She summonsed her mantra: 'Fall down seven times, Dawn, stand up eight.' (Sometimes during an attack she'd get the numbers round the wrong way) and went in search of Douglas's solid presence. She rushed into the hallway and opened the door that led to the attached cottage but he wasn't there. The cottage was to be for their use only, a place they could escape guests, if they ever got any. Glancing around the sitting room she noticed a brown stain along the entire front wall. What had caused that? She hadn't noticed it when they'd viewed but this room had been stuffed with Mrs Pook's furniture and clutter. Her gaze shifted to the narrow staircase that led up to the two small bedrooms where Becky and Chris could stay when they visited. But why would they? After uni they'd probably find work experience in London.

She thought of them, living their lives, they could be happy or sad, she wouldn't know. Suddenly, she needed to talk to them. She pulled her phone from her pocket. No signal. This place was the twilight zone.

Back in the hallway, she reached under a pile of mail, and found the curly flex of a house phone. After rubbing the receiver with a wipe, she put it to her ear but there was no dialling tone. Floorboards creaked, a door closed and she followed the sounds down the hallway towards where she thought the kitchen was, passing the two rooms that would be the sitting room and the dining room for the guests. A torn net curtain wafted at an open window. On the outside wall in both rooms she saw the same brown stain.

Wiping cobwebs from her face, she entered the kitchen. Cupboard doors were hanging from their hinges and inside one she noticed a chewed-up packet mingled with mice droppings. Two tin mugs sat next to a kettle on the Aga as if someone had been about to make tea. And to think Douglas expected her to churn out meals for up to ten guests in here! A vision flashed of her kitchen at home: quartz and limestone sparkling under spotlights.

He walked in and turned on a tap. 'The water looks like beer!'

'Call me when it looks like sauvignon blanc.'

'Very good, darling.' He laughed and jigged into the utility room singing about water tasting like wine.

God, she needed a shower and she'd only been here five minutes. She approached the heating controls and turned the wheel to 'on' but nothing happened. She balled her fists and dug her nails into her palms rhythmically. One, two, three, four, one, two, three, four. Oh, God. Not the counting. Her palms opened, revealing curved wheals where her nails had dug in.

She rushed out to join Douglas who was smiling at the old millwheel on the side of the house as if the rusty metal struts and rotting wooden wheel fired him with inspiration. 'Come on, let's go see the studio. The Pooks have made a start.'

They walked arm in arm across the sloping meadow behind the house to where the barn nestled in the long grass. It was a single storey stone building with slit windows and huge wooden double doors. As they stepped inside Douglas glanced up at the roof where light was streaming through. 'Good. Tony's put in the windows,' he said, smoothing his hand over a cupboard door.

The barn looked in better shape than the house. Electric cables snaked through holes in a new plasterboard wall but the three original stone walls remained intact. Dawn opened a door to reveal a brand new toilet and basin, and when she turned on the tap clear water ran out. She breathed through the knot in her chest. The barn, or rather, studio, was important but the contrast to the house was stark.

'I can see myself running art classes here. Out all day painting and drawing the wonderful landscapes and coming back to the studio to work on them. Painting portraits and still-lifes when it rains...'

He carried on talking but she drifted off. Why couldn't she feel more positive? It was as if positivity was finite, like oxygen in a small space, and Douglas was using it all up. He must have the same reservations, even if he was too afraid to say them out loud. She almost wanted them to fail so they could move back to London. But would Douglas go with her? He'd been so determined about this move. She could go back alone, rent a flat, apply for teaching jobs and then what? Find out no one would employ her? The schools she'd applied to last term hadn't even asked her for interview. The incident would be on her file. People would judge her harshly, like her former colleagues had done. She'd seen the doubt in their eyes, the looks they'd exchanged when she went into the staffroom, the whispers, 'how could she have done that?' And later, as she'd walked across the playground with her box of things, their eyes boring into her back, how she'd had to force her legs to walk as if they'd forgotten how. The shame of it. The roar of an engine snapped her out of it.

'That sounds like the removal lorry.' He said and rushed off. She followed him through the long grass to the front of the house. Maybe it wasn't so awful here. The Mill didn't look that bad from a distance if you half-closed your eyes, and the trees that surrounded the meadow gave them total privacy.

No one would find her here.

# Chapter 2

'Nothing goes into that kitchen!' Dawn instructed the removal men and led them to the dining room with their table and chairs, the fridge, microwave and boxes of kitchen stuff. The pieces of their bed and the cardboard wardrobes went into the extension bedroom and Douglas led them to a shed next to the barn with the tools and gardening things. It didn't take long as most of their belongings were in storage. Dawn found the kettle and made tea. In the failing light, they found some rickety chairs in the undergrowth out front and sat down.

'Well, that was the best organised move we've ever done, wasn't it Andy?' remarked Jim, the older removal man.

'That's because my wife has—'

'Organised it,' Dawn cut in, glaring at Douglas.

'Lovely spot.' Jim looked across the valley to rolling hills where horses grazed and pheasants strutted.

'Do you think so?' Dawn seized on his words as if this stranger's opinion validated their crazy move. Of course they were local so they would think that.

'Bit of a change from London. 'ow long you live there?'

'Since our early twenties. Over thirty years.'

Where had the time gone? The first eighteen years of her life had crawled by, elongated by the boredom of endless school days bookended with interminable weekends. Pace had picked up in the next eighteen, punctuated with university, career, love, heartbreak, love, more heartbreak, love, marriage, promotion and childbirth. The last eighteen had sped by with events blurring into one another, like the way sand drained through a timer, faster towards the end.

Douglas was speaking, 'We both moved there for work. We met there. Sort of got stuck, the way you do.'

Dawn flashed with anger. How dare he describe their life together as having been stuck? And imply she shared his feelings? He knew how much it had taken for her to give up her home. She raised her chin defiantly. 'I wasn't stuck. I loved it there.'

Jim nodded his head sympathetically. 'This house needs a bit of sorting out, of course. The old Pooks lived here for years. I don't reckon much changed since the sixties when they converted the Mill to a family home. Tony offered to update it but they wouldn't have it.'

'The Pooks brothers are doing the renovation,' Douglas said.

Dawn thought of the stain on the bedroom carpet. 'Did the old couple die here? In the house, I mean.'

'No. He died in a tractor accident and she lived in the hospice for over a year before she died. Luckily, she wasn't here when it flooded last year.'

'Flooded?' Dawn turned to Douglas who seemed fascinated by his cup. 'Did you know about this?'

'It wasn't a real flood,' he mumbled.

'I heard it was deliberate,' Jim said. 'Someone opened both sluice gates and a torrent of water came down the leat and flooded the house. It couldn't drain away because the bridge over the river was blocked with branches.'

So that was the cause of the brown stains in the rooms. But why hadn't Douglas told her? He'd assured her the flood report was fine.

After Andy and Jim left, Dawn confronted him. 'Tony Pooks saw us coming didn't he? He knew we were selling in London and wouldn't need a mortgage. Only outsiders would be stupid enough to buy this place. What if it floods again?'

He winced and glanced up at the house as if her harsh words might cause it offence. 'Well, one does expect a bit of moisture in a mill. Flooding may be overstating it somewhat. I didn't tell you because I didn't want to worry you.'

'You never tell me anything. Not even when you were sacked.'

He'd waited four months before he told her. 'I've lost my job,' he'd said casually, the way he would say, I've lost my keys, have you seen them? She preferred the word 'sacked' with its overtones of medieval rape and pillage. That was more how it felt.

'Oh, you're not bringing that up again.'

'We used to talk things through, make decisions together. Now, if you want to do anything, you go ahead and do it regardless. And you go to great lengths to bamboozle me. Who pretends to go to work every day for weeks?'

'It was only from September. I worked out my notice and was paid up until the end of the summer holiday. I didn't want to worry you. You were dealing with a lot.'

Dawn didn't know what was more worrying, the fact her husband had led a secret life or the fact she hadn't noticed. 'Every day you made sandwiches, set off on your bike, came home exhausted, pretending you'd been at work. Ingrid said you –'

'You talk to your therapist about me?' He had that glint in his eye, the one that signalled he couldn't believe she was his wife.

'Of course I do. Who else do you think I talk about? Prince William? Anyway, she said you have sociopathic tendencies.'

'I suppose it's better than psychopathic tendencies.'

'You may have those, too. I've been talking you up.'

Douglas looked at his feet.

'Look. I know you were trying to protect me but I'm bound to find things out sooner or later and I don't want another shock. So what are these sluice gates and leats they were talking about? I presume you know. If you don't we really are up shit creek.'

'I'll show you. Hang on. I just need to pick something up.'

He appeared with a large metal handle and she followed him round to the millwheel. He pointed to a stone channel that ended at the top of the wheel.

'That's the leat. It's dry now but when they wanted water to power the mill, they would open the sluice gate and water would flow down onto the buckets on the wheel and turn it.'

The channel went up the slope beside the house and veered off to the right where it met a wooden barrier. 'Is that the sluice gate?'

'Yes. It's permanently closed to stop water coming down to the wheel.'

Dawn walked up to the sluice gate. It was small but doing its job, forcing the water coming down the leat to run into a narrow side channel which flowed downhill to the river. Dawn was appeased that no water was coming anywhere near the house.

'That run off is called the spillway,' he said.

'So if someone opened this sluice gate, some of the water going down the spillway would run over the millwheel.'

'Exactly.'

'I can see why that might flood the house.' She noticed the leat disappeared into the trees. 'Where does the water come from?'

'It travels down the leat from the river upstream. There's another sluice gate there that controls the flow. Shall we take a look?'

They crossed a little bridge that spanned the leat and walked up the grassy lane that ran alongside it. The leat grew narrower and in places was completely overgrown. After ten minutes or so they came to a metal barrier about a metre and a half across.

'This is the main sluice gate,' Douglas said. Beyond it, the river meandered by.

He slotted the metal handle onto a large screw that ran up the centre of the gate and wound it round. The gate lowered a little into the mud. 'Now I've shut off the water completely.'

'How do you know all this?'

'Tony Pooks explained it when we met to discuss fixing up the barn.'

'But anyone could have raised this.' The shrillness in her voice caused him to look at her sharply.

'Well, they'd need a handle.'

'I'm sure they're not hard to come by. But who would have deliberately caused a flood? Someone who didn't like the Pooks?'

Douglas didn't respond but maybe he was just concentrating on raising the sluice gate to allow a little water to trickle through, explaining he wanted some to flow through the garden.

They were walking into the house when a loud bang rang out.

'What was that?' Dawn asked.

'I'll go look. You wait here.'

'This place is like Bates Motel,' she muttered, pulling her coat around her.

# Chapter 3

Douglas seized his chance to escape. Dawn would never let this flood business go. He hadn't exactly lied about it; he'd merely avoided mentioning it, for her sake. He'd promised to be honest since he'd kept his sacking a secret but now he'd been caught in another lie.

He glanced around the ground floor before running upstairs. From the first floor, he looked up to the second floor landing and saw the metal ladder that led to the attic had been pulled down and the hatch door was open. Odd. He ran downstairs, unzipped his case and pulled out a torch, congratulating himself on his foresight. He ran upstairs and climbed the ladder to the attic. As his head emerged into the roof space, he noticed daylight over in the corner. That must be the hole the roof tarpaulin was supposed to be covering. He should try and adjust it. The torch beam picked out a couple of cardboard boxes and a heap of old clothing on the floor. He stepped off the ladder and on to the boards, edging over to the hole, treading where he hoped the joists were.

He became aware of a rustling above his head and shone the torch at the rafters. Dark shapes were fluttering beneath the slates. What the hell were they? He stepped back and his foot struck something hard. He lowered the beam to see a face staring up at him: pale eyes wide with fear. Douglas gasped and jumped back. The mouth on the face opened and screamed a strange, high-pitched sound, and then it sprung up. He looked into the face of a boy. He felt the weight of the torch in his hand – he could use it as a weapon. But then the air filled with black shapes swooping and swirling. Man and boy dropped to the floor. Christ, he was trapped in the attic with bats and a lunatic. He felt papery beats against the side of his face, claws on his scalp, a beating on his back. He dropped the torch and covered his head with his hands. His fingers touched spiny, leathery things. The boy grabbed the torch, switched it off and dropped it with a thud and it rolled away out of reach. Douglas watched him crawl towards the hatch and look down. Then, he heard Dawn's voice.

'Douglas? Are you up there? I heard a scream.'

The boy didn't move. Dawn must be blocking his way. 'Dawn, do not come up the ladder!'

The boy shuffled back from the opening and Dawn's head appeared. A bat fluttered in her face, she screamed and the frenzied wing beats increased. Her disappearance was followed by a thud. The boy skimmed down the ladder first, Douglas close behind. As he reached her, he heard a door slam. Dawn lay on her back, groaning.

'Are you OK? Does it hurt anywhere?' He wanted to put his arms around her but feared she might be injured.

'I don't think so. I only fell the last few steps.' She tried to sit and he supported her weight. She rubbed the back of her head.

'Thank God you're OK. Any double vision?'

She blinked. 'No.'

He helped her to stand. 'I'll find a cold compress for your head.' She clung on to his arm. He hated seeing her like this, vulnerable and weak. He pushed the hair from her eyes.

'What was that boy doing in the attic? I saw a face in an upstairs window earlier but thought I'd imagined it. He looks a bit like … you know.'

He'd hoped moving down here would give her distance, but there was a reminder right here in their attic. 'I've no idea who that lad was.'

'And what sort of bird was that? It had glowing red eyes.'

He glanced up at the opening. He grabbed the bottom of the ladder, slid it into the attic and the hatch door slammed shut. A pulse thudded at his temple. Maybe Tony Pooks knew something about the lad. He pulled out his phone but had no signal.

## Chapter 4

Douglas settled Dawn at a table next to a roaring fire in a corner of the Darton Arms. He caught sight of himself in the mirror behind the bar. He looked and felt ten years older than when he'd left London this morning. His rigor mortis grin and the red patch on each cheek leant him a startling resemblance to a ventriloquist's dummy. He'd texted Tony from the car park: lad and bats in attic? As he stood at the bar, he checked he had enough signal to receive a reply.

He hoped the wine would relax her. He dropped a packet of her favourite crisps – prawn cocktail – on the table as if baiting a wild animal. She didn't touch them. Obviously, he should have told her about the flood and the bats, but he'd so wanted to buy the Mill and she'd never have agreed if she'd known. But he hadn't realised the bats were in the attic. Tony had told him they were in the barn. He should tell Dawn about the other problems, but this wasn't a good time.

You think you own a house but it owns you.

He looked around the pub, hoping that the driftwood sculptures, the dried hops hanging from the ceiling and the inglenook fireplace studded with horse brasses would provide a distraction. She was studying the menu as if for some future exam, doing that weird counting thing; he could see her jaw muscles moving in time. A trickle of sweat ran down his forehead.

'What a great local. What's the menu like? I bet I can guess what you're going to order.' He tried to make her smile; she looked lovely when she smiled. He knew she would order the scampi and, when it arrived, announce that she should have chosen whatever he was having.

Her face looked puffy and she had a definite double chin, no doubt due to all that comfort eating. Every time he'd

16

walked in on her recently – usually she'd been applying for jobs on her laptop – it looked as if there'd been an explosion in a cake factory. And this was the same woman who every morning for the last twenty years had packed plastic boxes with raw vegetables and cottage cheese for their lunches which took more calories to masticate than you gained from swallowing. He'd gone to a burger drive-thru most lunch times, when he had the car and Dawn wasn't insisting that they cycle to keep fit and protect the environment. Cycling through a drive-thru felt a bit like buying an abserciser and using it as a towel rail, something else he'd done. He'd hoped the move to Last Chance Mill would close the distance between them, give them new goals, a different perspective. But what if it opened up a chasm?

'I'm sorry I didn't tell you about the flood.'

Dawn ripped open the crisps, spilling some on the table. 'I'd never have agreed to buy a house with a flood risk. Even you can't think that's a good idea. You can see the flood damage to the walls in every room. The plaster must be rotten and the floor too. It's going to take all our money –'

'Tony's going to fix all that. It's in the budget.'

Some workmen walked in and Douglas peered to see if one of them was Tony. He caught the waitress's eye and she came over.

'What can I get you?'

'I'll have scampi, please.'

'The steak and kidney pie, thanks.'

'What if it floods again?' Dawn persisted.

'As the removal men said, it wasn't a natural flood. Someone deliberately opened the sluice gates. Tony told me about it and I checked his story...' he stopped, unsure whether he should mention her name, 'with Anastasia– '

'Anastasia! When did you see her?' Dawn accidentally spat a half-chewed crisp at his neck. He wiped it off.

Lady Anastasia Montague. They'd rented a cottage on her estate when they were house hunting. Dawn had disliked her.

The phrase 'stuck up bitch' sprung to mind, whereas he'd thought her jolly nice. Attractive too.

'I didn't see her. I emailed her.' He leaned forward and whispered. 'She confirmed Tony's story. A young lad did it. Her groom. He didn't want the Mill to be sold. He was worried that new owners would get rid of ...' He broke off.

'Get rid of what?'

Douglas swallowed. He'd walked right into this one. Dawn hated rodents of any description. Even Squirrel Nutkin made her shudder. 'Bats.'

She gasped. 'That thing was a bat! You knew they were there!' She swept her fingers through her hair.

'Tony told me they were in the barn. He said he'd got rid of them. I had no idea they were in the attic.'

'So let me see if I've got this straight. Anastasia's groom caused the flood so no one would buy the Mill, in order to save the bats. Hmm. And you believed it?'

He frowned. It had sounded a lot more plausible when Anastasia had said it.

'Was that him in the attic? With the bats?'

'I think so.' He checked his phone again. Where was Tony?

'What's to stop him from doing it again?'

'Anastasia assured me that she had talked to the lad and it wouldn't happen again.'

'That's all very well for her, sitting pretty in that hill-top castle while we battle bats and floods.' Dawn's voice rose. 'We should call the police. He broke into our house. I saw a window open downstairs. That must be how he got in.'

Douglas noticed several diners furtively glanced their way. She was probably right but he didn't want to stir up trouble; not on their first night. 'Dawn, keep your voice down.'

'Oh, that's typical. All you worry about is what other people think. These people aren't locals,' she gesticulated at their fellow diners with her wine glass, now worryingly empty, 'they're from the touring park up the road.'

A knife clattered noisily on to a plate. Douglas flushed hot, downed his pint as if extinguishing a fire, and skulked off to the gents where he locked himself in a cubicle. He took a calming breath. He wanted to take off his jumper but that would reveal the sweat marks on his shirt. He tore off some loo roll and wiped his forehead. He'd known this would be hard: taking Dawn from her comfort zone and subjecting her to chaos and filth. Her condition had worsened since the incident at work.

When he went back to their table Dawn had gone and two plates of food sat steaming. It crossed his mind that she'd left; not just the pub, but Devon. As he started on his steak and kidney pie, she appeared.

'The pie looks good. I should have ordered that. I had to stand on a bench to get signal, but I got through to the kids.' Dawn seemed more relaxed. 'They send their love. Becky's got an exam tomorrow. She sounded a bit stressed. Chris was at that bar job, so couldn't talk. Do you think it's a good idea for him to work while he's at uni?'

Douglas thought of their bank balance. 'Definitely,' he said. Thank God Becky was finishing at uni in May so those payments would stop. Since his redundancy, he'd become obsessed with money: money for repairs, money for bills and money for the kids. Leisure activity number one was reading bank statements and jabbing a calculator trying to make the zeros disappear. He was like one of those crazy cartoon characters with £££££ signs flashing in his eyes.

His phone buzzed. Tony. 'I'll have to go outside to take this.'

# CHAPTER 5

Tony sat among the smokers at a table under a canopy, drinking his pint, work overalls draping his boxer's build. 'Thought it best to speak to you alone. There's no point alarmin' the missus.' He tossed a peanut in the air and caught it in his mouth.

Douglas told Tony what had happened. 'Do you think the boy in the attic was the one who started the flood?'

'Samuel Grimes, the bat lover? Sounds like it. Red hair? Gormless? Can't speak?'

Douglas nodded. 'He could certainly scream. He had a camouflage hoody.'

'That's 'im. He must have thought the house was still empty. Bet 'e got the fright of his life.'

'Frightened me I can tell you.'

'He used to do the gardening for me mum. He got very attached to them bats. After he flooded the Mill, I threatened him with the police but 'e works for Lady Montague now and she said that if I reported him, she'd report me for smoking the bats out of the barn. I could be prosecuted, see. Fancy that. Them bats flew out the barn straight into the attic.'

'Yes, fancy that. Frankly, I would rather they were still in the barn. Dawn is freaked out. She wants to report him to the police for breaking and entering.'

'No need for that. I'll have a word with his family. They live just outside Darton. His brothers are all right. One of them's with the police. They'll set 'im straight.' Tony's phone buzzed and he turned away.

'So what do we do about the bats?' Douglas asked when he pocketed his phone.

'Not much you can do. They's protected, see. Bats 'ave the same rights as you and me.' Tony started texting furiously. 'Job done. My nephew, Jonno, is going round to see Samuel's brothers. He won't give you no more trouble.'

As they walked over to a van with both wings stove in and no registration plate, Tony told Douglas that he would be round in the morning with his brother, Pete the plumber, to fix the boiler but that the electric shower downstairs would work. Then he sped off, still talking into his phone.

Douglas told Dawn about Samuel, making up a few details to reassure her. 'Tony told me that he's a nature lover, a poor soul and completely harmless. He's going to have a word with the boy's family. His brother's a policeman apparently. To make sure he stays away.'

Dawn drained her glass.

As he paid the bill at the till, the landlord, a good looking chap in his forties, handed him a leaflet headed, Wild Swimming.

'Some of us are swimming on Saturday if you're interested. From Elberry Cove.' Douglas detected a south London twang.

'Yes, I know it.' He and Dawn had discovered it on one of their trips: a locals' beach, pebbly with crystal clear water. He loved sea swimming – so much better than in chlorinated pools. 'I'll try and make it, thank you.'

'I'm John.'

'Douglas.'

'You DFLs?'

'Sorry?'

'D. F. Ls,' he repeated. 'Down-From-London.'

'Oh! Yes. But we're not holiday makers, grockles.' Douglas was proud of this local slang. 'We've moved into Last Chance Mill.'

'You're like us then. Blow-ins.'

Douglas frowned.

'It's what the locals call unwelcome outsiders. We're the ones who keep the villages thriving and the villagers genetically modified. There're a lot of us about. We stick together.' He tapped the side of his nose with his finger.

'Very friendly barman,' Douglas remarked when he joined Dawn in the car.

'They seem a nice couple,' Dawn said.

'Oh, I didn't notice a woman around. Only the young waitress. '

'A very nice *gay* couple. His partner is the good looking black guy who's the chef.'

'I don't know how you glean this information, Dawn. They could use your skills at Scotland Yard.'

# CHAPTER 6

The house in darkness looked almost sinister. A phrase popped into Douglas's head: dark, satanic mill. Something flitted past – a bat? Luckily Dawn was preoccupied with the key at the front door. The hoot of an owl sounded suspiciously like someone pretending to be an owl. He retrieved his crate of art materials from the boot, staggered into the hallway and dropped it on the floor. Most of the lights didn't work so he found his trusty torch and stumbled around in the gloom checking all the windows and doors were locked.

Dawn had put sheets on their bed and seemed appeased by a warmish shower. He didn't reach for her. He tried not to touch her at all as if she were an unexploded bomb. His right leg, the one nearest her, twitched. When he eventually fell asleep, he dreamt that he was painting fish, actually painting their bodies, but the paint kept sliding off their scales and they kept slipping from his grasp. He woke with a start to Dawn shaking him.

'Douglas! Wake up! What was that? Did you hear it?'

For a moment, he didn't know where or who he was. 'Hear what?'

'A terrible scream. Like someone being murdered.'

'Murdered?' Then he heard it. Through the silence, cut a terrible shriek.

'Sounds more like someone witnessing a murder. If you're actually being murdered I don't think you could–'

'Oh, for God's sake, Douglas, let's ring the police or go and see what's happening!'

Dawn seemed to have forgotten that neither the phone nor the mobiles worked and wandering around in the dark looking for a murderer did not appeal. A horrible Hitchcockian scenario played in his head.

'Is my cricket bat under the bed?' He'd kept it under their bed in Crouch End.

'Of course not, it's in storage,' she snapped as if he were certifiable, which would be preferable right now.

'I'll go and check the doors are locked, you stay here and cover the windows.'

He stumbled off to check the front and back doors even though he knew he'd locked them before bed. He peered through a front window and saw no skulking murderer, no knife blade held aloft glinting in the moonlight, nothing at all but black. In London, the streetlights shone all night. He checked that the downstairs windows were shut in case the lad, Samuel, tried to get back in.

In the bedroom, Dawn was struggling to drape a sheet over the French windows.

'Did you check the window in the dining room was locked, the one the boy got in?'

'Yes, of course.'

'Do you think it was him screaming?'

Douglas wondered if Tony's nephew had spoken to the lad's brothers yet and hoped he wasn't lying in their driveway, a victim of Pooks' justice. 'No, I'm sure it wasn't.'

Dawn didn't insist on him patrolling outside so he climbed back into bed and made a mental note to fetch his spade from the shed and keep it under the bed. You couldn't be too careful.

'I'll never get back to sleep,' Dawn said. 'I'm used to nodding off to the comforting sound of screeching brakes and smashing bottles. Who'd have thought the countryside was so scary?'

He woke when the sun climbed above the trees and shone through the windows. Dawn's side of the bed lay empty. He wandered into the hall and called her name, his voice echoing in that eerie way that told him he was alone. When he peered through a window, he saw the car was gone. He dressed, pulled aside the sheet, unlocked the French windows and stepped out on to the dewy grass. Sunlight dappled the velvet green meadow, light then dark as clouds skimmed the sky. He felt moved to paint, to capture this fine chiaroscuro. Here, at Last Chance Mill, he had found his place, his time to shine. If only Dawn shared his vision. At this moment, it was a relief to be alone. His pleasure at her absence worried him but he refused to let it dampen his mood.

He checked the leat near the house. It was dry and the sluice gate was shut. After what Tony and Anastasia had told him he'd decided to keep a close eye on it.

He set off across the meadow intending to air the studio, which had smelt musty yesterday. He pushed open the heavy doors but stepped back in shock. Streaks of paint smeared the new plasterboard wall. He walked over, avoiding the twisted tubes of paints that littered the floor, their lids abandoned. Picking one up he recognised the labels. They were his paints. He picked up a paintbrush. It was one of his best badger hair brushes. The bristles were stiff with dried paint, it was ruined. When he touched an area of splatter with his finger, he found it wet. He swore as red paint squirted up his leg when he trod on an open tube. In a corner of the studio, he saw the storage crate he'd brought in from the car last night and left in the hallway of the house. Whoever had done this must have broken into the house, taken the crate, and brought it here.

Samuel?

He hurried back to the house, entering through the French windows. They'd been locked last night, as had the front and back doors; he'd checked them on his midnight patrol. He tried all the downstairs windows: also locked or sealed shut for years. Some of the upstairs windows were smashed but no one could have entered through there. So, with no sign of a break-in and with all the doors and downstairs windows secured, who had done it? And then it hit him.

Dawn. The mess, the bats, the flood and the boy must have triggered another episode. What if he'd pushed her over the edge with this move on top of everything else? He sat down on the stairs and gripped his head with his hands. A pulse beat in his temples. He couldn't do this without her but he needed her sane. He shook his head in disbelief. No. It couldn't have been Dawn. It must have been Samuel. Anything else was unthinkable.

He explored the house for more clues and found traces of red and blue paint in the kitchen sink. The culprit must have washed his hands here afterwards. But why would Samuel have come back to the house? Why not use the sink in the barn? Where the hell was Dawn? He bent over and drank brown water straight from the tap.

Then he heard a car.

He peered through the kitchen window and spied her hauling tubs of paint from the boot. Hah! She obviously regretted her actions and intended to paint over the mess before he noticed. The key clunked in the front door, the bags rustled as she dropped them in the dining room. He moved to the doorway.

'Good morning.'

Her hand shot to her chest. 'Good God! Don't creep up on me like that, not after the night I've had. I hardly slept a wink after that screaming. I expected to see a body lying in the brambles when I went out this morning.' She was pulling cartons of fruit juice and milk from a bag and putting them in the fridge.

He switched on the kettle. 'So, you had a busy night then.'

'Busy? Hardly. More like, sleepless. I woke up starving. I popped out to buy coffee and croissants and things for lunch. Darton village shop is surprisingly good. Great range of products. There's a butcher and a hairdresser too.'

Douglas frowned. She was acting innocent. 'And some paint, too,' he said slowly, eyeing her tell-tale purchase.

'Yes, I noticed a DIY place on the ring road yesterday. Thought we could make a start on the upstairs. Tony's only re-plastering downstairs isn't he?' She rummaged in one of the cardboard boxes and took out two plates wrapped in newspaper, wincing when a dead wood louse fell out.

'And now there's somewhere else we need to paint.' It came out with more of the tone of a psychiatric nurse than he'd intended.

She paused from spooning instant coffee into cups and gave him a sharp look. 'Like where?'

His heart sank. She couldn't remember? Or was in denial? 'The studio?' He smiled in what he hoped was a sympathetic manner.

'OK, I'll paint the barn too if you want. I realise that's your priority.' She poured boiling water into the cups.

'It won't take long to cover it up.'

She turned to look at him, hands on hips. 'Cover what up? What are you talking about? Oh! Is that blood?' She bent down and touched the red paint on his leg and lifted his trouser leg to inspect him for damage as if he were one of her wayward pupils.

'No, it's paint. It's OK, Dawn, I understand. I really do. I'm going to make this all right.'

'You're talking gibberish.' She stood abruptly and knocked the cups, spilling coffee on the table.

He opted for the passive tense, trying not to sound accusatory. 'The studio wall has been painted,' he said slowly, 'with my paints.'

'Really? How odd. Ooh...perhaps by the person who screamed in the night. The boy!' She grabbed a cloth and mopped up the coffee.

'I'm fairly sure those noises were foxes. It's no use. You can't blame—'

'What? You think I did it?' She stopped mopping and turned to face him.

'Well, yes. All the windows and doors were locked, it wasn't me so who else could it be?'

'Well, it wasn't me. It must have been the boy. He'll have a way of getting in and out. We must get Tony to fix the windows. We can't have some random boy vandalising the place.'

He wanted to examine her hands but didn't dare. 'Dawn…'

'What?'

He'd been about to ask if they were doing the right thing but stopped himself. He had to be the strong one. 'Nothing.'

But she sensed his doubt, his weakness and her face crumpled. 'If it doesn't work out, we can go back to London, can't we?'

At least she was saying we and not I. But she must realise that he'd never go back. And what could she get with half the money in London? Some poky flat? And that was dependent on selling a dilapidated bat hotel with a flood warning. For him, it was Last Chance or bust. He looked at her pleading face and his heart went out to her.

'Er, yes of course.'

# CHAPTER 7

'How much can I go to?' Anastasia was holding her phone in one hand and an auction catalogue in the other, leaning up against a marble column. She would kill to sit down. Her court shoes were agony. Too much time spent in wellingtons, she feared. Freddie was barely audible above the buzz of the auction room and she asked him to repeat the sum. Wow. It was only a drawing.

'Sounds a hell of a lot for, what looks like, a sketch knocked off between cocktails and dinner.' She turned the catalogue sideways and squinted at it.

'No. I don't suppose it *is* bad. It's a dying horse. Not really my cup of tea. But you didn't marry me for my knowledge of art. Thing is, I can't hang about all day. I need to get back to Dartcoombe. Coco's about to produce and the puppies are in breach like last time, so I need to be there. No, I cannot ask Sabrina to bid. She's far too busy sorting out the latest shipment from Bali.'

On cue, Anastasia's assistant, Sabrina, staggered to the top of the stairs with a cardboard cup filled with coffee in one hand and a giant Mulberry bag in the other.

Why on earth did she wear that dowdy suit? It made her look forty-five if she was a day. 'Thank you, darling,' Anastasia mouthed at her, 'life saver!' She tucked the catalogue under her arm and seized the cup.

'No, I was talking to a friend. I'd better go now, they're about to start. I'll do my best. I've cancelled an important meeting to be here. Will you be down tonight or are you ...' she cleared her throat, '...entertaining clients in London?' Her voice dripped with irony. Whoever he was entertaining, Anastasia knew she wouldn't be a client. He would be a client of hers, more likely. Anger bubbled at his response. Of course he wasn't coming down. Why would he deign to come back to his family home at the weekend?

Sabrina mouthed, 'They're about to start!'

'Got to go.' She rang off and headed for the auction room, vicious heels clicking on the parquet floor.

She noticed several admiring glances as she slid into a seat at the back of the room. She pushed a stray strand of blonde hair back into her chignon and smoothed down the skirt of her grey Chanel suit, picking off a dog hair. Why was she doing this favour for Freddie when he couldn't even spare the time to come home? Maybe she should just walk out now, tell him it went for too much. But he'd find out somehow. She could bid above the sum he'd given her just to spite him. She'd learned, though not from Freddie himself of course, that they were halving his bonus this quarter. God forbid he would tell her. Did he feel emasculated when they chopped his earnings? She hoped so. Not that it made much difference when his family owned the bank. She imagined him pocketing the bonuses that were due to the employees whilst whinging about having to cut back. Yes, that would be Freddie.

The auctioneer whizzed through the sales. Excitement fluttered in her chest as an assistant entered with the framed drawing and placed it on the easel. A murmur swept the room. Even from far away, the image chilled her to the bone: an animal in agony. The sight of her own darling Seraphim falling at the last fence, flashed fleetingly.

'And now we move to the Picasso drawing. A preparatory sketch for Guernica. It is a quality piece rarely seen on the market, with an exceptional and indisputable provenance. Let's start the bidding at two hundred thousand pounds, ladies and gentlemen. Am I bid two hundred thousand pounds?'

What an absurd sum for a few scribbles. Anyone able to hold a pencil could produce something similar, in fact you wouldn't even have to hold the pencil in your hand. One of those foot and mouth artists could do better, judging by their charity Christmas cards. But Freddie had got it into his head that Picassos were going to increase in value.

The drawing didn't excite her but the thrill of the chase did. She loved the theatre of the auction room and she played her part well. She eyed the bidders: the nod of a head, the flick of a catalogue, the raising of a hand by men in suits with phones wedged between ear and shoulder. She summed up her opponents and bided her time, as a lioness stalks a gazelle, waiting for the exact moment to pounce. You pathetic losers don't stand a chance. She waited until there were only two bidders battling. One was a dealer with a Poirot moustache, the other, a large man in a loud, checked jacket. Probably American.

'Three hundred thousand pounds,' the auctioneer proclaimed. Poirot bowed his head, defeated. Checked jacket looked across at him; triumph oozing from every pore. What a smug bastard.

The auctioneer continued, 'At three hundred thousand pounds, ladies and gentlemen, are there any advances on three hundred thousand?' He paused and looked around the room. 'Going ... going...'

'Three hundred and twenty,' Anastasia enunciated. The icy crispness of the vowels froze on her lips. A murmur swept the auction room and all heads turned, eyes searching for the face that went with the voice. Checked jacket swivelled his head so fast he should have auditioned for the Exorcist. The corners of Anastasia's mouth twitched. She always laughed when nervous – got her into no end of trouble at boarding school. And she *was* nervous. Despite her composed features and unerring stare, her heart was hammering against her ribs.

She and the auctioneer made eye contact and he nodded almost imperceptibly. But no one was looking at him, they were looking at her: looks of surprise and disproval. Damien's head swivelled back and his plaid shoulders slumped as if he'd been exorcised.

'Three hundred and twenty, I am bid. Any advance on three hundred and twenty?' The auctioneer scanned the room.

'Going... going... gone to Lady Anastasia Montague.' He looked at her over the top of his glasses with a smidgeon of a smirk. It occurred to her that she'd prevented another great work from flying across the Atlantic. Or rather Freddie had, although it would end up in the bank's vault.

She checked her phone. Nothing from Mary, so no puppies yet, thank God. She imagined the weekend ahead. Just her and the horses and dogs, wild swimming on Saturday and riding on Sunday. Bliss. The camellias and rhododendrons would be in bloom and she'd walk around the estate with Coco checking the pheasant feeding stations, the fences and streams. She'd always enjoyed her own company, hadn't she? She'd been a loner as a child: out riding or with her head in a horsey book. Come to think of it, her best relationship was with Coco. She certainly saw more of her than she did of Freddie. One bit of bad news: the new owners had moved into Last Chance Mill. Her Mill. DFLs, according to Mary's niece who'd married one of those ghastly Pooks. Their planning application must have been approved, despite her protests. Still, she had other tricks up her sleeve.

# CHAPTER 8

Scraps of wallpaper buried Dawn's feet. She'd been at it for an hour and had barely removed a square meter. She should be painting; that's what she'd planned when she got up this morning. Whitewash therapy. But Douglas had insisted that they remove the layers of old wallpaper and re-paper the walls. Even with both of them working flat out, Dawn realised the renovation was going to take all the money they'd made on the sale of the London house. Paying off the mortgage had taken a big chunk. She understood what he meant. They would need an income from guests by July. His lump sum hadn't amounted to much after all those years working part-time, trying and failing to make it as an artist. His pension, taken early, barely covered the kids' living expenses at uni.

It had been a relief when Douglas confessed he was having second thoughts and hadn't dismissed the idea of moving back to London. Since he'd admitted his doubts and stopped being so damned positive, she'd felt less negative. She just had to get through the next three and a half months. Their labour wouldn't be wasted: a partial renovation would increase the value of the Mill, which meant more money to spend on a house in London.

Douglas walked in holding up a weird contraption with a corrugated hose and a plastic tank that looked like an instrument of torture. 'Good news. We have a stripper. Tony found it in the back of his van. That van door is like the gateway to Narnia.'

Dawn frowned. 'I never thought I'd hear the words 'good news' and 'stripper' in the same sentence.'

He boiled a kettle and filled the stripper tank with a half-smile. She could see what an effort he was making to appear cheerful. A few days had passed since discovering the studio vandalised. They agreed it must have been Samuel Grimes. Who else? Secretly, Dawn was glad the boy existed and she hadn't imagined a face at the window. For weeks, she'd seen nothing but that face, the mouth contorted in anger as he advanced on the other boy. She'd only had a moment to react. A moment that had changed her life.

Douglas handed her the hissing steamer head and she slammed it against the wall, reeling as a cloud of steam hit her face. He attacked the soggy paper with his scraper, exclaiming with satisfaction when a large sheet peeled away, 'It's almost better than sex when it does that.'

'Thanks,' said Dawn.

'Not with you, of course.'

'Oh, you mean sex with other women.'

'Ur, sorry ...' Dawn swivelled and almost fell off the ladder. Tony Pooks smirked from the doorway, his face under the baseball cap was ghostly white with plaster dust. 'Do you want me to take away the bags of rubble or will you take 'em to the tip? They charge me to dump 'em see.' Tony bit into a giant sandwich.

'We'll take them to the tip.' They needed Tony to get the message that costs had to be kept down.

'How's it going down there?' Douglas asked wiping his forehead.

Tony told them that the old plaster would be off by the end of the day and that his brother, Pete the plumber, was fixing the boiler and moving some gas and water pipes in the kitchen. While he was talking, a piece of tomato fell from his mouth on to the floor.

'Have you decided which kitchen units you want? I'll need to get him ordered,' he asked, not bothering to pick up the tomato.

'I've circled the one in the brochure. The second cheapest.' She said, perplexed at Tony's use of 'him' for an object. Was that a Devon thing? 'And I've picked out the flooring.'

'I'll get him ordered too. I see you're doing a proper job 'ere.'

Dawn bit her tongue. She couldn't be rude about the four layers of wall paper they'd uncovered. It was his childhood home, after all. 'I've been wondering why you or your brothers didn't want to live here. To keep it in the family.'

'Mum left it to the four of us and none of us could buy out the others so we 'ad to sell. Anyway, my wife likes a nice modern 'ouse. Everything brand new. I built us a place on the edge of the village. She wants all mod cons. Not like you two.'

Dawn persevered, ignoring the slight. 'When the house flooded, why didn't you claim on insurance and fix the damage?'

Tony took a step back. 'We didn't have no insurance. Because the Mill's close to a river, insurance would have cost thousands. The bugg… I mean, the so-and-sos, put up the premiums after the floods a few years back.'

Dawn gripped the top of the ladder and glowered at Douglas.

'But it won't flood again. That was the first time since about two hundred years ago year when it flooded everywhere.' Tony glanced between Dawn and Douglas and backed out of the door mumbling something about fallout from a volcano blocking the sun.

Dawn wasn't listening. She climbed down the ladder and dropped the steamer head which spat boiling water on to the floorboards. She faced Douglas.

'I wanted to tell you, love,' he began, 'but I only found out after you'd agreed to the move. After we decided to stay together. If I'd told you, you would have refused to buy, you might have chosen to … you know–'

'You can say it. Split up.'

He switched off the steamer, walked over to the window and leant out.

'But you were right. Had I known about the flood and not being able to afford insurance I would never have agreed to buy. Oh, and the resident bats and lunatic in the attic might have put me off. Is there anything else you haven't told me?'

He had the dazed look of a man caught out. 'No.'

'Are you sure? Your lack of communication bothers me almost as much as the floods and the bats. We're supposed to be partners. You treat me like I'm the enemy. All your efforts go into covering things up.'

'You're making too much of it. I didn't want to worry you, that's all.'

She shook her head. He grasped her gloved hands which were covered in bits of gluey wallpaper. 'I still believe we have a good plan and that we can succeed if we stick together.'

She tried to pull her hands away but couldn't. 'We're certainly sticking together now. I miss London, I miss my friends.'

'I know.' He pulled a piece of wallpaper from her hair. 'We'll make new friends, and the old ones can come and stay.'

'How can I make friends when I'm stuck up a ladder every day?'

Douglas slipped an arm around her shoulders and pulled her close. She softened at his familiar feel. 'This won't be forever. We've just got to get through the next couple of months of hard labour. Shall I take over the steaming and you scrape off the wallpaper?'

'Five years of higher education and I've been reduced to labouring. It's like being a member of the intelligentsia in Maoist China.'

He broke away and switched on the steamer. A quick burst of affection and then he expected her back on the chain gang.

'Do you remember the last time we did this?' he asked climbing the ladder.

'When we moved into the flat and stripped everything. The walls, the floor, those awful ceiling tiles.' She'd hoped this project would re-kindle some of that sense of purpose and teamwork they'd felt then. But when you're young, it's a novelty and you have energy. Even though she'd been pregnant then, she'd rollered ceilings and painted radiators with paint she hoped wasn't toxic to the baby. They hadn't minded that they were poor. The future seemed a long and winding road lined with fun places, exciting opportunities and countless choices they would make together. Now, repeating the actions in their fifties, she missed that feeling of being young and in love, when everything was fun, even decorating. Now, it felt like a chore. The long and winding road had ended in a cul-de-sac. Did Douglas feel like that? Maybe he did and that was why she sometimes caught him looking at her in bewilderment. The thought emboldened her.

'Douglas, do you think I've passed my best before date?'

'What? No! I'd still pick you off the shelf. But I know what you mean. When I was sacked I definitely felt past my use by date.'

'I'm sorry. I wasn't much help.'

'Yeah, well you were dealing with your own issues. Can you pass that rag? My glasses have steamed up.'

'But it's looking brighter for you, isn't it? I mean, this is your dream. You gave it all up when Becky was born. This is your chance to do what you always wanted to do. To paint and draw, to be in the country.'

'I know leaving London was hard for you, Dawn. I do appreciate you being here.'

Dawn swallowed the lump in her throat. It was the first time he'd acknowledged it. Maybe there was a way back from the hole under the carpet where they swept everything they didn't want to talk about.

But then he asked her, 'Shall we eat in the pub again tonight?'

She winced at the abrupt change of subject. Let's not talk about our feelings and talk about our stomachs instead – so much safer. She duly complied. 'I bought some cheap wine and a lasagne when I went to the village shop.' She gripped the edge of a soggy sheet of wallpaper, pulled and the whole strip came away. She remembered Douglas's comment earlier. It was the closest they'd come to talking about sex, or rather their lack of it, in months. Their marriage had been stagnating when they'd still been in London and had money, the kids and friends around them. This project seemed to be prising them further apart rather than bringing them together.

They ate microwaved lasagne under a glaring light bulb. After supper, she rummaged through the books she'd brought with her and found The Thrifty Vegetarian. She decided to scrub the Aga and cook affordable, yet tasty and nutritious meals. Dhal bhat, lentils and rice, was the key. Two thirds of the world survived on that. She'd find a cheap Indian shop in the local town and buy all the ingredients: cumin, coriander, cardamom, turmeric, chilli, garam masala. She said the names out loud as she wrote them on her list, savouring their sounds.

Overcome with tiredness, she crawled into bed and dozed off with the books on top of her legs. She woke when he came to bed but when she turned towards him, he was already asleep.

# CHAPTER 9

A few days later, Dawn was cutting a length of wallpaper and smoothing it on a trestle table ready for Douglas to paste when a loud thump from downstairs shuddered through the bedroom floor and rattled the aluminium ladder. They looked at each other in alarm and sped downstairs to a clatter of falling plaster.

As the dust settled, Dawn made out piles of rubble heaped on the floor. A fluttering began in her chest. Don't panic, she told herself, it has to get worse before it gets better. A Pooks brother she didn't recognise was shovelling it into bags. She walked from room to room. The entire front wall of the house – the cottage sitting room, entrance hall, guest sitting room, dining room and kitchen – was down to bare stone. She noticed a patch of daylight about the size of a water melon in the hallway wall. 'Is that hole supposed to be there?'

'What hole?' Tony peered through the dust. 'Oh that hole,' he said, grinning. 'Oops. Overdid it with me sledgehammer. Matt, mix up some concrete will you? This is Matt by the way, Vinyl Matt we call him. Very 'andy with a paintbrush.'

'Any news about when you can repair the roof?' Douglas asked.

'Jonno will start when he's finished the job he's on.'

Dawn didn't want to think about what would happen when it rained. And it would rain; this was Devon.

'The stone is mostly dry at least,' Tony spluttered as he patted the wall, 'and the floorboards are OK. Luckily the water subsided pretty quick once we cleared the blockages under the bridges and we 'ad dehumidifiers in 'ere for days. We can start re-rendering when it's dried out and he'll be good as new.'

Upstairs, Dawn set down mugs of coffee. 'Really Douglas, he doesn't inspire confidence. Does he even know what he's doing? We've such a short time-scale.'

'I'll keep an eye on him,' he whispered. 'Well done for spotting the hole.'

'It was hard to miss. God forbid we employ another roofer. One from outside Don Antonio's family. Why are we whispering?'

Douglas turned up the paint-splattered radio and they listened to news about the war against so-called Islamic state. She thought of the children of asylum seekers she'd taught. First the Cypriots, (showing her age there) then the Vietnamese, Somalis, Eritreans, Kurds, Bosnians, Afghanis and now the Syrians. One of the most rewarding parts of her work had been to provide a safe haven for those children and their parents. But then she'd taken that job in the Pupil Referral Unit.

'Doug!'

Tony never called for her. Presumably women were too stupid to understand about demolition but for once, it was good news. When Tony and Pete had removed some kitchen units to adjust the pipe work, they ripped up the lino from the floor to reveal a yellowing layer of newspaper and underneath that, great slabs of limestone.

'Reckon he's a keeper.' Tony peeled away the sticky newspaper. 'Save you a fortune on floorin'.'

Douglas had knelt and was staring at it as if he'd just discovered America. 'It must be the original floor. This newspaper is dated 1939. It's all about the outbreak of war. Amazing!'

'Maybe the whole of the downstairs floor is flagstone,' Dawn suggested and she pulled on her gloves and they ripped up the lino in the hallway and the filthy carpets in the rooms, and revealed flagstones on the whole of the ground floor except for in the cottage sitting room which had black floorboards. She'd never been exposed to such filth. She heard the ringing in her ears that sometimes heralded a panic attack.

'Can we get rid of this now? Please?' Her voice quivered. Douglas looked at her with concern. He must realise how far out of her comfort zone this was.

They rolled up the lino and carpets, hauled them outside and dropped them next to the bags of rubble ready for the next tip run. She took some breaths and the men went back into the house. It looked like rain and the carpet would he heavier to move when wet.

Back inside, Tony was caressing the limestone. 'He needs a bit of scrubbin' but he'll come up lovely,'

'I'm sure he will.' Dawn knew whose job that would be.

Douglas was kneeling on the floor, peeling off the old newspaper as if restoring an ancient fresco. Dawn hopped from foot to foot. 'The tip closes in half an hour.' She wanted rid of those filthy rolls. Now. As they loaded them on to the roof-rack, decades of dusty carpet fibres swirled around them.

They took the short cut along narrow lanes. Dawn imagined a time when horses and carts ambled along, bearing loads of cider apples and sheaves of barley. She breathed in the rich smell of the hedgerows. This was Devon at its best.

The tip was Devon at its worst: huge skips filled with junk, rubbish underfoot, the stench of rotting garbage, the air thick with seagulls.

'I must say, the Mill is very handy for the tip,' said Douglas.

'Finally. A reason to have bought it.'

They dragged the carpet and lino up the metal steps and launched it into the 'household goods' skip.

'Are you alright, love?' he asked, pulling something that looked like a kidney off the bottom of his trainer. 'This would usually tip you over the edge, excuse the pun.'

'I feel as if I've accidentally enrolled in an OCD boot camp and I'm completing some sort of immunising assault course. Tell you what, cup rings on tables won't bother me again.'

She caught Douglas eyeing a shabby chair abandoned at the bottom of the stairs leading to the skip marked 'wood'. 'Don't even think about it. Can we go now? I need a shower.'

Her phone rang. Why did the kids never use the land line? She hated that the tip was her communication zone. 'Hi Mum, I can't talk long but just wanted to say I'm looking at internships for the summer and they're all in London. Do you think Aunty Sue would let me stay?'

Dawn pictured her sister and banker husband lounging on rattan furniture in the vaulted orangery of their Wandsworth home. The woman who had everything was now going to get her daughter as well. 'Probably. I'll text her for you.' She said, distracted by the sight of Douglas stashing the old chair in the boot while he thought she wasn't looking.

'Thanks Mum. Got to dash. Love you! Love to Dad!'

She rang off before Dawn had a chance to tell her their news. But what was their news? That she was at the tip, dumping carpet? That they were perfecting the art of stripping wallpaper?

'All OK?' Douglas asked when they were seated in the car, the windows sealed against the rotting stench, his face grey except for two circles around the eyes where his glasses had sat.

Dawn swatted away a fly. 'Becky's been looking at internships. They're all in London, of course. Wants to know if she can stay with Sue and Rich.' Repeating Becky's words she felt the stab of betrayal.

'Oh.' The disappointment in his voice showed he felt it too. 'I was hoping she'd come down here for the summer, Chris too. They'd love it here. Becky's such a beach babe and Chris could take up surfing again.'

'I thought we were supposed to be working by the summer. You make it sound like one long holiday. Becky at the beach, Chris on the surf, their friends sleeping on the floor, you painting the waves and me slogging away in the kitchen churning out three meals a day for a dozen hungry mouths. Come to think of it, it sounds just like our holidays. Anyway, once she samples the luxury of Wandsworth, I daresay we'll never see her again.'

She didn't say it, but they both knew that if they were still in London, the kids would live at home after uni. She'd so looked forward to them coming back. They filled the empty spaces and lit up the dark corners of their lives. Listening to their stories of adventures and disasters, Dawn re-lived her own youth vicariously through them, though some of it she was glad to have left behind. So many things happened to Becky and Chris in a short space of time. The notes she wrote in Christmas cards to friends were all about what the kids were doing. It was hardly worth wasting ink saying, 'Douglas and I are still in the same jobs, still in the same house, we went on holiday to France last summer. Again.'

Their kids bounced through life, adapting to whatever was thrown at them, whereas they, the older generation, struggled with major life decisions, fearful of making the wrong ones. Their maturity should have brought them experience and simplicity, not this confusion and fear of regret. How much easier to change nothing and convince oneself it was for the best. But after what happened, they'd had no choice but to move on. Time would tell if they'd made the right decisions. On the bright side, at least next Christmas she'd have something to write on the cards.

They drove along the lanes in the fading light. She started to text Sue but stopped. Sue would love it if she asked for a favour; another sign of Dawn's failure. She imagined Becky and her sister sipping coffee from witty mugs, looking out on their impeccable lawn, going to Peter Jones on a whim, accelerating up the King's Road in Sue's red Audi convertible. She switched off her phone and dropped her grimy hands onto paint-splattered track pants.

'I'm starving,' Douglas said. 'What's for supper?'

'Dhal bhat.'

'Not again.'

'Well one of us has got to economise with all these bills to pay.'

'I'm not sure my guts can take another dose. I dread to think the impact it's having on the cess pit. Can't we buy some meat on the way home?'

'I suppose we could afford some scrag end or pigs ears occasionally. Oooh! There's a pheasant. Go for it!'

'So that's what we're reduced to now.' He slammed on the brakes, allowing the bird to zig zag leisurely in front of the car. 'Eating roadkill.'

Dawn didn't hear him. She was thinking of a way to lure Becky to Last Chance.

## CHAPTER 10

On Saturday morning, Dawn pulled aside the sheet curtain in the bedroom to reveal a clear blue sky. There were no Pooks, no thumps, no dust and no snap decisions. For the first time since moving, her mood lightened.

They were eating breakfast outside, admiring the clumps of daffodils and primroses peeking through the weeds, when the post van drove up. Douglas rushed over to take the letters, pulled out a brown envelope, sat back down at the table and tucked it under the breakfast tray.

'What's that?'

He picked up a piece of toast. 'Nothing important.'

'No? Then why are you hiding it? You agreed to keep me in the loop.'

He reached for the marmalade. 'I'm not hiding it. I don't even know what it is.'

'Then open it!'

He spooned marmalade on to his toast. 'I don't want to.'

'Then I will!' She pulled the letter out from under the tray, read Douglas's name on the envelope and slapped it back down on the table. It might be private, a medical letter. 'You open it.'

He put down his toast, wiped his hands on his trousers and did as she asked.

'Well?' She watched him scan the letter and smile.

'It's something from the planning department I've been expecting.' He folded the letter up and put it back in the envelope. He didn't seem to know where to put it. He held it in one hand and ate toast with the other. She stared at the letter wondering why he wouldn't let go of it.

'What exactly?' Her heart thumped. She balled her fists and pressed her nails into her palms. Fresh wounds on old scars.

'It's an acknowledgement of our request for permission to change the Mill to commercial use. It's not going to be a problem. I talked to the planning department about it before we made an offer. It's a formality.'

'But they could refuse.'

Douglas drained his cup and stuffed the envelope in his trouser pocket. 'Technically, yes. But they won't.'

'But you don't know that. There could be local objections or it could be held up and then this whole renovation is a waste of time. How can you be so calm about this?'

He sighed. 'Because there is a precedent. Mrs Pooks used to do bed and breakfast. We just have to hope there aren't local objections.'

'But if permission doesn't come through soon, we can't advertise for the summer.'

'So we may as well carry on with the renovation so we'll get more money for the place. It's not worth much in this state.'

And then we can move back to London, thought Dawn. Hurray!

Douglas stood up and made for the door. 'Oh, by the way, I'm thinking about going on that wild swim today.'

'Don't be ridiculous. You don't have a wetsuit. You'll get hypothermia. I don't understand why it's called wild swimming. It's just plain swimming isn't it?'

He stalked off and, moments later, appeared with a swimming towel under his arm. 'Coming?'

She considered: a morning at the beach or a morning scrubbing flagstones? She grabbed her bag and a thick coat.

Dawn gazed at the sparkling green waters of Elberry Cove, along the coastline to towering red cliffs and beyond them to the hazy hills of Torquay, dotted with white buildings. Out to sea, below puffy clouds, lay the coast of Dorset. She could see why they called this stretch of coast the Riviera.

On the beach, about twenty people were gathered, some pulling on wetsuits, some swathed in towels, ranging in age from twenties to sixties, about half were women. There was a lot of flesh on view for March. She didn't feel like talking to anyone. She was still seething that Douglas hadn't told her about the planning permission.

'Morning,' Douglas hailed as they crunched over the pebbles, 'I thought I might join you.'

Several people called 'hello'. Among them she recognised the pub landlords, slinky in matching wetsuits, goggles positioned on their heads like designer sunglasses.

'Glad you could make it,' one of them held out his hand to Douglas. 'I'm John, this is Andy. We're swimming round to Fishcombe Cove today.'

'How far is that?' Dawn asked, already nervous for Douglas.

'Oh, not far. About a mile. We should be back in an hour.' Andy jogged on the spot and blew into his hands like a triathlete.

Douglas was sporting the tight-lipped smile he wore when England were losing at cricket. He pulled his jumper over his head, kicked off his trainers, peeled off his socks and slipped down his jeans as if stripping for the firing squad. Dawn was relieved to see he already had his trunks on. She folded his clothes and placed them in a plastic carrier bag.

'I told him he shouldn't swim without a wetsuit,' she informed Andy and John lest they think her as half-witted as her husband.

'He'll be fine,' John said, raising his voice above the chatter of Douglas's teeth.

'Are you joining us?' John asked Dawn.

To swim in this temperature wasn't wild swimming, it was crazy swimming. She drew her coat around her. 'No.'

'Very sensible,' piped up a slim woman in a wetsuit who looked pretty despite sporting a swimming hat embellished with psychedelic flowers. 'We must be barking mad.'

Dawn recognised Anastasia despite the attempt to look like an extra in a Buzby Berkeley movie. 'Hello. We're Dawn and Douglas Thompson. We stayed in your cottage last October half-term,' she said stiffly.

Anastasia glanced at them with the air of a TV talent show judge about to tell a particularly appalling act that they'd failed to make it through to the next round. 'Oh, yes?' she murmured, looking out to sea which, now the sun had gone behind a cloud, shimmered many shades of grey. 'Where has the sun gone?' she remarked as if it was one of her subjects and had left the estate without permission. Dawn flushed hot and loosened the scarf around her neck as she noticed Douglas gawping. Anastasia was attractive in an ice-queen sort of way: piercing blue eyes, chiselled cheek bones, well-defined lips.

The group moved down towards the water's edge and she considered dragging Douglas away before he committed this folly. As the only one not swimming, she offered to stay and look after everyone's things.

'Don't worry, we have a lookout.' Anastasia scanned the woods behind the beach. 'Samuel!' she yelled so loudly that Dawn jumped. A lanky lad with red hair ran over. He was the lad who'd been in their attic, the lad who'd vandalised the barn, the lad who'd opened the sluice gate and flooded their house a year ago, according to Tony. Close up, he didn't look anything like the boy from school at all. He was older than she'd thought, early twenties, Becky's age. She winced when she noticed his black eye. Instinct drove her to ask him how he'd done it and if it hurt, but she no longer trusted instinct. She watched him out of the corner of her eye, shifting from foot to foot, picking up pebbles from the beach and dropping them, throwing a stick for a dog belonging to one of the swimmers. Some radar told her to keep her distance. She stepped away from him.

'Right. Everyone ready? Nineteen of us today. Not a bad turnout. Good luck everyone,' said an older man in orange trunks who seemed to be in charge. 'You stick with me,' he told Douglas.

Dawn grabbed Douglas's hand. These people were obviously bonkers. He pulled away from her with a brave smile and waded into the water as if under torture. 'Tell them everything!' she yelled as she saw his body tense in the cold, his shoulders hunch up to his ears and then he dived under the waves, swimming towards the line of yellow buoys, flanked by the others. Soon she couldn't distinguish one swimmer from another. She dipped her fingers into the sea: icy cold. These Devonians were made of different stuff to her. When she turned, Samuel was sitting on the beach next to everyone's things, still throwing a stick for the dog. She walked away from him, to the end of the beach and into the woods. The path immediately started to climb. She couldn't see the sea through the trees but kept going, searching for a clearing that offered a glimpse of the swimmers.

She followed the path, careful not to trip on the roots that crisscrossed it. The towering trees dwarfed her and she forgot all about the swim and anything else other than putting one foot in front of the other. After half an hour or so, the path started to descend and she looked down on a rocky cove. Fishcombe Cove? She scanned the sea and beach for swimmers but saw only gulls bobbing on the water. She sat on a boulder and basked in the sun's feeble rays. It was wonderful to be breathing clean air rather than plaster dust, to not be wearing filthy clothes and pulling scraps of wallpaper from her hair.

Oddly, without Douglas at her side, she missed him. Since they'd moved down, she'd got used to having him constantly around but he was like a puppy that crossed back and forth across the line between heart-warming and irritating.

She still hadn't spotted the swimmers. Were they already back at Elberry Cove? Maybe her winding route through the woods had taken longer than swimming in a straight line and they were all waiting for her. She should have looked at her phone to see when exactly they'd set off. She left her tranquil spot and climbed the steep path into the woods. After twenty minutes or so, Samuel appeared on the path, striding towards her. She was about to ask him whether the mad swimmers were back, but he didn't make eye contact and brushed past her on the narrow path. Their shoulders

49

touched and he leapt away as if he'd been scalded. She looked back at him. He'd turned to glance at her too and opened his mouth as if to speak but said nothing. It hit her then, what it was that was familiar about him. She'd worked with many boys over the years for whom speech was their worst nightmare. They preferred no human interaction at all to the pain of trying. It wasn't her specialism but she'd had to communicate with them in class, watch them struggle to make themselves understood. But it might be best to leave this one alone.

It crossed her mind that if Samuel had left the beach, he was no longer needed to guard belongings so the swimmers must be back. But why he was walking into the woods? Panic stabbed her chest. What if all the swimmers weren't back? What if some, or one, were missing and he'd been sent to look out for them. She broke into a run, tripped on a tree root, slipped on mud, her breath came in ragged bursts. Emerging from the trees, she stopped and scanned the beach below: saw swimmers pulling on their clothes, towels littering the beach. She ran down some steps dangerously fast, not taking her eyes from the figures on the beach. Once her feet clattered on to the pebbles, faces turned to look at her. Unsmiling. She crunched the pebbles as she strode across the beach. Was that Douglas? No. She slowed as Anastasia approached. She held her breath, her legs stopped moving.

'Ah, you're here. Have you seen your husband? We thought maybe he was with you.'

## CHAPTER 11

Douglas smiled as he swam. He could do this. God knows, he'd made a mess of everything else. And now Dawn knew that the planning application could be refused. He'd hoped to keep that from her. He knew the only reason she hadn't gone ballistic was because she still thought they could sell up and move back to London. But he would never move back. He still hoped to win her round; he couldn't run this business on his own, nor afford to keep the Mill without her. He still loved her but he almost needed her more. They had to work as a team but she'd pulled away from him. He'd always thought their marriage was solid, but that had been easy when everything had been going smoothly. Since his redundancy and that business at her school, the relationship had been like mercury: toxic and impossible to grasp. He never knew whether her bad mood stemmed from one of his so-called wrong-doings or she was just grumpy these days. He preferred to believe the latter and live without self-blame.

He squinted into the sun. What a wonderful organ, the human brain! Even when plunged into, let's be honest, freezing water it could convince you the opposite as a means of survival. When he'd first hit the sea, his throat, neck and shoulders had throbbed with pain and he'd stopped doing the crawl and started breast stroke with his neck and shoulders as far out of the water as he could manage. He'd slowed down and started to lag behind the others who were soon a good swimming-pool length ahead of him. The chap who'd said, 'Stick with me,' obviously hadn't meant, 'I'll stick with you.' John and Andy, the only people he vaguely knew apart from Anastasia, had swum out of sight and Douglas wasn't sure he'd recognise them anyway. Most people looked the same with their hair slicked down. All the heads bobbing in the waves looked the same except for Anastasia. The psychedelic rubber flowers on her swim hat could be seen for miles. Maybe that was the idea. He should buy one himself, something more manly, with rubber sharks and anchors on it. Then they'd notice him. Anastasia hadn't recognised him. Had he grown so forgettable in his fifties? She, on the other hand, looked unforgettable in that slinky wetsuit.

The water no longer felt cold. He noticed dark shapes floating and swam towards them. As he approached, he saw they were large plastic floats like upturned dustbins with chains and ropes attached, trailing under the water, and they were covered with clusters of mussels. He thought about holding on to a float, but you could get a nasty cut brushing against those shells. He swam away from them, further out to sea. Looking towards the coast, he spied two small coves beyond the headland. 'Please God, let the first cove be Fishcombe.' For some odd reason he'd spoken out loud. He swallowed a mouthful of water. The salt burned his throat. His eyes watered as he coughed. His legs flailed. Don't panic, he told himself. After what seemed several minutes, he could breathe again. He squinted into the distance. Heads bobbed beyond the two coves and some were already disappearing around the next headland. Then the sun went behind a cloud. The sea darkened. A gust of wind whipped up the water. Azure blue to steel grey. He spun around. There was nothing but him and sea. No one around to help him. He turned his back on the mussel floats and trod water. Should he head back to Elberry? No. He would look like an idiot. He must follow the swimmers. He began swimming again, aching stroke by aching stroke, scanning the sea for specks in the distance, forcing himself to keep moving. After a while, he realised he could no longer feel his hands. The waves were growing larger and one slapped him on the side of the head, blocking his ear. Stinging water blinded him. Two senses down. He spat out salt water. Taste was the one sense he could do without.

His arms wouldn't do what he asked and no longer seemed attached to him but extended in front of him like pale pieces of meat. Again, water flooded his ears as he struggled to keep his head above the waves. It was now too choppy to carry on. He must make for the shore; to the cove he'd hoped was their destination. He willed his arms to move and, after an age, he passed the mussel floats again. He was tempted to stop and hang on to one but feared he'd never be able to let go. He kept swimming. His breath sounded like the bark of a seal. His chest felt fit to burst. He wanted to stop but didn't dare even tread water; he would sink. How far away was the shore? Everything was blurred. He saw stars on the edge of his vision.

He gasped as something gripped his leg. He kicked at it but it clung on. He managed to roll on to his back, raise his legs and flail at the slippery seaweed with his useless hands. He sunk like a stone. Icy water flooded his ears, his eyes and leaked into his head. It was dark all around Were his eyes closed? He heard the slow beat... beat ...beat of his heart. How much time had passed? The faces of Dawn, Chris and Becky wobbled on the edge of his vision, out of focus. When he turned to face them, they disappeared. They were shouting at him but he couldn't hear what they were saying.

## CHAPTER 12

'Douglas. Douglas Thompson,' Dawn called after Anastasia as she ran to higher ground to find a phone signal.

'Hello. Is that the coastguard?' Dawn heard her say as a thermos cup of tea was thrust into her hand.

'Don't worry dear, he probably made for shore and is walking back at this very moment,' said a large woman wrapped in a towel.

'I don't understand. Why did no one realise he'd fallen behind?' Dawn said. 'Surely someone noticed.' She scanned the group for the man who'd said he would stick with Douglas, but she couldn't recognise him without the orange trunks. Douglas was nothing to these people. Not worth keeping alive. 'Why did no one notice? When did someone last see him?' She wanted to grab every one of them and shake them.

No one spoke but the group exchanged worried glances. Then she realised the implication: they hadn't noticed him falling behind because he hadn't been there to be seen. He'd gone under. She turned her back on them and scanned the sea. A vision of him floating beneath the surface flashed in her head. She struggled to breathe.

'Dawn, we're really sorry but we've got to get back to open the pub.' John placed a hand on her shoulder. 'I'm sure he'll turn up.'

Dawn gripped the thermos cup. Her hand shook. It was their fault Douglas was there in the first place and all they were bothered about was selling pints. Did no one care? What was wrong with these people?

Anastasia appeared. 'I've alerted the coastguard. They're sending out a boat and a team to search the coast. I'm sure they'll find him.'

'Thanks,' Dawn mumbled. She hated her and all these stupid swimmers. She'd told Douglas it was a crazy idea. Why had he insisted on swimming in such cold? He should have listened to her. Yes, it's annoying that she always imagines the worst, but it's a tactic that keeps you alive.

'Look, try not to worry. The first timers usually turn up.'

'I heard that man over there talking about one of the swimmers who drowned two years ago.'

'I can't imagine why on earth he would bring that up,' said Anastasia. 'Some people have absolute shit for brains.'

Her anger took away some of Dawn's, but fear filled the space. Tears flowed down her face. She gritted her teeth as a sob rose in her chest but it burst out of her. Anastasia fumbled in the pocket of her body warmer, pulled out a tissue and handed it to Dawn.

'Look. I've been swimming down here all my life and in that entire time, almost forty five years if you must know, I've only known of one drowning. The bay is shallow, no cross currents or anything dangerous. I've sent Samuel along the coast path to see if he can spot him. These woods are his playground. If he's out there, Samuel will find him. I gave him Douglas's clothes in case he's ... well ... he's hypothermic.'

Then, out of the corner of her eye Dawn saw a figure step out of the woods. Her heart leapt.

'Douglas!'

But it was Samuel. Alone.

Another sob broke from her chest. Anastasia rushed over to Samuel and he turned on his heel and disappeared back into the wood. She should go and look too. The alternative, to stay with these uncaring excuses for human beings, was unthinkable.

## CHAPTER 13

Douglas is drifting. It feels good not to be battling water and waves. Even his lungs have stopped hurting. The family have gone now. They've dissolved into the black. It's peaceful. It's really not so bad...drowning.

'Douglas!'

His eyes jerk open. Dawn's voice. How... where... what? His eyes tell his brain to twist his neck to search for light. He finds a glimmer though it seems a long way off. He launches himself towards it. What if it's not daylight but merely an illusion? Maybe he's swimming deeper and further away from the air he craves. A pearl diver, he thinks, knife in mouth, can swim comfortably underwater for minutes. He raises his arms, reaching for the light, kicking with all his might. Then his head is out of the water. He gasps for air, feels himself choking. Oh, the pain in his lungs. His legs flail desperately. He mustn't go down again. A surge of energy courses through his body, like an electric current it moves through him. His arms, his hands and even his fingertips throb into life. He powers towards the shore: 1, 2, 3 stokes breathe, 1, 2, 3 breathe. He's at Crouch End baths. The water is warm and smells of chlorine. He's swimming down the roped-off lane, reaching the end, turning and pushing off again, dodging other swimmers. The shoreline is closer! He drops a foot hoping to find solid ground. Nothing. It takes every ounce of energy to raise his legs and kick them again. A little further and he tries again. A foot strikes a rock. He gasps with relief. His feet on solid ground! Then a wave knocks him off it.

He flounders. His arms ache as he pulls against the water but he keeps going and going until his toes scrape pebbles. He drags his body on to the shore, but the sea seems to cling on to him as if reluctant to let him go. He falls at one point and when he stands, his body feels heavy as lead. He stumbles ashore, drops to his knees, and flops face down on the beach. With the hard ground pressing into his chest, he struggles to breathe.

He rolls on to his back and gasps for air. The wind chills his wet skin and he starts to shiver. He knows he must get up. Keep moving. He pushes himself back into kneeling position, looks up at the cliff rising from the beach.

He stands and slaps his arms and legs. He can't feel them. He forces one leg, then another to move. His sees his ankles twist on the stones but he can't feel his feet at all. His eyes scan the cliff surrounding the beach, the huge boulders at each end and beyond them, to where more cliffs fall steeply into the sea. There's no way out. He turns back towards the sea. He can't go back in there. He looks again at the cliff behind the beach. Rocks have fallen one on top of the other and he sees spaces between them and ledges and holes and tree roots and fallen trees which might make it climbable. It's the only way out. He finds a gravelly bit of the beach and runs on the spot. He takes his pulse. It's slow, but he feels it speed up under his fingers. He notices a bluish tinge to his hands so he claps them together and shakes them and they tingle as the blood flows back in. He runs on the spot again before tackling the first boulder, crouching on all fours when he reaches the top. He scrambles up to another, groping for handholds, shoving his numb feet into footholds, grabbing at giant roots sticking out of the cliff, hanging on to fallen trees nestled on ledges. He feels his body heat up as he climbs. He must be near the top. A jagged chunk of rock is sticking out, overhanging. He'll never get over that. He spots a place to the left of it where a section of cliff has fallen away. It might be climbable, but he'll have to edge beneath the overhang. He takes a breath. Gripping on to a huge tree root, he lowers his left leg and feels for a foothold. He moves his right foot across to the same hold. Then he moves his left foot over again but can only see a foothold higher up. He goes for it, hurting his toe as he thrusts it into the gap between two rocks. He hoists himself up, his left leg taking all the weight, and grunts as he slams his right foot into the gap. His head is level with the top of the cliff. It's more soil than rock. He reaches up to touch it and red earth rains down on him, peppering his eyes and mouth. A strange noise escapes him, half sob, half wail. He tastes the iron of the soil.

He hears him first: sticks breaking in the undergrowth, the clatter of an empty can. And then his face is above his own, eyes wide under the mop of ginger hair. Samuel grunts and lowers his arm and Douglas grasps his hand but the boy shakes it off and points over to his left. He turns his head and sees a place where the cliff slopes up to the top, as if it has been cut away. He shuffles to his left and then across on to the slope where, on all fours, he makes his way to the top. He notices some crudely cut steps. Why the hell hadn't he seen that from the bottom?

At last he reaches the top of the cliff and sits, panting. He looks down at the cuts on his ankles and knees; a big toenail hangs loose. His knuckles are grazed. He notices the blood but the wounds don't hurt. Samuel sits beside him and pulls his folded clothes out of a bag. He thinks of Dawn, folding his clothes on the beach. He wipes his face on his T-shirt, smears it with tears and soil and blood, and pulls it over his head but can't get his arms into the sleeves. Samuel takes his wrist and stretches the T-shirt until he can hook his hand into a sleeve hole. He does the same with the other arm and then with his sweatshirt. Douglas extends his legs and Samuel feeds his jeans over them. It's hard because his legs are still wet and he has his trunks on but he feels better covered. He pulls up the zip while Samuel pushes socks over his feet. Douglas is reminded of dressing his kids when they were small; of how hard it was to push Becky's chubby legs into her tiny tights and how she would moan that he was crushing her toes when he pulled them up. Then Samuel picks up his trainers. He winces as his big toe stubs the hard leather. He's glad it's Samuel that's here and not one of the others. He wouldn't want anyone to see him like this. He bends his legs and tries to stand but rolls on to his side. Samuel faces him, plants his feet in front of Douglas's, grasps his arms above the elbows and hauls him up. Once standing, his head swims for a moment and he leans against the boy heavily. He feels him push something into his mouth and tastes the sickly sweet of a toffee. He smiles at him gratefully. The boy hasn't said a word. Samuel bends down to lace his trainers and as he is absorbed in the task, Douglas wipes away tears with the back of his sleeve. Then Samuel takes off his own jacket, lifts Douglas's arm and pushes it down the sleeve, wraps it around his back and pushes the other arm into the other sleeve hole.

Douglas looks around and sees they are standing next to a clearing littered with empty beer cans, cigarette packets and the remains of a fire. The evidence that he is returned to civilisation comforts him. Samuel holds his arm and manoeuvres Douglas along a path through the gorse and brambles to where it meets a wider path under the tree canopy. Water drips from his hair onto his face. He is still shivering. He wants to get back to Dawn and leave this place. The thought of her makes him want to cry. He doesn't want any of the swimmers to see him like this. He concentrates on putting one foot in front of the other.

# CHAPTER 14

Dawn turned away from the swimmers and moved across the beach towards the woods. She stopped dead. Samuel again, but moving slowly, a stooped figure at his side. Douglas?

The lump in her throat felt ready to burst. Relief flooded over her.

'Douglas!' she cried out.

'I'll call off the coastguard,' Anastasia said, striding off.

Dawn's emotions veered from wanting to rush up and start battering Douglas to weeping for pure joy. She scrubbed at her face with the tissue as she walked over to meet them in what she hoped was a dignified manner. The swimmers started to clap though Dawn couldn't imagine why he deserved applause. Maybe they were clapping Samuel for finding him. Douglas held out his arms and she fell into them but he was the one clinging to her. He felt damp and smelt of earth but she didn't care. She pulled back and saw his hands and face were smeared with blood but she couldn't see where the wounds were.

'Thank God you're all right. I thought... What the hell happened?'

'I did my best ... got left behind... panicked.... ran out of puff... swam for shore but had to... climb up a cliff.' His speech came in odd spurts, like a faulty phone connection.

Anastasia broke off from speaking into her phone, 'Are you OK?'

'Yes ... I don't know ... very cold.'

She cut him off and spoke into the phone, 'Yes he's fine, sorry about the false alarm but we can't be too careful after what happened before.' She pocketed her phone. 'Well, you had us all worried. The coastguard were about to send out the helicopter.'

'He's freezing,' Dawn told her to make the point that he wasn't fine at all. She took off her coat and draped it over his shoulders. Douglas didn't move. She saw his face was wet and heard his teeth chattering.

'You need a hot bath. Now,' Anastasia said.

'We've only got a warm shower at the Mill.'

Anastasia appeared to be considering something. 'Then you'd better come back to the Manor. Let's get going. You can follow my car.' She looked up and down the beach, 'Samuel!' she yelled and the lad scuttled out of the woods like a startled rabbit. 'Car now!'

'Thank you,' Dawn said, relieved that Anastasia was acting swiftly.

'See you next week,' a swimmer shouted to Douglas as they staggered across the pebbles.

'Make sure you bring your arm bands next time,' shouted another.

Douglas didn't look over. 'Very funny,' he said, but she doubted they heard him.

'Bastards,' she said under her breath. 'It's not a fucking joke.'

Inside the car, he started to shiver more violently and Dawn realised he was worse than he was letting on. Perhaps it was shock. 'Don't worry. We'll soon have you in a hot bath.' She placed her hand on his juddering knee, whammed the heating on full blast and accelerated after Anastasia's car. Cold air streamed out.

'I thought I was going to die. I saw you and the kids in the water. It was like they say …my whole life flashed in front of me. I almost gave in. You were all yelling at me. I knew I had to do something or you'd be really annoyed.' Dawn glanced over at him. He was blubbering like a child.

'Annoyed! I thought I'd lost you.' She told him about the man who'd drowned.

'Oh, my God. I'm such an idiot.' His teeth were chattering.

They slowed in a hamlet of pink cottages set around a huge oak tree. Dawn recognised the cottage they'd stayed in when house-hunting. She pulled up behind Anastasia in front of a pair of massive iron gates set in stone pillars which opened automatically. Once inside, Samuel got out and strode across the lawn, without a jacket even though it was drizzling.

'Did you notice his black eye? D'you think the Pooks did it?'

'Maybe. Hope not,' said Douglas. 'Was I glad to see him. He helped me. Don't think he can speak.'

At least Douglas's speech was improving. 'Can't speak or won't speak. He's certainly not comfortable with people. He hears when Anastasia yells at him, and she seems to understand him.' A grey stone mansion loomed through the trees. She saw turrets, columns, towers. 'Oh my God,' she murmured under her breath.

# CHAPTER 15

Anastasia phoned Mary from the car and told her to run a bath, light the fire and make tea. She parked in front of the house. The sooner that idiot immersed in hot water the better.

What a strange couple, she mused. For the first time she was optimistic about buying back Last Chance Mill. Those two couldn't organise a piss up in a cider house. They'd scuttle back to London like a couple of town mice at the first sign of trouble. They seemed oddly ill-matched: he so obviously up for anything, even drowning, and she so nervous. He was in rather good shape but she had let herself go with her grey roots, double chin and dowdy clothes. Easily done in the country where no one sees you from week to week but this pair had blown in from London. A shame as she must have been pretty once, with those with dark eyelashes and that creamy skin that tans easily, the envy of every real blonde. She checked herself out in the rear view mirror, squinted to form crows' feet around her eyes and frown lines between her brows and considered that it might be time for Botox.

She opened the door, surprised by the quiet. No click-clacking of Coco's claws as she trotted across the tiled floor to greet her, tail wagging. Poor thing must be sound asleep in her basket, exhausted by the prospect of giving birth at any moment. Anastasia could sympathise – she'd been exactly the same with Cosmo and Rollo. The doctor had ordered her to stay in bed for the last three months of the pregnancy with both of them. Bloody huge they'd been, like Freddie, and she so petite. Not really designed for childbirth, or mothering come to that. She'd been relieved when they'd both opted to go on the school skiing trip this Easter holiday. They took up so much space and made so much noise; it was exhausting.

She ushered the couple inside. 'MARY!!' She saw Mary flinch as she bustled up and took their wet coats. 'Could you dry these and make a big pot of tea? I'll show Donald where the bathroom is.'

'D…Douglas,' stuttered the man. 'It's Douglas.'

'Whatever… you can warm up by the fire in the sitting room,' she told the woman, gesturing to the door. 'Don… I mean Douglas you come with me,' she started up the stairs.

The man lagged behind and when she turned she saw him staring at the walls and muttering to himself. She hoped he wasn't hypothermic and delusional after the swimming ordeal.

'Munnings,' she heard him utter. 'Good God, is that a Sargeant? That has to be a …' Then she realised he was reciting the names of the artists of the paintings on the stairs. 'Surely that's not a … no it can't be…'

'Yes, it is a Monet. A lesser-known one. You know your art.'

'It's like the Tate Gallery here.' He looked up at her with a look of adoration reminiscent of Coco.

'My family have given quite a lot to the Tate over the years…' She continued up the staircase, enjoying the reverence.

'How generous.'

'… to avoid death duties. They were crippling in the seventies.' And the reason her father sold Last Chance Mill to that drunkard, Edward Pooks. Before then it had lain empty for twenty years, abandoned by the miller, their tenant, who couldn't compete with the cheap Canadian flour imports after the war.

She led him across the landing past a Constable he seemed reluctant to leave. 'Here's the bathroom. You'll find plenty of towels in the airing cupboard inside. I suggest you have a good long soak. I'll leave some clothes outside the door. You're a similar build to my husband. Come down when you're ready for hot tea and biscuits.' She had to push him in the door. He definitely looked a bit stunned. Perhaps he was in shock.

'Would you like me to call the vet? I mean doctor. Sorry. More used to dealing with animals than humans.'

'No, no I'm fine. Just a bit overwhelmed.'

'I see.' Perhaps she'll ask his wife what she thinks. Maybe he's always this odd.

The woman was standing in front of the fire with a cup of tea in the sitting room. 'Would you like something stronger?' She opened up the northern hemisphere of a huge globe and revealed an array of bottles. 'A brandy, perhaps? You've had a bit of a shock.' The woman had been distraught on the beach. Obviously loved the dolt of a husband. How would Freddie react if he thought she'd drowned? Probably ring up the mistress and arrange for her to come down for the weekend. Guess what? He'd say to her, we've got the place to ourselves, except for my dead wife's corpse on the dining room table.

She pushed a strand of blonde hair away from her face. 'Oh God, there's only a dribble of vodka left. MARY!' she yelled into the hallway. 'VODKA PLEASE!'

'Yes, I'll have whatever you're having, thank you,' said the woman.

Mary appeared in the doorway clutching the desired bottle. Anastasia cracked open the top and poured out two shots and handed one to the woman. '*Vashe zdorovie*,' she said and they clanked glasses.

'Thank you. For taking us in and looking after us.' She looked genuinely grateful. Anastasia realised it had been a long time since she'd deserved anyone's gratitude.

'Not at all. Least I could do after that arsehole lost your husband. He should have kept a better eye on him.'

'Quite. He just abandoned him.'

'I would have kept an eye out myself but he's in charge so I thought he would know better. I'll bring it up at the next meeting, don't you worry. I'll give him a really hard time. I'm good at that. I'd better go and find your husband some clothes. Won't be a tick.'

In Freddie's dressing room she found a pair of boxers, a T-shirt, some cords, a thick jumper and a body warmer. You couldn't be too careful with hypothermia. She placed them outside the bathroom. She listened at the door and heard splashing which reassured her. Then she remembered she'd forgotten socks. Back in the dressing room, she opened Freddie's sock drawer and rummaged around at the back to find a pair he didn't wear much. Her fingers brushed something hard and she pulled out a pair of socks with something stuffed inside. Odd. Freddie had hidden something here. It felt like a small box. She hesitated. Could it be a gift for her? Would she spoil the surprise if she were to look at it now? But what if it wasn't meant for her? What if it was for his mistress, whoever that was at the moment. She felt a wave of nausea. She needed to see exactly what this was. If she never received it, she'd know for sure that he'd given it to someone else. Plus, the gift would tell her the seriousness of the affair.

She pulled back the sock and revealed the robin-egg blue of a Tiffany box. Expensive and stylish but not antique-priceless. She flipped the lid: diamond earring. Enough to say, 'I care' but not enough to say, 'forever'. Not a complete disaster then. It suggested a casual rather than a serious relationship, same as the others.

Her mind started racing. She could have a bit of fun with this. Knowledge was power wasn't it? What if she took them and he found they'd gone? Would he come clean? Apologise, tell her she was the only one he loved and end it like last time? Better still, what if she wore them? She'd love to see the look on his face when he realised she'd found him out. She'd like to see him try and explain that one away. The smile froze on her lips. She couldn't do that. There was a chance he'd bought them for her birthday next month. Or not. A wave of sadness engulfed her and she sat heavily on the floor. Who was she kidding? Could she put up with this much longer? Should she finally end it with Freddie and start the process of disentangling herself from him? She imagined herself rattling around this house all alone, sharing the boys in the holidays, old friends gossiping, dividing up the spoils and feeling a failure. Would she even be able to keep the estate? It was in trust, along with the contents, but he could still claim half and she wouldn't be able to buy him out, even with half her share of the London flat. It seemed all wrong. Some of the paintings had been in her family for centuries. Why should he have half? She couldn't bear that. And there was the added shame that she would be the first Montague to divorce. The first dreadful 'd' would appear on the family tree.

She forced herself to take a few deep breaths. If only there were someone she could talk to about all this. It was too shameful to discuss with their London friends. Could she really call them friends anyway? She knew enough about friendship to acknowledge she didn't matter a jot to a single one of them. They probably all knew about Freddie's philandering anyway. Perhaps they didn't even blame him. They never asked her anywhere without Freddie. Everyone thought him amusing, a good conversationalist and a positive addition to any party. A couple of drinks propelled him from sullen to scintillating. Then she would see him as they did, as he'd once appeared to her. The friends mistook her watchful sadness for coldness and probably wondered why he put up with her. Without Freddie, she realised, she'd be even more alone. No. Separation or divorce simply weren't options. Better to keep things as they were. Perhaps she should stay at the London flat with him next week. Keep a closer eye on him; follow him and find out if he was having an affair; scour the flat for evidence, that sort of thing. And if he was, nip it in the bud before it bloomed.

She heard a shout and then Mary's voice calling her. Maybe Coco had started delivery. Dear, devoted Coco. Thank God somebody loved her. She knew where she was with a dog. She stuffed the box inside the socks, pushed them to the back of the drawer, grabbed another pair, dropped them outside the bathroom door and ran downstairs.

# CHAPTER 16

Samuel was cold and wet. He'd given his hoody to the blow-in. He'd lived by the sea his whole life but you wouldn't catch him in there. Outsiders don't know the dangers. When he was dressing him, he remembered how he'd dressed his dad. He mustn't think about that. He stared up at the pelting rain. Rainin' cats and dogs, he'd heard them say. How could anyone think that the rain was like cats and dogs? Rain was water. Water from clouds, nothing to do with cats and dogs. Why would anyone say that? He looked up, imagining cats and dogs falling from the sky. Rain stabbed his face like needles and his cheek stung where Nigel had punched him. He didn't care about that. He'd do anything for Her. He'd felt special when she'd asked him to do her that favour at Last Chance Mill that time. He didn't care what the Pooks did to him. He was sure it was them who'd told Nigel about him being inside the Mill.

He ran towards the shelter of the wood. Lying on a patch of ground, he listened to the sound of the rain lashing the trees. Spring was late. The branches and twigs were still bare. The rain was splattering and splotching his top, making a camouflage pattern. He felt like a commando stalking a target. He hoped Nigel wasn't out with his gun, after a fat pheasant or two. Nigel would take a shot at him and say it was an accident. He, Samuel, was a target. Grabbing leaf mould and twigs in his fists, he rubbed it over his clothing. He scooped handfuls of red mud and smeared it over his face. He could hide here for days. How quiet it was compared with the house with his brothers ordering him around and arguing, and his mother yelling at him about why his clothes were so dirty, why he didn't get the job, why he couldn't be like other twenty year olds, why he hadn't taken out the rubbish, why he'd dumped a pile of junk in the garden, why he kept a live bat in a shoebox in his room. He lay dead still. More of the earth than human.

They were on the edge of the wood. Two males and one female squatting not five metres away, their feathers shiny with rain, their red wattles glowing like fire. He stared at the colours of their plumage as they stood next to the feeding bin. When the rain stopped, he would move it to the middle of the field, like he moved the others, forcing the shooters to cross the open field where the birds would spot them and escape, flying off in a squadron. Vroom! The head of one of the males bobbed up as it spied him. He stared at Samuel out the corner of his eye and Samuel stared back. He knew their eyelids blinked from the bottom up and that they didn't need to blink as much as humans. If he didn't blink, the bird might think he wasn't human. He said the word over and over in his head: human, human, human until it was just a sound with no meaning. He wondered if the pheasant knew it was a pheasant and whether this even mattered to a pheasant. But pheasant is a human word and pheasants will have another pheasant-word for themselves. Nigel said pheasants were the pond life of birds as they lie in wait for cars, then dart out and run along in front of them as if they have a death wish. When he'd stammered that they were brave, his brother hooted with laughter and retorted that brave and stupid were the same thing and that's why he, Samuel, should join the army.

Three sleek heads jerked in unison as a large black shape lumbered towards them. At first he thought it was a sheep but then he recognised Her dog, Coco. The dog liked to lie near him when he worked in the Manor garden, to keep him company. He looked around for Her, the mistress, as dogs aren't usually out alone. The pheasants strutted and clucked, unsure what to do. Then they took off with a whir of pounding wings. Feathers rained down on him. The dog's pelt must be heavy with rain as she was moving slowly. He remembered she was pregnant but had no idea how far along. Surely if she was near her time, they wouldn't have let her out. His heart quickened as the dog approached, no doubt heading for shelter, but then she fell on her side in the long wet grass and growled, no, not a growl, more of a moan. If the dog had seen him, she gave no sign. Even when he sat up and crawled nearer, she showed no interest, not even raising her head. He crawled nearer and noticed the dog's body twitching as if something was shaking it and she groaned more loudly. It must be her time. She was in pain, maybe even dying. He stood and walked towards the quivering body. Teats peeked pink through the brown fur of her tummy. She didn't even turn her head to look at him. He could see the whites of her eyes, her teeth set in a grimace as she panted. He'd seen that look before. Leaning in close, he smelt her fear. He breathed his sounds into her ear and rested one hand on her head and the other on her heart. As soon as her pulse slowed and her breathing deepened, he took off.

He hared down into the coombe. His lungs hurt and his legs shook as he forced himself to run uphill. Finally, the house loomed through the mist and his feet hit gravel. He reached the front door, clanged the bell, banged his fists on the door and bent over, panting.

Mary opened it and looked him up and down as if she'd never seen a boy covered in mud and feathers before. 'Sam! What on earth?'

'D...d...' he stammered, but Mary just frowned. He looked past her into the hall. If She was there, She would understand. He shouted, shocked at the sound which came from his mouth which wasn't what he'd meant. Mary's eyes widened in alarm, she took a step back and called for Her, and then he saw Her coming down the stairs.

'C...C...' he tried again and saw Her face change. She turned on her heel and ran towards the back of the house.

'She's not there. Did you let her out?' she shouted at Mary. 'I told you not to let her out. Call the vet at once. Tell him the puppies are most likely in breach and Coco might need a caesarean. Tell him to come right away.'

She came up really close. Her eyes were flecked with violet. 'Where is she?'

He pointed across the valley to the wood and wrestled with his mouth forcing out the sound, 'Fe...fe.'

'Where the pheasants feed in Badgers Wood?'

He nodded madly. She understood him. Adults didn't normally get him, his own mother didn't get him but She always did. She pulled on wellies and a waterproof, and grabbed a blanket whilst yelling at Mary, 'Phone the vet. Tell him to take Sandy Lane to Badgers Wood and to sound the horn as he approaches. Now!'

Another woman stepped into the hallway, the other blow-in. 'What is it?'

'It's my dog. She's about to give birth out in the woods. The puppies may be in breach. She can't do it alone.'

'What can I do?'

'Come with us. We need someone to look out for the vet.'

The woman hopped around pulling on her trainers, found her coat and then they were running downhill after him, slipping on the wet grass. When he turned to check they were keeping up, he noticed Her hair lay sleek to Her head and he saw the fear in Her eyes, and she looked just like a frightened bird.

## CHAPTER 17

Dawn started to lag behind. She hadn't run for about ten years. If only she were as lithe as Anastasia. Her clothes were a bit looser since the dhal bhat diet but she munched biscuits on the sly. She was soaked and seriously out of breath when they reached the valley bottom. She looked at the grassy hill ahead and plodded up behind them, envying Douglas languishing in a hot bath. She followed Anastasia and Samuel into a wood but couldn't see them.

'Over here!' She heard Anastasia yell.

Dawn crashed through the undergrowth, ducked under branches and reached a clearing. The state of the dog shocked her. The animal's eyes were rolled back in her head, and she was whimpering in distress, her stomach pulsating and moving strangely. She looked as if she were dying. Anastasia sat on the wet grass stroking the dog's head and Samuel was kneeling and making strange clicking noises in her ear. He was covered in mud and feathers as if taking part in some weird ritual, a sort of witch doctor meets Morris man. She half expected him to dance around the dog, shaking sticks.

'See that tall pine over there?' Anastasia gestured with her head to a tree about five hundred yards away. 'That's on the lane the vet will take. Look out for him and bring him over.'

Dawn picked her way back through the wood into the field and headed for the tree. She approached a fence and ran alongside it looking for a gate but couldn't see one. She tried to squeeze between the fence wires but her shoulders got stuck and she pulled out. She held on to a fence post, climbed up the wires and ended up straddling the barbed wire at the top. As she was hoisting herself over, the sole of her trainer slipped and a barb snagged her jeans and scratched her thigh. With one foot on the ground, she struggled to unhook it. Free at last, she pulled her leg over and felt a sharp pain. Great. A groin strain. She limped across the field in a half-run but skidded and fell flat on her front. The fall knocked the wind out of her and for a moment, she couldn't move. Cautiously, she moved her arms, then her legs; nothing seemed to be broken. Luckily it had been a soft landing. She rolled on to her side, looked down and gasped at the greenish brown gunge plastered all over her coat, her jeans and even on her trainers. Cow manure. Her face hovered above anther pile. The stench made her want to retch. Her chest felt heavy. She couldn't breathe. Couldn't move. She screwed her eyes shut and held her nose. It's only dirt, only a cow pat, she told herself. She had to get to the lane. Moving one leg then the other, she forced herself to stand, eyes still shut. There's nothing there, Dawn, nothing there. Her eyes flashed open and she ran towards the fir tree. There was no sign of the vet. She dragged her limbs through the wet grass to try and wipe off the manure but that that only spread it. After a couple of minutes, came the sound of an engine and a huge 4x4 sped towards her. She waved her arms and it pulled up, but not before careering through a puddle and soaking her with muddy water. She gasped and looked down at her drenched, stinking clothes, and wished she could rip them from her body. A tall man with a beard jumped out clutching a bag.

'Hi. I'm the vet. Roger Masters. Where is she?'

'This way.' Dawn set off at a run, keeping an eye out for skidding hazards. Roger made for a gate at the top of the field that Dawn hadn't noticed.

She was relieved to find the dog still alive. Samuel was performing his ritual and Anastasia shot an anxious look in the vet's direction but her eyes rarely left the dog's. Dawn watched as Roger inserted his hands inside the dog and gently twisted and turned as the poor thing whimpered and shook. Dawn held her breath when the dog closed her eyes and went suddenly quiet. Anastasia looked sharply at Roger and Dawn knew what she was thinking.

Roger must have sensed her fear too. 'It's not breach. There's a puppy stuck in the birth canal. It feels quite large.'

He withdrew his hands and a tiny dark bundle squeezed out followed by some bloody gloop. Anastasia and Samuel were smiling and crying and making encouraging sounds and stroking Coco. And then another popped out and, with it, some more gloop and then another and another. Anastasia and Samuel were laughing. Roger seized a syringe from his bag and gave the dog a shot of something. The dog started licking the gloop. Dawn fought nausea. She had never witnessed anything like this before. She had never owned pets as a child (No, Dawn, they're too messy). Not even a goldfish (Sorry, Dawn, too smelly). She put her hand over her mouth and lowered her head and caught a whiff of excrement coming from the greenish stains on her front. What with that and the mud and blood mingling around the dog a sound, half laugh, half cry escaped her throat.

Roger picked up each of the five puppies to examine them, and then handed two to Samuel and two to Anastasia. He held out the big one, the one that had been stuck in the birth canal, to her. She wanted to protest. Sorry, she couldn't possibly touch a body covered in blood and slime that had emerged from inside an animal but she screwed up her face, held out her hands and Roger placed the tiny squirming bundle in them. She held it at arm's length, the fear of dropping it battling the fear of adding more bodily fluids to her person.

'Put them inside your coat and rub them. It will stimulate them to breathe.'

Really? Was he joking? Inside her coat was the only part of her not covered in filth. She gently pulled down the zip and rested the puppy inside, one hand cradling it from underneath. It felt damp and sticky and when she rubbed with her other hand, a fishy smell rose from its matted fur.

'Let's get this old girl back to the car.' Gently, Roger picked up Coco's mini stretcher.

Dawn stared down at the tiny face of the mewing puppy nestling inside her jacket and felt (of a) wave protection towards it. She carried it as carefully as she could over to the vet's car, trailing behind the others.

'Do you have something I can put over the seat?' she asked noticing, with dismay, the cream leather interior. Roger laid Coco in the boot and smoothed a sheet of plastic on the back seat.

'What's that smell?' Anastasia asked climbing in beside her.

'It's me. I skidded and fell on a cow pat.' Dawn raised her chin and gritted her teeth.

Anastasia looked over at Dawn's green stained front and shit covered leg and then the corner of her mouth twitched and she started to laugh.

'It's not funny. It's revolting! I need a shower. Now!'

Anastasia laughed even harder and Samuel turned round from the front seat to look and he was laughing too. Great guffaws followed by rasping breaths.

'Phew!' exclaimed Roger and made a show of holding his nose. The car rocked with laughter and soon Dawn's sides ached and she had no idea why she was laughing and not falling apart.

# CHAPTER 18

The Manor's oak and cream-painted kitchen filled Dawn with envy. She laid the tiny puppy next to Coco who settled in a basket beside a massive Aga. She and Samuel fussed over the puppies; the others were even tinier than hers. An odd lad, she decided, but harmless. Roger gave Anastasia instructions of what to do and what to look out for. Anastasia glowered at Mary when she handed them mugs of hot chocolate. Poor woman, Dawn wouldn't like to be on the wrong side of Anastasia.

Mary looked Dawn up and down. 'Lor' Lummee! What happened to you?'

'City girl,' Anastasia said.

Dawn smiled. 'Shitty girl, more like.'

Samuel seemed reluctant to leave the puppies but Anastasia reminded him there were stables to muck out and horses to bring in and Dawn remembered he worked as the groom.

'When they're old enough, you can have one,' Anastasia told him. 'If it hadn't been for you, they might have died. Coco included. But you must keep him here, after what happened to the last one. He'll be your responsibility. OK?'

Samuel smiled and nodded and his mouth moved but he seemed unable to speak. 'Now off you go. And you,' she turned to Dawn and held her nose, 'are the next one for the bath.'

'Oh, God! Douglas!' Dawn exclaimed suddenly, remembering she had a husband with suspected hypothermia.

'He's fine,' said Mary in a comforting west-country burr. 'He had a cup of tea and fell asleep on the settee.'

'Bathroom's upstairs, first door on the right, towels are in the cupboard. I'll find you some clean jeans.'

'Thanks. I couldn't put these back on.'

'It's as bad as having the boys at home with you two around. Take this plastic bag to put your dirty clothes in. Mary can wash them for you.'

Dawn started to protest then remembered that she didn't yet have a washing machine. With the drama, she realised she hadn't thought once about the Mill and the work and the bills.

'It's the least we can do after you helped us out,' Anastasia said. 'You were marvellous.'

'Well, I provided some comic relief, I suppose, if slapstick is your thing.'

Dawn took a peek at Douglas on her way upstairs, amused to see how at home he looked slumped on the settee, snoring lightly in the grand room with its high ceiling, mullioned windows and huge marble fireplace, sporting tan cords and a thick body warmer so tight it resembled a straight-jacket. She snorted with laughter at this country squire attire and he woke with a start. His face was grazed in several places and his hair askew as if he'd been electrocuted. Then his eyes focussed and his mouth fell open.

'Good God what happened to you? That's not what I think it is, is it? Are you alright? Why aren't you freaking out?'

Dawn shrugged nonchalantly; she didn't know herself. 'You seem better. I'm heading up for a bath.'

'I gather there was a puppy emergency. I must have fallen asleep. Country living is exhausting. Can you believe this place? I feel like what's-his-face in Downton Abbey, the chauffeur who can't cope with all the grandeur.'

Dawn found a pair of jogging bottoms placed outside the bathroom door. They were size eight but a baggy style which would fit her like a sausage skin. Thank goodness Anastasia had also put out a long baggy jumper that would cover her bum. Maybe she was more sensitive than she appeared. She went over to shut the bathroom window. Douglas must have opened it to let out the steam. She was about to close it when Anastasia's voice drifted up.

'I'm so sorry, Samuel. Roger said your eye will be fine, it's only bruised. If anyone asks you what happened, before, I mean, say nothing. What am I saying? You always say nothing. Don't tell them anything. Anything. You hear me?'

Dawn frowned. Why was Anastasia warning the mute lad to keep quiet?

She turned on the taps, peeled off her filthy clothes and dropped them in the bin bag. She smiled at how she and Anastasia had laughed together at the state of her. The ice-maiden had melted away. With Coco she'd been so emotional, so warm and caring and Samuel obviously adored her and yet he shied away from everyone else. She was not all she appeared to be, this woman. On the mantelpiece downstairs, Dawn had seen a photograph of her with an attractive man and two boys taken in a photographer's studio. They all looked happy and yet here she was, alone at the weekend.

Heaven is a hot bath, thought Dawn as she sunk under bubbles for the first time since leaving London. She made a mental note to thank Samuel for finding Douglas the next time she saw him. He'd found Coco too. That lad had an uncanny knack for being in the right place at the right time.

## CHAPTER 19

Douglas awoke with a start, his eyes flashing open. He'd dreamt he was under the water, drifting, watching bubbles escape from his mouth. He looked around: heavy damask covered furniture, a chandelier, brocade curtains framing a picture window, a marble fireplace topped with a gilt mirror and Anastasia opening the semi-sphere of a globe, pulling out a bottle and pouring the contents into a shot glass. Surely it wasn't drinks time already. Had he slept that long? A golden clock on the mantelpiece chimed three o'clock, reminding him of a clock at his grandparents' home. He realised he must have been dozing on and off for two hours, though it had been hard with Mary pacing the hallway muttering prayers to the Almighty the whole time they'd been away.

'Oh, you're awake.' She pushed a strand of hair behind her ear, revealing a chiselled cheek bone. 'How are you feeling?'

A face to paint, he thought, smoothing down his hair. He became aware of the scrapes on his face. He'd found some plasters in the bathroom and put them on the cuts on his legs and arms in case they bled on her husband's clothes 'Much better, thank you.'

'Drink?'

'I think I still have some tea left.' He picked up a cup and looked into it.

'Here, have a brandy.' She handed him a glass. 'Good for shock.'

'No really. OK thanks.' He took the glass thrust in front of him. 'Is your dog OK?' he asked her. She was clearly dog-mad. Every other painting in the room was of a dog and the ones that weren't, were of horses. He'd inspected them before falling asleep.

'Yes, thank you. I've got five more now. Your wife was a great help. Calm in a crisis. I like that.'

'Yes, well… plenty of experience in that department.' He took a sip of brandy. It burned his gullet.

'She wasn't so calm when she thought you'd drowned.'

He was on the verge of apologising but stopped himself. Nearly drowning wasn't entirely his fault. He lifted his chin and tried to look dignified. He caught sight of his wild hair in the gilt mirror above the fireplace. His shoulders slumped. 'Good to hear. Sometimes she looks at me as if she wants to murder me.' He regretted this comment when Anastasia's eyebrows shot up. It was a joke but he'd forgotten that this woman didn't know him or his quirky sense of humour. 'It's been hard,' he expanded, feeling the need to justify himself for some reason, 'leaving friends and family. Starting again in a new place. It's a big change from London. Dawn liked our previous life. She prefers London to the country.'

Anastasia screwed up her nose and nodded. Douglas felt a pang of disloyalty.

'You can always sell up.' She flashed a smile. He'd never seen such white teeth.

'We'd never do that,' he said with more vehemence than he'd intended.

She continued to smile, but her gaze shifted over his shoulder. He noticed a tiny spasm in the muscle of her right cheek. 'So, what do you plan to do with the place?'

'Run residential art holidays. Soon as we fix the place up,' he said with the conviction of a hotelier announcing a plan to build a luxury hotel on the rubbish tips of Rio de Janeiro.

'Has planning permission come through? I saw the application at the end of your drive.'

'Not yet. It's just a formality.' It crossed his mind that she might object. Who else but an immediate neighbour? She stood with her back to the window. He couldn't see her face.

'Have you drummed up any business yet?'

Douglas wilted under her interrogation. 'No. Our son's working on a web site.'

'So art holidays. Are you an artist?'

He took a breath. 'I was an art teacher. But I was let go, sacked.' He drained his glass and, as the warmth of the brandy entered his bloodstream, relief replaced the mild panic that gripped him when he usually said this out loud.

'Oh, I'm sorry to hear that. I suppose they boot out the old ones first.'

Douglas was stunned into silence. Most people pussy-footed around his redundancy, colleagues had avoided him completely as if it were catching. It took a moment to gain his composure. 'Actually, I think they did me a favour. You know when something awful happens and you think you'll never get over it. Then something better comes along, out of the blue, and you wonder why you put up with it for so long?'

Her face went completely blank. Even though she was looking right at him, he could tell she wasn't seeing him at all. 'Sorry,' she said after several seconds had passed. 'Miles away. Where were we?'

'Art holidays,' he said.

'Ah, yes. Freddy, my husband, is an art lover. He buys valuable paintings, locks them away in his bank vault until they increase in value then sells them.' She shuffled through a pile of books and magazines on a low table and handed him a catalogue opened at a page which showed a Picasso sketch for Guernica. 'He bought this last week.'

He stared open mouthed at the iconic image, momentarily speechless.

'I know. Ghastly, isn't it?'

'No. Well yes, that's the idea. Picasso wants us to view the sheer horror of war so we won't want to go there again. I've seen the original in the Reina Sofia in Madrid. It's magnificent. A powerful memorial to the horrors of the Franco regime.'

'Ah, you're a communist,' Anastasia remarked as if everything were now clear, 'how refreshing.' She sat in the chair opposite him.

Was she making fun of him? It was hard to tell as she had a dead pan delivery but a mischievous twinkle in her eye.

'I am not a communist,' he said in a slightly offended tone but he saw her smiling at him. Her eyes were the colour of corn flowers, their outer edges slightly inclined with fine lines like exquisite etchings on glass. If she were an object she would be a Lalique decanter. Not that he was objectifying her or anything but he was an artist; he noticed people's features. He became aware of holding her gaze a fraction too long.

'I prefer more realism in my paintings,' she said waving a hand in the direction of her animal portraits.

He stood and walked over to a painting of a dog. 'I noticed that the varnish on this one is peeling. Look here.' She came to stand beside him. 'The colour underneath is starting to fade.

'Oh, yes.'

'I also restore paintings,' he added.

'Well, we may have some work for you.'

They stood, heads inclined, examining the painting. Douglas became aware of her breathing, of the smell of roses.

'My grandfather painted it. The dog is Coco's ancestor. The first water spaniel brought over from Ireland. Perhaps you could–'

She turned abruptly at a sound, brushing his shoulder with her own and he felt a jolt of electricity. He followed her gaze to the doorway where Dawn stood, in black tights and a baggy red jumper, resembling a giant ladybird. He quickly stepped away from Anastasia.

## CHAPTER 20

Douglas tried not to look too disproving when Anastasia brandished the vodka bottle again. 'The other half?' she asked Dawn. He couldn't believe it when Dawn accepted. They clinked glasses, toasted in what sounded like Russian and downed the shot in one. What had he missed? Since when were these two drinking buddies?

It was strange, getting to know new people. He'd mixed only with old friends for so long. What he chose to reveal about himself and how he expressed it would determine what new people thought of him. This gradual unveiling of oneself could give the wrong impression. Right now, for example, he was coming across as a prudish, humourless Stalinist.

'My great-grandmother used to have Russian vodka imported,' Anastasia explained, 'couldn't abide anything else. It's a family tradition I like to maintain.'

'Was she Russian?' Douglas asked.

'Yes. Came over just before the Tsar fell and your lot overran the country.'

'Your lot?' Dawn turned to Douglas.

'Anastasia thinks I'm a communist.'

Dawn laughed. 'Has redundancy radicalised you, darling?' She turned back to Anastasia, 'Douglas would have been a Tsarist. All epaulettes and flashing sabres keeping down the revolting masses, which would have been me!'

'A loser then,' smiled Anastasia.

'Precisely. The mob wins every time!' And they hooted with laughter. Douglas looked from one to the other. They were poles apart but they shared the same sense of humour which at this moment comprised mainly of ridiculing him. Odd, as Dawn had loathed Anastasia on sight at their brief meeting at the cottage they'd rented back in November. He ignored Dawn and addressed Anastasia. 'I thought you were a typical English rose and it turns out you are–'

'A Russian daisy,' she cut in. 'The national flower of Russia is the chamomile daisy.'

'I love the tea,' he said.

Dawn giggled. The brandy made him flush and he quickly looked away. Through the window he saw Samuel working in the garden.

'So your groom and gardener, Samuel, is a bat fanatic we gather,' he began.

'Yes. I'm sure Tony Pooks has told you that Samuel got upset when he smoked the bats out of the barn. I went to investigate because I thought it was on fire,' Anastasia explained. 'Caught him in the act.'

'They escaped into our attic. That's where we found Samuel the night we arrived,' Dawn told her.

Anastasia looked surprised. 'So that's why his brother hit him. Samuel shouldn't have been in the house. I'll tell him to keep away.'

Douglas sighed softly. At least it wasn't one of the Pooks who'd hit him. 'We heard one of his brothers is in the police.'

'If 'in the police', means 'in police custody', then yes. You could say that.'

Typical Tony. Tell the blow-ins what they want to hear.

Dawn said, 'Tony told us it was Samuel who caused the flood a year ago to stop the house being sold. He said the lad opened the sluice gate so the river was channelled along our leat. The spillway was blocked with branches so it couldn't run off and it flooded the house.'

Anastasia flushed. 'Yes. Very unfortunate. But I couldn't let Pooks report Samuel to the police. He couldn't answer questions anyway. He's mute. You've probably realised. Tony Pooks was breaking the law himself. We reached an agreement.'

'Yes, Tony told us.' Dawn took a slug of vodka.

'He probably told you our families have been in dispute for some time.'

'No, he didn't,' said Douglas.

Anastasia looked surprised. 'Oh! I thought he didn't miss an opportunity to malign the Montagues. It's a favourite local sport.'

'What happened?' asked Dawn.

'Ancient history,' she said dismissively.

'Well the flood caused a lot of damage. Tony Pooks is sorting it out at the moment,' he said.

'We're worried it will happen again,' Dawn said, 'as we can't afford insurance.'

'It won't happen again. There's no question of that. I threatened Samuel with the sack if he tries anything like that again. The horses here are his life. He adores them. He wouldn't risk losing them.'

'There is something else we thought Samuel might have done. The first night we arrived, someone broke into the barn, Douglas's studio, and painted graffiti all over the wall.'

'That doesn't sound like something Samuel would do. He would protect things, yes, but not vandalise.'

Dawn looked puzzled. Douglas could tell what she was thinking. If it wasn't Samuel, who was it?

'I have an idea. Samuel also used to work in the garden for Mrs Pooks and you could probably use a gardener. It will get pretty overgrown now that spring is here. You'll get to know each other better. He's a good worker.'

Douglas wondered why Anastasia should be so protective of the lad.

'We could certainly use the help, couldn't we Dawn?' He noticed she was swaying. He had taken to Samuel since his ordeal, but thought Dawn might have a problem with a damaged lad around the place.

'Right. That's settled then,' said Anastasia, even though Dawn had said nothing. 'Top up anyone?'

Douglas was astonished to see Anastasia grasp the bottle again, her marble-sized diamond engagement ring flashing in the light. 'Actually we'd better go. We've got decorating to do,' he said at the same time as Dawn proffered her glass for a refill. Anastasia was clearly a very bad influence on her. They were giggling together like school girls banished to the back of the class. Dawn seemed oddly relaxed considering the cow poo ordeal. Only yesterday she'd gone into meltdown when she'd spotted a mouse dropping on the kitchen floor and today she was rolling in the stuff.

'I suppose having bats in the attic is going to make the roof repairs difficult and expensive,' Anastasia remarked. 'Are you sure the Pooks are up to the job?'

'Maybe not. But they're all we can afford. And they know the house.'

Douglas moved away and studied the photographs on the mantelpiece. He noticed a family photo: Anastasia looking glamorous, sitting in front of a haughty looking man, two blonde boys of about twelve and fourteen on either side.

'Cosmo and Rollo,' Anastasia said. 'My sons'

My sons, not our sons. Do people really call their children names like that? In Wood Green School they'd get the crap beaten out of them.

'Are they at school around here?' Dawn asked, peering at the photo.

'They were. Now they're at boarding school.'

Of course they were. Oddly, she didn't mention the collector-husband to Dawn. Maybe they were divorced. Hopefully.

'Is that your husband?' Dawn waded in.

'Freddie. Yes. He works in London.'

Dawn asked, 'And what about you? Do you work?'

He shot Dawn a look. Was she being deliberately provocative? Of course Anastasia didn't work. Since when did members of the landed gentry need jobs?

'Yes I do, actually. Not a lot of people ask me that. Sort of assume I'm a rich bitch with nothing to do except huntin', shootin' and fishin'.'

Dawn had the audacity to laugh as if this is the most ridiculous notion she'd ever heard. Duplicitous Dawn. He liked the way that sounded. He'd use it later.

'I have an online shop called Ends of the Earth. We import furniture and other goods from all over the world. We run it from a big warehouse off the ring road and a small office in London. I travel to the far flung quarters of the world scouring for things we can sell, employing local crafts people in their manufacture.'

'Sounds fascinating,' Douglas said.

'I love the name,' Dawn said, 'I'll check out the website. If the house is ever finished we're going to need some furniture. I love the colonial look.'

Colonial look? Dawn opposed colonialism and all its modern day manifestations. That vodka obviously held the power to turn you from a communist to a capitalist in minutes. So that was Gorbachev's secret. He had added it to the water supply and Putin must be keeping it regularly topped up.

'How about you? Do you have children?' Anastasia asked. She addressed Dawn, not him. He felt side-lined in this conversation.

Dawn swayed as if trying to keep her balance on a fairground waltzer – he couldn't see her going up a ladder this afternoon, unless it was to fall off. Her scrubbed face matched the red of her jumper and it took her a while to process the question in her inebriated state. Is this what life in the country was doing to her? Anastasia, on the other hand, looked as pale and lucid as a late-night talk show host.

'Yup,' he jumped in. 'Rebecca's twenty one, about to finish at Sussex. Christopher's nineteen and studying business at Bath.' It sounded pompous. Dawn giggled at his unusual use of their full names. They'd been Becky and Chris since birth.

'We're hoping they'll come down next month when term finishesh,' Dawn slurred. 'To help ush with the decorating. Though any whiff of hard work and they'll stay away, of coursh.'

He must get Dawn away before she necked another shot. 'Talking of which we need to get back. There's stripping to be done,' he said pointedly putting down his brandy glass.

'Sounds as if your afternoon is going to be more interesting than mine,' Anastasia said raising her eyebrows. Was it his imagination or was she flirting with him?

# CHAPTER 21

Douglas watched Dawn struggle with the car door, a puzzled expression on her face, as if the mechanism she'd been using for the last five years had been tampered with while she'd been downing vodka. He leant over and opened it from the inside. His backside felt wet again. The driver's side window didn't shut properly and his seat was soaked. He glanced over at Anastasia's gleaming Range Rover. Next to it their car resembled a skip on wheels.

'We'll return the clothes,' he called to Anastasia who was sheltering in the columned porch, 'and thanks again!'

Dawn lolled around trying to tune into a radio station but finding static.

'Please switch it off,' he said.

'Why so grumpy?'

'I'm not grumpy. I'm exhausted and starving. I haven't had anything to eat since breakfast. Is there anything to eat other than lentils? Just for once I'd like to eat something that has a pulse, not that is a pulse.'

'GO, GO, GO!' Dawn shouted as a pheasant on the verge danced the two step of indecision before heading for the safety of the wheel. Douglas automatically swerved to avoid it.

'You missed your chance there.'

'I told you before, I'm not eating roadkill.' Though pheasant breast would be nice.

'Why not? A wild bird is lot healthier than an anti-biotic fed chicken.'

'Would you have plucked it?'

'I had you down as the pheasant plucker. I mean the pleasant fucker. No, I do mean the pheasant plucker. I think I might have drunk a tad too much vodka.'

Douglas snorted. 'I'm going to the chippy to get a take away. '

They ate fish and chips from greasy polystyrene trays in the dining room. After she'd finished, Dawn lay her head on the table. 'I can't strip wallpaper. I really can't. Think I might go and die, I mean, lie... down.' She walked out of the dining room, listing to the right.

He looked at his phone. Five o' clock. It was getting dark. He was suddenly overcome with exhaustion. Memories of the swim kept coming back, unease came in waves, unbidden. He feared he wouldn't be able to sleep but decided there was nothing else he wanted to do.

When he went into the bedroom, Dawn was already in bed, fully clothed. He took off Freddie's clothes, reading their fancy labels, and laid them on top of his cardboard wardrobe. He got into his pyjamas, relaxing at the feel of their soft fabric. He looked across at Dawn. He tried to remember the last time they'd had sex and then he couldn't stop thinking about it. Definitely not since they'd been in Devon, and not a lot latterly in London. Sex between them had always been good, but demanding jobs meant they fell into bed exhausted every night. Even at the weekends they needed to schedule sex. The conversation went along these lines: we're out for dinner on Friday but maybe we could make time for ourselves before Saturday's supermarket shop but that's got to be done by ten so you can get Chris to football practice for eleven so we'd better set the alarm for seven. They invariably slept through the alarm. 'Time for ourselves', they euphemistically referred to it when talking in front of the kids. They fell into a routine and sex got knocked off; they were creatures of habit and got out of the habit. Though the kids had left home and they had fewer commitments, they were down to about once a fortnight. Sometimes he worried things would stop working or seize up like the brakes on his bicycle, also not used enough.

He remembered that during the first few years they couldn't keep their hands off each other. It had been a ridiculous sexathon. Maybe they'd used up all their sex allowance then.

Their first time had been the night they met. A fact he would never reveal to his kids. Their parental advice was, make sure you get to know someone really well first. Always test them in a crisis to see if they're really the person you want to be with. What hypocrites. Do as I say, not do as I do.

Dawn made snuffling noises like a truffling pig, threw off the duvet as if it were a marauding wolf and propelled a full glass of water off the bedside table. Douglas leapt out of bed, grabbed a towel and mopped it up listening to Dawn muttering incoherently, presumably to the wolf. He peered at her, trying to see the woman he'd fallen in love with.

That first night had been spectacular. She'd had a great body then: long, slim legs and high, firm breasts. They'd met at his friend's Halloween party. She'd just moved into the flat above. She'd worn a black lace dress, had bright pink hair and had overdone the black eye make-up. He was wearing his metal hook, a prosthetic hand that no one could tell was for real or not. She'd somehow managed to set her bag on fire in the crowded kitchen. She'd put it down on the cooker, leant against the knob and accidentally ignited the gas. He'd seen the flames rising and thrown a glass of water at them, soaking her in the process. He'd gone upstairs with her to change, and she'd asked him to unzip her sodden dress. His hook had got caught in the zip and they'd fallen on the bed, laughing. It seemed natural to progress to a kiss, a grope and then sex, though he remembered struggling to extricate his hook without fumbling and flopping.

He'd stayed the night and woken in an empty bed to the sound of the shower. Dawn's pillow was stained pink and smeared with thick black smudges and he felt nervous of how she'd metamorphosed in the night. The hair, it turned out, was chestnut brown and the eyes, well, mainly red.

'Don't look at me!' she said emerging from the shower. 'I've had an allergic reaction to that cheap eye make-up.'

He'd gone out for eggs and anti-histamine and, when he came back, all the bedding was in the washing machine and Dawn dressed in jeans and a jumper. They ate at a small table in her immaculate kitchen. At the time, he'd thought it was tidy because she'd just moved in. He'd made a note to clear up his place before she came round.

Yes. He was already planning a return match and he hadn't even tested her in a crisis.

'I don't usually do that,' she'd told him blinking slitty, crusty eyes.

'Me neither,' he'd said hoping her eyes didn't always look like that. 'Would you like dinner later? I mean, I'm sure you would, but with me? There's this Italian restaurant off Tottenham Court Road I've been meaning to try.'

'Thanks. I'd love to. I thought maybe this was a one night stand.'

'Shall we see if we can stretch it to a two night stand?'

They'd met at Casa Mia and he'd been relieved to see that her eyes did open and were not crusty slits at all, and amber, not red. She'd looked gorgeous in a wine-coloured velvet dress, cut low with a sparkly necklace he couldn't stop looking at. He saw the waiters ogling her and shooting him envious looks, but they were Italian and rather prone to that sort of thing.

He hadn't slept with anyone since. He hadn't wanted to. But, if the opportunity arose, would he now?

Had he actually said that he loved chamomile tea? He cringed with embarrassment. She wasn't so much out of his league as playing another sport entirely.

About midnight he woke up to Dawn shaking him and saying his name. For a moment he couldn't understand why the light was still on and why she was wearing a bright red jumper. His mouth felt like the inside of a deep fat fryer. 'What have I done now?' He was barely awake.

'Nothing. I was going to say we'll get steak for supper tomorrow but now I've changed my mind.' She fell back down on the pillow.

'No you weren't, you were about to tell me off. I know that tone.' He turned to look at her. Her face was contorted in the pillow like a rubbery mask.

She sighed theatrically. 'Promise me you will never, ever, ever swim again.'

'Well...'

'I thought I'd lost you! I thought you'd drowned. So did everyone. Please, Douglas, promise me.' She pulled the jumper over her head, threw it on the floor and kicked off her leggings, no doubt the onset of a hot flush. 'Look at the state of me. Look what you have done to me. I'm a total mess.'

'Oh yes, that's me. Not the vodka at all.'

He pulled the duvet back up over them. He had been hypothermic only a few hours ago. Dawn, now in bra and knickers, kicked it away.

'OK, I promise. No more wild swimming.'

'I'd give you a cuddle but I'm too hot at the moment.' She kissed his cheek. It was the most affectionate she'd been in months. He recoiled at the reek of alcohol.

Images of the day flashed though his brain: the grey expanse of sea, the mussel ropes, the overhang at the top of the cliff, the path to the side, the way Anastasia had turned to look at him on the stairs. His stomach churned. He must stop thinking about it. Instead, he began counting how many different types of sauces for steak he could think of. He managed a dozen.

# CHAPTER 22

Dawn sat at the dining room table counting out twenty pound notes. Over and over, the queen's tight smile mocked her. They had reached the end of Tony's fourth week and four Pooks had worked flat out all week: Tony rendering and plastering, Pete plumbing-in the showers and basins, Leccy Luke doing electrics and Vinyl Matt fitting the kitchen though, occasionally, a cry would go up and they would all rush to the aid of a brother in trouble. This week's wage bill was £2,500. She stared at a bill for kitchen units and work tops for £3,000 and another for a cooker and fridge freezer for £1,600. The shower enclosures, bought on ebay, were really cheap at £220 each though Pete complained they were tricky to install and it would probably have been cheaper to pay more for the units and less for his labour at £150 a day. It added up to £7,540. In a week. What was their income? Big fat zero. And they still had to pay for roof repairs, more rendering and plastering, another two toilets and basins, plumbing and re-wiring. Two more weeks at this rate and the money they'd set aside for renovation would be gone. There was always an unforeseen problem of some sort: a pipe had to be moved, the electrics had to be repositioned, a joist was rotten and had to be replaced, a ceiling was about to come down. The sight of Tony Pooks looming in a doorway triggered her heart rate to that of an Olympian hurdler. His brothers called him Muscle Tone, due to his hammer wielding skills and cement carrying ability. She and Douglas called him Dialling Tone as he spent so much time on his phone. He possessed the superpower of getting signal where no one else could. She had a horrible feeling this band of brothers was fleecing them and if they scratched the veneer of their Mickey Mouse names and Wurzel charm, they would reveal an Alan Sugar business sense and a Kray brothers' client relations policy.

Of course she blamed Douglas. The house was too big; it was more like two houses really. How on earth had he got her to agree to this foreseeable (at least by her) disaster? She could see the bills extending into the future; it would be like painting the Forth Road Bridge. As soon as you finished at one end you'd need to restart at the other.

He'd told her this morning that they still had no bookings through the website. Mind you, that was a blessing given how long the work was taking. The last thing they needed was guests arriving before the place was finished. Next thing they knew, Kevin Mc Cloud would be banging on the door and making a TV programme about it: Grand Disasters. She'd looked at the website Chris had put together and wasn't surprised. There were no photos except the one of the Mill from the estate agent's details. And Douglas hadn't spelt out exactly what the guests could expect in terms of art classes. She'd suggested he work on this tonight and email the website to every friend and acquaintance, except not her ex-colleagues, obviously.

She took off her glasses and rubbed her eyes. The thought of friends turning up was almost worse than strangers. They would put on a show, of course; living here was all wild roses and gooseberry jam, long walks and cosy pubs, sandy beaches and warm seas. Friends would nod and smile but sense their loss of civilisation. Envy would ooze from every pore as friends talked of plays: You must see The Play That Goes Wrong! And exhibitions: have you seen the Turner retrospective? And restaurants: there's a great place for bottomless brunch opened up on the corner of my street. Never mind the play that goes wrong, what about the life that goes wrong?

She stuffed the cash into an envelope and wrote the amount on the spread sheet. On the bright side, the Pooks were still here. You heard horror stories about builders starting a job and then abandoning it. The plastering was nearly finished downstairs, the kitchen units were in place and she could hear Pete installing the new hob and reconnecting the Aga in the kitchen as she sat at the dining room table. She and Douglas had papered and painted all six bedrooms and both bathrooms, and had start

ed painting the indoor window frames though repainting the outside would have to wait until the weather improved. They themselves were labouring eight hours a day, seven days a week, painting over the cracks. It was like trying to fix the Titanic's hole with a glue stick and brown paper: manageable but unlikely to last.

She looked out of the window at the sound of rain. Friday night. Keep it real. In London she would have been crawling along the North Circular, facing a weekend of paperwork and preparation for the week ahead. But at least they'd had an income. They would get a take-out from the Red Fort, watch TV programs they'd recorded during the week or have friends over for supper. They'd traded that for no social life, no leisure time and no money. With no foreseeable end to the haemorrhaging of their finances or parole from working on the chain gang, motivation drained from her and despondency flowed in, triggering a vision of the half-bottle of Pinot in the fridge door. She imagined the fresh, tangy taste on her tongue. Was this virtual drinking an indicator of real alcoholism? Frankly, who gave a shit? Was it too early to have a glass? She should wait until the Pooks left. She didn't want it all round the village that she was a soak. There was practically nothing else in the new fridge-freezer. When she'd opened the door earlier, the empty interior leered at her accusingly. Tomorrow, she would fill it with cut-price groceries, wine and cheap vodka. She'd got a taste for it at Anastasia's.

As she handed Tony one hundred and twenty five crisp £20 notes, he told her his nephew, Jonno, would have to put up scaffolding before fixing the roof as it couldn't be done from the inside because of the bats, and he could start on Monday.

Another Pooks brother on the payroll. When she'd asked Douglas what the roof was costing, he'd dashed off to take a phone call. After Tony left with their money, she put her head in her hands and kept it there for some time.

Lately, she found herself welling up a lot. Not at anything in particular but she suddenly felt overwhelmed and started blubbering. But not in front of Douglas; she couldn't risk another crazy swim episode. But it would be nice if, just once, he noticed her wet cheeks or red eyes and gave her a sympathetic hug. In films, a woman only had to draw in her brows slightly or sigh softly before her partner was all over her, massaging her back, cupping her chin in his hand, and asking her what was wrong. With Douglas she would have to prostrate herself at his feet and thump the ground with her fists to get his attention. Even then, he'd probably say, 'Shall I put the kettle on?' Part of the problem was that there was no escaping each other when you work together. When you go to jobs every day and only meet up in the evenings, it's an occasion of sorts where you drink a glass of wine, cook a nice meal, share a story about your day told in a witty way and laugh together. When you work together, you cross paths, share problems, exchange information on a need-to-know basis and communication becomes purely functional. Disagreements these days rarely came to a head and hung around like a storm cloud that didn't break for days. Were they afraid of where confrontation would take them? Or did they simply lack the energy to fight any more? She knew her simmering aloofness bothered Douglas more than a fight. He preferred a good storm to an oppressive grey cloud of resentment. When was the last time they'd laughed together? She blinked back tears. At some point they must talk about how this venture was affecting their relationship. Life is about more than just survival. That's a good line. She'll use that.

She opened up her laptop and checked a property website. Great! Two houses on the market on their road in London. Her mouth fell open as she read the price. Could prices really have gone up that much since they'd put theirs on the market seven months ago? If Douglas refused to move back, with her half of what they'd paid for the Mill, she couldn't even afford a two bedroom flat in their area. Anyway, they couldn't sell the Mill in its current state. She clicked to a London jobs website. A few teaching jobs came up. Her heart raced, her ears started ringing. Would they let her teach again? Was she finished? She scrunched up her eyes with the shame of it. She dashed to the fridge, reached for the bottle and poured herself a large glass congratulating herself that she'd lasted until a minute to six. She couldn't even feel excited using their new hob for the first time as she re-heated rice and dhal which stuck to the pan like orange cement.

Later, she lay in bed listening to Douglas snoring. He'd fallen asleep, or pretended to, immediately. Since the swimming episode, she'd felt more loving towards him. But when she was affectionate, she noticed him looking at her as if he was trying to puzzle something out. Yes, she'd kept him at arm's length for a while, and may have been a little vile, but now he was the one drifting away from her. A vision flashed into her head of Douglas and Anastasia standing close, heads bent, and shoulders touching. Had she left it too late to mend their marriage?

# CHAPTER 23

Dawn set off the next morning, a woman on a mission. Last night when she'd looked at the property website and seen what she could afford in London and realised she couldn't face teaching even if anyone would employ her, it had hit her. They had to finish the Mill and get the business running. To do that, they had to be a team again. To do that, she had to work on their marriage. She'd spent all night planning Operation Relationship Recovery.

She drove along single track lanes to the supermarket, peering through a part of the windscreen where the wipers hadn't smeared seagull poo. She rounded a bend, met another car head on and slammed on the brakes. There was no room to pass. She turned to look out of the back window, reversed towards a wider part of the road, turned back to face the front and saw the other driver had done the same. There then followed a ritual of flashing lights and hand signals before they both moved forward, squeezing passed each other with waves of thanks and flashes of ironic smiles. The etiquette of lane driving meant you spent almost as much time in reverse gear as in fourth.

The hedges were soft and dewy in the Spring sunshine, the hills a velvety patchwork of grass and ploughed pink earth, criss-crossed by wide Devon banks. She wound down the window and breathed in the sweet smell of grass. She should be grateful to be living in this beautiful place. She slowed down and followed a tractor, overtaking when the driver pulled into a layby to let her pass with a cheery wave.

The supermarket was empty compared with their one in London where, on Saturdays, shoppers wielded their trolleys like weapons. She walked past her usual buys: catering size packs of turmeric, the six types of lentils, and headed instead for the domain of meat. Then she wheeled her trolley over to the clothing section and fingered the silky lingerie. She chose a black, lacy chemise and laid it in the trolley where it nestled prettily between the chicken and sausages. She seized several bottles of wine, a large bottle of cheap vodka, a couple of bottles of tonic and then headed for the cleaning products, her favourite section. She grabbed a pack of j-cloths, a range of tantalising sprays and a pair of buttercup yellow rubber gloves. She covered the chemise with the j-cloths but, at the till, the female cashier insisted on waving it like a flag to find the bar code, and the man behind her in the queue shifted uncomfortably.

At home, she stashed her purchase in the cardboard wardrobe, put the food in the fridge and, though it was only midday, prepared the veg and mixed the stuffing for the special evening meal. Then she started lunch. Douglas was lured from painting window frames upstairs by the smell of sausages and bacon frying. He stood behind her and hugged her at the sight of this carnivore's delight. Maybe this was going to be easier than she thought.

Over lunch she announced her plan to start grouting the newly tiled showers. 'I've watched Matt. I know how to do it,' she told him. I, Dawn, the competent, supportive wife.

'Great.' He didn't look up from his plate; probably afraid she might snatch it away. 'I'll carry on with the windows.'

'Did you speak to Chris? Are there any bookings yet?' The interested, caring wife.

'Not yet. He needs photos for the website but we can't take any until we have some furniture in the rooms and the tarpaulin off the roof. At the moment it looks more like the set for Psycho than a holiday destination. '

You said it, she thought. 'Hmm,' she said, 'couldn't he use some computer tricks to add furniture and remove the tarp?' The inventive, creative wife.

'I hadn't thought of that. I'll ask him.'

'With some photos, I'm sure we'll get bookings.' The positive, optimistic wife but, from her lips, she feared it sounded like sarcasm.

Douglas looked up sharply, clearly unsure too. She cleared away the plates.

'Oh, and that was a great idea of yours to email everyone we know, even those we can't stand, to try and entice them here for an art holiday, maybe with a reduced rate.' The supportive, appreciative wife.

'But that was your ...' he began but stopped and shook his head. 'As soon as the website's updated, we'll get Chris to email all our contacts.'

'Do you think we should place adverts in art magazines?'

'Great idea.'

If it was so great then why didn't he think of it? He was the one with the expensive subscriptions to art magazines. But she kept her mouth shut lest the harping, resentful wife resurface. It crossed her mind that she might be developing a form of schizophrenia.

Grouting was not a job for those with OCD, even those trying to pretend they no longer had it. The grout either fell out of the gap on to the brand new shower tray, or she crammed too much into the gaps and smeared the new tiles as she wiped it off. She quickly abandoned the tool Matt used, donned rubber gloves (her saviours) and used her fingers to jam it in the gaps and clear away the excess with a piece of plastic, a method that worked for her. She listened to the afternoon play on the radio, imagined her new purchase hanging in the wardrobe and thought about what to mix the vodka with later. She wished she'd bought limes but they were too expensive. By six, she'd grouted the tiles in one shower and above a basin. She went down to scrub her hands, change her clothes and applied some powder and lip gloss. After fixing herself a tumbler of iced vodka and tonic she began cooking.

Douglas savoured every morsel of the roast chicken and trimmings, exclaiming over each mouthful. He held her hand and, with his other, poured them a glass of claret. He kissed her as they loaded the dishwasher. He hugged her as they turned off the kitchen light. Maybe this had been the problem all along: he needed meat for his libido. It boded well for her planned spontaneity in the bedroom.

She changed into the chemise in the bathroom and fluffed up her hair. When she emerged, like a butterfly from a chrysalis, Douglas was already in bed, carrying out his usual pre-bedtime activity of checking his emails. Self-consciously, she took off her dressing gown. She felt a bit silly in the clingy black lace which itched in places she didn't want to scratch. She'd lost weight. The chain gang regime and dhal-bhat diet had worked wonders and she was as slim as anyone in an Indian jail, a fact that Douglas had failed to notice. She glided awkwardly about the bedroom, bending down provocatively to pick up clothes, folding towels, cleaning her teeth, brushing her hair, smoothing the duvet and, when she had run out of things to do, picking specks of sock fluff off the floor in what she hoped was a beguiling manner.

'Ooh, I was getting really excited ...' Douglas said.

At last! He'd noticed! Just as she was about to give up and dive under the duvet. But, as she paused her provocative pillow plumping to reward him with a pouty smile, she saw that he wasn't looking at her at all. He was staring at his laptop.

'Amazing. I found this company who do humane bat relocation but then realised it was in the States. In the UK you can't do anything without applying for a licence and going through all sorts of rigmarole. Typical. It seems the UK is the foremost nation in the world when it comes to bat rights.'

Dawn picked up her pillow, debating whether to ram it over his face. Instead, she grabbed his laptop, flipped the lid shut and threw herself on top of him.

'Well Batman, Cat-woman's here now, so brace yourself.'

It wasn't the most subtle of approaches but at least she got his attention. It had been such a long time and, at first, they were awkward with each other, but they masked it with humour and each of them did what the other expected and when they'd finished she felt much closer to him, which was good. So why did she mentally tick 'sex' off her to-do list afterwards? She lay awake, listening to Douglas breathing, and wondered if Anastasia's husband was home for the weekend.

# CHAPTER 24

Dawn was standing in a shower grouting on Sunday afternoon when she heard the Skype melody ring out. She rushed downstairs to find she had a missed call from Becky. She rang back and Becky got straight to the point.

'I've finally handed in my dissertation. I've changed my mind about work experience.'

Yay! She wasn't going to Sue's luxury home, she was coming to Last Chance to help out. A few weeks ago, Dawn had reminded Becky about last Christmas dinner, when Uncle Rich had spent the entire time quizzing her about career prospects and Sue had asked her why she dressed like a lesbian hippy, while her Boden-clad, ten-year-old twin cousins sniggered behind their hands.

'I've decided to go travelling instead. I need to get a job. If I work in Brighton, all my wages will go on rent. I'm thinking about coming down to you in Cornwall so I can live at home, work and save up, like you suggested.'

'Devon. We live in Devon.'

'Right. Same thing.'

'Have you abandoned the work experience idea completely?' Travelling sounded even worse. Douglas would have a fit.

'I've decided to put it on hold until after travelling.'

'We'd love you to come home. In fact, we'd be really grateful for some hel–'

'There's just one thing,' Becky continued as though Dawn had said nothing. Wasn't there always?

'Is it OK if I bring a friend?'

'Of course. Who is she?'

'Actually it's a he and we're sort of seeing each other.'

'Oh, that's nice.' Dawn racked her brain for what 'seeing each other' meant. Did it mean the early stage when you're seeing other people too? Or, when it's more serious and you're sleeping with them? Or, when you're sleeping with them but it's not serious? Becky did explain the complicated protocol of dating in the social media age but she'd forgotten it. In her day you were either going out or you weren't.

'But he might not come.' Becky lowered her voice. 'Is Dad there?'

'No, he's painting the barn. I mean studio.' He'd finally got around to whitewashing over the graffiti.

'If my friend does come, do you think you can prime Dad? Like, tell him not to ask embarrassing questions or crack his so-called jokes. I'm worried he might be a bit weird with Barney.'

'Oh? Why's that? I mean, of course I'll have a word. You can have your own –' she was about to say room and that Barney could have one too if he wanted. Becky seemed oddly uncurious about the accommodation given that she'd never seen the house and didn't even seem to know what county they lived in.

'Thanks Mum. Gotta go. Love you!'

'Love you too! When will you–?'

Becky hung up and, as usual, Dawn found herself wishing she'd asked more questions or, more to the point, got some answers. The conversation had left her none the wiser as to her daughter's plans except that she was intending to travel to an unspecified place at an unspecified point in the future and that she might come down to Last Chance sometime with or without a boy called Barney who she may or may not be going out with.

Obviously, Becky had majored in the joint honours degree of Geography and Resisting Parental Questioning. Dawn obviously needed a course in Intelligence Gathering, majoring in Interrogation Techniques.

She made a cup of tea in the dining room. Waiting for the kettle to boil, she sneaked a mini-battenberg from her secret cache in the drawer, looked out of the window and frowned. She smiled at the thought of Becky coming to Devon but felt a pang of apprehension. During her teenage years, Douglas had considered Becky's appearance Dawn's domain. First there'd been the hemline wars, and when Becky had morphed into a Goth, dressed head to toe in black, cut her hair and spiked it, Douglas had expected Dawn to talk her out of it. Dawn believed these issues were to do with growing up but she'd still tackled them to keep the peace. When she adopted the hippy look before going off to uni - long skirts, piercings and dreadlocks - Dawn had felt vindicated.

Dawn had worried more about issues of safety, like going out clubbing mid-week during A levels (but it's cheaper) and returning at four in the morning (I couldn't get a cab). She would lie awake straining to hear the sound of the door above Douglas's snoring as she imagined Becky lying in a gutter. (Chill, Mum, my phone ran out of battery.) Oh, those sleepless nights filled with worst possible scenarios.

Since going away to uni, Becky came back periodically but had not stayed more than a couple of weeks before heading off inter-railing with friends or to a festival. But now she might come back for a while, and with a young man. She and Douglas were already distanced from each other enough without arguing about Becky. She needed to think it through.

'I'm going for a walk,' she called upstairs to Douglas. 'Do you want to come?'

'I'm in the middle of something.'

She grabbed her coat and headed out. She walked down the path towards the river, to the shore where the smell of seaweed and the call of the gulls reminded her of seaside holidays. She crossed the pebbly shore, clambered over the stile and climbed a steep, grassy hill dodging cow pats. These days her pace hardly slowed as she walked uphill. At the top of the field she crossed the farmyard with its old stone barns and entered the wood. The young beech leaves were lime green, the oaks were budding and sunlight pierced the canopy. Emerging from the wood, she stopped to admire the rolling hills that ended in the smooth horizon of Dartmoor, broken occasionally by distant tors. Then she walked back down to the river. She looked skywards at skein of geese winging their way to the coast. She followed this route whenever she had a spare half-hour and needed to think. It helped her to leave the mess and the filth behind, to look at surroundings she wasn't responsible for organising.

Dawn told Douglas of Becky's plan over a chicken salad supper. 'You will go easy on her, won't you? Not quiz the boy or anything. He could just be a friend.' She lied knowing that if Douglas thought him a boyfriend, he would be more critical.

He bridled as she knew he would but she had to say it for Becky's sake. 'I don't know why you even have to ask me that. You're implying that I don't know how to act around my own daughter. You were the one who used to fight with her the whole time.' He stormed out of the kitchen.

Dawn opened her mouth to protest but she couldn't confront him, not now she was trying to be the supportive wife. She felt she'd failed as a parent, her main role in life. She snuck off to the fridge, sloshed vodka into a teacup and sipped it, weeping silently while she pretended to read a cookbook. It was four in the afternoon and she was not proud.

But then something cleared in her head. That was in the past. She didn't have to play that role any more. Becky was a young woman of twenty-two. If she turned up with a spider tattooed across her face and a boyfriend on remand for armed robbery, Dawn would treat her as if she were her best friend and Barney as good a catch as Prince Harry. She would break this pattern of criticism and move on to a new era in their relationship. Douglas would have to fight his own battles and she would support him because she knew it could be hard.

The next morning, they awoke to the clang of scaffolding poles and the unmistakable shouting of the Pooks clan. They

met a member of the second generation: Jokin' Jonno, son of
Vinyl Matt, who had the upper body of a wrestler and short,
bandy legs. He skimmed around the building like a monkey
whilst singing along to Palm radio. The scaffolding had
solved the problem of how they were going to mend and
paint the upstairs window frames and Vinyl Matt had started
that job. Tony and Jonno began patching up the roof, leaving
a hole under the eaves where the bats could fly in and, more
importantly, fly out. Plumber Pete was on an emergency call
out so the bathroom work was on hold which meant there
were only three Pooks on the payroll this week.

But when Dawn went into the kitchen to make everyone
tea, she stopped dead. The cold tap was running and water
was pouring over the edge of the sink and on to the floor.
She splashed over to the sink and pulled out the plug. Had
she left the tap on after washing up last night? Perhaps. She'd
been distracted after their row. But they'd had salad for
supper so there'd been no pans to wash and everything had
gone in the dishwasher. No. It hadn't been her. Someone
had done this deliberately.

## CHAPTER 25

'Oh my God, this place is awesome,' exclaimed between hugs.

Douglas's heart felt fit to burst. He hadn't seen her since Christmas. His little girl was all grown up. He could hardly comprehend where the years had gone. He followed her gaze: the new paintwork on the windows and doors made the place look well cared for. The mess of sticks on the front wall had transformed into a wisteria, its massive purple blooms drooping prettily around rusty scaffolding poles.

'I love that it's so close to the river.'

'Hmm. We're not so sure that's a good idea. But we're doing our best. Considering money is tight.'

'I can't believe you got Mum to leave London,' she whispered.

Douglas hesitated. The kids didn't know what had happened. 'Oh, you know, my magical powers of persuasion.' Becky broke away to hug Dawn. Douglas's smile faded as a figure emerged from the end of the house and looked expectantly at Becky.

'Mum, Dad, this is Barney.' Becky broke away to link her arm through his. 'Barney, this is Mum and Dad.'

Douglas looked him up and down and his joy evaporated. Barney beamed through a wispy beard and several piercings glinted in the sunlight. His hair was scraped up in a top knot, his skinny legs clad in purple leggings and a bright green sarong flapped around his middle.

'Whad up Mr T, Mrs T,' he said hitching his rucksack over his shoulder.

Douglas wondered what Dawn's father would have made of him, Douglas, if he'd turned up to meet them for the first time wearing a skirt with his hair up. What was Becky thinking? Was this the best specimen available? With his narrow chest, hairy arms and stoop he looked like a TB victim. Why didn't she go for the sporty, healthy, wealthy-looking type? He didn't ask for much: jeans, a polo shirt and a nice pair of deck shoes would do it.

'Wow! I've heard so much about you guys.' Barney's head nodded up and down as if it was all too much to take in.

'That's odd because we've heard nothing about you.' Dawn shot him a look. Well, it was true!

'Douglas, why don't you make a cup of tea while I give Becky and Barney a tour of the house.'

He was pouring out tea in the dining room when Dawn appeared.

'Who the hell is he?' he asked her. 'She's had some weird boyfriends but this one takes the biscuit.'

'Shush! Keep your voice down. They're upstairs.' They both looked up at the sound of footsteps above.

'Is that a skirt he's wearing?'

'I suppose that's the fashion nowadays.'

'Maybe, in a hippy commune in Ibiza. And what's with the topknot? Is the oestrogen in the water supply causing boys to turn into girls?'

'As long as he can wield a paintbrush I don't care. I've shown them her room–'

'They're not sleeping together, surely.' He did not want to encourage this under his own roof.

'And Chris's room,' Dawn added, 'and told them we'll get her things out of storage if she wants. She hasn't said how long she's staying. He seems very polite, Barney.'

'Barmy more like. Oh! Hello. Here you are.' Douglas exclaimed as they appeared in the doorway.

'Oh my God, Mum, how are you coping with all this mess?' Becky turned to Barney, 'Mum has OCD,' she said in a tone that implied this explained everything.

Barney peered at Dawn and nodded sagely.

'I do not have OCD.'

'Barney's been studying psychology,' Becky explained.

At least he was studying something. Barney was looking at Dawn like a scientist examining a lab rat.

Dawn was protesting. 'You cannot reduce my nature to three letters. And anyway, real OCD sufferers have far more serious problems than me. I merely like things neat and tidy.'

'OK Mum.' Becky giggled, stroking her arm and giving her a pitying look. 'Take it easy. Nearly time for your pill.'

Douglas sprung to Dawn's defence. 'Actually your mum's a lot better. She was rolling in cow poo a few weeks ago and loving it.'

Dawn smiled at him. 'I'd had a bit to drink.'

'You've lost weight,' Becky said. 'Country life agrees with you.'

'I'm not so sure about that.'

Dawn never could take a compliment. He looked her up and down. It was true and he hadn't noticed. He saw her cringing with the attention.

'We live on dhal bhat, as we're broke, and being on the chain gang uses up the calories.'

The mention of their diet gave him an idea. 'Let's eat at the pub tonight.' He would commit murder for steak and chips but worried what the locals would think of Barney's attire.

Dawn linked arms with Becky. 'Come and see the kitchen.'

The dehumidifier Tony had lent them to dry out the floor was still humming but, as Dawn had said, at least the flagstones had benefitted from a good soak. He couldn't see how Samuel, or anyone come to that, had got in. All the windows had been fixed and the house had been locked that night. They hadn't seen Samuel since their visit to the Manor and Anastasia had assured them he wouldn't cause any more floods. But if not Samuel, who was it? Dawn had told him she'd overheard Anastasia ordering Samuel to 'say nothing'. What had she meant? Say nothing about what? The graffiti? The flood? He couldn't very well ask her and reveal that Dawn had been spying on them. It was probably nothing to do with the Mill at all.

Despite the setback, while Becky and Barney cooed over the shiny new hob, the old Aga, the oak units and granite worktops, it hit Douglas that they'd turned a corner. At some point they would climb out of the chaos and stop drawing thousands from the post office every Friday and handing it to Tony. Yes, there were planks of wood, copper pipes and bags of rubble everywhere, but they were getting there. He couldn't wait to show Becky the studio. Luckily, he'd painted over the mess a week ago so that was one less disaster to explain.

'It's so cool, Dad,' Becky said when he threw open the doors. 'I can picture you working here.' She turned to look at the view outside. 'And this meadow is idyllic.'

'Awesome,' said Barney and Douglas started to warm to him. 'Wow, we'd love to live somewhere like this, wouldn't we Becks?'

'We're hoping that you'll stay a while,' Douglas said. 'There's a lot of painting to be done, in here and in the house. You'd have free board and lodging. What do you think?

Becky and Barney exchanged a look. 'We were heading down to Cornwall.'

'To surf,' Barney cut in, 'but I guess we could stay for a bit, if Becky wants.'

'You can surf at some beaches near here,' Douglas pointed out.

'Then sure, we'll stay,' said Becky, 'it'll be fun.'

'That's great news!' Dawn said from the doorway. 'That was Anastasia on the phone. She's invited us all to supper. I bumped into her in the post office and she said she'd check with Freddie and call us back.'

Douglas wasn't sure he wanted to meet Freddie. He already hated him with his suave good looks and millions.

'Who's Anastasia?' asked Becky.

'Your mum's new best friend. They bonded over vodka shots.'

'Don't sneer, Douglas.' She turned to Becky. 'She's the only local we've met apart from the builders.'

'Poor Mum. Cooped up with dad all day.'

'Thanks, Becky,' said Douglas. 'Anyway, she happens to be Lady of the Manor.'

'Doesn't sound like your type, Mum.' She turned to Barney, 'Her friends are more save the whale types.'

'Cool,' said Barney.

Douglas interrupted. 'So tonight it's best attire and behaviour for all of us.' He looked pointedly at Barney though he doubted he had a smart outfit in the ripped rucksack he'd dropped at the door. Becky seemed to have even more piercings and dreadlocks, looking as if she'd been camping at a reggae festival for weeks. She'd always had the knack of spending hours getting ready only to emerge from her room looking like she'd been sleeping rough. But he knew better than to say anything. He'd leave that to Dawn.

'So what are your plans now Becky?' he asked, hoping they involved earning.

'Douglas! She's only just finished her final exam. Cut her some slack.' He'd forgotten how Dawn always stuck up for Becky and made him out to be the villain.

'It's OK, mum. I know Dad's the career police. Well, as you know, I never had a gap year. I'm thinking of going travelling. The Far East. I thought I could live at home for a bit, find a local job and go when I've enough saved. Then, when I get back, I might apply for a masters degree.'

Douglas's heart sunk. Another year of university living expenses to finance. At least she was talking about finding a job, but what the hell could she do in rural Devon? Dawn had gone ashen at the mention of the Far East. She backed away saying she was going to have a shower. Becky was oblivious to her mum's fears. Or was she ignoring them? Sometimes that was the best policy.

'But I'm spending the summer having fun. We're going to do the rounds of the music festivals. Barney has some contacts who can get us tickets.'

'I work as, like, a volunteer at festivals. Reckon I can get Becky in to do same. But like I'm totally happy to help out you guys. This place is really cool.'

'OK. Great. Shall we go back to the house and move your things into your room?'

'Oh, we're not sleeping in the house,' Becky said. 'Barney always sleeps in a tepee. Is it OK if we put it up in the meadow?'

'Er yes, why not? Tepee, eh? What a novel idea.' He nodded his head and smiled as if this was the most sensible thing he'd ever heard. He turned and stormed off to the house. He needed to tell Dawn this piece of news and find out what she intended to do about it.

# CHAPTER 26

Douglas barged into the shower room. 'Are you sure it's wise to take them to the Manor?' he asked Dawn. 'As we speak they are erecting a tepee in the meadow.'

Dawn started to rinse the shampoo from her hair. He took a step back to avoid getting splashed. 'Why?' she asked.

'To sleep in.'

'But the house isn't that bad, surely? They can use the inflatable mattresses until the furniture is delivered. Didn't you tell them that?' Dawn stepped out of the shower and reached for a towel.

He looked her up and down. She had lost weight. She looked years younger. He should have noticed that the other night when she'd worn that skimpy night dress but she'd been lying down most of the time. 'No, you're missing the point. That's where they live, apparently, in the tepee.'

'Oh. I wondered why she hadn't been asking for rent money. How very thrifty.' She wrapped the towel around her.

'Dawn, this isn't about money. It's about lifestyle. I've nothing against hippies but I would rather our daughter wasn't living in a tepee.' God, he sounded like his father. He'd been a bit of a hippy himself, back in the day he'd listened to Jefferson Airplane and Canned Heat. Going Up the Country was still his favourite song of all time. It hit him like a bolt of lightning. It was his life's anthem. No wonder Becky was a hippy, she was just like him.

'I'm sure it's just a phase. You had quite long hair in the seventies. I wore floppy hats and long skirts, smoked pot and listened to Joni Mitchell.' She wrapped a towel around her dripping hair.

Then another thought hit him. 'Do you think they're smoking weed?' He started to pull off his clothes, suddenly hot. He'd banned it when the kids were living at home but Becky had smoked rollups and he'd had his suspicions. Dawn had disagreed. She'd held the ridiculous notion that kids should experiment with drugs at home. What nonsense. You wouldn't encourage them to experiment with suicide would you?

'Chill out, Douglas. It could be worse.' Dawn said as she smeared cream over her face. 'She could have joined a cult instead.' She started to towel her hair dry.

He sat down on the bed, imagining Becky at some weird gathering, chanting and slaughtering a goat. 'I hadn't thought of that. You don't suppose –'

'No, I don't. They're just experimenting, dropping out, it's what kids do.' Dawn studied the contents of her cardboard wardrobe.

Becky was in a cult and all Dawn could think about was what to wear. Why was she so serene? She usually got het up about Becky's antics. 'You seem remarkably calm about the whole thing.'

'I'm just glad she's home. She's a grown-up now. Let's not chase her away by making her feel uncomfortable. The last thing I want is her to go travelling. You know how she is. She changes her mind all the time. Plus we could use a couple more members of the chain gang. More importantly, I didn't want to say anything in front of Becky, but tonight's a good opportunity to tell Anastasia about the flood in the kitchen. Get her to ask Samuel if he did it. I don't want us to confront him.'

'I don't see why not. He's done it before.' Douglas saw Dawn's face cloud over.

'It's better coming from her. We need to leave in half-an-hour. And we should take back those clothes that Anastasia leant us.'

He flushed hot and tried to keep his voice casual. 'Oh, I took those back last week.'

117

Dawn stopped towelling her hair and looked at him. 'Really? You didn't say. She didn't mention it when I saw her.'

'Oh, she probably forgot. I wanted to talk to her about Samuel starting work here so I popped round.' Douglas felt himself reddening. He busied himself folding up discarded clothes.

'I see. And is he?'

'Is he what?'

'Going to start work here?'

'We agreed next week. He's going to sort out the garden and mow the meadow on their sit-on mower. Do you want me to cancel?'

'No. It's probably a good idea to keep an eye on him.' Dawn picked up her hairbrush and sat on the bed. 'So are there any other attractive women with whom you've been having secret meetings?'

'A woman at the supermarket check-out flirted with me.'

'Sometimes, a smile is just a smile,' Dawn said and switched on the hair dryer.

He took it as his cue to escape to the shower. He didn't know why he was feeling guilty. He had nothing to hide about his visit to the Manor. They'd had a business-like chat about Samuel. She hadn't even asked him to come in. There was no flirtation on either side. Maybe he'd imagined it that day at the Manor after the swim.

Sometimes, a smile is just a smile. But sometimes it isn't.

## CHAPTER 27

Who the hell can come to supper at such short notice? She'd bumped into Dawn in Darton village shop on her way back from a lobster lunch at a cliff-top restaurant, and when Dawn had started banging on about manual labour and eating porridge for supper, the invitation had slipped out. What the hell was 'grouting' anyway? She'd had the feeling Dawn wanted to ask her about something. Anyway, it might be nice to behave like a family for once, and families ate meals with other families. The boys were home for half-term and Freddie had arrived last night. He'd taken them fishing on the river so he'd want adult time tonight. She found Mary in the kitchen and told her to prepare supper for an extra four and that the youngsters would eat in the snug.

Oddly, she found herself looking forward to seeing Dawn and Douglas again, D and D as she called them. Freddie would dislike them, naturally. She found them amusing. They were so different to anyone she knew, though she probably laughed at them rather than with them. But she admired the way they did everything together, as a team. She and Freddie were on opposing teams most of the time. Besides, she needed to keep track of what they were up to. Samuel had told her that the bats were still in the attic. They wouldn't be able to fix the roof with the bats there. Samuel was starting work next week so he could report any wrongdoings and things she could use to delay planning permission and their progress so they wouldn't get summer bookings. She'd made a point of mentioning the bat colony in her objections to their planning application, along with the increased traffic and the strain on local services caused by a holiday complex.

Upstairs, she checked Freddie's sock drawer. Her fingers closed around the box. Either the earrings were for her birthday next month or he'd thought twice about giving them to his mistress, whoever she was.

Of course, there were problems in their marriage. What marriage didn't have problems? They tacitly agreed not to bring them up as if talking about them would make them more serious. She'd stopped asking Freddie how he felt about her a while ago – he would accuse her of fishing for compliments and placate her with clichés about how she was the only one which worked for her because she hated scenes and messy displays of emotion. Their relationship functioned on some level though, every time she suspected him of another fling or found some piece of evidence, fear fluttered in her stomach and she could think of nothing else. Maybe her suspicions this time were unfounded. The earrings were still there, after all, and Freddie was spending more weekends than usual at Dartcoombe.

She ran downstairs with a spring in her step, opened the back door and Coco and the puppies rushed outside. She shaded her eyes from the sun, looked towards the river and spotted three figures on the bank: Freddie, Cosmo and Rollo. What a perfect picture of idyllic family life. She ran across the lawn with the puppies. She wanted to keep them all but Freddie said six dogs was too much. The same way he'd said two sons was quite enough but in that instance, she'd agreed with him. The vet had said Coco shouldn't risk another birth so she would keep a bitch puppy to breed from. That's what her family had done since the first spaniel arrived from Ireland and she intended to keep up the tradition. She would give one to Samuel, who adored them, but he would keep it at the Manor, after what had happened to his last dog.

It took her a couple of hours to walk the boundaries of her land, unchanged for centuries with one exception. She looked down into the valley at Last Chance Mill and smiled with satisfaction. Soon it would be reunited, and the estate intact again. She owed it to the Montague line to put right her father's mistake.

Back at the house she heard the sound of simulated machine gun fire. She opened the door of the snug where two blonde heads were bent over video consoles. In the sitting room, Freddie sat reading the paper, sipping a large scotch. He didn't look up.

'I've invited people for supper,' she told him. 'That couple I told you about who've moved into the Mill.'

'Do I need to change?' He looked handsome in cords, a cashmere sweater and polished loafers, his face tanned, his hair fairer. He was aging better than she was: his face was filling out slightly with age whereas hers seemed to be falling off her cheekbones on to her neck. She'd begun smiling just to try and hoist it up.

'No. They're very casual, very relaxed.' That was putting it mildly.

'So brief me.' He rattled ice cubes round his empty glass.

When had he stopped looking at her? Was it after Rollo was born? After his first fling? She didn't demand sex on the dining room table, but an arm slipped around her waist occasionally might be nice.

'Well, they're a couple of blow-ins, as I told you, I quite like them but they're hideously incompetent. I can't see them making a go of a business. He was sacked from his teaching job and she has some nervous disorder. I reckon they'll have to sell up soon.'

He stood and poured himself another scotch. 'To us, presumably. Lucky for you they bought it. The Pooks would never have sold it to you, not after–'

'Quite. So we're keeping it friendly.' She wondered how much Scotch he'd drunk.

'Whilst stabbing them in the back. That's what I like. A return to the good old Montague values.'

Anger stopped her breath. He used to love her family. She would overhear him boasting at parties that he'd married into one of the finest families in England, and one of the most beautiful women. He would beg her to come along to corporate events so he could show her off, wallowing in the envy of his colleagues. When had he last asked her anywhere? She couldn't remember; she must check the diary. There must have been something. Her memory was playing up. Wasn't there a theatre box last Christmas? No. That was the year before.

'How dare you criticise my family. Wasn't Marlows founded on slave trade money? At least my lot were anti-slavery.'

'Only because you had a plentiful pool of indigenous slaves.'

Once, they would have laughed together over her scheming and witty put downs. He'd found her refreshingly honest after all those simpering society types. Sometimes, she'd made a nasty comment just to make him laugh. Now he picked her up on everything, contradicted her, made her feel mean-spirited and unlovable. Did the sharpness and wit of youth appear as bitterness and hostility in middle age?

She stormed out and was still seething when she came out of the shower. She chose a linen dress and cashmere cardigan as it felt chilly for late May. At least she needn't dress up. Dawn would no doubt turn up in jeans.

She was still fuming when the doorbell rang and the dogs began barking. Downstairs, Mary was opening the door to Dawn and Douglas and two odd-looking young people who were being mauled by jumping puppies while Coco looked on from a dignified distance.

'I'm so sorry about the dogs.' She bent down and pulled a few of them away from her guests' feet.

'Don't be. They're adorable,' said the girl bending down to pet them. She would be quite pretty without that awful tangly hair and baggy tie-die clothing.

'This is Rebecca,' Dawn said, 'and her friend Barney. This is Lady Anastasia Montague.'

Barney resembled a pirate with his pony tail, gold nose ring and several others that Anastasia found it impossible to imagine how they'd been inserted. He was now being widdled over. She crouched down and pulled Mocha away.

'Oh, I'm so sorry. Mary, get this cleared up please.' She stood up and smoothed down her dress, now creased around the middle, and remembered why she hated linen. 'Delighted to meet you.'

'Likewise,' said Barney. 'Aw, don't worry, Lady A, I'm used to it. My uncle breeds dogs.'

She smiled at Lady A. That was a new one. Quite hip. Like Lady Gaga. The boys would love it. 'Really, what type?'

'Alsatians. For the police.'

She saw D and D exchange a look at this piece of information.

Rebecca said, 'Are you selling them? Mum can we have one?'

'What about me?' Douglas asked, 'I'll have to live with it too. Doesn't my opinion count?'

Freddie stepped out into the hall. 'Not in my experience, old man. Women rule the world now. Freddie Marlow. Pleased to meet you all. Come on through and I'll get you a drink.'

'Cosmo! Rollo!' Anastasia called. 'Come and meet Becky and Barney.' For once they appeared on cue, slouching into the hall. Mary rushed up from the kitchen with a mop and bucket.

'Boys, show Barney and Rebecca where the cider is. But only apple juice for you two.' She wagged a finger at them. 'Rebecca, you're in charge. Make sure they don't drink.'

'Don't worry, I have a little brother,' she said.

'Well, in that case you'll know not to trust these two an inch. The cider's made from our own apples. There's a farmer down the road that makes it for us. Jack Lustleigh. You should buy some. It's very good.'

'Wow, Cosmo and Rollo,' Barney said as they walked down the hall towards the kitchen tripping over puppies. 'Cool names, man. They're like wizard names from Harry Potter. Don't tell me you go to school at Hogwarts!' Anastasia watched them go, her two compact, blonde boys with the two hippies.

'It's pretty much like Hogwarts.' Cosmo actually smiled.

'Except without the magic,' Rollo piped up.

'We have this one master who's a dead ringer for Snape.'

'Hey, do you like Monster Hunt? We're in the middle of a game.'

Her boys were unusually chatty. Perhaps they were only moody with her. She warmed to Barney, she liked his openness; he wasn't closed and secretive like most young people nowadays. Dawn was watching them, a frown creasing her features.

'Let's get a drink, shall we?' Anastasia said.

# CHAPTER 28

In the sitting room, Freddie was giving Douglas a tour of the doggy and horsey portraits.

'Douglas says he can clean this one up for us,' Freddie told her as she poured two vodkas and added lots of ice. He turned to Douglas, 'If you do a good job, we've others that need doing.'

Anastasia smiled. 'What he means is, you can practice on that crappy one my grandfather did and them he'll let you into his vaults to advise on the Picassos.'

Douglas's eyes lit up. 'I'd love to see them.'

Freddie said nothing. Maybe she shouldn't have mentioned them but he hadn't told her to keep quiet about his small collection.

Dawn cut into the silence. 'Sorry about the kids.'

She was always apologising. She was looking better than usual in a rather nice turquoise dress. 'Sorry about what? I invited them. They're both delightful though I can't understand this need for the young to mutilate their bodies.'

'No, we struggle with it,' said Douglas. 'At least Becky doesn't have any tattoos.'

'Well ...' Dawn began.

'No! Don't tell me. I couldn't bear it.'

Dawn addressed Freddie. 'Fathers and daughters. You're lucky you have boys.'

Freddie chuckled. 'In my day we'd have been disowned if we'd pierced or tattooed. Nowadays, we're expected to let them do whatever they want otherwise they report us to social services. Bloody nanny state.'

'Careful, Freddie, Douglas is a communist.' Anastasia smiled.

'I am not a communist! I didn't even go to union meetings. I wish I had. The union might have fought harder for my job.'

'Sorry to hear about that, old man. Ana told me about your plans for the art holidays and it sounds on the button to me. About time someone did something with the Pooks' place. They let it go to rack and ruin. You should restore the old millwheel. There aren't many of those around these parts any more. You might get some heritage funding. The CEO of the Trust is a client. I could have a word with him if you like.'

Anastasia tried to catch Freddie's eye. Offering to help restore the wheel? Her wheel?

'We need any funding we can get,' Douglas said. 'The money's almost run out. Any more setbacks and we're finished.'

Anastasia perked up. Dawn took Douglas's hand.

'Dinner is served, madam,' Mary said from the doorway. 'The young people have taken the dogs down to the river. I'll give 'em theirs in the kitchen when they get back.'

'Freddie, take everyone through, would you? I just have to check something in the kitchen.' She shot out the door and followed Mary down the hall.

'Mary,' she spoke in a loud whisper. 'I need you to do something for me. Your niece is married to one of the Pooks isn't she?'

'Yes, madam. She's married to M – '

'I don't need the details. I want you to phone her and tell her that the Thompsons have RUN OUT OF MONEY. The Pooks won't get paid. Possibly not even for the work they've done. Do you understand?'

'That's terrible, madam. Matt and Jonno have been working –'

'Yes, yes. Terrible indeed. Can you phone her now?'

'Now, madam? I've got to assemble the pavlova.'

'Later, Mary, later. Make the call. Now.'

126

Mary looked over Anastasia's shoulder. Anastasia turned and saw Dawn standing in the hallway. How long had she been there?

'The loo's in here isn't it?' asked Dawn, opening the door.

When Anastasia entered the dining room she saw Mary had laid up the small table in the window rather than the formal dining table. She noticed Douglas staring at the chandelier, the family portraits and Regency furniture. Freddie was portioning a platter of whole salmon, one he'd caught in the river. She poured them each a glass of Chablis. When Dawn came back, she seemed OK. She couldn't have overheard. Mary said she'd just stepped into the hall.

During dinner the conversation flowed and Freddie acted his charming self. She glimpsed the old Freddie, the one who'd written her romantic poems and wooed her with Chanel jewellery, Riviera yachting trips and yellow tulips. He even paid her a compliment; he praised her skills in the auction room. Maybe she'd wear her satin negligee tonight and maybe he'd give her those earrings.

As they said their goodbyes in the hallway, Anastasia noticed the boys were giggling and glassy eyed.

'Let me smell your breath. Have you been drinking cider?' She saw Rebecca and Barney exchange a look but let it go. She noticed a pouch of tobacco sticking out of Barney's pocket. She turned to Rebecca. 'See if you can persuade your parents to have a puppy.'

'I will. Thank you. It's been fun.'

'Come back tomorrow and we'll walk the dogs,' said Rollo to Becky and Barney.

'Dad, can we take the rowing boat out?' asked Cosmo. 'There's a really cool island on the river we can go to,' he told Barney.

This rare display of enthusiasm to do anything other than play video games surprised Anastasia.

'Well, we're ... like... working on the house,' said Barney. 'But you guys should come over and help.'

'You could go over with Samuel and help him do the garden,' Anastasia told them. 'About time you did something useful.'

At the mention of Samuel, the boys made faces at each other.

'Don't be horrible about Samuel. He can't help it. What's the matter with you two tonight?'

'It's been a lovely evening, thank you,' Dawn cut in before anyone could answer. 'And lovely to meet the family. You will be our first guests once the kitchen is done.'

'So it's not finished yet?' Anastasia tried not to sound too interested.

'Sadly, no. There's a leak somewhere so they've dug up the floor.'

She watched Becky link a supportive arm through her mum's. Clearly the unfinished kitchen presented a challenge to her disorder, whatever it was. But there was something very genuine about Dawn. D and D were so wholesome. There was nothing devious or underhand about them. For her and Freddie, feelings were like paintings in the National Gallery – a select few on show and the rest hidden in the basement.

The thought that Dawn might have overheard her comments to Mary bothered her. 'Do you ride, Dawn? Why don't you come over tomorrow and we'll go out together?'

'No. I don't. I mean, not really.'

'Yes, you do!' said Becky, turning to Anastasia. 'We used to go riding together when I was going through my pony-mad stage. Though she did used to disappear when we had to groom them or muck them out.'

'I was allergic.' Dawn coloured. 'But I haven't ridden in ages.'

Anastasia was struck by her timidity. 'It's not something you forget how to do,' she said. 'We'll go easy I promise.'

'Well … OK,' Dawn said. 'It is Saturday tomorrow. I could take a couple of hours off.'

Anastasia relaxed. Dawn would not have accepted the invitation if she'd overheard. 'That's settled then,' she said before Douglas could contradict.

'That wasn't as bad as I expected,' Freddie said when they'd gone. His phone pinged and he read a text. 'I almost feel sorry for them now I know you have them within your sights. What have you got planned? You're not going to put her on Swallow with a loose girth and send her over a five-bar gate are you?'

She forced a laugh; pretending to take it as a joke rather than a slight. 'Don't be ridiculous. Coming to bed? I've been up since 5.30 with the puppies.'

She placed a hand on his shoulder; the cashmere warm and soft to the touch, the bone hard beneath. Her hand slid off as he walked into the drawing room, no doubt heading for the scotch decanter.

'No. I'm going lamping with Jack Lustleigh. To shoot that fox that's been after the pheasants.'

She tried to keep the disappointment from her voice. 'Make sure you don't shoot anything else.' She moved to the doorway. He was standing by the window, texting. 'Goodnight,' she said softly.

'Goodnight.' He didn't look up. No smile, no kiss. No airing for the negligee tonight.

## CHAPTER 29

'I can't believe you got those two boys stoned.' Douglas glared at Becky but aimed his comment at Barney who was staring at his bony, bare feet. Barney was the real culprit. You only had to look at him to see he was a druggie. They'd brought breakfast outside into the sunshine but Douglas wasn't hungry.

Becky seemed remorseless. 'They told us they smoke all the time at school. They get packages sent to them. The school thinks it's tuck from their parents. Not to mention the booze they get dropped over the wall.'

'Over the wall? Good God, it sounds like prison,' said Douglas.

Barney nodded in agreement. 'It wasn't Becky's fault, Mr. T.'

He wasn't sure if he liked being called the name of a member of the A team. He'd noticed Anastasia's lips twitching when Barney called her Lady A. Mister T and Lady A, like a couple of rappers.

'They begged and begged us. And they only had a tiny puff.'

'You know I don't like you smoking weed,' he said to Becky.

'Dad, I'm twenty-two. Didn't you smoke weed when you were twenty-two?'

'Oh, we were a veritable Cheech and Chong,' Dawn piped up placing a tray of coffee and croissants on the table.

Couldn't she back him up? Just once? 'Dawn, I don't think you should make light of this.'

'Yes, you're right. Don't move on to the hard stuff.' Becky gave her a withering look. 'And don't give it to our neighbours' children even if they are drug barons.'

Why did they trivialise everything he thought was important?

'So, Douglas, what are our jobs today?' Dawn smiled at him in a blatant attempt to change the subject. He couldn't believe how calmly she'd taken the revelation that their daughter was a pot head. Unless she'd known all along of course. He'd been duped again. He sipped his coffee and burnt his tongue. Mind you, if they worked, it might make up for the grief they were causing.

'Let's see …. Becky and Barney, you could start rollering the walls in the dining room and guest sitting room with the White Paint for New Plaster. The plaster in those rooms is now dry enough to paint. And you could paint Ordinary White Paint on the walls Mum and I have papered. Got that?'

Becky was trying not to laugh. The kids found him dated but quaint, like a lava lamp. 'Yes, Dad, Paint-for-New-Plaster on the New Plaster, I get it. I do have a degree you know.'

Douglas ignored her. 'There's a long arm roller you can use on the ceilings but put sheets on the floor. We're keeping those flagstones. Dawn, we'll start on the kitchen.'

After laying down ground sheets, locating brushes and rollers, opening tins, stirring paint and pouring it into roller trays without getting it on the floor, Douglas staggered into the kitchen wondering if it might have been easier to do the job himself. He poured himself a strong coffee.

'Douglas, you really mustn't confront Becky,' Dawn whispered as he started to roller paint around the kitchen window while she painted the edges with a brush. 'You'll only drive her away.'

He frowned. He seemed to remember that was always his line. 'I'm not going to apologise for disapproving of my daughter smoking weed and giving it to minors.'

'Quite right.' He noticed a hint of a smirk on her face.

'And what must Anastasia think of us?' I sound like my father, he thought.

'I think you may have blotted your copy book with Lady A. You're a communist and the father of a drug dealer. I dare say you won't receive another invite.' Dawn suppressed a snort of laughter. She was clearly enjoying pressing his buttons but he refused to react. Right now, all he wanted was to get out of the house and away from everyone. Perhaps he could sneak down to the beach later for a swim. It was so unfair. Dawn was going out for a ride with Anastasia and he was stuck here, outnumbered by the hippies.

'Remember to mention the flood in the kitchen. Get her to ask Samuel if he did it.' The opportunity hadn't come up last night.

Becky burst in and handed him the phone. 'It's Chris!'

Douglas knew Dawn was dying to talk to him but she let him take the call, leaning in to the receiver so she could hear, which irritated him more. But his bad mood evaporated when he learnt his nice, normal son was arriving later that day.

He beamed at Dawn. 'He'll be at Totnes at six fifteen. I'll go and pick him up.' She hugged him. He knew how thrilled she was to have both the kids home. Maybe Chris would inject a little normality into their lives. After living with the tepee folk for a couple of days, he needed it.

As Dawn headed off to the Manor, Samuel drove up on a mower. They had a brief, one-sided exchange where Douglas filled in Samuel's side of the conversation and Douglas smiled a lot. If Samuel was the vandal, it was a good idea to get him working with them rather than against them. He stood back and surveyed the house with some satisfaction. Everyone was busy. Great. He hoped by end of June, the work would be finished but it was only six weeks away. With all of them pulling together, they might be ready.

He walked over to the studio, passing the tepee. Dawn was right – he mustn't alienate Becky, they needed her and Barney. And, as they slept in the tepee, he and Dawn still had their space. Funny. You get used to having more space when the kids leave home and almost begrudge the loss of it when they come back. No, not begrudge, that's too strong, more like notice the loss of it. He hadn't expected that. He and Dawn had got used to living in one room and learnt how to step around each other quite skilfully. And things were definitely looking up in the bedroom department after a bit of a downturn.

His studio smelt of new wood and transported him back to afternoons spent pottering with his dad in the garden shed. He began stacking the shelves with pots of paintbrushes, crates of tools, packets of paper, drawers of paints and crayons. He thought of Chris and smiled; he'd definitely done a good job raising that one.

## CHAPTER 30

When Douglas left for the station Samuel, covered in mud and blood, was still digging out brambles from the front garden. Douglas made a mental note to find him a pair of gloves. It was the worst job. Attacking the brambles was a bit like the assault on ISIS; you thought you'd dug them all out but they only cropped up somewhere else.

'Would you like a lift home?'

Samuel looked up at him, puzzled, but wiped his hands on his trousers and walked over to the car. Samuel pointed out which turnings to take. They arrived at a small pink cottage fronting the road about a mile from the Mill. Beat-up cars and stacks of wood littered the small front garden.

The train was late and, when it pulled in, Douglas scanned the platform for Chris. The young man walking towards him was tall, smiling and exuded confidence. His dark hair was shorn at the sides and long on top; he had Dawn's dark-fringed eyes and his own broad-shouldered physique. He must have the girls flocking around. And he was aiming for a first in his business studies degree, even though he'd only just completed his first year. He'd told Douglas on the phone that he'd organised a work placement for his second year. How wonderful to be young and good looking and have great prospects! Douglas felt a rush of pride so strong he thought he might cry. Chris dropped a large holdall on the platform and, as they hugged, Douglas breathed in the smell of his leather jacket, checked out his face and found it mercifully free of metal. Well, at least fifty percent of the offspring were normal. Though he did notice Chris's jeans were slung abnormally low on his hips. Why did lads feel the need to display their underpants these days? He remembered

Dawn's caution and said nothing. He would offer him a belt later. Keep it subtle.

Douglas edged into the traffic. 'It's a lovely town,' he told Chris, 'but you can't tell from this road. Well done for getting that work experience with Adidas. What's the plan?' He turned off the main road on to the back lanes.

'I start in September. They'll pay me enough to cover rent and food. I've arranged to share a flat in Shoreditch with three others from my course. But I can stay for the next few weeks to help out. Maybe longer. Mum said you were really pushed.'

'That's marvellous!' Douglas exclaimed, relieved that Chris would be supporting himself in London and that he could help them at the Mill. 'By the way, did you set up the website to take bookings from July?'

'Yes. There've been a few enquiries but no bookings yet.'

'I'd appreciate it if you didn't say anything to your mum about that. The house isn't finished, as you'll see. I don't want her panicking that we might have guests in six weeks.'

'I haven't seen the place, but isn't that cutting it a bit fine?'

'Maybe. But the sooner we have money coming in the better. I've just found out what it's going to cost to fix the roof. We have to buy the original slates. Ten grands worth.' It was a relief to have Chris to confide in.

'Let me guess. Mum doesn't know.'

'We desperately need bookings, for the whole summer and early autumn if we can. Otherwise we'll run out of money. We can't get a loan. We've tried.'

'I'll do what I can but it's difficult with only one photo. Aren't any of the rooms ready yet?'

'The barn studio is finished. And some of the rooms. But we haven't any furniture. Mum suggested you use software to add some to the rooms, blot out the scaffolding poles, that sort of thing.'

'Sounds a bit dodgy, but I'll have a go.'

'Thanks. Good to have you on board, Chris. I really need your support right now with your mum freaking out about money.'

They drove passed a farm flanked by barns with rusty tin roofs. A sign read, Farm Cider for Sale. He remembered Anastasia mentioning a local cider farm. Becky said it was excellent and it was bound to be cheap which would put him in Dawn's good books. He rammed the car into reverse.

They rapped on the door and it was opened by a man in his fifties sporting a stained vest moulded over a massive beer, or rather, cider belly. He appeared to be eating something at the same time as smoking a cigarette. At their request for cider, he yelled over his shoulder, 'Mother, I'm off to the barn!' And they followed him through a five bar gate and into a large barn containing a press and vats.

"ow much you want?' he asked in a gruff voice. They agreed on three gallons.

'Bring them flagons back when you're done and I'll fill 'em for cheaper.'

Douglas read the label on the flagons: Farmer Jack's Cider. 'Is that you? Jack?'

'Yup. Jack Lustleigh. There's been Lustleighs here since Doomsday.'

Doom is right, Douglas thought, looking around the dark muddy barn filled with old bits of tractor, musty sacks and plastic crates. Why were farms always like junk yards? He was starting to sound like Dawn; the OCD must be rubbing off.

Jack syphoned the cider. 'You grockles?'

'No, we live here. We bought the Pooks' place. Last Chance Mill.'

Jack pursed his lips as if he wanted to say something but thought better of it. 'My daughter used to work for old Mrs Pooks,' Jack told them, 'cleaning and changing the beds and what not when it was a B&B.'

They each grabbed a flagon and walked over to the car. 'We'll have guests too. When we've sorted the place. My son and daughter are helping out. But in a few weeks we might need to take someone on. Could we have your daughter's phone number?'

'Better still, you can meet her.' He kept them on the doorstep and yelled, 'Suzy!' up the stairs. 'She's doing Hair and Beauty at South Devon College. Saturdays, she works in the village hairdressers. Curl up & Dye. You know it?'

Chris stifled a snort of laughter. Douglas mumbled, 'Yes, I've seen it.'

But their smiles faded when, in the doorway, appeared a pre-Raphaelite vision: long blond hair, pale blue eyes and full pink lips set in a sneer as she stood on the doorstep and scowled down at them, clearly annoyed at her father's summons to meet two gawping idiots. Pre-Raphaelite women always looked moody; presumably because of pre-Raphaelite men. Douglas tried not to stare.

'Yeah?' She pronounced it with two syllables.

'These two gentlemen live at Last Chance and might have some work,' Jack told her lighting another cigarette.

'Oh?' She sounded disinterested, almost suspicious.

'Y…yes indeed,' Douglas stuttered, rendered almost speechless at how anyone so lovely could come from someone so unlovely as Farmer Jack. Christ, maybe that's what people said about him and Becky. In order to concentrate, he averted his eyes from her face but unfortunately they fell on an exquisite midriff, exposed between a skimpy top and low cut jeans, adorned with a glistening jewel.

Chris picked up the thread. 'We'll need some help in the summer. Cooking, laundry, that sort of thing.'

Douglas marvelled at his son's self-possession. There was no way he would have managed the smooth speech and open-faced friendliness in the face of such beauty when he'd been his age. He was struggling even now.

Suzy folded her arms across chest which only served to accentuate the gravity-defying cleavage.

'Suzy didn't have a nice time there,' Jack explained. 'Them Pooks brothers is a randy bunch. I went over with my shot gun and sorted them out.' Jack set his chin and Douglas believed a warning had been issued.

'Well, how about I send you my phone number?' Chris reached for his phone. 'You can text me if you're interested.'

Douglas snorted.

'In the job, I mean.'

Douglas glanced at Chris and saw him grinning at Suzy, as if sharing a joke. 'You won't get no signal round 'ere.' Suzy pulled her phone from her jeans' pocket, 'But let's swap landlines. I work in the pub at weekends. The Darton Arms in the village? So you can always find me there. I dare say I won't see you in Curl Up & Dye. Like your hair, by the way.'

Douglas felt himself reddening. 'Oh. Thank you –'

'I was talking to 'im.' She jerked her head at Chris.

Douglas cringed.

'Where d'you have it done?'

'London. Turkish barbers.'

'Nice. You from London?'

'Yep.'

'Nice.'

Douglas looked between the two of them. There was a definite attraction on both sides. 'What's the landline, Dad?'

'Oh, er, not sure.' He struggled to remember his own phone number, gave up, fumbled in his pocket for his mobile and found it in contacts. All the while Suzy quizzed Chris about what clubs he went to in London.

As they drove away, Douglas could hardly see the road through tears of laughter. 'Text me if you're interested,' he spluttered, wiping his eyes, 'What sort of line was that?'

Chris laughed. 'You thought she liked your hair! I just wanted to curl up and die!'

Douglas, crying with laughter, swerved around a bend. 'Do you think she has that effect on all men? She must think we're a total bunch of inarticulate morons.'

'How old do you think she is?' Chris asked.

'Becky's age? Too old for you. And a father with a shotgun. Don't forget that.'

'Talking of Becky, she told me she's staying the whole summer. When the house is finished, if I can find some paid work round here I might stay down till September. I'm getting dangerously close to my overdraft limit.'

Douglas thought of the obvious rapport between Chris and Suzy. Had meeting her influenced him? 'Well there's always the Darton Arms,' Douglas suggested.

'Yeah, I was just thinking that myself.'

Who'd have thought cider buying would be a father-son bonding activity? He felt closer to Chris than he had in years. He would be a valuable ally against the tepee folk. He'd not said a word about Barney. The last thing he wanted to do was to supply ammo for a sibling spat where his negative comments were thrown back at Becky to undermine her. Oh yes, he was learning.

Dawn stood in the kitchen marinating steak. Thank God for Chris's return. She'd never have bought steak for him. She gave a little yelp when she saw Chris and hugged him until he squirmed.

'What a lovely evening. Thought we'd fire up the barbeque. Becky and Barney have lit it. There's beer in the fridge.'

'Mum, I have to say, this place is amazing.'

'There's still a lot to be done. As you can see we have a rather large hole in the middle of the floor and the cooker's not connected. But we're getting there. Now go and say hello to your sister. She's dying to see you. Dad and I will bring the food out.'

Douglas grabbed a beer for himself and topped up Dawn's wine glass. 'Chris seems well. We had some fun at the cider farm.'

Dawn grabbed armfuls of salad stuff from the fridge. 'Oh yes? Tell me over dinner. Can you cut up the French bread?'

'How was your ride with Anastasia?'

She started slicing onions. 'Interesting. I told her about the flood in the kitchen. She said she'd bring it up with Samuel. Can you pass me that knife if you've finished with it? Thanks. I like her but I feel she's keeping something back all the time. Since I overheard her talking to Samuel that time, I don't really trust her.'

'That mightn't have been about the Mill at all.'

Dawn scraped onions into a bowl. 'No. But there was something else. The other night I saw her talking to Mary but she stopped when she saw me. She looked guilty. They were talking about the Pooks but I didn't hear what they were saying. Can you grab a couple of bottles and put them on the tray?'

Douglas opened the fridge door. 'Well, they do have some sort of running dispute.' Women were so much more sensitive about reading other people but Dawn could be a little over-sensitive. In his opinion, she'd over-reacted to her colleagues. He'd told her that once. Never again. 'Do you think she's hiding something?'

'I don't know. I can't help feeling a bit sorry for her. It's the first time we've talked when she hasn't been sloshed, well, we've both been sloshed. I think she's lonely. Freddie isn't down in Devon that much. She obviously adores the boys, her horses, the estate. She's a bit negative about Freddie.'

'Oh?' Douglas envied him less. 'I found him a bit cold.'

Dawn sliced tomatoes and tossed them into the bowl. 'Well, obviously you hate him.'

'What? No! Why would I?'

'Because you fancy her.' She turned to face him, hands on hips, the knife still in her hand.

'No, I don't. I just find her ...' beguiling, alluring, 'different, that's all. Unpredictable. Not what you'd expect someone with her wealth and status to be like.'

'Ok. Maybe you just fancy her art.' She picked up a bottle of salad dressing and splattered the tomatoes.

'Now that is true.'

'I don't think she has many friends. Otherwise why would she bother with me? Unless ...'

'What?'

'Nothing. Can you grab that salad bowl and the French bread? I'll bring the –'

'Dawn. Just stop a minute.' Douglas reached out and held her arms. 'Both the kids are back. Both of them. We weren't sure they'd ever come down.' He smiled at the thought of their two grown-up kids tending the barbeque and winding each other up.

She moved into his arms and laid her head on his shoulder.

'I know. How lucky are we?'

## CHAPTER 31

Becky looked completely at home in Totnes, as Dawn had known she would. Beck stopped to roll a cigarette outside a shop selling goods from India. An array of sparkling clothing, bags and trinkets filled the window.

'This place is really cool,' she said, taking a drag and coughing. She was smoking a lot but Dawn knew better than to point this out. How did some parents manage to turn out immaculate, fit, motivated kids? Possibly through instilling fear, using bribery or passing the job on to a boarding school. As she'd aged, she'd come down more on the nature side of the nature-nurture debate as it involved less self-blame. Both Becky and Chris had emerged from the womb with their own distinctive personalities already stamped in their DNA. They'd never paid any attention to her and Douglas's attempts at nurture.

'I want to visit India when I go travelling.'

She'd only just got her daughter back and she was planning to go again, to somewhere full of dangers. Anxiety kicked in.

When had her anxiety started? She remembered after Becky was born, that feeling of exhaustion and not being in control of her life: unable to eat, shower, go out, sleep or even go to the loo when she wanted. There was no time to clear up or clean, and the house piled up with dirty plates, mounds of grubby washing, stacks of unopened letters and piles of bills and papers. She noticed peeling wallpaper, chipped paintwork, worn carpets, filthy windows and broken cupboard doors. After a few months of this building up and frequent outbursts of tears, something clicked inside her foggy head and she started to clear up the mess and then she couldn't stop. For months she hadn't been able to lift a finger and now her fingers and her hands and feet and her whole self were spinning in activity. She seized the moments Becky slept, not to sleep, but to sort and clean, unable to rest until everything was in its place, and if it didn't have a place she made one. Storage became an obsession. She trawled the local shops with Becky in her pushchair looking for clever storage ideas, favouring attractive crates and boxes that could house any offending homeless objects. 'Come to bed, I'll clear up in the morning,' Douglas would say wearily but she would lie in bed and fret if the curtains weren't arranged in correct folds, the draining board emptied, every surface cleared of objects, and Becky's toys back in their huge wicker basket. She knew she was out of control but she couldn't stop. She didn't want to stop! Look how pretty everything looked! She was in control! During these frantic episodes Becky lay on her back under her baby gym or slept in her rocking chair. When Becky wouldn't settle, Dawn wore her in a papoose on her front and once, she was ashamed to say, tiny Becky fell on to a pile of washing as she was stuffing it into the machine and nearly ended up inside. Of course she exhausted herself and broke down that time the vacuum cleaner bag split open on the kitchen floor, and Douglas came home to find the baby playing in the dirt while Dawn sobbed hysterically. After that, he'd spent his weekends mending, gluing and painting and never complained. But at least, back then, she'd always known where Becky was.

'India? Dad and I talked about going once, but never got round to it.' Dawn had never had the urge to travel; she found Europe enough of a challenge.

'Cool bookshop. Have we got time for a browse?'

'Of course. If you see anything you like I'll buy it. We need to keep our bookshops thriving.'

It had been hard for Douglas too. He had to live with this new woman, a far cry from the carefree, laid-back one he'd fallen in love with. It must have been like picking a ripe apple from the bowl and then noticing halfway through eating that it was rotten. Nothing changed a relationship like having a baby.

Becky found a book on wild Devon, and Dawn bought one about wild swimming for Douglas.

'Shall we get a coffee?'

'Yeah, but where? I've never seen so many cafés.'

They picked one and sat in the window watching the passers-by.

'Will Barney go travelling with you?' Dawn ventured, stirring the creamy top of her coffee.

'He's said he will.'

'Oh, good.' Better than going alone.

'I don't think Dad likes Barney.'

'Dad's always a bit reserved with new people in the beginning. I'm sure he'll come around.'

'I know Barney will always treat me right. At uni I dated a couple of guys. One got drunk the whole time. I never knew where he was. And the other was dating someone else behind my back. Creep.'

'What shits,' Dawn said, lapsing into Becky-speak. 'You don't need that. Unfortunately most twenty-something boys do exactly what they want and think later.'

'True that. Barney's not like that. He's a bit older than the others. He's loyal. I can depend on him. If he says he's going to do something, he does it. He doesn't bail.'

'He seems really into you. I've noticed he follows your lead.' Dawn had seen the way Barney looked at Becky. Every woman should be looked at like that. Yes, Barney was a bit different and the surfer talk jarred, but apart from that he was quite conventional, rather like Douglas in fact. 'We'll do our best to make him feel welcome. You can stay as long as you like.' Please don't go travelling, she thought.

'Thanks, Mum. He'll be useful too. I know Samuel's doing the garden but Barney can plant veggies and fruit bushes. He's really into all that. Working on the land.'

'That would be great.'

'And how are you? I know I tease you about having OCD but you seem better.'

'I am.'

144

'Country life agrees with you. But there's one thing I don't get.' She bit into a flapjack. 'How come you left London? You said you'd never leave. Then all of a sudden ...'

Dawn's head started spinning. It wasn't the caffeine. She'd forgotten how Becky could read her, sense her every mood, tell when she was holding back. She picked up a teaspoon and twiddled it between her thumb and forefinger. 'I had a problem. At work.'

The coffee grinder stopped its harsh rattle and a hush fell over the café. Why had she said that? What had compelled her to reveal? She and Douglas had agreed it should never be mentioned. Why hadn't she deflected with something like, it's your dad's dream so I wanted to support him. That was the line she'd been using with friends. But this was her daughter. She hadn't been prepared for how that bond could wrench the truth from you. Unconditional love meant just that. But she doubted it worked in reverse. Kids set high standards for their parents who usually came up lacking.

'What sort of problem?'

Dawn glanced around at the couples eating cake, the groups sipping coffee. They were listening, she was sure of it. Two women sitting by the toilets looked familiar. Where did she know them from? She should never have mentioned a problem. Becky was looking at her expectantly and she was on the verge of confessing when she remembered the bird killer episode. On the way to work one day, she'd accidentally run over a pigeon. Becky had gone on about it for months, calling her the bird killer. It became a joke, but in the beginning Becky, who was going through a Buddhist phase, had been genuinely outraged. She'd made Dawn feel awful.

She faced her daughter and scrabbled around in her brain for a problem. A minor problem. Lying was hard. How did people do it? She'd never even lied to her parents; everyone did that. How much easier it would have been to say, I'm staying at a friend's tonight, rather than, I'm going to the disco in town and you can't stop me. She'd always thought telling the truth to be a virtue. Lies tripped you up and came back at you.

That's what she'd thought before.

'The new Head was horrible. I couldn't work with her. Dad had been sacked by then. So we agreed on a fresh start.' It was true. The Head had been horrible. She'd told her to leave immediately, not to come back, not to speak to anyone before she left. If she'd have just had the chance to explain, maybe they'd have understood.

'But you could have found another job in London.'

How could she tell her daughter she was unemployable? That the thought of running into anyone from work made her blood run cold? She couldn't bear for Becky to know, for Becky to think of her the way the others did.

'Dad's always wanted to live in the country. You know that.'

'I'm surprised you gave in, that's all.'

She dropped the teaspoon and it clattered into the saucer. 'Relationships are based on compromise.'

'As long as you both compromise and not just one of you.'

Dawn smiled. Becky was growing up.

Becky drained her cup. 'Let's go and trawl those charity shops.'

Dawn stood up so fast her chair fell backwards. 'Yes, lets. Or we could just go for a walk along the river. I hate trying on clothes.'

'Mum, your clothes are hanging off you. You need new stuff. We can swap clothes now.'

Dawn imagined herself in a pair of ripped jeans and a holey alpaca jumper. They walked past a couple of smart boutiques, barely glancing at the window displays with elegant mannequins trying to entice them in. From charity shops she bought a pair of jeans, two summer skirts, a pair of linen trousers, a flowery dress and three tops. All for thirty quid. Good brands, too. Becky bought a tie-dye top and silver flip flops. It was as much fun charity shopping as buying in expensive shops with the additional rush of getting a bargain. It took her mind off things. Dull unease had replaced the sharp pains of anxiety. She linked arms with Becky on the way back to the car. She felt she'd managed the situation. Nothing had changed between them; that was the most important thing. To Becky she was still only a bird killer.

# CHAPTER 32

Excitement rose in Dawn's chest as they sped down the motorway in the ten-year-old people carrier they'd bought to transport guests when the business got up and running. They'd saved some money when Tony had sourced the roof slates cheaper than expected. Now they were going to spend more money. How she'd looked forward to this day! Of course, the house wasn't finished. The kitchen looked awful and they hadn't ordered enough units and yesterday, Tony had prised up the huge floor slabs to access the water pipes because of some plumbing problem and cracked one. Also, Jonno was still fixing the roof – some rafters were rotten and needed replacing – but carpets had been fitted in the cottage sitting room, on the stairs and in the bedrooms and the removal company had delivered their furniture. But they needed more.

Her phone pinged and she read a message. 'Anastasia's just texted me,' she said to Douglas. 'She asked Samuel about the flood in the kitchen and it definitely wasn't him.'

Douglas sighed. 'I don't see who else it could have been. If it was him, her bringing it up might have warned him off. What has he got against us? We've befriended his boss, put him on the payroll and we're accommodating his bloody bats. What more does he want?'

Dawn draped her arm around Douglas's shoulder. 'Let's forget about Samuel for now. I feel as if I've been let out of prison. I don't want to be reminded of the other inmates.'

God, I've missed this, she thought as she manoeuvred the oversize trolley over to the bedroom display area. Shopping. A day away from steam and dust, paint and Pooks.

'Steady on!' Douglas glared at her, 'that was my ankle.'

He hated Flatpack World. She loved it: the caffeine and sugar high after elevenses, the bright lights and rampant display of consumerism they could almost afford. Oh, the joys of middle-age, where sparkling kitchens, polished wood and storage solutions were more exciting than sex.

Dawn studied her list: four single beds and two doubles, several chests of drawers and bedside tables, a small table for the kitchen and eight chairs to go around the big dining room table and clothes rails for those bedrooms without built in wardrobes. The snag was, it wasn't furniture at all but merely piles of wood which might become furniture once assembled. She read further down the list: bed linen, towels, curtains, bedside lamps and throws for the two small settees and comfy chairs she'd bought on the internet for the guest sitting room. She felt like a kid in a sweet shop.

Douglas lay down on one side of a display bed and patted the other side with his hand.

'That's the best offer I'm likely to get for a while.' She lay down beside him.

'Can we get what we need and go?'

'Don't spoil my day out Douglas.' She rolled on to her side and rested her head in her hand. 'I'm scalded, cut, bruised and exhausted. I deserve a day out without your whingeing.'

'Point taken. So will this do? It's the cheapest,' he asked, indicating the bed. 'Shall I write down the numbers? The sooner we hit that warehouse and checkout the better. All I want are picture frames to display that newspaper we found under the lino.'

His phone buzzed. 'It's Chris. We have our very first booking! Rajesh. Remember him? He used to be the PE teacher? Left at the same time I did. And another couple. Let's go have lunch and celebrate.'

'When are they coming?'

'Er, not until next month. Plenty of time to get ready.'

Dawn took a deep breath. 'Hope so.'

'Soooo…' Douglas began, attacking a plate of meatballs. Dawn knew what was coming. After twenty-five years she knew almost before he did what would spout from his mouth.

'Becky and Barney, Barney and Becky. Do we think this is serious?'

Dawn bristled. 'You know Becky has never confided in me about her relationships and I don't think I'd get very far by prying. All I know is that he treats her well and that's what matters.' Her strategy of feigning indifference to her daughter's life and not making judgements had improved their relationship no end.

'I don't like Becky smoking weed and I think Barney encourages it.' Douglas reached for a plastic tomato sauce bottle, turned it upside down and squeezed it. Of course he only noticed the superficial things: the piercings, tattoos, speech ticks and dope smoking.

'I don't like it much either but I think of it as a phase. She won't still be smoking dope in a few years when she's got a proper job. She'll stop when it no longer fits her lifestyle.'

'Let's hope that it doesn't become her lifestyle.' The tomato sauce bottle farted feebly.

'Douglas, do you remember when Becky was born, how she didn't sleep at night and we'd be up every two hours trying to pacify her?' Dawn had visited a sleep clinic, during the day, of course, where Becky slept like, well a baby, which made her point hard to make.

'Yes, I do. It was awful. I used to kip in the art room during the lunch break and nod off during staff meetings.'

This was news to Dawn. She was surprised they hadn't sacked him sooner. 'I used to say don't worry, she'll grow out of it, she won't be doing this when she's a teenager.'

'She still prefers to sleep all day and stay up all night. I anticipate a glittering career as a night watchperson.' Douglas grabbed another tomato sauce bottle and shook it vigorously.

'The point I'm making is it's a phase. It won't last. You know what kids are like. As soon as you get used to them doing something, they stop and do something else.'

'I was worried about you after Becky's birth. I thought you were suffering from post-natal depression.' He cursed at another empty bottle of tomato sauce, complained that they were never re-filled, took another bottle from a nearby table and started prising off the lid with his knife.

'I did not have post-natal depression. I was exhausted by a baby that demanded constant attention. I couldn't eat, sleep, wash, do anything. It's the same for all new mothers. I think mothers who don't feel overwhelmed should be labelled as having post-natal delusion. And, as a working mother, I was panicking about going back to work. We hadn't made any childcare arrangements, if you remember. Douglas?'

'Bugger.' A pool of tomato sauce flooded his plate.

'Douglas, are you even listening to me?' He seemed unable to do two things at once any more. He was the same with walking and talking. He'd developed this habit when they were walking of stopping when he said something, making it sound more important than it was.

'Yes, yes, we had no childcare arrangements.' He spooned the sauce back into the bottle.

'Do you remember those baby kidnappings in the early nineties? One was taken by a nanny who left the country, another taken from a hospital.'

'Nanny,' he muttered vaguely, finally managing to get a meatball in his mouth. 'You were better with Chris.'

'By then I knew what to expect. I'd grown used to the constant vigilance and the lack of personal time. My expectations had plummeted. I remember when I went back to work when Becky was three months, having lunch in the staffroom and thinking: this is nice, sitting down and eating a sandwich without a helpless infant demanding food or milk or winding or a nappy change or a teething ring or some other demand I can't understand.' Dawn broke off, realising she sounded shrill. My God, what a terrible mother she'd been. Why hadn't she been cooing, rocking the cradle and singing lullabies?

Douglas put down his knife and fork and reached for her hand. 'They were wonderful days,' he said dreamily and she realised he'd missed the point entirely. 'We haven't talked about those times for ages.'

Dawn sighed. 'It's because the kids are back. We're focusing on them again. We dealt with empty nest syndrome but failed to realise our chicks are homing pigeons and we can't get rid of them. An alarming amount of twenty-year-olds still live at home.'

'Doesn't surprise me. There aren't proper jobs and rents are ridiculous. Us parents are expected to foot the bill. We have to cling to jobs we should have left years ago.'

'We left ours,' she pointed out.

'We didn't have a choice.'

She could tell Douglas wished he hadn't said that. 'Checkout?'

His hand shook as he handed over the credit card at the till and when he gave her the metre long bill with his I-want-to-kill-myself face, she shoved it into her bag without looking at it. They wheeled the two giant trolleys out to the car and all the purchases fitted in, and what didn't, went on the roof.

Two hours later, they were driving down the hill into Darton, past the modern bungalows, through the heart of the village with its rows of pretty terraced cottages and the odd big house set back from the road. As they passed the Darton Arms, she admired the hanging baskets and clematis around the porch and waved to John who was collecting glasses from the outside tables. As they passed the village shop, she waved to the owners who were tending the flower bed out front. For the first time, she felt as if she were coming home.

Pulling up outside Last Chance, they noticed a strange car parked in the driveway. Becky ran over, her face serious.

## CHAPTER 33

'Becky? What is it?'

'I wanted to catch you before you came in. There's someone here,' she whispered. 'We told him you'd be back soon so he waited. Sorry.'

'Who is it?' She looked up at the sound of Jonno hammering. A slate skittered down the roof and smashed on the ground.

'He's from environmental health. He's in the kitchen.'

Dawn turned to Douglas. 'Did you know about this?'

He paled and shook his head.

Becky opened the front door. The floor was wet; they'd scrubbed the flagstones. Dawn could have kissed her.

In the kitchen, littered with cement bags, paint pots and wood shavings, a man in a suit stood astride the newly dug channel in the floor clutching a clip board. A half-eaten pizza lay in its box next to the overflowing bin. A mouse scurried into the utility room.

'Good afternoon,' the man said. 'I'm here from the local authority to register the premises under the Food and Public Health Wellbeing Act.'

'Isn't this visit premature?' Douglas asked. 'As you can see, the kitchen's not finished yet.'

'You completed this application form,' he thrust a piece of paper at them. 'You are preparing and cooking meals for more than five people here?'

'No. Not yet,' Dawn said. 'We didn't apply for an inspection, did we Douglas?' Don't say this was something else he hadn't told her.

'No,' he responded as adamantly as her and she knew he wasn't lying, for once. 'My wife has OCD and I can assure you that this kitchen will be as spotless and sanitised as an operating theatre before she will allow any food preparation.'

Dawn felt herself grow red.

'The inspection is more to do with facilities and equipment than cleanliness,' he explained. 'I'm afraid it falls down on three of fourteen counts so I have to list it as unfit for use.'

Dawn's shoulders slumped with relief. Only three things.

'It clearly is unfit for use at the moment. The point is, it's NOT FINISHED!' Douglas shouted. She looked at him in alarm.

The inspector stepped backwards, his calf narrowly missing the blade of a jig saw. 'What three things?' Dawn asked quickly, placing a restraining hand on Douglas's arm.

He consulted his list, glancing nervously at Douglas. 'Er, smoke detectors in every room, fly screens on all opening windows in the kitchen and a separate wash hand basin with a single faucet tap in addition to the kitchen sink.'

'We have a sink in the utility room,' Dawn said, picking up the jig saw, 'won't that do?'

The inspector glanced nervously at the saw, as if she were about to fire it up and advance on him. She laid it on the kitchen counter. 'You need to fix a new tap,' he said.

'No problem. And did you try and open any of these windows? They haven't opened since 1901. See?' She demonstrated that they were painted shut. 'No access for flies. And as for smoke detectors, we'll fit those immediately. No problem.'

'You also need a plan of the accommodation including the room sizes and the numbers of people in each room. And each room has to have a plan clearly displayed showing the fire escape.'

'Fine. Who do we send it to?'

'The address is on the top of this checklist. You'll have to apply for a re-inspection after the actions are completed. I suggest you log on soon as there is a waiting list for appeals and re-inspection. A back log,' he added as if they were too dumb to understand the meaning of waiting list. Dawn watched Douglas's face turn from red to white.

'But we have guests arriving next week!' Douglas shouted, breaking away from her grip and advancing on the inspector.

She stepped between them. Guests next week? Surely he meant next month. It must be a ploy to get an early re-inspection. 'Douglas, I can hear the phone. Would you answer it please?'

'I didn't hear the phone.'

'Dad, it's for you!' Becky said from the doorway where she'd been lurking. 'Dad!' she said again, sharply. Douglas blinked in surprise but walked out. Becky shut the kitchen door behind him. Dawn breathed again.

'Look,' she smiled her sweetest smile at the inspector who pulled a hanky from his pocket and wiped his brow. 'This is all a bit of a shock. If there's any way you could pop back next week, we'd be very grateful. We really want to comply and have everything above board.'

The inspector said nothing. Was this the time to whip out a fifty pound note? If only she had one.

She threw a worried glance towards the door. 'Can I fix you a cup of tea? Perhaps a piece of lemon drizzle cake? I made it this morning,' she said switching on the kettle and reaching for the cake tin she stashed on a high shelf out of Barney's eye line.

The inspector opened a diary. 'You're in luck. I'm in the Darton Arms on Tuesday morning. I could come round after that if you think you'll be ready by then?'

Douglas came in. He must have been listening at the door. 'Yes. Definitely. We have a crack team working round the clock –'

A loud crash reverberated through the house. Dawn clutched a work top. They all looked up at the ceiling.

'I have every confidence in them,' Douglas continued, as Jonno staggered into the kitchen, white with plaster dust, grinning from ear to ear.

'I just fell through the ceiling,' he said. 'Ooh. Is that lemon drizzle?'

## CHAPTER 34

Douglas and Dawn stared up at the hole in the bedroom ceiling. Another Pooks fuck up, thought Douglas. One step forward, two steps backward. Above them, something fluttered. The crash had disturbed the residents. He ushered Dawn out of the bedroom.

Chris appeared on the landing. 'I thought you could use some good news. We've another booking for next week. We've seven guests now.'

Douglas glanced at Dawn who blinked a lot. 'That's great news,' he said.

'Please tell me it's not true,' she said slowly.

'I thought you'd be pleased,' Chris said.

'You told me next month, Douglas. Next month.'

He had told her that, implying in a month's time. 'Er, next week is next month. It's July next week, isn't it Chris?'

'Yes.'

Douglas tried not to meet Chris's eyes. He wished Chris hadn't heard this exchange.

Dawn sat down on the stairs. 'This is a nightmare. There's a hole in the kitchen floor, the furniture is in flat packs and now we have the latest Pooks disaster. A hole in a bedroom ceiling. Not to mention that the scaffolding is still up, we haven't had our change of use application approved yet, and we just failed a Public Health inspection.' She delivered this without taking a single breath. Chris sat down beside her and wrapped an arm around her.

'It'll all work out,' Douglas said. Chris looked at him sharply. 'You were marvellous, Dawn, with that idiot. I wanted to punch his lights out. You saved the day. Thanks to you, we'll pass next week. I didn't even know we had to register so I've no idea how he had that form.'

'When you get hold of Tony, tell him we need Pete to put in the right tap.'

'The Pooks will have to work over the weekend,' Douglas agreed.

'And we need a job lot of smoke alarms and have them all installed by Monday night.'

Chris put his hand on her shoulder, 'We'll get it finished, Mum, don't worry. Anything I can do to help right now?'

'Yes, please Chris,' said Douglas, 'we need all the flat packs out of the car and into the right rooms ready to assemble. Can the three of you do that while I clear up here?'

'And could you do the room plans the inspector asked for?'

'Consider it done.'

'Thanks, love.' Dawn turned to Douglas, 'We'll have to eat at the pub tonight. We don't have a functioning cooker and it's just started raining so it's too wet for a barbeque.'

'Great.'

'Can we afford it?'

'Fifty quid isn't going to make a lot of difference to the credit card debt and we deserve it after all this. I'll phone Tony now.'

He picked up the house phone and dialled. When Tony answered he explained about needing to get the work done before Tuesday's re-inspection.

'Sorry, mate,' Tony said, 'we've had to move to another job.'

Douglas went hot; was that a blood pressure thing? 'But why? You've not finished here. There are two holes now, an unfinished roof and a couple of jobs we need done to pass the health inspection. I don't understand. What's the problem?'

'We can't work for no money, see?'

'Of course not. We've always given you cash on time, haven't we? And paid up front for materials?'

'A little bird told me you don't 'ave no more money. And you never paid us today, did you? For last week's work. So I presume it's true.'

'I'm sorry but we left early for Bristol and you'd left by the time we got back. The Inspector turning up threw me. I can bring it round now if you want.'

A silence followed.

'Please, Tony. We need you. I know we're only blow-ins but we're your blow-ins. We're ... we're practically family.' He had no idea where that came from.

'Family, eh?' Tony chuckled. 'I s'pose you do live in my family home. You'll be asking us round for Christmas dinner next.'

'Yes! Please come for Christmas dinner. That's a great idea. Bring all your brothers and wives and children and nieces and nephews. The more the merrier!'

'Ok. We'll be round tomorrow. To work, I mean, not for Christmas dinner. Eight o'clock sharp. We got a match to watch in the afternoon.'

'Of course. Thank you. Thank you so much.'

'Family, eh?' Dawn said from the doorway. 'You can still surprise me, Douglas Thompson. That's what I love about you.'

A vein in his temple throbbed as she picked up the mail from the hallway table and shuffled through the letters. A brown envelope flashed like hazard warning lights.

'Oh, God. It's a letter from planning.' She held it out but he couldn't take it.

'Shall I open it?'

'No!' But he had to know what lay inside. He grabbed it, tore it open, his heart thudding as he read an entire paragraph before he found a sentence which made sense. 'We've got it! Permission for a commercial property granted!'

'No! Let me see that.' She stepped forward to take it from him but he scooped her up in his arms, staggered through to their bedroom and dropped her on the bed.

'That was amazing,' she said five minutes later, when they lay on their backs, stunned. 'Do you think all the Pooks have such fast sex, or is it just our branch of the family?'

Douglas rolled on to his side and rested his head in his hand. Dawn looked flushed and happy, despite the roller coaster of a day. She was his rock, he realised with a start.

'Tony said a little bird told him we were broke. Who could that have been?'

'The whole world knows we're broke,' said Dawn. 'Except …do you remember I told you I overheard Anastasia talking to Mary when we went round to dinner at the Manor? Saying something about the Pooks. Anastasia said, 'phone her'. She could have meant phone Mary's niece. She's married to Matt Pooks isn't she?'

'That could have been about anything,' said Douglas. 'And the Pooks hate the Montagues so why would they listen to Anastasia?'

'But it came from Mary. Not Anastasia. Maybe we should find out why the Pooks hate the Montagues. Maybe then we'd find out what this is all about.'

# CHAPTER 35

Friday night. Most of the village had congregated in the Darton Arms. Funny, Dawn thought, how I lose track of the days. Teaching in schools, her whole life had revolved around dates and times, buzzers and bells. How come she'd missed that next week was July? She knew Douglas hadn't been totally honest with her but, as their marriage was finally getting back on track and they had the prospect of guests, she wasn't going to spoil that by quibbling.

'Hello!' She turned and saw Freddie perched on a bar stool, sporty in tweed Plus Fours and waistcoat, though spoiling the country gent effect with a white shirt unbuttoned to his navel, Mr Darcy style.

'Hello,' Dawn shouted back above the noise.

'Can I get you a drink?' he slurred.

'Thanks, but Douglas is buying. We're here for a family meal. Our son is home.'

Freddie was drunk. She could tell from the set of his mouth and his bloodshot eyes. She looked past him to see if Douglas was being served. 'So you're down for the weekend.' She was surprised to see him down again so soon and during term time because Anastasia had told her he didn't come down to Dartcoombe often and preferred London. She thought back to the snippet of conversation between Anastasia and Mary that she'd overheard. What kind of a person would act as their friend yet plot against them?

Freddie held up his empty pint glass and, without a word, a pretty blonde barmaid took it from his hand. Dawn glanced down the bar and saw Douglas still hadn't been served. Well, he wasn't Lord of the Manor. She saw Chris following the barmaid's every move with his eyes, presumably trying to get her attention too. When the girl plonked Freddie's pint down in front of him, he handed her a ten pound note and said, 'Keep the change and have one later.' So that's how he got served so quickly. The girl didn't say, 'thanks' or register him at all, not a smile or nod or anything. Not even eye-contact. As she moved down the bar to serve Douglas, Freddie watched her over the top of his pint so intently that Dawn felt uncomfortable. He turned his attention back to her.

'I changed my plans. Spur of the moment. Wanted to surprise Ana. I'll be down next weekend too. For her birthday.'

'How nice. I must go and find the others. Tell Anastasia I said hello and that I'll ring her soon to arrange a supper. We've had a bit of a setback with the kitchen ...' but Freddie's attention had wandered so she slipped away.

'Hi, Dawn.' She turned and saw the landlord, John. 'Great to see you. I've just been chatting to Douglas and I met your son. What a nice lad.'

'Thanks. When they leave for uni you worry that they'll never come home.'

'I never did,' said John. 'Couldn't wait to get away from the parents. But I'm sure you and Douglas are very supportive.'

'We try. I must go and find our daughter and her boyfriend. You must meet them too.'

Dawn found Becky and Barney sitting at a table in the back room.

'Chris has got himself a job,' Douglas announced proudly, sloshing beer as he laid the tray on to the table. Dawn wondered how Becky must feel to be constantly in the presence of the favoured child. 'Turns out their last KP resigned so Chris is in. John and Andy just hired him.'

She seized the bottle of wine and poured herself a glass. 'What's a KP?'

'Kitchen Porter!' They said in unison.

'How did you know there was a job going?' she asked Chris.

'I talked to Suzy, the barmaid. She's the girl we told you about, who used to work for Mrs Pooks. She says she'll work for us if we want.'

162

'So that's Suzy.' Douglas had told her about their meeting. 'She's as pretty as you said.'

'Yeah, in a kind of obvious way,' Barney said smiling at Becky. Dawn liked him more each day.

'Well, duhhh,' Chris mocked. 'Don't worry, Mum. I won't start until the work at the Mill is finished.'

'It's all hands on deck now we have guests arriving,' Douglas said. 'By the way, I spoke to Tony and he and Pete are fixing the smoke alarms and tap tomorrow so we'll be ready for the re-inspection on Tuesday. The holes will be fixed next week and then it's just more painting. Your mum and I can't thank you enough for all your help. You too Barney.'

'Aw, thanks Dad, I mean Mr T,' Barney joked.

'It's all happening too fast,' said Becky, echoing Dawn's thoughts. 'We'll never be ready in time. It's exhausting.'

'Don't be such a downer! Just 'cos I got the business,' Chris said.

Becky chipped in, 'You didn't scrub all those flagstones. Oh, by the way Mum, Freddie told me that the puppies are old enough to go to other homes. Can we have one please? Please?'

'But you're not even going to be here. You're going off to Laos or Vietnam or some other country America bombed. Who do you think will look after him then?' Douglas pointed out.

'Maybe I won't go. Barney and I might just settle down here.'

Dawn's mouth fell open. She couldn't get used to the way the kids changed their plans continually. She caught Douglas's eye and they raised their eyebrows. They never could refuse their children's demands. They each looked into the defeated face of the other.

'Dad and I will think about it,' she said. How could she refuse the girl who scrubbed an acre of filthy flagstones without being asked? After all, the main problem with having a dog was what to do with it when you were on holiday and she couldn't imagine having one of those for several years.

'Hello. Dawn isn't it? Anastasia's friend?' She looked up and saw a tall man with a short grey beard looking down at her. It was the vet who delivered the puppies.

'Hi. Well remembered. Roger isn't it?'

'Roger Masters and this is my wife Penny.' Penny was blonde and smiley. 'I almost didn't recognise you without your coating of cow excrement.'

'Roger!' Penny scolded.

Dawn laughed and explained to Becky and Chris about how she'd been at the birth of the puppies. Penny asked them to come along to the pub on Thursdays for the pub quiz.

'We'd love to,' Douglas enthused, always keen to show off his general knowledge.

'Great! What's your specialist subject?' Penny asked Douglas.

'Art!' shouted Becky and Chris in unison.

'Excellent,' said Penny. 'None of the team know anything about art. And you, Dawn?' Penny looked at her expectantly and so did her children. Douglas grinned at her stupidly, his smile fading as the seconds dragged on. She couldn't think of what to say, not even to make a joke about it. Had she reached her fifties and knew nothing about anything? She knew how to provide a safe haven for children with troubled pasts. She knew the best ways to teach children to read and write. She was an expert at procuring grants for educational projects. But she doubted that any of that would come up in a pub quiz.

'Mum's really good on literature and films,' Becky chimed in. Dawn could have kissed her.

'She always wins at Trivial Pursuits so I'd say she's an all-rounder,' Chris said. 'She can recite the names and sizes of all the Japanese islands. Who knows that?'

She let out a breath. Thank God for sibling rivalry.

Penny looked relieved. 'You'll both be a welcome addition to the team.'

'Thanks,' Dawn said to Becky and Chris as she sat back down to eat her duck and mash after Roger and Penny had left. Douglas poured her another glass of wine, his way of saying sorry perhaps. 'The only thing I could think of as my specialist subject was remedies for wet rot and opening times at the tip.'

'Jolly useful specialisms both,' said Douglas.

As they left, Dawn noticed Freddie still sitting on the same bar stool. Douglas might be a pain sometimes but at least he wasn't a pub fixture. Why did Freddie spend so much time in the Darton Arms when he could be spending time at Dartcoombe Manor?

They sat in the kitchen with a glass of wine while the kids watched television in the sitting room.

'You seem very pensive tonight. Is everything all right?'

Dawn looked up in surprise. He'd noticed. She wasn't even sure she should say out loud what was on her mind. That usually caused an argument but the wine had mellowed her.

'Do you sometimes wish you could start over again? I mean, do things differently?'

'You mean with the benefit of hindsight.'

'Yes.'

'What would you change? Not me, I hope.'

'No. I think we've worked out OK. I'd just have liked …'

'What?'

'I wish we'd had more fun. We were always working, striving towards some goal or other. I wish we'd taken time out and travelled before we had kids. No routine. No obligations. No jobs.'

'That's what I imagined retirement would be like. Sitting in a deckchair, doing crossword puzzles, cruising –'

'Cruising? You can't stand being cooped up with other Brits. Or did you mean cruising for sex? That's about all you can afford.'

Douglas shot her a withering look. 'You know what we need?'

Dawn nodded.

'A gap year!' they said together.

# CHAPTER 36

Anastasia was stepping out of the bath when she heard the front door. She pulled her robe around her and rushed downstairs. Cosmo and Rollo were almost as tall as her as she stood in her bare feet. 'You've both grown,' she said, hugging them.

'It's only been four weeks, Mummy. Happy Birthday!'

'Yes, happy birthday, darling,' said Freddie, planting a kiss on her cheek.

'I've booked a cab for seven thirty and the restaurant for eight. Shall we meet up in the drawing room at seven?'

'Have we got time to take the dogs down to the river?' Cosmo asked.

'You've one hour but take your phones and don't be late. And don't get all muddy.'

'I need a shower.' Freddie picked up his leather holdall and walked upstairs.

'Shall I bring you up a cup of tea?'

'Thanks. I'd love one. The traffic was ghastly.'

She gave him some space. The Tiffany box was still in the drawer. He'd need time to wrap it.

He was still in the shower when she went into the bedroom. She sat at her dressing table, applied make up and styled her hair. Not bad for forty-six she thought as she studied her reflection. Freddie came into the bedroom, a towel around his waist. He had the beginnings of a six-pack. He must be working out again. Maybe she should go to the gym; she'd noticed cellulite on her thighs.

He bent down and kissed her neck. She smelt alcohol on his breath and her eyes scanned the room and picked out his silver hip flask on the bedside table. He hadn't kissed her like that in longer than she cared to remember so she was not about to reprimand him for his drinking. It was nearly six o' clock after all.

'I feel old,' she said instead.

'Guess what the boys told me on the way down. Their dorm voted you the sexiest Mum.'

'Really? That's boys' boarding schools for you. I told you they should have gone to co-ed.'

'You've still got it.' He opened her robe. She wished she'd put on a bra and panties. She closed her eyes and gave herself up to the sensation of his hands running over her. The next thing she knew they were on the floor. She glanced anxiously at the door and hoped the boys were still at the river. Without the bed covers she felt exposed. She remembered how they used to make love in his office, behind the desk, the possibility that someone might walk in and find them excited him but terrified her. That was her worst nightmare, akin to finding herself walking down a street, naked. She felt his breath on her neck, the urgency of his kisses. His desire turned her on. He really wanted her. She welled up with relief.

When it was over, he lay on top of her and she stroked his hair. To think she'd worried that he'd gone off her! You couldn't be having an affair with another woman when you made love to your wife like that.

'We'd better get dressed,' she said. 'The boys will be waiting.'

When she went downstairs, she called the boys from their games consoles and they rushed into the drawing room. Freddie came in with a large present wrapped in shiny paper and she tried to keep the smile on her face. He cracked open a bottle of champagne and she had several sips before ripping off the wrapping paper. She revealed a Chanel bag. She ran her hand around the inside feeling for a small box. Nothing. The boys took a small present out from behind the settee cushions. She beamed; it was about the right size. She took another gulp of champagne, tore at the paper and relief flooded over her as she glimpsed the robin-egg blue. She pulled off the lid. A bracelet. A sodding bracelet. She forced a smile, kissed them all and put out her hand so the boys could fasten it to her wrist. She ran upstairs on the pretext of grabbing a pashmina. She checked the sock drawer. The box was still there. He must have forgotten about it, that's all. He'd probably remember later. She smiled when she saw her robe lying on the floor. He'd come down to Dartcoombe the last four weekends so, even if he had been having an affair, it must be over. She sat down at her dressing table and looked at her reflection. She was now nearer to fifty than forty. Men weren't exactly flocking around. It must be nice to have that feeling of security that growing old with someone brings. An image of Dawn and Douglas flashed into her head.

She ran downstairs as the taxi pulled up and drove to a new seafood restaurant in Dartmouth. The boys told amusing stories about school and explained why they wanted to go to a summer camp in Scotland. She and Freddie drank too much and fell into bed at the end of the evening, Freddie asleep as his head hit the pillow. In the morning, she woke late, alone.

'He's gone fishing, madam,' Mary told her when she asked after him.

'With the boys?'

'No. They're in Cosmo's room watching a video.' That was odd. He usually took them when he went down to the river.

She went upstairs to dress. She was drawn to the sock drawer like a heroin addict to a source. Heart pounding, she went into his dressing room and opened the drawer.

The box had gone.

## CHAPTER 37

Anastasia cried into Truffle's soft fur. Cosmo and Rollo took turns to console her. 'It's OK Mummy, you'll be able to see him whenever you want. Becky will love him. You've got three others.'

She stared at the boys through her tears. She didn't deserve their sympathy. She'd never comforted them when they needed it. She and Freddie had hired a full-time nanny when Rollo was born; a large, matronly woman. Anastasia had believed that children should not affect your life. When they'd started boarding school, she'd been relieved, as were all her friends. She could refocus on Ends of the Earth, enjoy intimate suppers with Freddie and resume champagne brunches with her London chums. 'Now boys, buck up and stop crying,' she'd tell them at the start of every term, 'it's only for twelve weeks. We all have to go through it. You have to go to school. It's the law.' They'd been seven years old and for them twelve weeks was a lifetime. She hadn't even shed a tear. She and Freddie had never considered not sending them to boarding school. Her parents had done it and their parents before them. But now the boys were thirteen and fourteen, it struck her that she was the one who'd missed out.

One of them stroked her hair. When had someone last done that? She hugged them back. 'I love you both so much.' She'd squeezed them until they wriggled away complaining, unused to such affection.

'Will you be wanting lunch, madam?' Mary asked from the doorway.

'No thanks, Mary. And we're out tonight. We've been invited to the Mill for supper so you've a night off.'

'Yay!' The boys punched the air.

'Becky and Barney made quite an impression on you two didn't they?' She couldn't understand why. Becky seemed a nice enough girl, not that she knew much about girls, but she was friendly, outgoing and kind. But Dawn worried about Becky. Well, she would be worried too if she had a daughter who wanted to live like a gypsy. Barney was sweet. Fine as a pet but not as a boyfriend. And Dawn was fretting, quite understandably, about them travelling around the Far East. Anastasia spent a lot of time there, trawling for goods and arranging for them to be shipped. From the safety of five star hotels, she watched the news and read the newspapers. It was a dangerous place. Last year, a young woman had been killed in a tourist resort in Thailand, in a safer place than where Becky and Barney were heading. She shuddered to think of Cosmo and Rollo exposed to all that. If they insisted on a gap year she would pay some organisation a small fortune to arrange for them to paint huts on the slopes of Kilimanjaro or rehabilitate orangutans in the Borneo jungle. No backpacking for them. But she doesn't think they'll want to. Neither of them was adventurous. They would probably head for the City as soon as possible and buy Maseratis. They were mini-Freddies. She used to think this was a good thing, but now she isn't so sure.

'Not a word about Truffle tonight as he's going to be a surprise for Becky. Her brother, Chris, is back from university but he's about twenty. So...' she looked at them indulgently, 'who would like to go to McDonalds and then watch Iron Man Three?' She laughed as the boys whooped with delight. Teenagers were so easily pleased.

Later, as she sat at her dressing table, dabbing at the blotches on her face, Freddie walked in. She was wearing her slinkiest slip but she could have been dressed in a bin bag. He didn't even glance at her. How different from last night. What had that been? A dutiful birthday shag? To keep the little wifey happy? Her features looked pinched as if she'd eaten something bitter.

'You went out early.' It sounded more accusatory than she'd intended.

'I went fishing in the Bay. Thought I'd told you. Caught lots of mackerel. We can take some over tonight. Can you drive, darling?' That meant he was planning on getting tanked up.

Anger rose in her chest. She opened her mouth to ask where the box had gone and demand an explanation. The boys' shouts reached her as they raced up and down the corridor. She knew what he would say: that she was the only one he loved, that it wouldn't happen again, beg her to forgive him, blah, blah, blah. And she would forgive him because she didn't want to risk losing Dartcoombe. No. She wouldn't confront him now but would wait until the boys were back at school, avoiding an ugly scene in front of them just before they were going out as a happy family.

She hoped Dawn had a bottle of decent vodka. Would it be rude to take one over? Probably. She'd down a couple of shots before she left to deaden the tornado of emotions swirling around inside her. Hopefully it would be good news. They'd failed to get permission for a commercial property or they couldn't complete the renovation. They must have failed that inspection too. Samuel had told her the kitchen floor had been dug up at the time. Thank God. She needed something to cheer her up.

# CHAPTER 38

Anastasia's kitten heels clacked across the flagstones and she feared she may have overdressed.

Douglas led them to a small sitting room with a new-carpet smell, sparsely furnished with a worn corner sofa, a coffee table, empty book shelves and stacks of cardboard boxes. He offered her a vodka, a good brand thank God, and Freddie accepted a single malt.

'I've just had a vodka myself,' Douglas confessed handing Anastasia a glass. 'Flat pack furniture is enough to turn anyone to serious drink.'

'All the comrades love a vodka.' She clinked his glass, caught his eye and smiled. She enjoyed teasing Douglas. It made him flustered and say silly things. She hoped Freddie noticed the way Douglas acted around her. He looked dashing tonight in a pale blue shirt and jeans and flirting with him in front of Freddie felt good.

But tonight, Douglas quickly looked away. 'Yes well, us communists find communal living goes much better when drunk. Talking of which, it turns out that Barney is a dab hand at constructing furniture from sticks even when parts are missing.' He turned to Cosmo and Rollo, 'Why don't you go upstairs and find them? They're in one of the bedrooms assembling a wardrobe and could probably use a hand. Shall we go and find Dawn? I don't think she heard your car.'

The kitchen looked like a bombsite.

'Mind that piece of wood on the floor,' said Douglas as Anastasia tripped on it. She looked down into a gaping trench. Hopefully, the kitchen had looked like this when the inspector called. How she could ask without giving herself away? Dawn, red-faced and wild-eyed, was juggling pots and bowls and mixers. She was wearing a floaty summer dress and had had her hair done which made her face look slimmer. Anastasia found herself hugged, and suppressed a laugh when Dawn tried this on Freddie who used his bag of mackerel as a shield.

Dawn grasped the smelly bag. 'Thank you. Douglas, put these in the freezer, would you?'

As she held it out, Anastasia noticed the bag had the logo of a fish shop in Brixham. So much for a fishing expedition. Where had he been?

Dawn continued, 'We've got Red Devon beef in ale tonight, from the village butcher who gets it from the farm up the road. Fruit salad and local cheeses to finish. The local vineyard makes the most delicious cheese. Wine's a bit pricey but we must support our local businesses. I think that trip to Flatpack World set me off. We've been spending money like water.'

Anastasia winced at Dawn's manic laughter. She was high as a kite, possibly drunk. A wave of exhaustion overcame Anastasia just looking at her. She looked around at the bubbling saucepans, mounds of vegetable peelings and soiled cutting boards. She'd never been to a dinner party where the hostess had cooked the food and even bought it herself. 'It looks as if you've gone to a lot of trouble.'

'I only stepped off the ladder an hour ago. Jonno fell through the ceiling last night. Didn't Douglas tell you? And we've seven guests arriving on Saturday! It's been a crazy day!'

Anastasia leant against a cupboard. They had guests. She never thought they'd be ready for this summer which meant they wouldn't survive the winter. But, now they had guests. Could this day get any worse? She forced a smile.

'We failed a Public Health Inspection but the chap's coming back on Tuesday to re-inspect. Tony and Pete have been here all day getting things in place so we can pass. And we've finally had planning permission confirmed. It's official. This is a commercial premises.'

Anastasia drained her glass. The Pooks were conspiring against her. Mary had assured her they weren't coming back, damn them. Some informer Samuel had turned out to be. He hadn't said a word about any of this. The planning department had told her she was entitled to appeal, and she could do so anonymously. She started to mentally draft a letter. Maybe she could play up the bat angle. Only last week she'd read about a barn conversion that had been stopped when they'd found a rare species of bat. Perhaps one could buy them on the internet. Samuel would know.

She became aware of Dawn jabbering on about employing a girl from the pub but she wasn't concentrating.

'From the Darton Arms?' Freddie piped up, sounding suddenly interested, breaking off from a conversation about fishing with Douglas.

'Chris is working there, too. I think he's sweet on her,' Douglas said with a suggestive raise of the eyebrows. 'They're going to the pictures next week.'

'You haven't met Chris yet,' Dawn said as she pulled hot pans in and out of Aga drawers. 'Where is he?' she asked Douglas.

'He's in the studio sorting out the art delivery that arrived today. Would you like to see the studio?' Douglas asked them, emptying ice from a tray into a jug and putting some in Freddie's glass.

Anastasia wasn't keen but Freddie expressed an interest so they set out across the meadow. Her shoes weren't suitable for walking across grass. The heels dug in and she held on to Freddie to steady herself. He didn't talk on the way over and had drained his glass by the time they reached the barn.

'I say, you've done a great job here,' said Freddie admiring cupboards of all things. 'Kept it rustic. Very nice.'

Douglas glowed with pride. He really was quite sweet.

A good-looking boy of around twenty stopped unpacking tubes of paint from a large cardboard box and walked over. 'Hi I'm Chris,' he said, holding out his hand. What a self-possessed young man. They'd managed to produce one normal child. Good-looking, too, with Dawn's colouring and Douglas's height though he was stick thin.

'Is that the tepee?' Anastasia asked spying a conical tent that looked like a sagging, canvas kennel. 'How cosy.' How did Becky and Barney live in that? She imagined Truffle asleep on their bed. She never let the dogs upstairs at home, let alone on a bed. But a mattress in a tepee would be acceptable. Truffle will be a spoiled, hippie puppy – a pippie? Wild and crazy like his human role models. He already had the required doggy dreadlocks.

'So, Chris, you're working at the Darton Arms,' Freddie said, ignoring her. 'Enjoying it there?'

'Yes. The people are really nice. John and Andy are great to work for and I can cycle there and back which is handy.'

'Your father says you've met a nice girl there,' Anastasia said.

'Mum and Dad are obsessed with me making new friends here. I'm heading back to London in a couple of months anyway.' If Chris was embarrassed he dealt with it well.

'I'm sure you'll make lots of new friends now you're working there,' Freddie said. 'It's the hub of local life.'

'You should know. You spend enough time there,' Anastasia said. She liked going there occasionally but couldn't see the attraction.

'I thought you looked familiar,' Chris said, 'that must be where I've seen you.'

'Guilty as charged.' Freddie held up his hands and feigned a sheepish look.

Douglas led them around to the front of the Mill and they sat on rickety chairs. Anastasia felt chilly in her summer dress but soon Dawn called them in for supper.

Nine of them sat around a large, bare wooden table in a small dining room that smelt of paint, sitting on chairs that the kids foraged from around the house. Chatter filled the room. Three conversations were playing out at once but she sat listening. Cosmo and Douglas were jabbering on about bats and vampires, a subject they both appeared to know a lot about. Rollo and Chris were discussing an IT assignment he had for homework. Freddie was talking to Becky and Barney about music, of all things. How come he knew so much about current bands? She watched Dawn dashing back and forth between the dining room and the kitchen, offering more food, bringing in more bottles and joining in everyone's conversations when she could. The poor woman appeared to be shopper, cook, waitress, cleaner, hostess and decorator all rolled into one. She was clearly struggling with it, though she seemed happy, as if it were a normal state of affairs.

She glanced across the table at Freddie, sitting upright as a board, squeezed between Becky and Barney. He caught her eye and looked away. Dawn kept drawing Cosmo and Rollo into the conversation and Anastasia felt uncomfortable remembering the pleasure she'd felt when Dawn had told her only last week that the renovation was not going well and that their marriage was under strain. You had to hand it to D and D; they'd pulled the cat out of the bag. She looked around the dingy room, thought of the messy kitchen and wondered if this was the right environment for Truffle. After the grandeur and parkland at the Manor this place would be a come down.

She couldn't bear to be in the room a minute longer. She excused herself and went in search of a decent loo.

## CHAPTER 39

Suzy was very pretty, Dawn thought as she walked into the kitchen, too pretty if there were such a thing. And like most pretty girls, she knew it. Pretty in an obvious way, Barney had said in the pub. Dawn knew she shouldn't put down beauty in this clichéd way. Beauty could be a burden after all: the staring, the unwanted come-ons, the bitchiness of others less beautiful, not to mention the lack of expectation of personality or intelligence. But strip Suzy of her elaborate make up and the fancy hairdo that she worked on for hours at college and Becky would compare favourably. When Suzy looked at Becky, Dawn could tell she was thinking the same thing as her: for God's sake brush your hair and bin those ripped jeans.

She pulled a tray of flapjacks from the Aga. She would never make comments on Becky's appearance ever again. Not New Dawn. She loved New Dawn, though regretted its connotations with Marxist splinter groups and whacky Christian sects. New Dawn was fun, fearless and accepting of others. Out loud, anyway. Her internal monologue suggested Old Dawn was creeping up behind New Dawn with a chloroform pad whilst she projected her fun persona. Old Dawn considered New Dawn to be the result of late-onset schizophrenia.

'Lovely earrings,' she said to Suzy as they stood side by side, one buttering bread, and the other mashing mayonnaise into tuna. The stones sparkled in a shaft of July sunshine. They must be zircon, but the way they caught the light. How would she afford real diamonds? Mind you, Suzy wouldn't be short on admirers. Even Dawn stared at her in jaw-dropping admiration.

'Thanks,' said Suzy. 'They were a birthday present. What's the sandwich order for today?'

Dawn picked up the list the guests had filled in at breakfast. 'Two tuna mayo, two cheese and pickle and three ham and tomato. And put a flapjack and an apple in their pack along with a bottle of water.'

Suzy had worked with Dawn for the past two mornings, since the guests had arrived. Becky could have helped, but even before she'd started working nights at the Darton Arms, she'd operated on Californian time, waking at four in the afternoon rather than eight in the morning. She'd promised to help on changeover days. Dawn shuddered at the thought of her going off to the Far East. Hopefully, she wouldn't manage to save enough money. Dawn had another idea to make her stay.

Dawn yawned. She'd been getting up at six o'clock to have breakfast ready for eight so the guests were ready for their art class at nine. They worked with Douglas until dinner time which gave her some time to herself, after she'd cleared the breakfast table, washed up, cleaned and tidied the whole house and bought and prepared the evening meal. Last night, she'd fallen into bed at midnight.

She opened the chest freezer, took out a joint of beef and put it in the fridge to defrost for tomorrow's evening meal. They'd spent a fortune stocking it after she'd planned a fortnight's meals. She looked up at the flagons of Farmer Jack's cider on the shelf; plenty to keep them going. All last week, she'd had an underlying sense of anxiety about the imminent arrival of guests. It reminded her of school before the kids arrived, the calm before the storm. She hadn't been so nervous since waiting for the verdict of the hearing. She hadn't voiced this to Douglas who didn't need her anxiety heaped on his own. He'd been chivvying the Pooks to finish and clear out their stuff.

Through the window she saw Barney constructing raised vegetable beds and a fruit cage at the far end of the meadow. The kids had been brilliant this past week: assembling furniture, cleaning windows, putting up curtains, making the beds and stocking the bathrooms. She'd scrubbed, tidied and binned in an OCD spin, the familiar panic rising in her chest drove her to order, sort and create space to breathe.

'Where are they going today?' Suzy asked putting sandwiches into the cold box.

'Dartcoombe. To paint those chocolate-box cottages.' Dawn threw chunks of lamb into an industrial-size frying pan.

'I might join in,' Suzy said.

'Could your interest have anything to do with a certain Rajesh?' Rajesh, a disgustingly fit PE teacher from Douglas's old school, had caught the eye of both Suzy and Debbie, another guest, recently divorced who didn't seem to be missing her ex-husband one bit. 'I think you might have a bit of competition there.' Dawn scraped the browned lamb into the slow cooker along with carrots, onions and swedes.

'Eeeuuw, from that old woman? That's revolting.'

'She's only thirty-five.' What must she think of me? Amazed I'm still alive I suppose. 'And he's thirty-two so rather too old for you.'

'I like older men. They know how to treat a girl.'

'You mean buy you diamond earrings.'

'Sommat like that.' She coloured slightly.

Dawn looked at her watch and untied her apron. Suzy looked as if she were about to say something, but turned away and washed her hands.

Chris was on an early shift at the pub and had asked Dawn to make sure he was up before she left. She crept upstairs and listened at the door. She opened it and tiptoed over to the bed, unsure whether to wake him. He lay on his back, one arm draped above his head. In sleep his face looked softer, vulnerable. Her perfect boy. He'd always hidden his emotions, grown cagey if she'd asked questions. But he had a trusting nature, a desire to please. Over the years she'd seen the way other boys manipulated him, used him to cover for them, asked him to write their essays, hung out in his room when their own parents had thrown them out. A person like that could get their heart broken. Girlfriends had come and gone. Girl mates she now suspected they'd been. They had two attractive girls staying, Zoe and Alice, and Chris hadn't even looked at them. She could read girls, she'd been one herself. Boys were harder. How would she know if one cared for her son or was just using him? Did he even know that she knew he was gay? Did he think a mother would know these things without them having to be spoken? Or did he not trust her with the information? She leant closer, listening for his breathing, as she'd done from the moment he was born, always fearful he would be snatched away from her. She knew nothing of this world he'd entered. She looked around his bedroom for a clue. His lap top sat on the desk next to a pile of books – course books by the look of them – his sports trophies perched on a shelf that he and Douglas had put up, along with his hair products. Clothes spilled out of his sports bag, she could smell their boyish mustiness. The lack of personal items saddened her for some reason. What a contrast to Becky who displayed it all. Chris either had nothing to hide or he was good at hiding. She used to think it was the former but now she knows it's the latter. On the bedside table – an upturned wine box that Douglas had rescued from the tip – Chris's phone flashed into life and began a strange incantation. Dawn tiptoed backwards towards the door, closing it silently as Chris began to stir.

As Dawn entered the utility room, she heard a splashing, opened the door and saw Samuel running his hand under the outside tap. The water running off was red with blood. She stepped back. Panic gripped her. Samuel's eyes flitted towards her and she saw his pained expression. She snapped out of it. The boy was in trouble and needed her help. Gently, she pulled his hand away from the stream of water. She was frightened to look but forced herself. Blood pooled around his thumb. The cut looked deep and ragged.

'Don't worry. It's not that deep. I'll take you to the doctor. We'll get it checked out to be on the safe side. Suzy!'

Suzy appeared in the doorway. 'Sam! What have you done?'

'Suzy, grab a clean tea towel.' Suzy stood transfixed. 'Quick!'

Dawn wrapped the tea towel tight around his wrist and gently over his thumb and instructed him to hold his arm above his head. She held onto his good arm, walked him over to the car and helped him into the back seat. Suzy slid in beside him and Dawn couldn't help smiling as Suzy laid her head on Samuel's shoulder and he leaned into her.

A doctor at Darton medical practice saw him immediately. When the doctor asked Samuel how he'd cut it, he struggled to squeeze out an 's', gave up and mimed sawing. Dawn and Suzy looked away while the doctor cleaned the wound and stitched it.

The doctor looked at her computer screen and gave him a tetanus shot. 'I see from my notes that we referred you for speech therapy two years ago Samuel. Have you attended any sessions?' She asked as she applied a dressing.

Samuel shook his head. Suzy frowned at him. 'Is it because of the bus?' she asked.

Dawn noticed Sam blink and look at the floor. He had a problem with buses? 'I can drive you, Sam,' she said.

'That would be great wouldn't it, Sam?' Suzy beamed at him, he paused, then gave a brief nod. Dawn had a feeling he would jump off a roof if Suzy asked him.

The doctor smiled. 'The clinic will send you a letter with an appointment, Sam. No work with your hands for a week and wear thick gloves at all times.'

'Don't worry, doctor. We'll look after him,' Dawn said. Sam rewarded her with the briefest of smiles. She left the surgery with a lighter step. How did someone develop a bus phobia? At least that was one she didn't have.

## CHAPTER 40

Sam raced upstairs without a word when his mum opened the door, leaving Dawn standing on the doorstep like a Jehovah's Witness without a pamphlet.

'I hope he hasn't been up to no good,' Mrs Grimes said, ushering her along a dark hallway to a kitchen. 'You know what boys are like. When you have four, there's always one causing you grief and I wouldn't be at all surprised if–'

Dawn sat down at a table covered with chopped vegetables. 'No, Mrs Grimes, Samuel isn't in any trouble. In fact we're very grateful to him for–'

'Take Joshua,' she continued completely ignoring what Dawn had said. 'I warned him about buying an MOT down the pub but would he listen? And now he's in trouble with the police.'

'I'm very sorry to hear that but–'

'Nigel is the worst. He's a bully…'

Dawn realised she was getting nowhere. She'd almost become an elective mute herself. She sympathised with Gillian Grimes. Four boys living at home must be a strain but how could she be so oblivious to Samuel's problems? Gillian looked to be in her sixties, her hair steel-grey, and her eyes red-rimmed as if she hadn't slept. Something that reminded Dawn of school dinners was rattling the lid of a saucepan on the cooker. But she wasn't here to discuss the whole family. She dug deep for some remnant of her inner school teacher. 'Mrs Grimes, Gillian, I'm sorry to cut you off but I haven't much time. Samuel cut his thumb today when he was working in our garden. We took him to the doctor and she stitched it up and he's fine.'

'Oh. That's why you brought him home. He should be up at the Manor. '

'I'll call in there on my way back and explain. But I need to ask you about Samuel, more specifically about his speech. Has he ever spoken? Or has he always been mute?'

Gillian Grimes wiped her hands on her apron and sat down at the table, deep in thought. 'He used to stutter. He couldn't get his words out. They used to make fun of 'im at school. So he stopped trying. They moved 'im to a special school but it didn't make no difference.'

'Did he speak at home? Some children who stammer are embarrassed to speak at school but they speak in the safe environment of the home.'

'His brothers teased 'im too. He's not very bright see? None of them did well at school but my other boys are sharp. Samuel was always different, always special.'

And probably couldn't get a word in even if he'd wanted to.

Gillian continued, 'But when he needs to speak, he can make sounds.'

'Did he have speech therapy at school?'

'Oh, yes. But he didn't go to school that much. It was a long bus journey, to the special school. He always hated buses. I couldn't understand why until …' She looked out of the window and fell quiet for the first time. 'He likes being outside, Samuel, he hates being shut in. If he goes in a car he sticks 'is head out the window. Like a dog.'

'I would like to drive Samuel to his appointment. Would you be happy for me to do that?'

'You can try but he won't go. He didn't before.'

'I have an idea that might give him a reason.'

'Thank you, Mrs Thompson.'

'Dawn, please.'

'You and Mr Thompson have helped Samuel and we're grateful for it, even if he can't say it. You gave him a job and I hear Suzy Lustleigh's working for you too. People complain about blow-ins, but your family has done a lot for the locals.' Gillian began an anecdote about yet another brother, Daniel. But something nagged in the back of Dawn's mind. She interrupted Gillian in mid-flow. 'You just said, 'after we got him back'. Where had he been?'

'He lived on the streets for a while. Nigel accidentally shot Samuel's dog. Thought it was a fox 'e did, an easy mistake as she 'ad a long bushy tail. But Samuel couldn't see it. They had a big fight and Samuel left with only the clothes he stood up in. We looked for him everywhere but it was Suzy who spotted him living in the doorway of the supermarket in Exeter. Jim, his dad, went off to bring him home. When he saw Samuel, 'e ran over the road, beaming all over his face, the witnesses said. He got hit by a bus. Died in Samuel's arms.'

Dawn's hand went to her mouth. She and Gillian stared at each other across the table. Dawn reached out and took her hand.

Gillian's wedding ring pressed into the palm of her hand. 'When was this?'

'Four year ago. Now you know why we have bigger worries than Sam not speaking. I'm just glad I got 'im back.'

Poor Samuel. How can you grieve properly if you can't talk about it? Seeing a therapist had helped Dawn. She was more determined than ever to help Samuel speak.

'So his fear of buses, it stems from then?'

'No. That's the strange thing. He's had it his whole life. As if he knew what was coming.' Gillian's face creased in bafflement.

'I'm going to try and help Samuel, Gillian.'

'Bless you, Dawn.' Gillian pulled a hanky from inside her sleeve and wiped away a tear.

# CHAPTER 41

Dawn found Anastasia at the stables. The horses, Swallow and Symphony, stood dozing in the sun, occasionally flicking flies with their tails and stamping their feet on the cobblestones.

'I had to drop Samuel home,' Dawn explained. 'He's not supposed to use his hand for a few days. I talked to his mother. She told me what happened to his father.'

'It was a terrible tragedy. That family have so much bad luck.'

Dawn told her about Samuel's speech therapy appointment. She thought Anastasia, as his employer, could have been more pro-active in helping Samuel but bit her tongue.

Anastasia tightened Swallow's girth. 'I saw Douglas this morning when I took the dogs out. They'd set up their easels on the green and it all looked terribly professional. Is he enjoying it?'

'Hmm, maybe 'enjoying' is a bit strong. He's coping. He used to work with one of them, Rajesh, a PE teacher. There's an elderly couple who knit pictures. They make sketches when they're out and, when they get home, they get out the needles and the wool and start knitting up their drawings. I think it's quite clever but it seems to grate on Douglas's nerves. I don't think knitting is a pure enough art form for him. And then there's Debbie the divorcee, who seemed normal until she set her sights on Rajesh and became a weapon of mass flirtation.'

Anastasia laughed. 'I can imagine Douglas seething whilst having to grin and bear it.'

'But he likes Zoe and Alice, who work at Saddler's Wells. One's a scene painter and the other works in wardrobe, costumes or something.'

'So everything's going well, then. With the business?'

'Yes fine, surprisingly. No major disasters. But it's early days.'

Anastasia raised her eyebrows as if this weren't the answer she'd been expecting.

'Is Freddie down again this weekend?'

'Yes. He's taken up fishing in a big way. Lately, he's been down virtually every weekend. Not that I see much of him. Last weekend he stayed over on a friend's estate after fishing.'

She looked pensive but Dawn didn't want to pry. 'I have the opposite problem. Every time I turn around Douglas is there. I have to lock myself in the bathroom when I need personal space and even then he stands outside and talks to me through the door.'

'Are you ready for Truffle yet? I could bring him over tomorrow about ten?' Anastasia asked.

Dawn smiled gratefully. Operation Keep Becky in Devon was underway.

Driving back to the Mill, she thought about Anastasia's reaction when she'd told her everything was going well. She hadn't seemed at all happy for them. She still suspected her of telling the Pooks they had no money to pay them. But now the renovation was finished and the business was up and running, it didn't seem so important. She liked Anastasia. It amused Dawn when she swore and threw out insults with those cut glass vowels and sounded like the queen impersonating Gordon Ramsay but she didn't trust her.

When she got back to the Mill, a white sports car was gracing the parking area, looking as out of place as Beyonce at a school disco. A dark haired man wearing jeans and a leather jacket was sitting at their new Ends of the Earth table and chairs.

'Hi! Sorry, I wasn't expecting you until later,' she called over, slamming the door of their ancient car. The wing mirror dropped off and swung by a wire. She ignored it and walked over the bridge.

The man stood, hitched up his jeans and towered above her. 'No problem. I was enjoying listening to the river.' He gave a wry smile. 'Rex Holman. Pleased to make your acquaintance.' He held out his hand. She looked up into his smiling brown eyes with their lattice of laughter lines. Her knees weakened.

'Dawn Thompson,' she said, pushing the hair off her face and smoothing down her T-shirt. Her hands flapped at her sides. 'I think you've spoken to Douglas on the phone. He's out sketching with the group at the moment.' She looked at her watch. 'He should be back soon.' Rex's eyes seemed to penetrate hers and see right inside her.

He strode over to her car and manipulated the wing mirror back into position. Practical, too. Dawn took the opportunity to fluff up her hair and hitch up the shoulder straps of her bra so her boobs were nearer where they should be. Trust her to be wearing a blood spattered T-shirt and shapeless leggings when the first attractive man she'd seen in weeks arrived at her door. That is, the first attractive man except for Douglas, she reminded herself. With a pang of annoyance she remembered Douglas's attraction to Anastasia. She could have some fun with this.

'If you'd like to bring your bags in, I'll show you to your room. Then I'll make us some tea, or would you prefer coffee?'

'When in Devon I intend to do as the Devonians do. Tea will be just fine.' He smiled, revealing teeth that could only result from expensive dentistry. Dawn shut her mouth and used her tongue as a suction cleaner.

Rex pulled a large leather holdall from the boot of his car and followed her inside. 'Mind your head,' she said at the doorway. She became aware of how her backside looked. She sucked in her stomach though feared that would have no effect. 'Be careful with the beams. Some of them are a bit low.'

'Your house has real character.'

'That's one word for it,' she laughed. She was laughing a lot.

She showed him to his room which, she now regretted, was one of the smallest and looked even smaller with him in it. But it did have a double bed and the en suite bathroom with a brand new shower as its saving grace. He ducked his head and looked out of the window across to the hills, just as she had done when she'd first come into this room.

'Mighty pretty. Looks just like it's supposed to.'

Dawn smiled at him gratefully. He had perfect manners but the comment seemed genuine. She left him to unpack, ran downstairs and made a pot of tea. She arranged her granny's tea set on a tray – only the best for Rex – and carried it outside.

Rex came out wearing a T-shirt and tracksuit bottoms. He had that muscly physique you can see through clothing. He would have great abs, she decided, and then struggled to remove the image from her head. He sipped the tea, staring into the cup as if it were some magical potion.

'So what brings you to Devon?' she asked as she offered him a custard cream. He took one, turned it over and studied the writing on it, clearly puzzled, and bit off a corner.

'Ooh, these are good. Which bit is the cus*tard*?'

'The bit in the middle but we pronounce it *cus*tard.'

'*Cus*tard,' Rex repeated as if practicing a foreign language.

Surely they had custard in America?

'Isn't the bit in the middle the cream?'

'Yes … I suppose it is … I suppose it's a custardy cream… though custard is usually runny … mind you, so is cream… I've never given it much thought before, to be honest.' Why was she wittering on about custard creams to this gorgeous man? Four months in Devon had reduced her topics of conversation to biscuits and dry rot.

'In answer to your question, my company transferred me to London from California but I don't start work for a couple of weeks. They put me up in a hotel which I hate. My mom came from this area. I checked out places to stay and found you.'

'Lucky me.' Dawn beamed and then blushed with embarrassment. Of course he didn't mean 'you' as in 'her', he meant Last Chance Mill. 'I mean lucky us. You want to develop your art skills?'

'Art was my first love. I went to art college in the eighties but sold out and ended up designing software for an IT company my friend was setting up. Sort of got locked in and couldn't escape. Then last year my wife died. I felt like a change. So I'm in London.'

'Oh, I'm sorry to hear that, about your wife, I mean. How awful.'

He looked at her levelly. 'She was ill for years. I had a long time to consider life without her. Our kids are grown. Life doesn't always work out the way you expect.' His delivery suggested this was a precis of a longer speech he'd grown tired of reciting. She warmed to him even more after this revelation.

'It certainly doesn't. Would you like another cup of tea?'

'You British think everything is cured by tea, right?'

'If tea doesn't work, there's always custard creams.'

Rex chuckled. His eyes were perceptive, calculating and she knew that if she frowned, he'd notice.

'I'm making some scones for tea. Would you like to help? I can show you how to make a real Devon cream tea.'

'I was intending on going for a run, but I have a real sweet tooth and no self-control.'

Maybe the abs weren't so great. 'Me too. Have you ever tried Battenberg cake?'

'No. We don't have any of that stuff in the States.'

'You are in for such a treat.'

He followed her inside and paused in the hallway, in front of the newspaper pages about the war Douglas had displayed in clip frames. He pulled a pair of glasses from his top pocket and peered at the yellowing paper. 'How interesting.'

'Douglas thinks so too. Hence the frames.'

'My dad was stationed here in the war. At Agatha Christie's house. Greenway?'

'Greenway House? It's a fifteen minute walk.'

'He could be in this photo. He and my mom met there. She was working in the garden, growing vegetables and fruit for the war effort. She was a great gardener.' A smile lit his face. 'She could make things bloom in the desert. After the war, she came over to the States and they married.'

'Do you know anything about your mother's family?'

'Not much. She came from Darton. Her parents and sister are long dead. The sister never married. I've no family here.'

'You should go and look around the house. Douglas and I did a tour. There's a mural in the library that I think was painted by one of the American officers stationed there.'

'How interesting. The Texas-Greenway connection.'

Douglas would be thrilled when she told him. He and Rex were going to get along really well. She reckoned they were about the same age, too. She greased a baking tray while Rex weighed flour and butter. She smiled when he spilled a little flour on the floor and didn't bother to wipe it up. She guessed Rex liked his women laid back.

# CHAPTER 42

They sat in the shade of the oak tree that dominated the hamlet of Dartcoombe. Douglas mixed the exact shade of pink for the cottage but the sun disappeared behind a cloud and it changed to a darker shade: more orangey. He added a smidgeon of greenish-grey and the sun came out and changed it back again. Was this a metaphor for his life? That he dealt with one thing only to be confounded by another? The sun disappeared behind a cloud again.

He liked how light changed the colour and feel of things. This particular cottage was the same one they'd stayed in when they'd viewed the Mill. He planned to give the painting to Dawn on their wedding anniversary. He loved this enforced time to paint and sketch; he hadn't spent this much time painting in years. If he hadn't been doing this, he'd have found other things to do: repairs to the house, research on places to visit, buying supplies on-line; now that was a time-sucker right there. Having this time to build his skills was a gift and the flip side of having to spend his days with annoying adults who thought themselves experts.

When he offered them advice, they acted as if he were violating their human right to free expression. They didn't seem to understand that painting was a skill they could improve upon.

Len and Deirdre were in their element painting the chocolate box cottages of Dartcoombe. A perfect subject for one of their knitted pictures. He'd noticed similar clichéd scenes in the photo album they'd shown him of their work. Who would have thought picture knitting was a thing? Why couldn't they knit jumpers for their grandchildren like everyone else? He didn't paint clothes on his body did he? Still, they were a sweet old couple and once Len had exhausted his joke repertoire, he'd felt a lot less like hitting him.

He noted that Debbie had positioned herself as close as possible to Rajesh without actually sitting on his knee. Rajesh's obvious lack of any artistic skill must be boosting her confidence no end. Douglas found it hard not to look down the front of her blouse – she'd undone most of the buttons – as he stood behind her watching her daub the leaves of the ancient oak, adding the finishing touches to her painting.

'You've captured the age of the building well, Debbie. It's got a lovely rustic feel. Try using a looser brush style when you paint the leaves. Think impression rather than detail.'

'But I like detail,' Debbie retorted, cocking her head to one side to contemplate her masterpiece and sticking the paintbrush in her mouth provocatively. He'd never seen anyone use a paintbrush as a flirtation device before. 'I don't like pictures that are all blurry.'

A century of artworks dismissed at a stroke. Amazing. He bit his tongue. According to Chris's research, return custom was vital in this business and he wanted the guests to write nice things on the website and spread the word. They had some guests booked for each week of the summer but they weren't yet fully booked.

He turned his attention to Rajesh who was painting what looked like a shocking-pink Barrett home. Douglas looked up abruptly at the seventeenth century cottage in case they weren't looking at the same object.

'Hmm, what do you think about the colour you're using, Raj? Does it look authentic to you?'

'I'm going for a Paul Klee look,' Rajesh blurted pretentiously, 'I saw his show recently at the Tate.' He put down his brush and pushed back his quiff which looked more like moulded clay than hair.

'Right,' Douglas concurred. 'Very original I must say.'

'Is that art teacher speak for, 'what a load of crap'?'

'Not at all.' Douglas congratulated himself for conveying the exact message he'd intended.

'At our school,' Rajesh flashed Debbie a smile and Douglas cringed in anticipation, 'they used to send all the naughty kids to the art room. Doug had this way of calming them down. He'd make them catatonic through art and they'd stumble out like zombies.'

Debbie giggled. 'What will they be doing without you?'

'Rioting, I imagine,' Douglas said wistfully.

'I can't say I have any regrets about taking that job in Dubai,' Rajesh boasted. 'I'm looking forward to the ex-pat life. Sitting beside a pool, sipping cocktails at sunset, lunching at the beach club.'

'Ooh, that sounds lovely.' Debbie looked at Rajesh adoringly. It was hard to imagine she was the same woman who'd collapsed in tears when Dawn opened the door of her room and revealed single beds. 'I'll never need a double bed again!' she'd wailed, 'he told me her didn't want children and now he's got some floozy pregnant and he's marrying her and wants a divorce.' Dawn had marshalled Debbie into the kitchen, given her a large vodka and tonic and introduced her to Rajesh who was standing at the Aga stirring rice pudding, wearing an apron over a pair of mini shorts. They'd flirted outrageously and Dawn had bragged about her matchmaking skills ever since. Funny, as he'd always thought Rajesh was gay. Would a straight man wear short-shorts? Surely not. He hoped Debbie wasn't barking up the wrong tree. He watched the way Rajesh leant over to dip his brush in Debbie's water jar and sniffed her hair. Would a straight man do that? Douglas certainly wouldn't.

For about the hundredth time today he thought of his old job. Rajesh had stimulated his memories. Last night, he'd dreamt he hadn't been going to work and no one had noticed. In his dream, he was weighing up whether to go in and draw attention to himself and thus have to explain his absence, or whether to continue not showing up and see how long he could get away with it. He'd woken up in a cold sweat. Relief had flooded in when he'd recognised his Devon bedroom. Never again would he wake up and dread driving through the rush hour traffic to face class after class of volatile kids. And to think he'd been upset at the prospect of leaving! His first reaction had been to try and cling on somehow, or to find a similar job. Now he was here and happy, truly happy for the first time in ages. Funny, how he'd never realised he was unhappy until he left; whilst in the thick of it, he hadn't dared confront his feelings. And Dawn was happier now that they'd fixed up the house and had bookings. She hadn't mentioned selling up in weeks. True, credit card debt hung over them, and they badly needed more guests, but bookings were trickling in. Chris was already working on website placement. The boy was genius on the computer.

Finally he turned his attention to the lovely Zoe and Alice. They knew what they were doing. Both had been to art college and were more on his wave length. Soon, it would be time to pack up. He wondered if their final guest had arrived, the IT nerd. Poor Dawn. He was probably boring her tears.

# CHAPTER 43

Douglas drove up the lane and frowned at the sight of a white sports car parked in his spot. It must belong to the IT nerd. He decided to leave the easels in the back of the car; they'd need them tomorrow wherever they went, he hadn't decided yet. He staggered into the kitchen in need of a cup of tea but stopped in the doorway. At the island in the middle of the kitchen, wearing a pinny and stirring something in a mixing bowl with a wooden spoon, a fit looking man stood close to Dawn as she poured milk, drop by drop, into the bowl. They looked very comfortable with each other. Too comfortable. Douglas cleared his throat and Dawn jumped in surprise as if *he* were the intruder. She looked different somehow; a new hairstyle perhaps? She glowed despite the smudge of flour on her cheek.

'Douglas! There you are. I thought I heard a car. This is Rex. Rex, this is Douglas. Rex is making his first Devon scones.'

Rex wiped floury hands on his pinny and extended a hand. He smiled wryly at Douglas.

'Welcome, Rex. I gather you've come all the way from silicone valley.'

'That's right but they've let me out to fresh pastures.'

'To the UK?'

'Yup. The company is thinking about setting up a research and development facility here. Your scientists are leading the field in some areas that we'd like to get into. I'm here to see if it's feasible.'

Douglas's neck strained from looking up at him. 'Good to hear we have something that the yanks don't.' He turned away to pour himself a cup of tea.

'Rex is from Texas originally,' Dawn said. 'And his mother came from these parts.'

She said the last two words in a Devon accent and sounded like Jolene from the Archers, his least favourite character. He sipped the tea. Cold.

'Really? How interesting.' He looked out of the window. 'Looks like everyone's gathering for tea.'

'I'll make a fresh pot.' She stepped closer to Rex. 'Now shape them into balls and place them on the baking sheet. Like this.' She threw Douglas a pointed look. 'Tell the guests there'll be fresh scones in fifteen minutes.'

He made a face at her as if to say, what? But he knew what she meant; he was being unsociable. But right now he was desperate for a lie down.

'Rex is going for a run later. He's training for the Iron Man Challenge.'

Of course he was.

'You should go with him. You did a marathon once didn't you?'

It had been a half marathon for Children in Need. His whole school had done it. He'd pulled a muscle in the first fifty yards and ended up limping it, holding on to a colleague's wheelchair.

'Er, yes. Long time ago. Before the doctor warned me off exercise. Excuse me but I have to sort out the studio for tomorrow. I'll see you at dinner, Rex.'

He scowled at her. She had no idea how exhausting it was, jollying-along the guests all day and having his teaching points rejected when all he wanted to do was to shut himself in his studio and paint. Alone.

# CHAPTER 44

'Douglas? What are you doing in here all on your own?' Dawn flopped down beside him on the bed.

'Getting some peace and quiet. What do you think? Not all of us want to hang out with Iron Man.'

'Oh, my God, you're jealous! You're jealous of me getting cosy in the kitchen with Sexy Rexy!' She snorted with laughter.

He lay still, his eyes firmly shut. She'd successfully wound him up. He was so predictable. She lay down beside him and snuggled against his rigid form. So much for her idea that Douglas and Rex would bond. Douglas was obviously intimidated by the tall, handsome and worse still, wealthy, American: the deadly trilogy. He had more chance of bonding with a wood louse.

'Don't you have dinner to cook?'

'Nope. I made it this morning in the slow cooker. I just have to chuck in the dumplings. Rex has never eaten dumplings before. Do you remember when you used to call me dumpling?' She tickled him. 'Do you?'

'I can't call you that any more. You're more like a stick of celery.'

At least he'd noticed. 'I'll take that as a compliment though I'm not sure you meant it as such. It's been ridiculously busy here. I had to take Sam to the doctor today.' Dawn recounted the accident and the talk with Gillian Grimes.

'Poor Sam,' Douglas rubbed his eyes, visibly moved. 'Why didn't Anastasia tell us?'

'Maybe he doesn't want people knowing and bringing it up. I can't imagine what it must be like for him.' She took off her jeans and T-shirt. It was probably best not to mention the speech therapy. Douglas would tell her not to get involved in case it triggered something. Maybe it would; but doing this for Samuel, she felt better about herself than she had in a long time. So she changed the subject. 'How did it go today at Dartcoombe?'

Douglas closed his eyes. 'The knitters loved it. Just their sort of kitsch. I can visualise the cushion covers already. Debbie was all over Rajesh and obviously he's playing along. He is the most outrageous flirt.'

'Do you think he has any intention of following through?' Dawn peered into the mirror, applying mascara and lip gloss in the same slapdash style she decorated and hoped Douglas thought she was doing it for Rex.

'Between you and me, I always thought he batted for the other side.'

'Nonsense. You've always had the worst gaydar. I've seen the way he looks at Suzy.'

'Good God, that's disgusting. She's Becky's age.'

'Some girls do like the more mature man.' Dawn leaned down to give Douglas a noisy kiss. 'Talking of Suzy, she wants to join your sketching class tomorrow.'

'Oh, great. I'll have a ghastly jealous threesome to deal with. I was thinking of taking them to the beach afterwards.'

'Text me when you're finished and I'll come and join you. Anastasia is bringing Truffle over in the morning. Becky doesn't know. We could bring him along.'

'You still don't trust me alone in the water, do you?'

'Of course I do. I know you'll be careful. You wouldn't want to leave me a merry widow would you? Who knows what I'd get up to.'

'Can we stop this now please, Dawn?'

She'd really got to him. She slipped into a scoop neck floral dress she'd bought in the charity shop with Becky and fluffed up her hair with a brush and some spray. It looked good. Suzy had tinted it last week and added some softening highlights. The girl had talent.

'I saw Anastasia earlier.'

'Oh? How was she?'

'She was a bit weird, actually. She asked me how we were getting on and when I said fine, she looked surprised and disappointed as if she'd hoped we'd fail. I still don't trust her. Or maybe she's just the type who relishes in other's misfortune. Schadenfreude, I think it's called. She said Freddie was home at the weekends but that she hardly ever saw him which I thought was a bit odd.'

'I don't like him.'

'Well, we know why that it is.'

'Because he's an upper class prat?'

'No. Because you fancy Anastasia.' Dawn said, folding up clothes, and stuffing them into over-full drawers, grazing her knuckles in the process. No matter how many drawers and wardrobes you possessed, there was never enough room.

'I do not! Although, she does flirt outrageously with me.'

'What rubbish! You think every woman flirts with you. It's your age.' She picked up a shirt Douglas has discarded on the floor, sniffed it and shoved it in the washing basket. 'Right. I'm off to put in the dumplings and steam the veg. It'll be ready in half an hour. I thought we'd eat with the guests tonight. You'd better set the alarm. You look like you might nod off.' She smoothed down her dress.

'You look very nice tonight. You always do in fact. You even looked good in those paint-spattered track pants and T-shirt you wore for months and had to be surgically extracted from.'

Wow! A compliment. She couldn't remember the last time he'd said anything nice about her appearance. Mind you, she hadn't been making much of an effort. Her strategy was yielding results. 'You carry on talking like this and I'm going to think you have a guilty conscience.'

'I can't win can I? If I don't compliment you, I'm taking you for granted, and, if I do, then I'm having an affair.'

'No you can't win. I'm glad you admit defeat.' She dodged the pillow he threw at her as she made for the door.

## CHAPTER 45

Douglas heard laughter as he approached the dining room. He hoped Dawn didn't expect him to eat with the guests every night now Rex had arrived. He was irritated to see Rex sitting at the head of the table. He had to squeeze in between Zoe and Len. Dawn sat opposite Rex at the end of the table nearest the door, doling out stew and dumplings.

Rajesh was leaning across poor Deidre, quizzing Rex. To hear him going on you'd have thought Rex had single-handedly invented the mobile phone. Debbie was filling glasses from a flagon of cider but Douglas needed glass of wine. He took a bottle from the sideboard and offered it round the table.

He turned to Zoe. 'So which art college was it you went to?'

'Just a minute, Douglas,' she said peering past him towards the end of the table where Rex was holding forth. 'I want to listen to what Rex is saying.'

'Oh ... er ... OK.'

Debbie had just asked Rex how his journey had been.

'The roads got narrower and narrower. I drove the last few miles on what would pass for a sidewalk in Texas.'

'Oh, that's hysterical,' said Alice. 'And did your sat nav die? Our taxi driver's did.'

'Absolutely. And it seems you Brits took down all the signposts at the start of World War Two and never put 'em back up.'

Douglas felt deeply affronted for some reason about this view of the state of British roads. He was on the point of extolling the virtues of single track lanes when he was distracted by Dawn placing a plate of stew in front of him with only one dumpling. He'd noticed two dumplings on

Rex's plate. His obvious lack of the requisite number of dumplings enraged him.

'If you yanks had entered the war a bit sooner, I daresay we wouldn't have been so worried about being invaded,' he said, spooning too many peas on to his plate.

Dawn cleared her throat. 'Douglas...'

Oh, no. There was an edge to that *Douglas* he knew all too well.

'...don't forget Rex's father fought in the war.'

Don't say it, don't say it.

'Douglas's father was a conscientious objector.'

A hush fell around the table. Douglas heard himself swallow. Surely everyone had heard that.

'You know what? If there was a war now, I think I'd be one too,' Rex said.

He hadn't needed to say that. It was generous. Somehow it made him hate Rex all the more. 'More wine anyone?' He picked up the bottle and brandished it, unfortunately drawing attention to the fact it was empty.

'Help yourself to veg, everyone, and tuck in,' said Dawn beaming prettily at Rex. He watched her features transform into a scowl as she glared at him.

Rex was smiling back at Dawn, his teeth glinting. 'So tuck-in means dig in, right?'

'As in tuck, meaning food,' Len piped up. 'I think tucker is an Ozzie expression. Our daughters live there.'

'Have you found any other differences in the language, Rex?' asked Alice.

Oh please, did she have to encourage him?

'Plenty. It's weird considering it's the same language. You have so many words for underwear: pants, knickers and something called Y fronts?'

Everyone laughed. What was wrong with Y fronts for Christ's sake?

'I know, right? And don't get me started on all the slang words for sex. Shagging, bonking, leg over...'

Debbie hooted with laughter as if this was the funniest thing she'd ever heard. 'The thing is,' she said, 'we know all the Americanisms because of TV shows. I nearly died when I heard someone talking about a fanny pack.'

'Oh, I know that one,' said Rex. 'That's a bum bag.'

Douglas stood up, intending to fetch another bottle of wine from the kitchen and knocked over his glass. Nobody noticed the clatter above the peals of laughter.

'Oh, and this is my favourite expression...' There was no stopping Rex. He was out of control. Douglas wondered if he was a cider virgin. 'I don't give a monkey's. A monkey's *what* for God's sake!'

'It sounds so funny when you say it,' said Dawn. 'I never realised how ridiculous an expression it was until now.'

Rex beamed at her. 'This meal is delicious. These dumplings are a real treat.'

'Thank you.'

Douglas grew hot as he saw her blush and simper. He noticed she was wearing a very low-cut dress and wondered if it was new. He wolfed down his food, and stacked the plates, glad for an excuse to leave the room.

He heard Dawn saying, 'Pudding anyone? That's dessert to you, Rex.'

'Douglas, you're being very quiet,' Dawn said as he loaded the dishwasher and she eased a summer pudding out of a bowl onto a plate.

'It's hard to get a word in edgeways.'

'Why don't you tell everyone what you're doing tomorrow? Where you're going? What they'll be seeing and such like.'

Really? Dawn was giving him a lesson in communication? He picked up the pudding bowls saying, 'because I don't give a monkey's.'

After dinner, Len and Deidre excused themselves saying they were tired and he was about to slope off himself when Zoe grabbed his arm and he found himself propelled into the guest sitting room to play poker. Dawn appeared with coffees and a jar of change and they played until nearly midnight. Naturally, Rex won.

Later, in bed Dawn asked him if he was OK. What was the point of that? After the conscientious objector comment it was like a matador patting the bull after stabbing it. He grunted and turned his back on her.

'You could make more of an effort to lighten up. You've been weird ever since Rex arrived. Is someone a little bit envious of the attention he's getting?' She traced a finger along his back.

'I don't know what you mean.' He squirmed when she kissed his neck but then turned towards her and kissed her. At some point he noticed her eyes were closed and wondered if she were imagining herself with someone else.

# CHAPTER 46

Dawn awoke to sun streaming in through the French windows. Douglas had drawn back the curtains so she had a clear view across the meadow, its edges flanked with towering trees, their leaves shimmering in the sunlight against the backdrop of a cloudless sky. Steam seeped from the shower room where Douglas was singing some old Supremes number. She watched the light creep across the meadow and wished she could hold the contentment of this moment, that the next time anxiety gripped she could picture this scene and calm herself.

Suzy arrived as Dawn was clearing away the breakfast things. 'I saw one of Sam's brothers at the pub and he said to tell you that a letter arrived from speech therapy. He has an appointment tomorrow at eleven.'

'Great. Can you come too? You have a calming influence on him.'

'Sure.'

'Douglas says you can go to Elberry with them today,' Dawn told her while they made sandwiches and stuffed them into plastic bags. 'So make yourself a sandwich too. I'm coming down later with Becky and Chris for a swim.'

'Cool. Can you manage without me on Sunday morning? I've got a twenty-first and a sleepover in Exeter. It might be hard to get here for nine.'

'Yes, of course. You go and enjoy yourself.' Dawn lugged the cold box across the kitchen. 'Now off you go. Take this box out will you? I'll see you later.'

She smiled at Suzy who looked particularly lovely today, with her hair tied up in an elaborate knot and then she noticed. 'Have you lost an earring?'

'Yeah, but I know where it is.'

'Knock, Knock.' Anastasia's distinctive voice rung out from the doorway, 'Delivering one puppy. Under duress, but I'll get over it.'

She held up a gorgeous, cuddly bundle of chocolate brown. Dawn dissolved in adoration. 'I'm going to put him in the tepee so Becky wakes up with him. He is the most adorable puppy ever. We will give him such a good home. You can come and see him whenever you like.'

Anastasia had fallen quiet. She was staring at Suzy as she fussed over Truffle, kissing his tiny muzzle, stroking his curls and rubbing his ears.

'Best be off!' Suzy picked up the cold box. 'Be sure to bring him to the beach later. I think I've fallen in love.'

Anastasia looked ashen. Dawn suddenly regretted taking Truffle from her. 'Look, if this is hard for you we can get Becky another puppy. I haven't said anything to her yet. I don't want you upset.'

'No, it's fine. Like I say, I'll get over it.' She flashed a brave smile but Dawn wasn't fooled.

'We're all going to Elberry Cove later. Why don't you come?'

'I …maybe… must dash…the vet's due. One of the puppies is off her food.'

Poor Anastasia. She was so attached to her animals.

Dawn crept out to the tepee, undid the ties and slipped Truffle inside. It took a minute for Becky and Barney to squeal and coo.

'Mum? Are you out there?'

Dawn opened the flap and peered in. Becky was beaming. 'Thank you so much. What an amazing surprise.'

'He's yours Becky. Your responsibility. Dad and I don't have time to look after a puppy.' Now please bond and never, ever be able to leave him.

She picked up the post on her way in and opened a brown envelope. As she read, her heart sank. There'd been an appeal against the Mill being used as commercial premises.

The letter informed them there would be another ruling. Dawn shuddered. It was horrible to think someone was conspiring against them; possibly someone they knew.

## CHAPTER 47

'Really look at all the colours in the sea, Rajesh. There are more than just blue.' Rajesh had squeezed blue paint straight from the tube – about twos quid's worth – and smeared it on the canvas in a straight line to represent the water.

'I'm doing it like Monet and Van Gogh.'

Talk about pretentious. Douglas circulated amongst his flock. Len and Deidre had set up their easels and fold-up seats slightly apart from the others and had opted for water colours. Douglas crossed the beach and sat down next to Zoe, Alice and Suzy. As he approached, he heard Suzy asking them about London: how much it cost to rent a flat, where they lived, how much they got paid.

'Don't look at my work it's rubbish,' Suzy said to Douglas, glancing at Zoe and Alice's work.

'Don't compare yourself to them,' he told her. 'They're artists.'

'I would go and sit next to Rajesh. He's crap. But Debbie'll get the hump.'

Alice giggled. 'She is quite possessive, considering they've just met. I can't get that boat right,' Alice told Douglas.

'Try using less white', he advised. 'You have the white of the paper too.'

'Thanks.'

'Zoe, you should try layering the paint more. Adding some texture. That might work. Give it some more depth.'

'I'll try.'

'You two are both so talented. I'm sure you could teach me a thing or two.'

'You should come and see our work, shouldn't he Zoe? Maybe you and Dawn could come up for our next show. We'll take you backstage.'

'We'd love to. Though once Dawn got back to London I'm not sure I'd ever get her out again.'

'It was quite an adventure for both of you, coming down here wasn't it? I do admire you. My parents have lived in the same house all of their married lives.'

'That's nothing,' said Suzy. 'Us Lustleighs have been here since Doomsday. I can't imagine living all my life here. I need to get away.'

'When you've finished your course you should look for work in London,' Alice said. 'Hairdressers charge a fortune there.'

Douglas stood up and stretched. Since lunch he'd wanted nothing more than to lie down on the pebbles and snooze. He scanned the beach and saw Rex over by the cliff at the end of the beach, perching on a fold up seat, absorbed in painting. Despite his popularity, or perhaps because of it, Rex often separated himself from the group. Douglas now saw vulnerability beneath the brash, jokey exterior – perhaps due to the loss he'd suffered. He imagined for a moment his life without Dawn. It was a dark, desolate place where one had to rely on the kindness of others. Douglas crunched over the pebbles. Rex looked up.

'This place is magical, buddy. In this sunshine, it beats the Caribbean. Just look at the colour of that water.'

'I've never been there but I believe you. You know this place was a desert, millions of years ago. That's why the cliffs are orange. Geologists come from all over the world to examine the rock formations.'

'With that colour, you could be in Arizona. If you block out the sea.'

Douglas looked at Rex's painting. It was really good. 'Your painting reminds me a bit of a Winslow Homer,' he told him. 'I've a book on his work that I'll show you when we get home.'

'Thanks. I like his work. I've seen it in the Met. Painting water is the hardest, isn't it? That and sky.'

'And don't forget land,' Douglas joked. Rex laughed.

Douglas sat down on a large stone. 'Did you ever consider a career in art?'

'I was brought up by a military man. When I announced I was going to art college in California you'd have thought I'd told him I was joining a brothel. I went, and I finished the course. But in the end, I went for the money. I'm not proud of it.'

'Dawn told me your father was stationed at Greenway House during the war. That your parents met there. I thought we'd go there tomorrow to sketch.'

'It's weird. I think about them a lot since I got here. How little I knew about them, mostly. But they were that generation. They hid everything from us.'

Douglas thought of his own parents. 'How true. Whereas, our kids know every embarrassing detail about us.'

'And they know how to work us. We're the generation that did everything our parents wanted us to do and now we do everything that our kids want us to do.'

'With a few short years in our twenties for rebellion.'

They both laughed. He and Rex got on a lot better when Dawn wasn't around flirting with him. She was always patting him and giving him treats, the same way she did with Truffle. Douglas spied a pack of choc rolls in his picnic bag. Everyone else had those tasteless flapjacks that welded your teeth together and ensured future root canal. He knew what Dawn was up to, of course. He probably had been neglectful of late and been taking her for granted. But she had his attention now.

# CHAPTER 48

That little bitch. How could he? How could she? How the hell old was she?

She felt sick. She never threw up. Like a horse, she was physically incapable of it, until now. Her foot floored the brake, she flung open the door and vomited on the verge. Get home and shut yourself away, she told herself. Mary must know. Everyone in Darton must know. They'd have been flaunting their affair in the pub. She was the only idiot who didn't. He'd forced into the role of a hapless, stupid victim worthy only of betrayal and shame. Thank God the boys were camping on Dartmoor; she didn't have to pretend everything was normal. There was no normal. She climbed back into the car. The sun, cruelly bright, prismed her tears and blinded her.

She'd found it on Monday morning. Glittering up at her like an evil eye from the driver's foot well in the Range Rover. She'd picked it up and recognised it immediately as one of the Tiffany diamonds. She might be too stupid to realise Freddie was screwing a local woman, but she knew her jewellery. She scrutinised the earring as if it could tell how it got there and what act had been performed in the losing of it. She'd realised then that the owner must be local, as Freddie only drove the Range Rover in Devon; he used the Porsche in London. And today she'd seen the other one. In the ear of the Lustleigh girl. Nothing could have prepared her for that revelation. The earring she'd found in the car lay in her own jewellery box having pierced the flesh of that foul creature.

How could he stoop so low? He hadn't the sense to keep his dick in his pants on his home ground. The affair explained why he'd been spending more weekends at home.

And to think she'd believed it was a fishing fad! All those nights he'd told her he'd been staying at friends after a day's fishing up country, he'd been screwing Barbie in the Range Rover, probably taking her to fancy hotels.

She was used to the odd, discreet affair. When the woman lived in London, it was distanced from their life together. But an affair with a village girl was rubbing her nose in it. She fumbled in the car door for her sunglasses and speeded up, desperate to run to ground, to assemble her thoughts and decide what to do.

This betrayal was unforgivable; Freddie had crossed a line. She had hoped they could muddle along until Cosmo left school but that would be another five years. The main blow was that she would have to give up the estate; she couldn't afford to buy him out. Her mind see-sawed: lose the estate or forgive Freddie. She caught sight of her face in the rear view mirror and hated what she saw: the lines of distress, the blotchy skin, red eyes, the ugly downturned mouth. She fumbled again for her sunglasses and this time found them. She was stunned at the power of betrayal. It could turn a well-adjusted person into a tormented soul in seconds. Maybe she wasn't as well-adjusted as she'd thought. Doubts flooded in. Oddly, she heard her father's voice, 'Pull yourself together, Daisy. The Montagues are made of tougher stuff.' She sniffed and smiled. She would not give Freddie the satisfaction of seeing what this had done to her.

She decided against phoning him and risk sounding hysterical. He was expected at the weekend and she would state her position in a calm, dignified manner. They would instruct their lawyers to value their assets: the estate, the London flat, the art collection and arrive at a settlement figure. Freddie could have the boys whenever they wanted. As it was, he only saw them during the holidays and for the odd sporting event at school. Divorce was so much easier if one's children were used to not seeing their parents much anyway. Freddie usually attended their matches as, being in London, he was nearer and team sports held no interest for her. The boys rarely spoke to her even when she did turn up and seemed embarrassed that she'd bothered to come, as if it were uncool to have parents who cared, and humiliating to be shown up in front of their friends for not having been spawned in the ghetto.

Coco, Mocha and Sprinkles jumped up at her as she stepped down from the car. She missed Truffle already. Damn Freddie for saying she had too many dogs. Why couldn't men be more like dogs? Loyal, loving, dependable, adorable and one always knew where they were.

Remembering her latest plan to reclaim Last Chance, she found Samuel in the stables, mucking out. 'I need you to do something for me, Samuel. The same as before.' He stopped shovelling but didn't look at her. 'Do you know what I mean?'

He nodded.

'You know what to do.'

He went back to his shovelling. The smell of manure hit her nostrils, pungent and penetrating. She turned on her heel and strode off. It was regrettable but everything else had failed. She grabbed a bottle of vodka from the pantry and headed up to her bedroom, trailed by her fluffy shadows. She lay on the bed, poured herself a glass and found an episode of Midsomer Murders to watch. She picked up a bottle of No 5 from her bedside table, dabbed it on her wrists and sniffed but she couldn't mask the smell of manure.

## CHAPTER 49

Dawn strolled down the slope to the beach with Chris, Becky and Barney with Truffle trotting alongside. The sea was a different colour every time she came. Today, it was deep blue on the horizon, teal within the cove and pale turquoise where the waves lapped the white-pebbled shore. Sometimes it was a colour she had no name for: lapis or cerulean? Douglas would know. Even as she watched, the colours changed. At dusk, it would shimmer in tones of pale blue and soft pink, opalescent against a dark sky. She wondered if an artist had ever managed to capture it. The scene would look too magical to be real. If she were a painter she would paint only sea, summoning the skills of an alchemist to turn liquid to solid.

She was determined to forget the brown envelope from the planning department that had arrived this morning.

Douglas and the group were folding up their easels and he was laying out their work on the rocks to dry. She waved at them and sat down on her towel. She took off her dress, self-conscious of wearing a bikini around these younger women. Becky and Barney wandered over to the ruined bath house. Suzy ran over when she saw Chis and they began throwing sticks into the sea for Truffle, encouraging him to paddle, but he stood on the shore and watched baffled as the sticks drifted out to sea. But when Dawn walked into the waves, he followed and started swimming. Well, he was a water spaniel.

The sea was cold but she wanted to show everyone how wonderful it was. As she waded in, the tide sucked at her legs and she turned her back on an incoming wave which sprayed her with icy droplets. She waded out further, urgently before another wave broke. She sank below the waves, then rose to the surface and floated. The water was liquid silk against her skin. She dipped her leg for reassurance. Below the surface, the water was colder and her toes skimmed sand. Comforted, she raised them to the warmth of the surface. She swam through pockets of warm then cold which sat side by side without mixing. She felt something brush up against her. She trod water, swooshing her arms back and forth and then she realised it was only her movement through the water causing the sensation. Douglas swam over to her and she wrapped her arms around his shoulders.

'Isn't this great?' she said, watching Becky paddling in the shallows with Truffle. 'I'm hoping Truffle will convince Becky to stay.'

'I wouldn't count on it, love. She'll probably get him a passport and take him with her.'

Dawn giggled. 'Truffle Thompson. International jet setter.'

'International jet spaniel, you mean. But I agree. It's great being all together again. This is our life now. Sometimes I have to pinch myself. I can't believe it.'

'Me too. I never thought we'd get here. To this stage. I was so bogged down with all the work and filth and bills. You were the one with the vision.'

'I couldn't have done it without you.'

Douglas was being so nice to her at the moment. He was always complimenting her or thanking her, as if he'd recently noticed she was there. Thank God for Rex.

'I was awful in the beginning. I know I was. I feel differently now.'

'You are different. You've changed.'

'I'm still a bit worried about money. But if we're fully booked until the end of September, we'll clear our debts.' She wished she hadn't spoiled the moment by saying this as Douglas's face clouded over. They had a tacit agreement not to discuss credit card debt. Wait till he found out about the appeal.

'We've no bookings yet for September. And even if we get them, we'll have to survive the winter with virtually no money.'

She tried to lighten his mood. 'I'm looking forward to lying in bed with all my clothes on, reading novels, living on dhal bhatt if necessary.'

'I might start keeping hens,' he said, 'for an occasional bit of meat.'

'You know what they say: when a poor man eats chicken, one of them is sick.'

They trod water and looked towards the shore, watching Rex recoil as he dipped his toe in the water.

'Wow! Check out the muscles on Rex,' Dawn thought, and then realised she'd spoken out loud.

'How does anyone working in IT get muscles like that?' Douglas snapped. 'Why do you even need muscles if you work at a computer? You should have well developed finger muscles. That's all.'

'Come on in!' she yelled at Rex. 'What are you waiting for?'

'I know. It's warm when you're in,' he yelled back. 'It's always warm when you're in!'

Rex howled as Suzy ran in, splashing him. She was wearing a T-shirt over underwear. She must have forgotten her costume, Dawn thought as she watched her dive through a wave.

'Hah!' said Douglas triumphantly, when Rex walked out. 'Now who's the real man?'

Chris followed Suzy into the water. She was always relaxed around Chris; he had a way of putting people at their ease. Only yesterday she'd seen them deep in conversation in the garden. Suzy had looked upset and Chris had his arm around her. Boyfriend troubles, probably. Chris was a hit at the pub too. John had told her they were going to train him up to work behind the bar. Dawn felt proud as she thought of how he made friends so easily and always saw the good in people.

Barney and Becky were playing with Truffle on the shore. Rajesh and Debbie sat on their towels deep in conversation and Dawn hoped he wasn't giving her the brush off; a distraught Debbie was not what she needed. Len and Deirdre were sitting on a rug, knitting, and Zoe and Alice were sunbathing. Douglas headed for the shore but she didn't want to leave yet. The sea washed away her anxiety and relaxed her.

She swam towards a buoy, one of a row that separated off the swimmers' area from where the water-skiing boat came in. Halfway there, she realised she could no longer touch the bottom, but kept going. She'd never swum out of her depth before. She held on to a buoy and caught her breath. She let go and swam on to the next one and then the next until the figures on the shore looked tiny. She rested a while and then swam back along the line, taking it one stroke at a time, not stopping; not for a moment.

# CHAPTER 50

'Holy cow. Will you look at that?' Rex was staring up at the frieze around the top of the wall of the library in Greenway House. 'Here it is. The connection: Houston, Orange County, Galveston…' he read aloud, '… painted on a wall of an old house on the River Dart. Unbelievable.'

'By a Lieutenant Marshall Lee, according to the guidebook,' Douglas said. 'Apparently, fifty-one captains and members of the planning team arrived in a flotilla of twenty-four landing craft to be used for the Normandy Landings. They were billeted here, in the house.' Standing beside Rex, Douglas, at nearly six foot, was shorter than him. The woman who'd sold them the entrance tickets had blushed when Rex asked her for a guide book. She obviously fancied him; everyone fancied Rex. If Douglas were female or gay, he would fancy Rex. His fanciability, which put normal blokes like Douglas in the shade, should render him detestable, but Rex's obvious bafflement about this quality made it impossible.

'And my dad was one of them,' Rex said wistfully. 'He worked for the US coastguard, based in Galveston. The landing craft were built in Houston.'

'They were innovatory. It says here the craft could land two hundred men directly onto the beach.' Images from films about D-Day played in Douglas's head.

'He told me that the journey here was the worst time of his life. Or so he thought. Until D Day. My mom said she didn't think he'd make it back. She prayed for the men every day. She wasn't even religious.' Rex took out his phone, tapped the camera and panned around the frieze.

Douglas pointed to the other place names on the frieze. 'Look at that. It shows all the places they went before arriving here. Port Lyautey. Where's that?'

'It was a US base. North Africa somewhere. And look, they were in Italy.'

He looked at where Rex was pointing. 'Licata and Salerno. All those places saw action. It must have been a relief for them to arrive here. Look at their faces as they sailed into Dartmouth, how happy they look.'

'My dad never talked about the war. Too painful, I guess. But they both talked about his time here. It was something they shared.'

'Dawn tells me your mother worked here, in the garden. The men probably ate well.'

'Oh, yeah. She'd have spoiled them all right.' Rex moved away and peered at another image. 'Who's the nude?' he asked Douglas as he stared up at a dark haired woman languishing on pillows.

Douglas skimmed down the page. 'It says here that it's a mystery. It might not have been painted by the same hand. You don't suppose—'

'That's my mom?' Rex chuckled. 'That would be cool. But she was the biggest prude. And way too fidgety to sit for a portrait. She never even sat down properly in a chair. She always perched on the arm, ready to run off on some errand or other.'

Rex took off his glasses and rubbed his eyes. He looked around him like a ship-wrecked sailor surveying the shore he'd washed up on. The man was visibly moved.

Alice and Zoe appeared in the doorway. 'Here you are,' Zoe said. 'We lost you. We've been up in Agatha's bedroom. Her clothes are fabulous!'

Alice sighed. 'Wish I could dress only in silk and fur. But if you do that in Hackney, people think you're a bag lady.'

Zoe giggled. 'We're off to the café. The others are already there.' The last time Douglas had seen Len and Deirdre, they'd been examining tiny boxes made from matchsticks. Raj and Debbie had probably found an empty bedroom on the top floor to make out in. But there was something he wanted to clear up with Rex before they joined the others.

'What Dawn said the other night…about my father being a consci.'

'You don't have to explain, buddy.'

Douglas carried on. 'I know. But I'd like to. As we're looking at these pictures of heroes I think I owe him that. He was conscripted when he reached eighteen in 1944. His father, my grandfather, was killed at Dunkirk. My grandmother pleaded with him not to join up. So he didn't. I think he regretted it. He certainly seemed unhappy most of his life.'

'Sounds like our dads were peas in a pod. The only time mine smiled was when the Dallas Cowboys scored a touchdown.'

Douglas went outside to set up the easels on the front lawn while Rex went off with a female volunteer who'd offered to show him the greenhouses. This was Douglas's fourth trip here. No one had offered him a private tour. He cheered up when he thought of how happy Dawn had been yesterday at the beach. He must take her out somewhere nice soon, maybe when the guests left, before the next ones arrived. They needed some quality time together.

## CHAPTER 51

Dawn doubted Sam would have got out of the car if Suzy hadn't been there. She'd sensed his agitation since they'd picked him up. Suzy had plugged him into music on her phone and that calmed him down, but when Dawn turned into the car park, a bus overtook them and, in the rear-view mirror, she saw his eyes widen in alarm. He reminded her of a wild colt who might bolt at any moment. She'd known boys like that at the PRU. Any hint of trouble and they'd run off and leave you standing, wondering if you could have handled things better.

She'd phoned the clinic and asked if she could meet the speech therapist before she saw Sam. They'd agreed, though were surprised given that Dawn wasn't a family member. As soon as the automatic door whirred open and she stepped inside and breathed that clinical cocktail of plastic and bleach, it brought it all back. Her pulse thumped in her ears. While they waited in reception, Dawn leafed through a magazine, trying not to show her agitation. When she was called into the therapist's room her throat closed up. Suzy waited outside with Sam.

Jane Shaw was in her thirties with dark hair and glasses, softly spoken with a gentle manner. Dawn immediately calmed down and hoped Sam would do the same. She explained about Sam's school life, his family and the trauma of his father's death while Jane took notes. She ended by saying, 'I had the impression from his mother that he's always had a bad stammer but that since the accident he's been virtually mute. I wondered if it could be due to post traumatic stress disorder.' Several of her former pupils with childhood traumas had manifest symptoms of PTSD, she explained, and they'd improved with talking therapy and cognitive behavioural therapy. 'But what can we do for Sam if he's unable to speak?'

Jane stopped writing and tapped her pen on the desk.

'Can he write?' she asked. As soon as she said it, Dawn felt stupid. She'd never even thought to find out. But she wasn't acting in a professional capacity here, just as a concerned adult. Jane suggested that Sam could work with a psychologist as well as a speech therapist and Dawn left her office with the impression that Sam was in the right place.

'I'll wait outside with Suzy. She's his friend. She has a calming influence on him. If he doesn't settle …' Was she being paranoid? Why did she expect something to go wrong? It was fairly obvious why.

'We'll find you. Don't worry.'

Once Sam was in Jane's room, Dawn found the loos. She closed the door and took deep breaths. She hadn't considered how this visit might affect her. She'd had no time to herself recently and it had turned out that was exactly what she'd needed, no time to think. The smell had brought it all back. All those hours spent in the hospital waiting for the lad to come round.

Back in the waiting room Suzy was on her phone but had the grace to switch it off as Dawn sat down which was more than her own kids would have done.

'It's really good what you're doing,' Suzy told her. 'His mum's not in a good place and she can't drive anyway.'

'Thank you for coming. He's lucky to have a friend like you.'

'I don't know about that. I'm no good to any one.'

'That's not true, Suzy–'

'I've done something stupid. I don't–'

'Mrs Thompson?' Jane called from the doorway of her office. 'Could you come back in please?' Dawn looked between Suzy and Jane and back again.

Jane explained that Sam had done well, and that she was scheduling two sessions a week and that she would like him to bring a friend or family member in on the next session to build up the people he felt comfortable talking in front of.

'That will be Suzy. She's in the waiting room. I'll bring her for the next appointment. His mother would like to be involved too, I'm sure,' Dawn said, wishing to include Gillian.

Jane called Sam and Suzy into her room and asked if he was happy with Suzy attending. Dawn was relieved when he nodded. He trusted Suzy. She was the ideal candidate. Dawn felt sick at the thought of dealing with her clinic phobia twice a week, but it had to be done. Maybe Anastasia could bring them sometimes.

Suzy linked arms with Sam and as they walked towards the car, Dawn heard Suzy encouraging him to sing along with the words of a song she was playing. She made a mental note to mention that to Jane next time; it could be a possible way forward. Suzy was such a good friend to Sam so why had she said she wasn't? Was it linked to the stupid thing she'd done? Tomorrow, she'd ask her what she'd meant.

# CHAPTER 52

Douglas woke before the alarm to the sound of rain lashing the French windows. Yesterday, the weather forecast for today had been sun all day. Typical. He blinked up at the ceiling light. Why was that on? He looked over at Dawn and decided to surprise her with tea in bed.

The hallway lights were also on, which was odd as they usually switched off the downstairs lights before they went to bed, and left on the landing light for guests. The kitchen, too, was ablaze with lights: ceiling spots, the strips above the worktops and, more alarmingly, the hot plates on the hob were glowing orange. He turned them off, wincing at the heat. He felt sure Dawn would have checked them before bed as she always did. A greasy frying pan sat almost touching the hot plate; any nearer and it might have caught fire. He moved it away. It was red hot. He stepped back and rubbed his head. Had someone had a midnight feast and left everything on? Had one of the kids got drunk and fancied a fry up? The utility room lights were also on. He took the teas into the bedroom. He'd better not mention the midnight feaster. Thank God he'd got up first.

Dawn was sitting up in bed, applying cream to her face and checking the weather on her laptop.

'Ooh, thanks for the tea. Looks as if a beach trip is off. What's plan B?'

'Plan B is to come up with a plan B.'

'You mean there isn't one. I'm taking Sam to his next speech therapy appointment today. Suzy's going in with him.'

'Did it upset you? Being back in that environment?'

'A little bit. But at least I'm not the one in the spotlight. Sam's the one who's suffering.'

That was so typical of her. He admired her and feared for her in equal measure. He planted a kiss on top of her head.

'You need that plan B,' she said sipping tea. 'It looks as if rain's setting in for the rest of the week, according to the Met Office.'

'In that case, we'd better prepare for a heat wave,' Douglas said drawing back the curtains. He should check the level of the leat later, in case it had risen with the increased rain. He went into the shower room, lathered his face, pulled his weird shaver's expression and picked up his razor. 'We'll have to take refuge in the studio. I can conjure up a still life using those old cider flagons we unearthed when we first moved in, add some fruit, a bottle or two and any bits of material you can find to display them?' That would take time. He speeded up his shaving and cut himself.

'I'll see what I can find. There are a couple of table cloths in the kitchen drawer. Maybe a glass and a full bottle would come in handy.'

'And there starts my slippery decline.' Douglas emerged from the bathroom, pieces of tissue glued to his face with blood.

'There's no point making packed lunches. I could put together a hot lunch in the dining room. That would be nice change.' The lightness in her voice irritated him for some reason. He knew she was trying to cheer him up but it only made him glummer.

'I suppose it will kill a bit of time. God knows how I'm going to fill their day productively.' The bed springs pinged as he lowered himself on to the bed with a grunt. When did he start grunting when he sat down?

Dawn peered at him. 'Self-mutilation won't help you know. Here,' she rummaged in her bedside drawer and handed him a tube of cream, 'put this on instead of the tissue, 'You'll look less like an extra from a Mummy film.'

After serving breakfast, Dawn left for the village shop and Douglas began rooting around in the kitchen for objects for his still life. He jumped as the backdoor flew open and, with a gust of wind and a splatter of rain, in walked Suzy. Douglas stared at the dripping goddess.

'You should have called. Dawn would have picked you up.'

Despite the weather she was wearing a T-shirt, now so transparent he could see a red bra through it, and tight jeans dark with rain. The mound of the famously bejewelled belly was covered. Maybe she felt it more appropriate for work or had simply grown tired of old men leering. He didn't leer, did he? He quickly averted his eyes. Grunting and leering, whatever next?

'It's only a bit of rain. We're famous for it down 'ere, don't you know,' she scoffed.

'The rain here is so much wetter than in London…' His voice tailed off at the withering look Suzy shot him. She shook her head like a dog, her hair flying wildly and he stepped back to avoid a splattering. She grabbed a tea towel and rubbed her hair.

'What you doing today?' she asked, 'Can I join in? I enjoyed it yesterday. After I've done the soup and salads,' she added after picking up the instructions Dawn had left her.

'Be my guest. It's a bit dull I'm afraid. Life drawing. I mean still life drawing.'

'I've done some life modelling. At college. I model for the students in the art classes. Nude,' she added with no hint of shyness lest he didn't understand what life modelling entailed.

A vision of Suzy posing in front of a class of admiring artists planted itself in his head. He imagined her as a Botticellian Devonian Venus, rising from the half-shell, long hair ruffling in the breeze, soft flesh and inviting curves. He shut his mouth, snapped out of this reverie and grabbed a blue vase from the shelf. And then he had a brainwave.

'I don't suppose you'd model for the group tomorrow? If they draw flagons and pots for days on end, they'll go potty, if you'll excuse the pun. Drawing from life would be something special.' He blushed at this gushing and his shaving wounds started to throb. He considered the group: Rajesh might enjoy it a little too much and Debbie might be jealous. Dawn was right again. Rajesh wasn't gay, just 'metropolitan' as Becky eloquently put it. The knitters might not be so enamoured. He imagined knitted cushions depicting Suzy's curves adorning their settee at home. Note to self: business idea: pornographic cushion covers. But he could offer the group a choice.

'Sure,' she said, donning an apron and starting to wash the greasy frying pan and egg-encrusted pot left by the midnight feaster.

'Great. I'll pay the going rate.' He turned at a sound and Chris shuffled into the kitchen, clothed only in tartan pyjama bottoms that looked as if they were about to slip from his impossibly narrow hips. Why were young men so thin these days? Suzy suppressed a giggle. How long had Chis been standing in the doorway? He hoped not long enough to hear his last comment which, even to him, sounded alarmingly like solicitation.

'Hiya,' Chris drawled. Luckily, he was in his usual morning state of semi-consciousness.

'Sexy PJs, Crispy.' Suzy flashed him a flirty smile and for one awful moment Douglas thought they were about to hug but they went through some elaborate hand shaking ritual which, at one point, was interrupted by Crispy having to grab his PJ bottoms as they shifted south. Oh, dear God. Don't say they were sleeping together. If he wasn't there, they'd be making out on the chest freezer. Douglas rooted around in a drawer, trying to appear nonchalant.

'You're all wet,' Chris complained, pulling away from their final huggy thing.

'Want to work in the bedrooms with me now? I'm going with your mum to Sam's appointment later.'

Douglas shot Chris a look, pulled a cloth from the drawer and placed it on top of his cache of weird objects. He should go and set up; he could hear the guests leaving the breakfast room but he couldn't tear himself away from this scene of seduction. His presence was the only thing preventing actual sex.

'I'll make it worth your while,' she breathed.

He suddenly feared for his son. What if Suzy was using Chris? He was moving back to London, where she was desperate to go. Perhaps she was planning to live with him, rent free, while she looked for a job.

'Actually, I need Chris in the studio now to help me set up for the day,' Douglas said brusquely, pleased at his quick thinking. 'So get dressed and I'll see you out there.'

'Maybe Chris would like to help tomorrow, too.'

Douglas shot her a look. He imagined his son drooling over Suzy's naked body, reddening with jealousy as others gawped at her. When had they started sleeping together? Did Dawn know about this? Maybe the life drawing session hadn't been such a good idea.

'Sorry. Can't help either of you,' Chis said. 'Andy wants a deep clean of the kitchen before opening time for the next three days. That's why I'm up so early. And I'm working till closing time. I'll be a zombie by Friday.'

'Thanks again for walking me home last night,' Suzy purred as she wiped her hands on her apron, picked up a tray and brushed past Chris on her way to the breakfast room with a sway of her hips.

Douglas hadn't known what it meant, to bat one's eyelashes, until that moment. Thanks for walking me home, she'd said. Shit. It was worse than he thought. Walking her all the way from the pub to the Lustleigh's farm, and then back here in the dark. It must be love. He had a sudden vision of a cider-sodden, red-faced Farmer Jack chasing his son down the road with a shot gun. He picked up his box, ready to retreat, defeated.

'Chris, by the way, did you have a fry up last night when you got in?'

'No. I went straight to bed. Why?'

'No reason. Did you hear anything in the night?'

'No. But I was shattered. Didn't get in till after one.'

Dawn walked in with shopping bags. 'Douglas why are you still here? They're making their way over to the studio now. I thought you were setting up.'

'Just off,' he said, relieved that she could take over chaperoning. For some reason he didn't think that Suzy would behave so provocatively with Dawn in the room. 'Back here for lunch at one?'

'Can't wait.' They exchanged a brief kiss.

The still life drawing wasn't as dull as he thought it would be.

'We're using charcoal today,' he told the group, 'I want you to capture the tonal variation. Focus on where the light hits the objects and what's obscured. The light and dark, the chiaroscuro, as the Italians say.'

He'd constructed a Cezanne-style arrangement in five minutes flat. It presented a good opportunity to work on their drawing skills. Suzy arrived after bed-changing duties with coffee and warm biscuits. Good old Dawn. And she produced a fabulous lunch too: soup and warm Greek spinach pie with a name that sounded like spina bifida, and lots of salads followed by strawberries and meringues. The chatter was lively and he cheered up.

In the afternoon he had them painting the same display in acrylics on canvas boards. They were building up a nice repertoire of works to take home and show their friends and, hopefully, drum up more business.

At four, Suzy left for the pub. 'Still OK for tomorrow?' she asked him.

'Yes, please,' he said. Now he knew Chris would be at work he felt better about it. He wondered whether he should mention it to Dawn. He decided against it. She would only throw in his face all the reasons why it wasn't a good idea and make him question his decision. He went off to find Becky and Barney in his quest to find the midnight feaster. There was something else he'd meant to do, but he couldn't remember what it was.

## CHAPTER 53

As dusk, Samuel walked out of the stables and headed into the coombe. He didn't want to sneak inside the Mill and steal the winch handle and open the sluice gate but She'd asked him to. He'd done it before when the Mill was empty, when the bat-killing Pooks had owned it, but he didn't want to cause trouble for Dawn and Douglas. He liked them. They didn't judge him and they helped him. But he had to do what She asked.

He walked uphill to Badgers' Wood. As he walked along the lane, he saw it. Her 4x4. What was She doing in the woods? Mind you, it was Friday evening so it could be the Master. The car was rocking and squeaking. Was someone harming Her? He hit the ground and crawled towards the car, commando-style.

The windows were tinted and he never expected to see inside. Slowly, he raised his head. Lit up by the dashboard lights, a blond head bobbed up and down in front of his face. The head flicked up and the eyes met his and flashed so wide he could see white all around them. She blinked as if she couldn't believe what she was seeing, then her brow furrowed and she looked scared. For a moment she stopped moving but then began bobbing again. His eyes flicked from Suzy to what lay underneath. Flat on his back, head pressed up against the car door, face screwed up, wearing his shooting jacket, lay the Master.

Samuel jolted as if he'd been hit by a bullet. He walked backwards, away from the car, climbed the gate and ran down the coombe. Anger pulsed through his veins. He and Suzy had been getting closer, or so he'd thought. Today, after speech therapy as they were walking to the car, she'd taken his hand when a bus roared past. What an idiot what an idiot what an idiot. His old mantra streaked through his brain. And with the Master! What would She do when She found out? The rain lashed him as if trying to wash away the memory but he couldn't get Suzy's face out of his head. The fear. But what was she afraid of? That he would tell the mistress? Suzy would be in trouble that's for sure. He stopped running and grabbed his head in both hands. He didn't want to hurt anyone – Suzy, Her, Dawn or Douglas – but the throbbing in his head told him they were all going to be hurt. And all because of him.

## CHAPTER 54

After breakfast, Douglas grabbed the inflatable mattress and jogged over to the studio through the drizzle.

One by one the guests appeared, leaving their waterproofs and umbrellas at the door and sitting down at the same chairs and easels they'd occupied yesterday. When they looked up at him, Douglas's heart pounded.

'We have a choice today, ladies and gentlemen. You may either carry on with your still life work from yesterday,' he gestured to the potty composition, 'or, if you prefer, you can draw from life. Our life model today is, Miss Suzy Lustleigh.'

A deathly hush. A paintbrush clattered to the floor. Heads turned as the loo door squeaked open and Suzy, draped in a white sheet which trailed behind her like a wedding train, walked into the centre of the circle of easels and lowered herself on to the mattress. Rajesh gasped and Debbie glared at him, Deidre giggled and Len wiped the sweat from his brow. Alice and Zoe eyed Suzy with professional appraisal. Rex seemed unperturbed but he had a daughter, too, so he probably viewed Suzy in the same fatherly way that Douglas did. Suzy clutched the sheet to her chest as he'd asked. He hoped she was following his other instruction.

'As you can see, we're drawing with charcoal again today and using large sheets of paper. I would like you to treat the human form as a landscape: capture the hills and valleys, the shadows and light as you would do with a landscape. Move your seats to the angle you prefer.' His students looked more comfortable with this comparison. Then he nodded at Suzy, their signal for her to release the sheet and smooth it over the mattress.

He let out the breath he'd been holding when he saw she was wearing the g string they'd agreed upon. Her legs were closed and nothing down below was displayed, though that would change when he asked her to move around. He noted with relief that her breasts were smaller than he'd expected; the gravity defying cleavage must be the result of a special bra. With a lot of throat-clearing, the group shifted their seats and easels, all of them had chosen to sketch Suzy. Rajesh used his easel to bulldoze his way to a spot where he could see both bottom and breast. Deidre took the longest to settle – perhaps this was out of her comfort zone – he expected she'd tell the women's institute all about it when she got home, not that they were strangers to nudity since Calendar Girls. He went over to help her start on the contours of Suzy's curves, and noticed that the glittering jewel Suzy wore in her navel was no longer there and that she appeared to be quite thick around the middle.

They drew for two hours and then broke for lunch. Suzy gathered the sheet around her and went into the loo to dress. He took the sandwiches Dawn had made before she went to the cash and carry from the cold box and poured everyone a hot drink. It was chilly so he switched on the fan heater. Suzy had dressed for lunch in track pants and a thick jumper he recognised as Chris's. He felt a stab in his gut and a mouthful of bread and ham stuck to the roof of his mouth.

After lunch, Douglas told them they were going to try something different. 'I want you to loosen up your style. Most of you are adding too much detail. Try working with a looser hand. Suzy will keep a pose for only five minutes. You must complete your sketch in that time.' As he talked, he handed out three fresh sheets of paper to each of them and placed a chair in the centre of the circle. The group clipped the paper to their easels and sat poised. 'We're ready, Suzy.' She came out of the loo, clad in the sheet and sat on the chair, knees pressed firmly together and let the sheet fall, as he'd told her. 'Ready? Off you go.'

After five minutes he told them to stop, flip over their drawing and start another sheet. Suzy stood and clasped her hands behind her head. The group were engaged. There was no sniggering now; they were concentrating too hard.

'Much better', he encouraged as he circulated, looking over their shoulders. 'Now Suzy is going to move around the room for two minutes and I want you to really loosen up, think with your fingertips not your brain, let your hands and arms do the work, try and capture the movement, the gesture and be less descriptive. Does anyone need more charcoal?'

Suzy glided and skipped, crouched and stretched, slumped and twisted. Every eye followed her. Hands flew fast and wild. Douglas beamed. He hadn't felt this good about his teaching since that time the Royal Academy ran a life modelling class in his school. He offered more sheets of paper and these were grabbed by blackened hands and filled in minutes. Charcoal snapped and paper ripped. Alice and Zoe moved around their paper like dancers, swooping to make a line here, a curve there.

By four o'clock, the rain had stopped and sun was streaming through the windows. He suggested they call it a day, and go for a walk or to the pub before supper. Suzy disappeared into the loo to dress. She was due for work at the Darton Arms at five.

'Great session, Douglas,' said Rajesh. 'Reminded me of that time the RA came in and you ran that workshop for teachers after school.'

'I really enjoyed that,' said Deidre. Len gave Douglas a fat wink.

'Me too,' said Debbie.

Rex thumped him on the back. 'That was something.'

'Brilliant,' said Zoe. 'I thought it would be dull in the studio.'

Alice added, 'I haven't done anything like that since art school.'

Douglas beamed. 'I'm glad you enjoyed it,' he called out to them as they filed out. When they'd gone, he breathed a sigh of relief and went over to the loo door. 'That was wonderful, Suzy. You're a natural. Is thirty quid all right?' He peeled some notes from his wallet. 'Do you need a lift to the …?' His voice tailed off when he realised they were not alone.

## CHAPTER 55

Douglas looked up. A bulky figure stood in the doorway, silhouetted against the light, holding something long and dark.

'Hello. Can I help you?'

The figure stepped forward, the barn door shut with a bang and Douglas's heart somersaulted as he recognised Jack Lustleigh. He was pointing a shotgun at Douglas's middle.

For some silly reason, probably because he'd seen it in films, he raised his hands.

'Steady on,' he said, willing Suzy to stay in the loo. He heard the click of the lock, the squeak as the door opened. He glanced over his shoulder and saw Suzy pulling up the zip of her jeans, her blouse open to reveal the red bra. She raised her head and yelped. It sounded like the noise Truffle made if you trod on his paw.

'Dad! What d'you think you're doing? Put the gun down!'

Douglas turned back to face Jack. 'I can explain,' he began. 'It's not what it looks like.' He saw the thirty quid in his hand and wondered how long Jack had been standing outside the door and exactly what he'd heard him say to Suzy. He tried to hide the notes by balling them in his fist, but a ten pound note wafted to the floor and stared up at him accusingly. Jack's eyes narrowed and he barred his teeth.

Suddenly, the barn door swung open and light flooded in. Jack swivelled towards the door and Douglas took a breath. The gun no longer pointed at him. Dread followed relief when he saw who stood there, the gun trained on her: Dawn. His stomach lurched. 'What's going on?' she asked and her eyes narrowed in confusion as she spotted Suzy in the back of the studio in a state of undress.

'It's not how it looks…' he began again but broke off as another figure stepped out from behind Dawn. Chris. Wasn't be supposed to be cleaning the pub? Then it dawned on Douglas. This was about Chris. Jack had found out about him and Suzy. They hadn't exactly been discreet; even he'd worked out they were an item.

'Dad?' Chris eloquently managed to convey both disgust and disbelief in that one syllable.

'I can explain. Suzy was doing some…some life modelling for the class. That's all. Tell them Suzy!'

'That's right,' she said flatly. Was that all she had to say? Jack didn't move the gun an inch. 'Put the gun down, Dad. You're embarrassing me!'

Embarrassing her! He was about to get shot and Suzy was embarrassed?

'I found it,' Jack growled. 'In the bathroom. I'm not such a stupid old man I don't know what it is.'

Out of the corner of his eye, Douglas saw Suzy drop to her knees.

Douglas shifted his weight. 'Help me out here, Suzy. What did Jack find?'

He heard a sob behind him and then she blurted out: 'A pregnancy test!' followed by more sobs.

Dawn spoke now. 'Suzy, you're pregnant?' She walked further into the barn as if Jack wasn't pointing a gun at him and this wasn't a provocative move. Dawn looked from Suzy to Douglas and back again.

Douglas's brain joined the gymnastics of his other organs. Pregnant? But surely Jack didn't think that he was culpable? But who was? Oh, God. No.

Chris.

He shot a wide eyed look at his son and mouthed, Run! Now!

Chris ignored him and repeated, 'Dad?'

'Run!' Douglas yelled and this time and everyone looked at him except for Jack who was glowering at Rajesh's drawing

237

of his naked daughter, her assets grossly over-emphasized in a Jessica Rabbit cartoon style.

'What the hell is goin' on here?' He jerked the gun and advanced on Douglas.

'Yes, that is a very inappropriate drawing I would agree,' Douglas mumbled.

'Yes, what *is* going on here?' asked Dawn looking almost as scary as Jack.

Chris wasn't getting the message. 'Chris, go and call the police. I'm being threatened by a man with a gun.'

'I was modelling for the artists, Dad,' said Suzy. 'That's all.'

Jack ignored her. 'Who's the father?' he barked.

If there was ever a time for heroics, it was now, Douglas thought as he imagined his son with a Tarantino-style hole through his middle. He had always wanted to be the sort of father who would make a big gesture for his children. My father died to save me, Chris would say. It would be on his tombstone: Douglas Thompson, bravely died saving his son.

'I am,' Douglas said, raising his hands again. 'It's me,' he repeated unnecessarily as if there could be any misunderstanding.

'What the fuck?' He heard Suzy exclaim behind him.

He watched Jack's chin jerk up; his face contort into a snarl. Dawn's mouth opened but no sound came out. He was unsure which one he feared most right now but it was probably the one with the gun.

'God, Dad, you make me sick,' roared Chris.

Well, that's gratitude for you! He was about to get shot for his son's mistake and the boy was acting disgusted by him. He'd learnt to expect disdain rather than gratitude from his kids, but this was too much to bear.

'You said it was an older man but you neglected to say it was my father,' Chris spat at Suzy.

Douglas's head swivelled from Suzy to Chris to Dawn and back again. Older man? What older man?

'No! You got it wrong!' screamed Suzy bringing her hands to her head as Jack raised the butt of his gun, pressed it into his shoulder, closed one eye and looked along the sights with the other. The barrel now pointed at Douglas's head. His insides turned to liquid. He sank to his knees.

'J...Jack, please! P...put the gun down,' he stuttered. 'You don't want to shoot me. It wasn't me. I'm not the father. I've never even touched your daughter. I was lying. I swear! Ask Suzy! Suzy, tell him!'

Behind Jack, a crack of light appeared as the door opened. He held his breath, terrified that the noise would startle Jack, as if perfect stillness and silence would somehow protect him. The gun still pointing at Douglas, Jack lurched forwards. Douglas shut his eyes and braced himself for the bang.

# CHAPTER 56

Anastasia walked out of Madeline Mason's Exeter office with a lighter step, grateful Madeline was on her side. She was a middle aged dynamo: direct, calculating, experienced and slick, combining vindictiveness and motherly concern in a lethal cocktail. Things were in motion. She was doing the right thing. She wouldn't even miss Freddie. He was hardly ever around anyway and when he was, they were cold with each other. No more would she be forced to suffer the indignity of stumbling upon one of his affairs.

He'd broken down and cried when she'd told him she wanted a divorce, he'd actually cried. He'd lied of course and told her he'd only screwed Suzy once, when drunk, but she'd checked his bank accounts, she had all the passwords, and had seen the hotel bills and the receipts for goods from shops of which Suzy could only dream. He'd begged her to take him back, told her he would break it off with Suzy and drove off to talk to her. Anastasia made sure she was in bed when he arrived home. She didn't want to see him. She'd let him stay in the spare room but asked him to be gone by morning. He'd wanted to see the boys, forgetting they were doing the Ten Tors challenge. She enjoyed seeing him realise what he'd lost. Yes, she'd enjoyed it.

She'd almost reached home and was trying to conjure up things she would miss about Freddie (surely there must be something) when Jack Lustleigh's tatty Land Rover hurtled towards her on the lane close to Dartcoombe. She slammed on the brakes and swerved. The car skidded on mud, slid into the verge and stalled just short of the wall. That bastard Jack Lustleigh! Cuckolded by the daughter and nearly killed by the father. Had she stepped onto the set of a Shakespearian tragedy? Her heart was still thumping as the gates to the Manor opened. Rain or no rain, she needed to go out for a gallop and let off some steam. She shed the suit for jodhpurs. She was striding off to the stables with the dogs when a bedraggled looking Samuel ran up the driveway.

'Samuel, what are you doing out in this? You look like a drowned rat.' He was shaking or shivering, she couldn't tell which, but he was clearly disturbed by something. She wondered if he'd opened the sluice gate yet. Oh God. What if something had gone wrong? Had he been discovered? He was mouthing at her the way he did, expecting her to conjure up psychic abilities. She pushed the wet curls off her face and turned on her full powers of deduction

'J...J...J...a,' he stammered. His speech seemed a little better.

'Jack Lustleigh, yes, I've just seen him twenty minutes ago. Ran me off the road. What about him?'

'G...G...' He mimed someone aiming a gun.

'He's got a gun. So where is he Sam? With this gun.'

'D...D...'

'Darton? He's in the village?'

'Mi...mi,' he managed with such effort that he had a violent attack of coughing.

'At the Mill? What's he doing there? Never mind. Let's go.'

In the hallway she opened the gunroom door, seized her shotgun and pocketed some ammunition. She was not going up against crazy Jack Lustleigh without it. It crossed her mind he might be about to shoot his daughter. She'd pay good money to see that.

The rain had eased as she sped down the lane towards Last Chance Mill, Samuel riding shotgun, literally. She swerved into the parking area, spraying gravel and nearly clipping Jack Luscombe's beaten up Land Rover. She slammed on the brakes as Truffle bounded towards the car. She leapt out and scooped him up. He jumped up at her face, trying to lick her, quivering and wriggling. Samuel tried to hand her the gun; he was clearly not comfortable with it. They were crossing the footbridge when the front door opened and out stepped a tall man in running gear eating biscuits from a packet.

'Hey, you,' she called over. 'Take this puppy and don't let him anywhere near a gun.'

'Yes ma'am,' he said, smiling. As she thrust Truffle at him, warm brown eyes met hers and held her gaze for a moment longer than was comfortable. She seized the gun from Samuel and followed him at a jog towards the barn. What was Jack doing there with a gun? The huge door was ajar and she and Samuel paused outside, listening.

Douglas was saying something about not being the father and that he'd never even touched Suzy. She felt her recently glued-together-self fall apart again. A jumble of thoughts bombarded her. The slut was pregnant? Freddie must be the father. Did he know? Why hadn't he told her? He'd got her pregnant and left her, Anastasia, to deal with the fall out? Was there no end to the harm Freddie had caused? Her breath came in ragged bursts and her hands were quivering dangerously, especially the finger on the trigger. She wished Freddie were here in front of her so she could... she could... Grief overcame her and the gun dropped as if she no longer had the strength to hold it up. She heard Douglas asking Jack to put the gun down. Shit. Jack had a gun? She motioned for Samuel to push the door open, not knowing whether Jack would be facing her or not but hoping he would have his back to her. She sensed the bulk of the tall man behind her and it emboldened her to make the next move.

She stepped into the barn and jabbed the barrel of the gun into Jack's back, her heart banging against her ribs. 'Put the gun down, Jack. It's not him that got Suzy pregnant. It's my husband.'

Jack's body jolted as if she'd tasered him. Douglas made a strange sound. Slowly, Jack bent down, set the gun on the floor and turned to face her, his features a picture of disbelief.

She stared past him to the girl standing across from her, the girl carrying her husband's child; a child that would be a stepsibling to her own. Her eyes strayed from the girl's terrified eyes to the belly protruding through an unbuttoned blouse. The gun was pointing at her. She would like to shoot the slut in the face, not blow her brains out or kill her or anything, but just disfigure her horribly so she would learn the hard way that personality was more important than looks because she deserved a grotesque souvenir of the damage she had done.

A voice behind her spoke. 'Wow. This sure beats Texas.' She felt the gun being eased from her grip.

## CHAPTER 57

Dawn couldn't help thinking this was all Douglas's fault. Even though he wasn't the culprit – and for a moment she'd thought he was – he'd still provoked a gun fight. Douglas was walking with Jack, ahead of her; she could hear him explaining why he'd confessed. Chris was behind her, his arm around Suzy's heaving shoulders. Rex followed them, carrying both guns on his shoulders like an extra from Django Unchained. Anastasia, clutching Truffle, was at his side. Sam had disappeared. Before Suzy climbed into the ancient Land Rover with her dad, she asked Dawn whether she should come to work the next day. She shrugged and said she'd call her. Dawn was furious with Freddie and disappointed with Suzy but she couldn't abandon a pregnant girl. Jack might throw her out. She'd ask Chris later. He'd know what to do.

She was also upset for Sam. She'd sensed something between him and Suzy. His haunted look as he'd stood transfixed in the barn matched her feelings. Just as things were going so well with his speech therapy; this could be a set-back.

And what about Freddie? The bastard was swanning around London, boozing at his club and going to swanky parties completely oblivious to the fact that his girlfriend was pregnant and that his wife had collapsed sobbing on their barn floor. Not that she'd sobbed for long. In true aristocratic style she wiped her tears with the puppy, stood up and walked off with the tall, handsome stranger.

'Take her into the sitting room and stay with her. I'll make a pot of tea,' Dawn instructed Rex. Anastasia's arms were wrapped tightly around Truffle.

Rex manoeuvred Anastasia through the doorway. 'Doesn't she need something stronger? No offence to your tea or anything.'

'She knows where it is. If she wants it, she'll find it, trust me.'

Dawn gripped the granite worktop whilst waiting for the kettle to boil. She wished she still smoked. If ever there were a time for smoking it was now. She couldn't quite believe what had happened, how very nearly someone could have got shot. Did everyone own guns in Devon? She thought London was supposed to be the hotspot for gun crime but she'd never seen one the entire thirty years she'd lived there.

She took the tea tray into the sitting room and felt like an intruder. Anastasia sat, glass in hand, slumming it with a bottle of cheap Polish vodka. She and Rex were deep in conversation, heads bowed, Truffle asleep on her lap. Dawn poured out three cups of tea but left them and took hers. She didn't know where Douglas had disappeared to and she didn't care. She bumped into Chris in the hallway.

'I need your advice about Suzy, love. I don't know what to do.'

'I'm late for work.' Chris pulled on his trainers.

'I take it you didn't know about Suzy and Freddie.'

'No. She said she was pregnant, and the father was an older man. I didn't know it was Freddie. He used to give her a lift home from the pub occasionally. But I thought he was being nice.'

'That's one word for it.'

'What about Dad? What he said? For a moment I believed it, didn't you? What a shock.'

Shock was an understatement. For a minute Dawn had thought the unthinkable.

'It was good of Dad to take the rap. I can't believe he still … I mean, that he hasn't … you know.'

'You really need to tell him, love. That was a hideous misunderstanding. Do you want me to talk to him?'

Chris chewed his lip. 'No. I'll do it. I've got to go to work now.'

'Do you want a lift?'

'I'll take the bike. I could use the exercise.'

'Love you, Chris.'

'Love you, Mum.' He kissed the top of her head.

She needed to talk to someone. Becky. She didn't know yet what had happened.

'Hello!' she called from outside the tepee, 'Anyone at home? Can I come in?'

No reply. It crossed her mind that she might be interrupting some intimacy but, frankly, didn't care. Sometimes your daughter needs to be there for you. She swept aside the canvas flap. They were lying on their backs napping, headphones plugged in. Despite the fact that there was almost a shotgun fight ten metres from their abode, the tepee folk were completely oblivious. Had she slept as much in her twenties? Her daughter seemed to need thirteen hours sleep at a go, most of it in daylight. Barney was no better. Were they, in fact, vampires? Should she hang some garlic around the tepee to test her theory? How the hell would they ever enter the realm of real work?

'Mum!' Becky squealed as Dawn sat down on top of her feet. 'You woke me up!'

'It's five o'clock and, anyway, don't you have to be at the pub for six? Chris just left.'

Becky scowled. 'Of course he did. He's always showing me up.'

Barney snuffled awake. With his spiky dreadlocks he resembled a large hedgehog.

'Could you roll me a ciggie?' Dawn asked.

'What? Why? You don't smoke!'

'And put some of that wacky backy in it. I need something to calm me down.'

'Way to go Mrs T!' said Barney propping himself up on his elbows, revealing a scrawny chest with indecipherable black symbols tattooed across it, and reaching for a pouch. 'Here's some I harvested earlier.'

'Harvested?' Surely they weren't growing it.

'Barney,' Becky chastised.

Dawn looked from Becky to Barney expectantly. 'Well?'

'Barney has been growing a few marijuana plants in the vegetable garden.'

'What? That's illegal!'

'Don't worry. No one will see it. You haven't, have you?' Becky pointed out as Barney rolled and lit a spliff in record time. If only it were an Olympic sport.

'I did notice some rather tall tomato plants but with no tomatoes,' Dawn said. 'Is that them?'

Barney nodded sagely and handed Dawn the spliff.

'You'd better make sure your father doesn't find out.'

'About the fact we're growing weed or that you're a pot head?'

'Both,' Dawn snapped. 'And don't think I'm condoning it just because I'm having a tiny puff.'

'So what's Dad done? You only refer to him as 'your father' when he's in your bad books. What's up?'

At last, Becky had asked. Why were the young so uncurious of their elders? But as she started to tell them, she had their attention.

'What?' Becky sat up and knocked over a half-empty cup of cold tea. 'Why didn't you wake us up? Did you film it? Oh my God, that would have been so cool. We could have put it on You Tube and got millions of hits. Was Chris there? Maybe he filmed it,' she said to Barney.

'I can't believe that your only comment is that it's a missed social media opportunity.' Dawn took another puff. It wasn't having much of an effect so she took a hefty draw.

'How's Mr T taking it?' Barney asked. 'And why did he confess if he didn't do it?'

At least Barney was listening. 'He thought Chris might be responsible. He thought Chris and Suzy were having a thing.'

Becky's eyes widened. 'What? That's crazy. Chris is … I mean … everyone knows Suzy is screwing Freddie. He used to prop up the bar and leer at her and drop her home after work, if you know what I mean.' Becky gave a pantomime wink.

'Why didn't you say something?' Dawn asked.

'I didn't think it was anything important. I didn't know she was pregnant.'

'What about Anastasia?' Dawn asked. 'Didn't you feel bad for her?'

'No. I mean, I know I should but she's hard to feel sorry for. Her type always comes out on top.'

She pictured Anastasia being consoled by sexy Rexy as they spoke. Maybe Becky had something there.

'That was nice of Mr T,' Barney said, 'takin' the rap an' all. My dad would never have done that.'

Dawn had to admit that Douglas had stepped up as a dad. He'd probably expected that she would understand instantly what he was doing. But what was she supposed to think when he said he was the father? For a moment there, she'd believed it. To doubt him had been wrong of her, but he should have told her about the life modelling. She would have said it was a bad idea. He'd behaved like an idiot.

'Mum, are you all right?'

Stars twinkled in front of Dawn's eyes. 'No, not really. I'd forgotten how paranoid this stuff makes me. I'll take you to the pub. See you at the car in ten minutes.'

She staggered into the kitchen puzzled by a wonderful spicy smell. Of course; she'd assembled a lamb tagine in the slow cooker hours ago. She glanced at the kitchen clock. 'Christ! It's nearly supper time.' She lifted the lid, the tagine had dried out so slopped in a tin of tomatoes. The couscous would take minutes. She clicked the kettle on. What ingredient had she forgotten? Who cared?

'Dawn, where've you been?' She jumped at the sound of his voice. 'I've been looking everywhere for you.'

'I'll tell you where I haven't been. I haven't been in the studio with the naked daughter of an armed maniac. Because that would have been stupid.'

He stepped closer. 'I'm so sorry. I confessed because I thought it was Chris that had got Suzy pregnant. I wanted to take the bullet rather than him.'

'Oh, for God's sake, Douglas, if you weren't so preoccupied with yourself then you'd realise that it couldn't have been Chris. And I'm not annoyed about that.'

'What then? And why couldn't it be Chris?'

'You really don't know?'

Douglas looked sheepish. 'The life drawing. I should have told you. I'm sorry. Your eyes look red. Have you been crying?'

Dawn pursed her lips and glared at him. Jack would have shot him for that alone, never mind the affair and pregnancy. She wasn't going to pursue the Chris bombshell now and anyway, he'd asked her not to.

The kettle boiled and she poured water over the couscous. She'd been planning to tart it up with herbs from the veggie garden that were not narcotic but she couldn't be bothered. She went over to the fridge for yoghurt.

'Please don't stand in front of the fridge when I need to get things out. Do the guests know?' she asked him as he moved aside.

'Only Rex. They all went out for a walk after the class.'

'That's something at least. A Mexican stand-off isn't good publicity for relaxing art breaks.'

'No, it's not and, again, I apologise for that.'

'Call everyone for supper and take this through would you? Anastasia's staying. The table's laid, the red wine is open, and there's a fruit crumble in the Aga and clotted cream in the fridge.' She gave these orders in an even more brusque fashion than usual, whilst fluffing up the couscous which had solidified and moulded itself to the bottom of the bowl like a Frisbee. Douglas opened and closed four Aga doors as if to verify the crumble's existence. Then he squinted into the fridge as if dazzled by the tiny light.

'Where's the thingy?'

'What thingy?'

'The cream.'

'Oh, for God's sake! Do you want me to draw you a map?' She took a breath. 'I'm taking Becky to the pub for her shift now,' she said untying her apron. 'I don't feel very sociable for some reason.'

She needed to get out of the house. She was looking forward to a large glass of sauvignon blanc and would kill for a piece of Andy's chocolate cheesecake. She was craving sweet food all of a sudden.

# CHAPTER 58

Suzy didn't show up for her shift at the pub.

'Does Chris know where she is?' Dawn asked Becky as she placed a huge wedge of cheesecake in front of her saying, 'That should ease the munchies.' She sat down and rested her chin in her hands. 'God, I'm so bored. It's worse when it's empty like this.'

The wedge had a crack in it. 'Did you drop this?'

'Of course not.' Becky licked her fingers. 'She's gone to London. She texted Chris from the train. But don't say anything. Officially, she's got flu.'

Presumably she'd left to find Freddie, so he must know by now what had happened, or he would do soon. Should she tell Anastasia? Once Freddie heard his secret was out, he'd rush home and she might appreciate a warning. Or she might be upset with Dawn. There was a reason that a person needed to be told not to shoot the messenger and this one had access to firearms. Dope-induced paranoia battled neighbourliness. After the first mouthful of cheesecake she decided to risk a bullet and went outside to text

She stayed in the pub for an hour. She loved being close to Becky and Chris like this. She and Douglas hadn't had a local in London; it was one of the pluses living near Darton, to have a pub where she felt at home and could always find someone to talk to; half of her family were here after all. She watched Chris through the kitchen door whenever it opened. He looked so grown up these days, chatting easily with customers, taking instructions from John and Andy. A wave of sadness engulfed her. Chris hadn't actually told her he was gay. She'd worked it out, and he knew that she knew. But Douglas needed to know and it should come from Chris. He was the golden boy. That was a lot to live up to. She wanted to rush over and hug him, tell him how proud she was of him.

Becky was pulling pints behind the bar sporting her usual just-got-out-of-bed look, which in this case was accurate. She was lucky that Andy and John didn't mind her unkempt appearance. She watched Becky reach for a glass, fill it with wine, take the customer's cash and ring up the till, biting her lower lip in concentration. Dawn felt a stab of love so strong it stopped her breath. Her daughter, for all her faults, wrenched such intense love that it hurt, like a corkscrew tugging at her heart. She felt bad about thinking these things that she'd never say out loud. To whom would she utter them anyway? With Douglas, a problem shared was a problem doubled. She fought the urge to rush over to Becks and hug her. She thought of the disdain with which that would be received, and the lump in her chest melted like ice in the sun. All you can do is love them and show them that you do. She needed another drink but she had to drive home. She imagined being stopped by the police and protesting: No officer, I am not under the affluence of incohol.

The kitchen door opened again and through it Dawn saw a guy she didn't recognise standing with his arm around Chris. Was he a boyfriend? Chris turned his head; their faces were close. It certainly looked like it. She'd never seen Chris with a boyfriend. She could be wrong; she wasn't exactly at her sharpest. Becky would know. She called her over and was about to ask when Becky dropped her bombshell.

'Mum. There's something I need to tell you. Don't freak out."

Dawn's mouth fell open. Was she ill? Don't say she was pregnant.

'You know I've been really bored working here. Well I did the sums and saw it was going to take me nine months to save up to go away. So I, well, I applied for another job.'

'Great!'

'Wait. You haven't heard what it is yet.' She paused and took a breath. 'It's working in a surf shack.'

'Lovely! In Devon or Cornwall?'

'It's in Bali.'

'Bali? Was there a Bali beach in Devon? There was a California Cross. 'You don't mean Bali in Indonesia?'

Becky rolled her eyes. 'Yes. Bali in Indonesia.'

'Why not work in a surf shack round here? Have you booked the flights?'

'Yes. We're flying out next week... spending time in Thailand and Laos before I take up the job.'

'Barney's going too?' Becky nodded. Thank God for that. 'When are you coming back?'

'We've only booked the flight out. I don't know when we'll come back.'

Not even a return date to hang on to. 'You will be careful, won't you? You hear such terrible tales. Only last year that lovely young couple were murdered.'

'Oh, here we go. You really suffer from worst-possible-scenario-disease. I'm seriously worried you're going to infect me with it. If I thought about every dreadful thing that could happen, I wouldn't go.'

'What about tropical diseases?' Dawn persisted.

'I've booked the jabs in the travel clinic. While we're in Exeter we'll get a travel card and load it with money. If it's stolen, we don't lose anything.'

As she talked, Dawn imagined Becky lying dead by the side of the road, a victim of robbery or a bus crash or lying ill in a filthy hospital bed.

'Oops, there's a customer. I'd better go.'

By the time Dawn arrived home, the house was quiet. In two days the guests would leave and a new lot arrive. She was just starting to get used to them. She hoped she could keep it together. Heading for the fridge, she poured herself a glass of wine and took it into the bedroom. Douglas needed to know about Becky but he was asleep, or pretending to be, on the far edge of the bed.

In the night she woke to a strange scrabbling sound, as if Truffle was trying to get in the door, but he was in the tepee.

She turned on the light and saw Douglas spread-eagled against the door, his arms clawing upwards as if trying to scale the wall. 'Douglas!' she exclaimed before it occurred to her that he might be sleep walking and you shouldn't wake sleep-walkers. Sod that. She leapt out of bed and grabbed him and pulled him on to the bed. His eyes were wide open and he started gabbling.

'I dreamt I was trying to crawl along the floor but I couldn't get anywhere.'

She fought the urge to laugh. 'That's because you weren't on the floor, you were trying to climb up the wall. Did you think you were Spiderman?'

'Are you still annoyed with me?'

He was probably in shock. Sometimes you just have to get over yourself, as Chris would say. She sighed heavily. 'No. Nobody's dead. That's the best we can say about the day.'

# CHAPTER 59

Douglas took a deep breath and scanned the moor and sky. From the top of Hound Tor, Dartmoor extended for miles into the distance, bare of trees, gorse glowing gold in the sunshine.

It was amazing how being threatened by a gun-toting madman put everything in perspective; he wanted to enjoy every moment. Aside from the swimming incident, it was the closest he'd come to death. He'd thought this new life in the country was going to be relaxing, instead it was like an episode of Emmerdale; not that he'd ever watched it.

'Time to pack up for lunch,' he told the guests. He drove them down the steep hill into Widecombe. Dawn had suggested lunch out. She was struggling without Suzy. Becky and Chris were working at the pub until midnight and weren't around to help in the mornings, and Barney ate more food than he prepared.

'Are you OK?' Rex asked as they stood at the bar waiting to order. 'You seem a little distracted.'

Douglas had warmed towards Rex. He was a good confidant and he kept cool in a crisis which seemed a necessity at Last Chance Mill. Since Dawn had stopped flirting with him they were getting on well.

'I've been better. I'm climbing the walls in my sleep, we've still no bookings for September, and one of our neighbours has appealed against the Mill being used for commercial premises so our license might be revoked. Oh, I forgot, I nearly got shot the other day.'

'That was insane. It must have been a shock for Dawn. Hearing you confess to getting a pretty girl pregnant. I believed you!'

'I could have handled it better.' At last, he thought, a title for my autobiography. 'I haven't thanked Anastasia properly yet. For stopping Jack from shooting me.'

'You should thank Sam too. He fetched her. He saw Jack arrive with the gun and ran over to the Manor.'

'Really?' So Sam must have known about Freddie and Suzy. Otherwise, why would he have fetched Anastasia? 'He's devoted to Anastasia.' Douglas remarked setting down his easel. 'Though how she understands him, beats me.'

'She has a way of inspiring devotion.'

Poor bloke, he'd obviously succumbed to Anastasia's charms. That wouldn't end well. He and Dawn had noticed Rex slipping off after dinner since that fateful day, but he was always at the Mill for breakfast. They did seem the most unlikely couple although, as the polar opposite of Freddie, Douglas could see the appeal.

'How's she doing? Since the revelation?'

'OK. She wants to get you guys over.'

After lunch, they walked uphill to another tor, easels under arm, sketchpads in hand. Douglas took photos, capturing the dark rocks against the pale landscape. Next time the rain forced them into the studio, the group could paint from the photos. He sat on a rock a little away from the others, bathed in the warmth of the sun and wished he could lie down and sleep. He'd known the first year in a new business would be hard, or first few years, who was he kidding? But the very day they'd finished renovating, guests had arrived and now the initial excitement and adrenaline had worn off he was exhausted. He felt like the leading racehorse that collapses just before the finishing line.

Back home, he saw Sam carrying spades and hoes walking down from the lane that ran alongside the leat. He must have been working at the vegetable beds. Douglas waved, Sam stopped dead and for a moment it looked as if he was about to turn and run but he seemed to change his mind and kept walking. As he approached, Douglas noticed he had that haunted look again. Funny. Dawn had told him that Sam was happier now.

'I wanted to say, thank you for fetching Lady Montague that day when Jack Lustleigh…well…you know.'

Sam stared at him with his pale eyes and Douglas wondered if he'd offended him in some way. 'Is everything all right, Sam?'

He nodded brusquely and walked off. 'See you tomorrow!' Douglas called after him.

He found Dawn in the kitchen.

'We've had a huge energy bill,' she told him as she filled the kettle. 'They want to increase our monthly payment. Can we raise our prices? Even if we get bookings for September we'll struggle to pay off the credit card debt.'

'I'm loath to put up prices. I'll ask Chris to come up with some marketing ideas,'

She rested her head in her hands. 'We can't cut back our spending any more. We're using our own garden produce, thanks to Barney, and we're not paying Suzy at the moment. This is a cheap period.'

He could sense her sinking. Only last week everything had looked positive and now they were plunged into uncertainty again. He didn't mention his encounter with Sam. She had enough to worry about now that Becky was leaving.

# CHAPTER 60

Anastasia dropped the bloody chunk of beef into the middle of the rolled-out pastry, smeared it with the honey-mustard concoction she'd prepared earlier, wrapped it up, coated it with egg yolk and set it aside while she tossed the sweet potatoes and roasted peppers in oil and tipped them into a roasting tin. Nothing to this cooking lark, she thought, a lot of fuss and fluff about nothing that people pretend is an art and exploit to make money. She ran upstairs to change out of her riding gear.

The bed was still unmade; the duvet heaped in the middle and an empty champagne bottle lay on the floor where it had dropped. Last night, Rex had stayed over. His eyes had lit up when she'd told him the boys were on a sleepover and she'd felt, not exactly obliged, but that he expected her to ask him to stay. Having sex was one thing, but waking up next to someone was another. Clearly, she was not a good picker of men. She'd always gone for good looks and money and this one was no exception (she'd trawled the internet and unearthed his net worth.) But at this stage of her life, kindness and loyalty were probably more important traits than being good breeding stock. She had thought they were a good match for a casual liaison: he so obviously into rescuing the damsel in distress, and she enjoying the attention of an attractive man to get over rejection. It seemed an ideal arrangement. But last night she'd noticed a worrying post-coital gleam in his eye. It struck her that he didn't view this as a holiday fling that would end when he went back to London.

The face in the mirror smiled back at her. The sex had been easy and good. With Freddie, pleasure cowered behind a barrier of emotions: did he still love her? Did he still want her? Last night had simply been two people enjoying each other and that had been refreshing. She deserved to feel the desire of a man again.

By the time the bell rang at eight and the dogs rushed to the door, she'd laid the table, warmed the plates and whipped up a gooseberry fool. She wiped her hands on her jeans. Rex liked her in jeans. To think she'd changed for dinner every night with Freddie! Why had she put up with him for so long? The boys rushed into the hallway at the sound of barking and she remembered why. A pang of fear exploded in her middle followed by the familiar wave of doubt. Was divorcing Freddie the right thing to do? How could anyone ever know? But she knew one thing. She didn't want to be a woman reduced to spying on her husband and feeling inadequate, as if it were her fault for him straying.

Dawn, Douglas, Rex and the boys stood in the hallway. She smiled as Rex ruffled her boys' hair and joshed with them. Rollo, the elder, was more reserved, like his father, but Cosmo loved Rex.

'Show me that magic trick again!' he demanded and before she could protest that he leave her guests in peace, Rex was down on the floor with the pack of cards.

She greeted Dawn and Douglas with a peck on each cheek. Dawn looked pale and tired but she knew better than to comment. Douglas looked flushed and tired or maybe it was a tan as he spent a lot of time outdoors. She started to greet Rex the same way but he kissed her full on the lips. Their first public kiss. She stepped back, her cheeks flushed. Dawn and Douglas discreetly looked the other way.

'Oh God, the beef wellington!' she shrieked as a burning smell reached them. She ran towards the kitchen.

Dawn followed her. 'You're actually cooking. Who are you and what have you done with Anastasia?'

'Mary's on holiday,' she said. 'She's gone to fetch the Lustleigh brat.' She'd been about to say 'tart', which was how she referred to her, but sensed Dawn had developed some weird kind of sisterhood with Suzy. Maybe it was because she had a daughter of that age, or maybe because Suzy worked for her, or because she was a feminist, whatever that was. 'By the way, thanks for your text. For giving me the heads up.'

'Is she staying with Freddie?'

Anastasia bristled. Really! Dawn could be so naïve. As if Freddie would take her into her London home.

'Freddie drove down here the night she left. He said it only happened once which is a lie of course. He's claiming the baby isn't his. There'll be a DNA test once it's born.'

'So where's she staying?'

'I don't know and I don't care.' Why did Dawn care about Suzy after everything she'd done? She'd wrecked their family. She wanted to tell Dawn about the divorce proceedings but she seemed more interested in Suzy. She faced her, hands on hips. 'Is it a problem for you, now she's gone?'

'We're coping. Becky's doing fewer shifts at the pub and more for us. John and Andy are suddenly two staff down so they're not happy though they've taken on a new guy. Chris has been promoted to bar staff.'

Anastasia scraped the pastry and burnt bits flew everywhere. 'That girl certainly screwed things up for a lot of people.'

Dawn started to clear up the mess. 'She's screwed things up for herself more than anything.'

Really! Listen to her. She sounded as if she were on the girl's side.

'And how are you coping with it?'

Finally! Dawn was asking her, the victim, how she was. 'It's hard.' Her voice wobbled. She put down the knife and pressed the back of her hand to her mouth. They crept up on her, these moments of grief, it was like bereavement.

'Oh Anastasia, I'm sorry. I've been really insensitive talking about Suzy when it must be so awful for you!'

She stiffened as Dawn tried to hug her. She was about as huggable as an eel but she clung on like someone used to having hugs rejected. Anastasia broke away and poured two vodka shots.

'When did you find out about him and Suzy?'

'The day I brought Truffle over. She was wearing only one earring. I'd found the other in the Range Rover.'

'Oh my God. That must have been awful.'

'I thought he was having an affair. He's had them before.' Dawn's eyes flashed wide. 'With women in London. But here in Darton? With a local girl? That was unforgivable.'

'And what about the boys? How are they taking it?'

'I told them we were splitting up, that they would see Freddie in London and me here which is pretty much what they do at the moment. They didn't seem that concerned.' They'd both gone back to their x-boxes though she wondered if Rollo had texted Freddie. She hadn't told them about Freddie's affairs – that was up to him – but if he didn't, then she certainly would. She didn't want them thinking she'd kicked him out on a whim or that he'd left because she was the one who'd done something wrong. 'Did a certain American influence your decision?'

She knew Dawn would jump to that conclusion. Rex was gorgeous; Dawn probably fancied him herself. Was there a hint of jealousy there?

'No. This has been a long time coming. Rex is a darling. A very welcome distraction. A harmless flirtation. Anyway, he's going back to London next week, as you well know.'

Perhaps Dawn had noticed that Rex hadn't slept at the Mill last night but Anastasia really didn't want to discuss her sex life. 'Right, dinner's ready. Be a dear and bring through those bottles of red wine. Boys!' she yelled, 'Come and get it!'

In the dining room, they grouped at one end of the table. She carved the beef and they helped themselves to the rest. Douglas stared at his plate as if it were Christmas and picked up his glass. 'Cheers everyone! Here's to the chef.'

She smiled graciously and looked over at Rex. His eyes locked with hers and he gave a half-smile, a flick of his eyebrows and she wondered if she should ask him to stay tonight. Her boys rarely rose before eleven so were unlikely to twig he'd stayed over but she couldn't risk giving Freddie ammunition. She hoped D and D didn't think that her screwing Rex balanced out Suzy screwing Freddie. Just because she didn't show how hurt she was, didn't mean she wasn't hurting: a fact that Rex had intuited right from the start.

'Thank you both for coming. I have a couple of things I'd like to say. Firstly, I am so sorry that you all got mixed up in, what should have been, our family's business.' She took a breath. 'I wanted you to know that Freddie and I have separated. I've filed for divorce. And Freddie is going for half of the estate so I'll have to sell up to pay him off. I'll contest it of course, but my lawyer isn't hopeful.'

There followed a stunned silence. Anastasia took a slug of wine. Douglas had picked up his knife and fork, but put them down again.

Dawn broke the silence. 'Surely you won't have to sell the Manor. It's been in your family for generations.'

'My lawyer tells me that Freddie is arguing that the estate should be included in the settlement. It's the family home.'

'Surely you could sell some land and pay him off?' Douglas asked.

'We haven't that much land. It's grazing land, anyway. Not worth much. The big money is in land for development, which we're not allowed to do. Not that I'd want that anyway.'

'What about selling a painting?' asked Douglas.

'The paintings are in a trust my family set up. They're not mine to sell.'

'But surely he's wealthy in his own right. All those Picassos,' Douglas persisted. It was gratifying to see how outraged he was.

'They're late-period drawings, most of them. There's one small painting. They're not worth much.' This was awkward. They'd been valued at a million, a huge sum to D and D, but her half of that added to half the value of the London flat still wouldn't be enough to buy Freddie's share of the estate. 'Let's change the subject. It's too depressing. How's business going?'

Douglas gulped his wine. 'Not great. We're not fully booked in August and we've no bookings for September.'

Anastasia refilled his glass. 'What? None at all?' Maybe things were about to go her way and they would have to sell up. Now she was about to lose the Manor, it didn't seem at all important. She offered Douglas more beef; he accepted eagerly and abandoned conversation in favour of eating.

She listened as Rex told D and D about visiting the cottage in a nearby village where his mother's family had lived and searching the local churchyard looking for the gravestones of his grandparents and an aunt he'd never met. The aunt had never married – probably because of the lack of men after the war – so Rex's family was the end of the line. As he explained his pride in discovering his Devon roots and described his emotional attachment to the landscape, Freddie's voice crept into her head, ridiculing the cliché of yet another American trying to find his roots in Britain. She wondered if Freddie held imaginary conversations with her too, and if he missed her. She hoped he did and that he regretted destroying their home. She caught Rex's eye and he winked as if they shared a secret. In all her years with Freddie she'd never seen him wink.

## CHAPTER 61

Dawn stripped the beds, listening to Becky singing along to some tune on her headphones as she cleaned the toilets. Becky appeared in the doorway.

'Can I ask you something, love? Is Chris, I mean, does he have a boyfriend? I thought I saw him with someone at work.'

'You should probably ask him but, yes, I think so. It's the guy John and Andy took on to replace Chris now he's taken Suzy's job behind the bar. Carl.'

So she hadn't imagined it. She must remind Chris to tell Douglas. She staggered outside with a basket of wet sheets to peg on the line and noticed Sam deadheading the climbing rose, and with him was Suzy. He had his back to her and she was standing with her arms folded, staring at the ground. Neither of them looked happy.

Suzy spotted her and came over to help her peg sheets on the line. She got to the point. 'I need my old job back. I've gotta pay for Hair and Beauty next term.'

Dawn worried how Anastasia would feel about them accepting Suzy back. Anastasia had accused Dawn of being sympathetic towards Suzy, even though she was trying to stay neutral. No doubt Suzy thought she was siding with Anastasia. But with Becky and Barney leaving, the timing couldn't have been worse.

'What about the baby?'

'I had a miscarriage.'

Dawn stopped pegging and touched Suzy's arm. 'Oh! I'm so sorry.'

Suzy didn't meet her eye. 'I'm not. It was for the best.'

'Are you back home?'

'Yes. Dad drove my mum away years ago. He realised he didn't want to do that to me.'

'Well, that's good ... I mean about you being at home, not about your mum. Becky and Barney are going away soon so we'll need some help. Will you be going back to the Darton Arms?'

'I hope so. Curl Up & Dye won't take me back. Pat, who runs the place, sympathises with Lady Montague.'

'He's annoyed with me. Said he won't go speech therapy again.'

'Oh, no. I was afraid that might happen.'

Her phone pinged. Anastasia: I know you're busy but could you pop round?

How intriguing. Something must have happened. She noticed the time. 'I'd better go and fix dinner. I'll phone you later.'


Anastasia attempted a smile as she opened the door but Dawn could see she'd been crying. She steered Dawn into the drawing room and poured two vodka shots. She sank into the sofa and tucked her legs underneath her. 'I hoped he'd feel guilty about the affair and I could talk him out of it, but he's still insisting on half the estate.' She wiped her eyes. Mascara smeared everywhere.

Dawn wasn't sure why Anastasia was confiding in her and not a closer friend but supposed it was because their friends knew Freddie too. Or perhaps it was because the revelation had happened at the Mill. Would she confide in Anastasia? No. She still didn't trust her.

'I'm so sorry.'

'I knew he'd pull a stunt like this. That's why I stuck with him for so long.'

The boys flitted in and out, asking when dinner would be ready and if they had time for a bike ride. Dawn saw their worried glances and handed Anastasia a tissue. When they'd gone Dawn said, 'Perhaps it will be worth it. To be rid of him.'

'Maybe. I keep wondering if I've made the right decision.'

'You and Rex seemed happy the other night.'

'We're both having a bit of fun. God knows I deserve it. But that's all it is.'

Dawn thought of the way Rex looked at Anastasia and wondered if he knew he was a bit of fun.

'I hate Freddie. What he's done to us. He's the one who had the affairs and now he's punishing me.'

'The law's all wrong.'

'You can say that again. Here, have another shot. Just when I was starting to feel better. Things were dark. I was drinking a lot.'

Stolichnaya must have had to build a new factory. Dawn nodded sympathetically. 'I know.'

'No. Really dark. I wanted to murder someone, three or four people actually, until I realised Freddie wasn't worth it.'

Dawn remembered Anastasia pointing her gun at Suzy in the barn and shuddered. She'd had motive and opportunity. If Rex hadn't seized the gun she might have shot Suzy. At least Rex knew what he was letting himself in for. That must be his type: the femme fatale. No wonder Rex hadn't been interested in Dawn; she was about as fatale as the Easter bunny.

Dawn leant over and whispered, 'Did you know she had a miscarriage?'

Anastasia's eyes widened in surprise.

'I only found out this afternoon. She came round asking for her job back. Becky's leaving soon so we'll be short staffed but we can find someone else.'

'I suppose that's a blessing. I feel sick when I hear her name. If you do take her back I never want to run into her.'

'No. I understand. You'll never see her and I won't mention her name again. I promise.'

'Fine then.' She poured them another shot. '*Vashe zdorovie,*' they chorused. Anastasia downed it in one. Dawn sipped hers and considered that what she'd thought was Anastasia's eccentricity might be nothing more than alcoholism.

She noticed a new painting on the mantle-piece in place of the family photo. How easily people are obliterated. 'Is that a new painting?'

'Yes. Rex painted it on one of Douglas's trips to Dartmoor. I love it. He's captured the dark, brooding undercurrent of the moor. Douglas must be an excellent teacher. I've seen some of Rex's paintings and they're shite. Talking of Douglas, where is he? Why aren't you together on a Saturday night?'

'He went to the pub with the guests. I didn't feel like socialising.'

'Is everything all right between you two? Last time you were here you weren't quite team D and D.'

Again, she picked up a hint of Anastasia's pleasure at their misfortune. 'We've still money worries, and we're waiting to hear the result of the appeal. And...' Dawn broke off. She'd rather confide in Cruella de Vil that her pedigree bitch was pregnant, but she was grateful for Anastasia's intervention with Jack Lustleigh.

'There, there, have another vodka and tell the hapless, betrayed wife all about it.' Anastasia topped up Dawn's glass like a KGB agent attempting to lubricate the tongue of an informant.

'I'm still annoyed about the near shoot out. I dread to think what would have happened if you hadn't shown up. He's such a fool!'

'Yes, but he's a lovable fool. No malice there. And don't forget that he loves you, and I think you love him. I know he's an annoying prick ...'

Dawn laughed.

'Sorry. Was that too strong? Rex says I'm rude. I thought I was honest but he can be –'

'An annoying prick?'

'Especially when he insists on diluting my vodka with tonic. That's like watering down Chanel No 5 with toilet cleaner. I've never known anyone so into health and fitness. The most Freddie did was walk across the room to refill his glass.

The other night he consulted that thing he wears on his wrist and told me how many calories he'd burned during sex as if I were an exercise bike.'

Dawn giggled. 'I'm worried about Becky too. She's off to the Far East next week. I admit I'm a worrier, but I am convinced she's never coming back, that she'll end up dead or, at best, horribly disabled. Douglas doesn't seem at all worried.'

'Dawn, she's not going to war in Afghanistan! She's going to be touring ancient monuments, watching the sunset over the ocean, riding around in rickshaws and on elephants. All the kids do it now.'

'It's all very well being glib while your boys are sitting next door watching telly. You'll see how it feels soon.'

Anastasia frowned. 'There's something I need to tell you.'

'That sounds serious. What is it?'

Anastasia jumped up. Coco's head shot up, her ears cocked and she began to growl. 'Did you hear that?'

Dawn had heard nothing. Anastasia tiptoed into the hallway, opened the front door and called out, 'Who's there?'

Dawn peered through the door and heard a familiar voice. 'Thank God you're in. I think I've broken my wrist. It hurts like hell.'

'Douglas!' she exclaimed, rushing over. 'I thought you were in the pub.' His trousers were muddy, his hair full of grass cuttings and he was holding his wrist. Anastasia ushered him into the hall. 'What the hell happened?'

'I thought I'd walk here across the fields. It was light when I set off. I fell into a hole as I got into the garden.'

'Oh! The ha-ha,' Anastasia said.

'It wasn't bloody funny!' he retorted.

'No, I mean you fell into the ha-ha. It's a bank with a ditch on one side that goes around the garden to keep the deer out.'

Dawn giggled. 'Yes, Douglas, the ha-ha. Don't tell me you've never noticed it.'

'It was dark. It's a bloody man-trap.'

'Busted!' Anastasia said. 'Now you know how I get my men!' She and Dawn high-fived.

'How much have you two had to drink?'

Anastasia hiccupped. 'I think you need to go to Eccident and Amergency.'

'I've drunk too much to drive,' said Dawn.

'Me too,' said Anastasia.

'Now there's a surprise. I've only had a couple of beers, but I'd have to drive with one hand. I could operate the foot pedals and you could steer from the passenger seat, Dawn.'

'I suppose I could manage that.'

'That's the most absurd thing I've ever heard,' Anastasia protested. Dawn and Douglas exchanged a smile. 'Oh, I see, that was a joke. Rex says I don't get dead-pan humour. Freddie used to laugh at his own jokes so I knew when he was joking. That was about the most considerate thing he ever did.'

'Calling for an ambulance seems a little dramatic,' Douglas protested. 'It's probably not broken.'

'I'll phone Samuel's house. One of his brothers drives a cab.'

'What are you doing here anyway?' Dawn asked him while Anastasia phoned.

'I found out something I thought would interest Anastasia.'

Anastasia put down the phone. 'Oh? What's happened now?'

'It was something I read in Artist Quarterly. You should get a new valuation of Freddie's Picassos. You told us you didn't pay much for late-period drawings a few years ago, but they've rocketed in price. Paintings even more so. The Russians are buying them up. Look at this.' He pulled a muddy folded magazine out of his pocket and handed it to Anastasia. 'There. Read that,' said Douglas, jabbing his finger on a page.

Dawn looked over Anastasia's shoulder as she read aloud.

'Medium-sized paintings which would have fetched two million pounds a few years ago are now selling for up to eight million. Russian and East Asian collectors have been pushing up the prices.'

Anastasia smiled at Douglas. Dawn felt so proud of him. 'That is interesting. Freddie always said he was onto a good thing with those Picassos.'

'Do you know which ones he has?'

Anastasia nodded. 'Absolutely. I bid for all of them. Five drawings and a painting.'

Minutes later a car pulled up and they were speeding through the lanes towards town, attempting a conversation with Sam's brother, Josh, who spoke in a weird Devon-cockney accent and was as unintelligible as his brother. She'd wanted to ask Anastasia what she'd been about to tell her, but not in front of Douglas. She had a feeling it was something to do with him.

## CHAPTER 62

Accident and Emergency. A mass of messy people milling around, either drunk, deranged or both. Clearly this was normal behaviour in Devon on a Saturday night, as in London. They waited hours for the triage nurse who gave him a morphine shot, more hours for a doctor who examined his wrist, more hours for an ultrasound – x ray wasn't operating at that late hour – and still more hours for a nurse who bandaged his wrist and fitted a sling, telling him that it was a bad strain.

Dawn started off perky, fuelled by vodka, but faded fast and after two hours, looked as if she wanted to cry.

'Go home,' he implored, but she wouldn't leave without him. She'd always been an affectionate drunk. When he came back from having his sling fitted, he found her asleep with her head on the shoulder of a shaven-headed teenager who was bleeding from his ear.

It was five in the morning when the cab dropped them off. Their bats were swooping, their owls hooting, their foxes screeching; it was great to be back in the peace and quiet of the countryside. 'I need to be up in two hours to make breakfast,' Dawn croaked, pulling the covers over her fully-clothed body.

After only two hours sleep, he waded through the long grass in the meadow. He hadn't prepared for his art class. His trousers were wet with dew, his wrist throbbing as the morphine shot wore off, and his eyes gritty from lack of sleep. He blinked back the brutal rays of early morning sunshine.

'Knock, knock,' he called patting the outside of the tepee and getting his good hand wet. 'Becky? Barney? Are you awake? We really need your help.'

271

He heard the nasal tones of Barney, 'What up Mr T?'

'Dawn needs Becky in the kitchen and I need you to help set up the studio asap. Please.' Then he remembered. 'Shit. I left the people carrier at the pub.' Douglas heard mumbling from within and the tepee flap opened to reveal the illustrated body of Barney. It was too much to bear before his first cup of tea.

'No. It's here. You left me the keys and I drove it home,' Barney said rubbing his eyes. He started to roll a cigarette and a bag of weed fell out of his pocket.

'Really? Oh yes, I remember now,' he lied.

'And, no, he wasn't drinking,' Becky chimed in removing a pink eye mask with 'fuck off' written in sequins on it.

Douglas didn't suppose driving under the influence of cannabis was a lot better.

'What happened to your arm?' Becky asked.

'Long story. I'll tell you later.'

Becky pulled a jumper over her pyjamas, donned a pair of wellies and went to help Dawn prepare breakfast. In the studio, Douglas organised paper, charcoal and pencils and Barney set up the easels. Becky reappeared with a tray of scrambled eggs on toast, tea and his painkillers.

'Mum says eat before you take the pills or you'll get stomach bleeding or start hallucinating or something. I swear, the inside of her head is like a Final Destination film. Chris is making breakfast with Mum so I can help out here. You look pale, Dad. Are you in pain? Mum told me about the ha-ha.' She had the cheek to start giggling. Why did his offspring love it when he was accidentally damaged in some way? Without exception they found it hilarious. When he told a funny joke or related a humorous story he was met with stony, puzzled faces. But when hurt himself, it provided hours of mirth.

'What do you call a deer that falls into a ha-ha and gouges out its eyes?' she asked him.

'No idea.'

'No-eye-deer! That's right! Well done Dad!' She exclaimed as if he'd surprised her with his intelligence. Barney doubled up with laughter.

'What about if it knocks itself out too?' Becky persisted.

'Absolutely no idea?' Douglas suggested.

'No. STILL no-eye-deer. Get it, Dad?'

Barney laughed so much it sounded as if he was coughing up a lung. 'Sorry, Mr T,' he wheezed, 'But you walked right into that one.' This set them both off again.

'So, Dad, what are you planning on doing today?'

'I don't know. Having a nervous breakdown? Running away to sea?' His wrist started to throb and he downed the painkillers. Hallucinations would be preferable.

Becky gave Douglas her 'poor thing' look. 'Are you all right, Dad?'

'I worry about this drugs stuff, Becky. I know you all do it and I puffed the odd joint myself at your age, but you hear such awful stories about other people's ch –' don't say children, 'I mean young people.'

'You know too much because we live at home. If we had our own places you wouldn't know what we got up to, would you?'

'No. That's true. But there's a reason why they call it blissful ignorance, you know.'

'I know. If I have kids I'm booting them out as soon as they hit adolescence.'

'Why didn't I think of that? Hang on. Does that mean they'll end up with Mum and me?'

'You'll be dead by then, I expect. I don't plan to start a family until I'm in my forties.'

So he would never know his grandchildren. Becky faked a rueful smile. The young were so cruel these days. Perhaps mobile phones had fried the empathy part of their brains or staring at screens had burnt out their sympathy receptors. How easy it was for them to callously pursue their dreams with no thought for others! Life was one big social media experience where you commented with no repercussions and moved on to the next posting. He was moments away from asking, what is the world coming to? And then the metamorphosis into his father would be complete. A wave of exhaustion hit him. Caffeine. That was what he needed. He set off towards the house.

He heard the water before he saw it. The leat level was higher than usual and the water was racing down the spillway. Why was there so much water? Tony had told him it overflowed occasionally but it hadn't rained that much in the last week. He strode along the grassy lane that ran beside the leat, to where it met the river. From a few paces he saw the problem: the sluice gate had been raised slightly, allowing water to trickle through underneath. He shook off the shiver that crept down his spine. That sluice gate hadn't raised itself. Someone had done it. Was it the same person who'd vandalised the studio, flooded the kitchen and left the cooker on? He looked around, expecting to see someone watching him. He raced home and retrieved the winch handle from the utility room. The door was usually open; anyone could have entered and taken it. As he rushed back to the sluice gate he remembered he'd seen Sam walking down this lane the other day. He'd looked uncomfortable, as if he wanted to run off. Had that look been guilt? Douglas wound the winch handle until the sluice gate was down to its usual level.

## CHAPTER 63

Rap music blared from Becky's window as Dawn walked up the drive. Who'd have thought so many words rhymed with motherfucker? She'd gone for a walk to clear her head. The people carrier wasn't back yet. She might manage a quiet cup of tea with Becky and Chris. She knocked gently on Becky's door.

'What?' Becky barked. Dawn took a step back and considered retreat.

'Anything I can do to help, darling?' she said a little too brightly, sticking her head around the door.

Becky sat on the floor, along with the rest of the contents of her room, wrestling with a rucksack the size of a small wardrobe, pulling at its webbed straps and angrily pushing back her hair. 'This rucksack isn't big enough. I need a bigger one.'

Dawn pointed out that it might be better not to take a bigger one. How would she lift it? She earned herself a snarling. Becky refused advice even on a good day, and she'd been so snappy recently which did make her leaving a little easier to bear. 'Have you got your–?'

'Do-not-run-through-a-checklist,' Becky seethed.

'Ok,' Dawn squeaked, 'I'll go and put the kettle on. Can you spare a minute to come and sit outside?'

'Too busy,' Becky snapped, jumping over a pile of clothes and narrowly missing a camera discarded on the floor. Dawn resisted the urge to pick it up and put it somewhere safe. All moments with Becky were so precious now, but it was like spending time with an injured hyena. Perhaps she was wrong, but she was not convinced that her daughter, who used to forget her PE kit for school and her purse when they went out shopping, had everything she needed for a six month trip to the Far East.

A new rap blasted out. She couldn't take it any longer. She opened the door and Truffle, who obviously shared her sentiments, shot out. She knocked on Chris's door.

'Can you do me a favour, Chris? Sam is refusing to go to speech therapy but he likes singing along to rap. Can you lend him a CD or get him Spotify or whatever you kids do for music this week.'

'Sure. I'll ask him what he's into.'

She found Truffle curled up in his basket with his paws over his ears. As she was pouring tea, Barney appeared.

'Becky,' Dawn began, 'is so short with me. I can't say anything without her jumping down my throat.'

'It's not you,' Barney said sticking his hand in the biscuit tin and picking out three. 'She's pretty weirded out. Of course she's psyched about it. But she's also… like… nervous. And there's so much to organise, man. She hates that! You can't tell her about all the bad stuff that might happen. That's projection Mrs T!' He tapped the side of his nose. 'Yeah, we need to avoid that. Did an essay on it.'

It seemed obvious now Barney pointed it out. She should be telling Becky that travelling would expand her horizons, rather than worry she'd end up bedridden after catching a tropical disease. She should be reminding her that it will be a life-changing experience, rather than a life-ending experience where she'd end up dead in a ditch after a mugging.

'It's been really good of you to let me … like stay here, Mrs T. You've been better to me than my own family. They booted me out. Was a lucky day I met Becks at that festival. It was like … karma.'

It was the most she'd heard Barney say in one go. 'Why did they kick you out?'

Barney shook his head, 'They wanted me to go into the family business. I didn't want to. Told them I wanted to see the world. They think I'm this alcoholic drug addict which I'm not by the way.'

'I think you kids have the right idea,' Dawn said. 'Our generation couldn't wait to leave home and start earning. We had to scrimp and save for a deposit to buy a flat. Life was hard, I can tell you. But at least we could get on the bottom of the property ladder. Goodness knows how all of you are going to manage that.'

'It's cool Mrs T. Some of us are happy in tepees.'

'And now, in our enforced retirement, we're still struggling to make ends meet. No. You kids definitely have the right idea. Delay the onset of slave labour as long as possible.'

'Barney!' boomed Becky's voice from upstairs.

Dawn gave him a 'rather you than me' look and he dutifully trotted off without complaint. Anyone who could put up with Becky in this mood was definitely a keeper. Tomorrow, Becky would be in Thailand. Dawn rode the customary wave of dread that overtook her when she thought of Becky thousands of miles from home. She prepared the shepherds' pies, washed Barney's kale, chard and green beans, put the gooseberry and redcurrant pie in the bottom oven and all the while, she cried. Then she had a large shot of cash and carry vodka. It stemmed her tears like a knife cauterising a wound.

# CHAPTER 64

'We won't be joining you tonight,' Douglas told the guests, placing a shepherds' pie on the dining room table and cutting it into portions. 'It's Becky's last night before she goes off on her travels. We're having a family meal in the kitchen later.'

'Becky's trip sounds really exciting,' said Alice.

'She's going with a big group isn't she?' Rajesh asked.

'No. Just Barney.'

'Crikey!' exclaimed Debbie, dropping her knife and fork onto her plate, 'How will you sleep at night?'

'Exactly!' Dawn exclaimed as she and Chris carried in bowls of vegetables.

'It's a well-trodden travellers' route,' Douglas said quickly.

'The travellers are worse than the natives! Haven't you seen The Beach?' asked Rajesh.

Images of dirty syringes and shark bites flooded Douglas's head. Even he felt nervous now.

'He looked over at Dawn. She looked close to tears. He wanted to rush over and hug her but it would only draw more attention.

'I'm sure she'll have a lovely time,' Deidre piped up. 'Our daughters went to India in their twenties, ended up in Australia, got married and never came back. We haven't seen them for ten years. But we hope to go this winter. Don't we Len?'

Len flashed his tombstone teeth.

Dawn's face was ashen and she started to sway. That was her other fear: Becky wouldn't come back. She rushed out of the room. Douglas followed and found her outside the back door, sobbing. 'I'm so sorry, love,' he said. 'Don't pay any attention. Becky's a sensible girl and will keep herself safe.'

'You can't know that!'

He couldn't, but he still had to proclaim it as if it were the truth. It was his husbandly duty to look on the bright side. But he couldn't win. If he acknowledged the dangers, he was fuelling her fears and if presented a positive view, she accused him of being uncaring. 'The time will pass quickly. We managed when the kids went to uni didn't we? She'll skype and phone and post online the whole time. We'll soon get used to the lack of verbal abuse.'

Dawn gave a strangled half sob, half laugh.

'Come back in and let's have a nice evening together.' He pulled her towards him. She resisted at first but then yielded. He stroked her hair. 'I'll fix us both a stiff drink so we can grin and bear it.'

He led her inside and poured her a vodka which she downed just as Becky and Barney breezed in chattering away as if they hadn't a care in the world, which of course they hadn't. Becky was carrying Truffle, kissing him on the nose and telling him how much she was going to miss him. If she noticed Dawn's blotchy face, she didn't remark on it.

'I made your favourite, shepherds' pie,' Dawn said with barely a quaver in her voice. Good stuff that vodka. Made him wish he'd got her on to it years ago, though that cash and carry stuff smelt similar to his brush cleaner.

'Great,' Becky said flatly in that monosyllabic way she'd been using with them for days. By contrast, she chatted animatedly with Barney and Chris about a full moon festival on some island. Douglas opened a bottle of Prosecco and poured five glasses.

'Cheers! Here's to your wonderful travels ahead. We'll miss you but we know you'll have a great time.'

Becky smiled. 'Thank you. Oh, Dad, can you take us to the station tomorrow for ten?'

He looked from Dawn to Becky, puzzled. He'd presumed that he and Dawn would both go. Dawn would want to be there. 'Umm, Mum and I thought we'd both come.' Dawn was looking at Becky like a death row prisoner regards their executioner.

'OK. I presumed Mum would be doing breakfast that's all.'

'I can ask Suzy to come in to do breakfast,' Dawn said quickly. 'I didn't know the time of your train.'

How typical of Becky to conceal important information until the last moment as if she were co-ordinating a top-secret parachute drop behind enemy lines.

'I won't come if you'd rather I didn't.'

'Oh, for God's sake Mum, of course I want you to come,' Becky snapped. Douglas could see Dawn was close to tears.

'I can do breakfast,' Chris volunteered. 'I don't have to be in until eleven tomorrow.'

Douglas smiled at him gratefully as he served up the shepherds' pie. Barney and Becky cleaned their plates in five minutes flat and left saying they had to finalise their packing.

'She doesn't mean it, Mum,' said Chris coming over to give Dawn a hug. 'I'm off to work now. See you later.'

'Try not to be upset, love. It'll be good for her to travel. Make her realise everything she has here. She's ready for this. We'll probably have more conversations with her than we do now. Let's face it, she's not very communicative at the moment. Not unless you count 'get out' and 'fuck off'.'

Dawn took a deep breath. 'I'm not going to miss that gangster rap.'

'There you go. Now you're looking on the bright side.'

# CHAPTER 65

The next morning at seven, Dawn woke everyone with cups of tea and she and Douglas ate toast while Becky and Barney dragged their giant rucksacks downstairs.

She was determined not to cry and managed until the London train pulled in. Why were trains so gut-wrenchingly sad? She hugged Becky, clinging on as if for the last time. The guard blew the final whistle, the train crept away and as it gathered momentum, so did her sense of loss. As she looked up the empty track, she felt Douglas's arm around her giving her a reassuring squeeze.

When they got home, Dawn realised she'd been so focussed on Becky that she hadn't talked to Sam about his refusal to go to speech therapy. She found him strimming brambles in the meadow. As she approached, he stopped. The birdsong resumed.

'I thought you might be thirsty,' she said sitting down on the grass and handing him a can of lemonade. She must get to the point but she hadn't thought this through.

'Suzy told me you don't want to go back to speech therapy.' Sam's head shot up. That was something. He usually avoided eye contact. He took a swig of lemonade.

'I'll take you to your next appointment. Suzy would like to come too.'

He shook his head.

'Are you annoyed with Suzy?'

He chewed his lip.

'She did something…silly. But we all do silly things. I know I do. Can you forgive her? Be her friend again? You know, if you could speak, you could ask Suzy out. How cool would that be?'

Sam's head jerked up as if she'd slapped him.

281

'She likes you too. I can see it, when you're together.'

Samuel's eyes softened. She breathed a sigh of relief. 'Shall we try one more session?'

Samuel shifted from foot to foot but then nodded.

'Good. I really think it will help you. Your mum told me what happened with your dad and—'

The word 'dad' had slipped out. The shock on his face told her she'd made a huge mistake. He stepped back, knocked over the can of lemonade, turned on his heel and strode off. This was her only chance and she'd blown it. She clawed her brain for one thing that might make him listen to her.

'Sam!' she called after him. 'I know what happened to you. It's only fair that I tell you…' Could she do this? 'What happened to me.'

He stopped and turned to look at her. She caught up with him and grabbed his wrist. Her heart thumped. She didn't know where to start but she had to start soon. He put his head on one side and frowned, his pale blue eyes locked on to hers. She let go of his wrist and rubbed the back of her neck. She was the one who wanted to run away now.

'Something bad happened to me too. I…' Was she really doing this? Would she regret it later? 'I was working in a Pupil Referral Unit. It's a place where they put students who've been excluded from school. I hurt a boy. Accidentally. His name was Tom. I sort of…I shoved him and he fell and hit his head. He was in hospital. In intensive care, in a coma. They weren't sure he'd recover. But he did. Eventually.' There. She'd said it. And the ground hadn't opened up and swallowed her.

Samuel cocked his head to one side. 'W…w…why?'

'Oh, Sam, that's brilliant! You're talking! I knew you could—'

He made a tutting sound, shook his head and raised his eyebrows.

'Why did I do it?' Her heart began to race. She'd been over this moment so many times. 'He stormed into my classroom and started shouting at this year nine boy. He picked up a chair, raised it above his head and I thought he was going to hit the boy with it. I froze. He was bigger than me. I was frightened. I…' Dawn's voice faltered. This was the part she didn't remember well. 'I knew I had to do something to stop him so I shouted his name and he turned away from the boy to face me. I thought he was going to hit me with the chair. I guess I panicked.' She remembered the prickly sensation as anger swelled red in her head. 'So I ran at him, put my hands on his chest and shoved him. Hard. I don't know whether it was because his arms were above his head and the chair was heavy, but he lost his balance. He sort of staggered backwards and as he fell, he hit his head on the corner of a desk and was knocked out. It was horrific.' She closed her eyes tight. She could still hear the sickening crack, and the thud when he hit the floor. When she opened her eyes, Sam was still there.

'When the police questioned me, I couldn't remember the exact order of things. They were trying to catch me out, as if I were a criminal, a murderer. It looked as if he might die, you see. I was suspended and told not to go back to work. Later, there was a hearing. They decided that I'd used too much force.' A red hot bolt of shame shot through her. It never went away. Her therapist claimed it was worse because she'd been ushered out of the school and instructed not to talk about it with any of her colleagues.

Sam nodded slowly. His eyes weren't judging her, as the eyes of the Head teacher and the police had done, they were full of sympathy. 'S…self …defence,' he stammered.

'Maybe. But maybe he wasn't going to hit me with the chair. Maybe I did over react. Afterwards I had a breakdown. Post-Traumatic Stress Disorder. I kept replaying the event in my head, over and over, trying to make sense of why I acted like that. Therapy helped me.' Mind you, she'd talked to a therapist for months but she'd never thrown off the shame. She should have walked away, called for help, restrained him and not used so much force. She could have explained better what happened, to the school, at the hearing, and to the police.

'So now you understand why, when I heard what you went through, I thought it might help if, one day, you could talk about it. I'm sorry if I was pushy. I can be pushy. Chris and Becky are always saying that.' She broke off, her head throbbing, her mind racing.

He reached out, placed both hands on her shoulders and closed his eyes. Then he lowered his arms and flicked his hands as if trying to remove something sticky. Her body felt lighter, she stood taller and she didn't need to blink even though the sun was shining in her eyes. For a few moments she allowed herself to see the accident for what it was: an instinctive reaction to protect a student and herself that had consequences. Sam wasn't blaming her; she saw pity on his face.

# CHAPTER 66

The glass door closed with a sigh. She stepped onto the Mayfair pavement, the slabs as white and shiny as marble. A smile quivered on her lips. Her hand fingered the card in her pocket. She wasn't shaking so much as vibrating. She looked down expecting to see herself glowing.

'Piccadilly,' she told the taxi driver.

The restaurant was filled with chatter and the clatter of heavy silver on expensive china. Light from chandeliers glittered on gold fittings and sparkled off the tiled walls. Heads turned as she walked over to the table. The highlights and botox were worth it. Only one head didn't turn: Freddie's. He was staring at his phone. No change there. He stood as she pulled out her own chair with a scrape. She slipped her arms out of the silky sleeves of her coat.

'Would you like a drink?' he asked, his hand firmly grasping a whisky and ice even though it was mid-day and he must be going back to work.

'No. Let's order,' she said, simultaneously picking up the menu and raising a hand to attract a waiter. Salad was the best option – something she could eat fast. Freddie ordered steak; he always ordered steak. His face was flushed and the twinkling blue eyes she used to love were drooping and bloodshot. She poured herself a glass of water.

'Cheers!' said Freddie, smiling broadly. 'So…I think I can guess what this is all about.'

'Can you?'

'Yes. Since you've heard from my lawyer that I intend to make a claim on the estate, you've had a change of heart.'

'Really? Is that what you think?'

'It goes without saying that I am prepared to make things work. I'm sorry for what I did and it won't happen again. It's our marriage which is important.' He reached across the table for her hand. She let him take it but slowly turned it over and uncurled her fingers. Freddie frowned at what lay in her palm. 'What's that?'

'It's the business card of an art dealer who's prepared to pay you up to 10 million pounds for the Picasso drawings and the painting. He has a waiting list of Russian clients.'

Freddie's mouth fell open. He took a swig of scotch.

'Your lawyer told mine you'd had them valued at 1 million. Was it a typo? A zero missing?'

'No! I know what it looks like. But I didn't know. Seriously. I had the valuation done two years ago for insurance purposes. I had no idea they'd increased. Late-period, too. Who'd have thought?'

'Yes, indeed. Who'd have thought?'

He drained his glass. 'Well, that's great news, isn't it?'

'It means the estate needn't be part of the settlement.'

'Of course. I can see that,' he snapped, throwing his napkin on the table. 'Will you excuse me a moment?'

He was on the phone before he'd crossed the floor – no doubt hassling his lawyer to come up with some other scheme to stop the divorce. The waiter brought their food. 'Can you bring me a large vodka, please? He'll have another scotch.'

Freddie returned to the table and started tucking into his steak. 'I suppose you're living with the American.' A waiter put drinks in front of them and rained pepper on his steak.

Was he having her followed? Employing a grubby private eye to gather proof of her infidelity? 'Actually I've been at friends, but I'm glad you brought that up. I need somewhere to stay when I visit the boys and come up for work. I can't rely on the kindness of friends forever.'

'You can stay at the flat whenever you want.'

'I don't want to run into your latest floozy. You can either buy me out of the flat, 1.75 was the valuation, or we'll sell it so I can buy another. Of course you'll have to sell a drawing or two.'

'I suppose you'll want half of what the drawings are worth.' Freddie sawed at his steak as if he wished it were her neck. It was swimming in butter and she imagined it solidifying in his arteries. She popped a radish into her mouth.

'No, Freddie. I just want Dartcoombe to stay in trust for our boys. And I want half the London flat. Not everyone wants to screw other people out of their inheritance. Talking of screwing, your little tart is back in Darton badmouthing you. 'I've been vaccinated slower' was the expression she used.'

Freddie's cheeks bulged as if he couldn't swallow. His eyes widened and looked about to pop. His mouth gaped like a fish and his head dropped towards his plate.

'Waiter!' she called over, 'this man is choking. Please perform the Heimlich manoeuvre.'

The waiter hauled Freddie up, grasped him around the middle and pumped him violently from behind. A half-chewed lump of steak shot out of his mouth in an arc and landed in her salad. Freddie slumped back into his chair, saliva trickling down his chin. She tried to stop him as he reached for her glass, but he brushed her hand aside and downed it in one. He went bright red in the face and gasped for breath.

'Oh dear. Did you think that was water?'

'That was uncalled for,' he said at last.

'I saved your life.'

'I don't mean that, I mean what you said about Suzy. I know you're angry but I'm sorry, Ana, truly sorry. How many times do I have to say it?'

She leaned across the table, aware that most of the clientele were watching them. 'Sometimes sorry isn't enough.' She leant back.

'Are you going to stop me from seeing the boys?'

'Of course not. Cosmo said to tell you he has a match next Saturday, if you want to go that is.'

'Of course I want to go,' Freddie hissed. 'Why are you implying otherwise?'

'You never went to them before I filed for divorce. We've all noticed your renewed interest in the boys.'

Freddie slammed down his glass. 'What's that supposed to mean?'

'Nothing at all,' she said coolly.

Freddie crumpled back into his chair. He had sauce on his tie and the waiter had popped two buttons on his shirt. He was weak. Now was the time. She could get him to agree to settle out of court. Under the table, she activated the record button on her phone.

'So that's why you wanted to meet for lunch. To tell me how much the Picassos were worth?'

'Yes. Why? What did you think? That I would trust you and accept your valuation?'

'I suppose I hoped you'd decided to come back to me.'

'No, Freddie not this time. If you agree, we can settle out of court and save ourselves a packet.'

'Fine.' Freddie closed his eyes and rested his head in his hands.

She pressed 'stop' on her phone and dropped it into her bag.

'Goodbye, Freddie.' She donned her camel coat and walked out. Her big smile hardly moved the rest of her face at all.

She put in a few hours at the office, listening to Sabrina's ideas for Christmas goods to add to the website, approving carved tables and chairs from Bali, which always sold well before Christmas, colourful Turkish carpets and pretty Thai silk tree decorations. Now the puppies were older, she should take another trip. She quite fancied Sri Lanka. At six o'clock she wandered down to Covent Garden, to a little bar with tables on the street. It was a beautiful late summer evening, balmy, the way evenings never were in Devon. She touched up her makeup in the bathroom, slightly disconcerted when applying mascara that her eyes didn't seem to widen as much as they used to. She ordered a white wine spritzer, took it outside, admired the late rays of sunshine, watched the shoppers and listened to a murmuration of starlings in the trees. She sipped the wine and let it melt away her tension.

Her heart skipped a beat when she saw him. It actually did; it was not a cliché for once. She'd gone into this thing with Rex viewing it as a fling. She'd only slept with him because she thought it would come to a natural end when he left Devon. But when he'd gone, she'd missed their long walks (she still refused to jog), their rides and, of course, the sex (he'd assured her she wasn't part of his exercise routine). When, a week ago, he'd suggested that they meet up in London she'd thought, why not? She was surprised at how excited she'd been to see him, at the feelings he wrenched from her. Last night, for example, when he'd told her how he'd cared for his wife and, despite her illness over many years, he'd stayed faithful and not been with a woman since her death, she'd felt a wave of warmth, even love towards him. Loyalty was a positive trait and Rex had it in spades. She was loath to admit it, but he was rivalling Coco in her affections.

He leant over and kissed her, grinned and then kissed her again. 'You smell good,' he said. 'Have you done something different with your hair? You look younger, brighter somehow.' He looked puzzled.

'Highlights.' An observant man, whilst desirable, has its downside. 'To cover the grey.' This aspect of anti-aging she would own up to.

'I'd still love you if your hair were grey.'

How could you not love a man who said things like that? 'While there's peroxide in the world and breath in my body, it will never be grey.'

He ordered a beer and they talked about their days. Well, he talked about his day and she gave him the edited highlights of her meeting with Freddie. 'He thought going after the estate would change my mind about the divorce,' she concluded.

'I can't blame him for wanting you back.' He looked at her in that way he did and she pictured them making love later.

Concentrate woman! 'But now, thanks to that tip off from Douglas, you won't have to sell. What do you say we head back to mine, freshen up and I'll cook for you?'

'Sounds wonderful,' she said feeling intimate parts of herself melting in the warmth of his brown eyes. But his comment had made her uneasy. It was Douglas who had saved her. And with all the excitement over the Picassos she'd forgotten her appeal to planning and her instruction to Samuel to open the sluice. She pulled out her phone, emailed the planning department and withdrew her appeal. Then she sent Samuel a text. Would he read it? He rarely got reception and wasn't great at picking up texts or voicemail. Perhaps she should drive back to Dartcoombe tomorrow, just to be sure.

# CHAPTER 67

When Douglas staggered in the back door after a day's teaching, the delightful aroma of tomato and oregano wafted from a pan of bubbling Bolognese sauce, and transported him to a little restaurant with red and white checked table cloths in the back streets of Venice where he and Dawn had lunch one time. He hugged her, hoping she might offer him a taste.

'Could you call Chris? Tell him the spag-bol's ready. He needs to eat something before he goes out.'

'Don't they feed him there?'

She drained a portion of spaghetti. 'He only gets the stuff they can't sell. Desserts Becky dropped on the floor, that sort of thing. I've started cooking earlier so I can feed him before he leaves.'

Douglas stood at the bottom of the stairs and called up. Music blared from his room; Chris wouldn't be able to hear him so he dragged himself upstairs, rapped on the door and walked in.

He stopped dead. The first things that caught his eye were the dope plants. A hanging forest suspended from a complex network of strings criss-crossing the ceiling. Then his gaze drifted to what lay beneath: two figures sprawled on the bed in a tangle of skinny limbs, mercifully, fully clothed. Chris raised his head and their eyes met. Douglas saw another face he didn't recognise. A man's face. He stepped back, shut the door and tiptoed downstairs, as if his silence would negate what he'd just witnessed.

'Dinner's ready,' he called up the stairs before closing his bedroom door. He collapsed on his bed and stared at the ceiling. His son, whose achievements and victories he celebrated daily as his twilight years denied him triumphs of his own, was a drug-growing homosexual. How had he missed that? It was like looking both ways before crossing a road and being hit by a train.

There was a knock at the door. 'Dad, can I come in? We need to talk.'

Memories flooded back of times his father had said the same to him or rather: son, we need to talk, after his mother caught him 'discovering himself' in the bathroom. Oh God, he put both hands over his mouth. His son should not ever feel shame like that.

Chris sat down on the bed.

'Firstly, the dope plants aren't mine. They're Barney's. He just needed somewhere to hang them after harvesting. I don't even smoke.'

'I didn't think you did.'

'And me and Carl. It just sort of happened.'

'It's OK. You don't need to explain. It was well...' the shock of my life, '... a surprise, that's all.'

'I guess because I've had girlfriends. When I was younger.' His voice tailed off and he bowed his head.

Douglas's heart lurched and he felt a wave of sadness that he knew Chris would hate but he couldn't help. He sat up and put an arm around his son.

'But I've seen you flirting with Suzy.'

'What? No. That's just banter. We're good mates. She spotted I was gay right away. She was relieved to find a bloke who didn't go all weird around her.'

'But we laughed about...about how alluring she was.'

'I guess I played along. If you're uncomfortable with this I can leave for London sooner.'

'No, don't do that,' he said quickly. Dawn would kill him, especially with Becky going, but he was finding it hard to look at Chris.

'You really had no idea?'

'Well, no.' Though now he can remember Dawn and Becky letting slip a couple of things, but he thought he'd misunderstood. Or he'd chosen to.

'I told Becky and Barney, or rather, they asked. Mum sort of guessed. She asked me to tell you. But there never seemed to be a right time.' Chris wrung his hands and looked at the floor. 'I knew you wouldn't take it well.'

Douglas knew what he said next would be crucial to any future relationship. Now was not the time to express concerns or reservations or prejudices or any opinion at all frankly. 'What do you mean, I wouldn't like it! I'm perfectly fine with it! You know I have lots of gay friends, well, two or three. As I said before, I'm surprised that's all. Your mother's right. I have the observation skills of a sonically impaired bat.'

'So you are OK with it?'

'Of course I am! So who is this—?'

'Carl.'

'Where did you meet?'

'He works at the pub.'

Quite the gay centre. 'Well, I hope you'll introduce me properly next time we meet. I'm so sorry I barged in like that. I heard music and thought you hadn't heard me knock.'

'It's OK. Just a bit embarrassing.' His voice was thick with irony.

'You'd better go and eat now. I know you're late for work. Is Carl eating too?'

'No. He left.'

When Chris had gone, Douglas opened the French windows and stepped outside. He needed to clear his head. Why had nobody told him? Why hadn't Dawn told him? He clenched and unclenched his fists. They'd made him look like a fool. He didn't know his own son.

## CHAPTER 68

Douglas parked the car, grabbed his swimming things and took the path to the beach. He saw a tent and beside it, a normal looking family having a barbeque: a mum, dad, girl and two boys. Douglas envied their blissful ignorance. The kids were too young to be gay or straight. The father didn't need to worry about how to be a good father to a gay son, to know the right thing to say, and the right thing not to say to make everything OK. He didn't need to build a supportive, trusting relationship with the son he loved more than anything in the world so that he didn't walk out of his life forever. One fact tormented him: Chris hadn't talked to him about it. He hadn't been there for his son at the one time Chris needed him most. His own son couldn't talk to him.

Had Chris not told him because he came across as homophobic? If he'd known, he'd have gone out of his way to show he wasn't. His negative thoughts about Chris's gayness were not rational. Douglas had gay friends in college and in his art and teaching career. He'd met their partners and been to their houses. One of Dawn's best friends from uni was gay. He found himself running through an inventory of everyone he'd ever known who was gay as if immersing himself in gayness would immunise him.

He stripped off under a towel, pulled on his trunks, stepped across the pebbles, waded through the seaweed and dived into the flat, turquoise water. It struck him that Dawn had known in the barn that day, with Jack Lustleigh's gun pointing at his middle, that Chris and Suzy weren't a couple. That was why, for a few seconds, she'd believed it when he'd said he was the father. She hadn't understood he was only saying it to save Chris. No wonder she was pissed off with him. She knew Chris didn't need saving. Of course she knew.

She was the better parent after all. He'd made an error of judgement with the life-drawing and his stupid confession and now he was banished, like an ailing family pet shut out in the garden after an unfortunate incontinence episode.

The sun had sunk behind the hill by the time he dragged himself from the water. He shivered as he pulled clothes over his wet body and wished he could warm himself on the happy family's barbeque. How he'd loved it when the kids were small, when they were loving, uncomplicated and didn't answer back and would crawl into his arms with a thumb in their mouth and fall asleep. He'd known how to be a good parent then. How could you be a good parent to a gay son who didn't trust you? He suddenly knew where he should be.

'Hiya, Douglas,' Andy's voice boomed across the pub as he walked in. 'I'm advertising for staff. Do you want a job? Dawn could be assistant chef, then we could employ the whole family.'

'Still trying to make a go of the art breaks, thanks Andy. But it might come to that.'

Andy and John must have spotted Chris was gay immediately. 'Can you ask Chris to come over? Just for a minute.'

'Sure.' Andy went into the kitchen.

Chris appeared with a cloth and wiped the already clean table. Douglas spoke in a loud whisper. 'Chris, I want to apologise. I've been such a fool. I want you to know I'm … ashamed of myself. I love you so much and nothing, nothing will ever change that.'

Chris smiled but didn't look at him.

'I'm so proud of you and I always will be. I don't want this to come between us. I want to know about your life, your partners or whatever.'

'It's cool, Dad. Really. I've always known you'd have my back. In the barn that day. You were barking up the wrong tree, but you'd have taken a bullet for me.'

Relief flooded over Douglas. 'Thanks. I don't deserve your forgiveness.'

'There's nothing to forgive.'

'Yes, there is. I've not seen what's been right in front of me.'

'Dad, I hid it. OK? Don't beat yourself up.'

'I'm so sorry about barging in on you, Chris. I want you to know that I will never go into your room again.'

'Great. Can we forget it now, Dad? Please? Just talk to each other normally? I think that's why I couldn't tell you. I knew you'd act weird with me. I get that you're shocked. If you told me you were gay, I'd be shocked.'

'Especially if you caught me with Rajesh.'

'That would be a shock as Rajesh isn't gay.'

'Apparently not. It's a shame. He was my best gay friend.'

'And that's a horrible thought. Thanks for planting that in my brain.'

'Now we're even,' said Douglas with a grin, and Chris burst out laughing.

Douglas caught sight of himself in the rear view mirror driving home and saw a piece of seaweed stuck to his cheek. Not only did no one talk to him, no one looked at him either.

Dawn had dozed off with her glasses on and her book had slid to the floor. She woke with a start as he sat on the bed.

'I take it that you knew about this,' he began. He sounded more confrontational than he'd intended but wasn't withholding information one of his major crimes? And he'd only withheld information about losing his job, the problems at the Mill and the life drawing, not about their children.

'What are you talking about? Have you been drinking?'

'I'm talking about the fact that Becky is growing weed and Chris is gay.'

'Oh, that.'

'Well?'

'I only found out about the dope after the incident with Jack and I was afraid to bring it up, to be honest. I knew you'd react like this and I couldn't deal with it.'

'And Chris?'

'I had my suspicions. He's never confided in me if that's what you're thinking. I asked him to talk to you. He said he wanted to be the one to tell you.'

'I caught him and Carl in bed together.'

Dawn sat up. 'No! Poor Chris. He must have been mortified. They weren't–?'

'No, thank God. They were fully clothed on the bed. Dry humping I believe it's called.'

'Where on earth did you learn an expression like that?' She giggled.

'Oh, I'm quite the man of the world, Dawn.'

'No, you're not. It's not nice, is it?'

'What's not nice?'

'Imagining one's kids doing it. An image flashes into my head and I have to erase it quickly.'

'It's going to be a while before I can erase what I saw, I can tell you. I can't believe you all kept me in the dark. Have you any idea how angry that makes me? You've made me look stupid.'

'Why do you always act as if you're the wronged party? We all love you, Douglas, but you can be very annoying.'

Typical Dawn. Wrap up an insult in a compliment and hope to get it past him undetected but he knew better than to answer back. He knew when to back down.

'Are you and Chris OK now?' she asked.

'Oh, yes. I sort of envy him. He has his whole life ahead of him, new job, new flat, new boyfriend. There. I said it.'

'Well done. Now go and shower. You've seaweed on your face.' She leant over and gave him a peck on the cheek. 'You taste salty. Let's go swimming together tomorrow when you finish teaching. I think we have to try and work in some quality time rather than just talking shop or harping on about each other's faults, extensive and fascinating though they may be.'

He glimpsed the winch handle sticking out from under the bed. Dammit. He'd meant to check the water level in the leat before he came to bed but with the Chris business, he wasn't thinking straight.

# CHAPTER 69

A figure stood in the shadows, partially lit by the moonlight streaming through the skylights. They'd decided to sleep in the studio as Carl didn't feel comfortable staying over in the house. Neither did Chris come to that. He wasn't sure he'd ever be able to have sex under the same roof as Dad. So here they were, with Truffle lying between them.

But who the hell was this?

Several easels stood between their mattress and the figure, so it was hard to see what it was doing. Chris realised it didn't know that he and Carl were there, tucked away in the corner under a pile of blankets.

He watched the figure bend down, stand up and then turn towards the wall. A man or a woman? Old or young? The oily smell of fresh paint wafted to the back of the studio. The figure was painting? And then it struck him. This must be him, or her, the vandal, the graffiti artist or whatever. Mum and Dad had told him how graffiti had appeared on their first night in the Mill. They'd thought Sam must have done it. After all, he'd caused the flood and he'd been in the attic when they arrived. But then there had been the flood in the kitchen and he remembered that time Dad had asked him if he'd been cooking late at night because someone had left the cooker on. He'd asked him not to mention it to Mum.

But the figure wasn't Sam. It wasn't tall enough. So who was it? His eyes had adjusted to the light and he saw hands flying. He was making a right mess of the wall. Should he shine his phone torch and see his face? Now he was sure it was a man. Or should he shout and scare him off? Or should he blend into the shadows in case he was dangerous? What would Dad do? A paintbrush clattered to the floor. Truffle's little head shot up and his ears pricked. Chris gasped and tried to pull him under the blankets but he struggled and clawed his chest. He growled and slipped through his hands and bounded towards the figure, yapping his puppy bark.

Chris froze.

As Truffle reached the figure, Chris's heart thumped. Would he lash out at the puppy? He sat up, ready to defend him but the figure didn't do anything at all, as if Truffle wasn't there, snuffling around his feet. Truffle even jumped up to his knees as if he wanted to be picked up. Some guard dog. Chris shook Carl awake and raised his finger to his lips and then to his. Carl propped himself up on his elbows. They looked at each other, puzzled.

'It's the vandal,' Chris whispered. 'What do we do?'

Carl reached for his phone and, to Chris's horror, shone the torch at the figure's face.

Chris couldn't believe his eyes.

# CHAPTER 70

'Mum wake up!'

Dawn took off her sleep mask. Why were Chris and Douglas standing at the end of her bed in the middle of the night?

'We found Dad in the studio. Sleepwalking.'

She sat bolt upright.

'We woke him up. He was painting on the wall.' Chris looked concerned. 'He didn't know where he was or what he was doing. He was talking gibberish. Has he done it before?'

'Talking gibberish? Constantly. Sleepwalking? Only once, so far as I know. I found him trying to climb that wall a few nights ago. Douglas, are you all right?'

'Of course I'm not all right. I've been vandalising my own home. I've gone stark, staring mad!'

'You're just stressed. Sleep walking is normal in times of stress.'

'No, it's not normal. It's...it's the opposite of normal.'

'Abnormal?' suggested Chris.

'Thanks Chris,' Douglas said.

Chris said, 'You realise all those things you blamed on Sam must have been done by you,' he told Douglas.

'What do you mean, all those things?' she asked. 'Apart from the graffiti, there was only the flood in the kitchen. I didn't blame Sam for that. I presumed I must have left the tap on.'

A look passed between Chris and Douglas but she couldn't summon the energy to unearth more revelations. If it were true, that all the weird happenings had been Douglas all along, she was relieved in a way. She'd always believed that Sam wasn't malevolent, though of course she doubted her instincts. She was indebted to Sam. Ever since she'd told him about the accident and his reaction had been sympathy rather than horror, she'd lost that feeling of shame and the blame had evaporated. Douglas had said all of this before, of course, but he was her husband and hardly impartial. She might even tell the kids now. 'Why were you in the studio?' she asked Chris.

'Carl came over. To listen to music.' He flushed red.

Poor Chris. Douglas had barged in on him again, though at least this time he hadn't been conscious. Chris was such a private person. It must have been so embarrassing. Unlike Becky, he took such pains to hide everything from them. Dawn thought back to when she was young. She'd never even taken a boyfriend home, let alone had sex in her parents' house. She hadn't even wanted to sleep there with Douglas when she was married. She quite understood him retreating to the studio.

'Douglas, go and wash your hands and come to bed. We'll talk about this in the morning.'

'So sorry, love,' she said to Chris when Douglas left. 'I gather he barged in on you last night. And now this. I'll have to start tying him to the bed at night.'

'Very Fifty Shades, Mum.' They giggled but stopped abruptly when Douglas returned.

She listened to Douglas snoring but couldn't get back to sleep. Was this sleepwalking episode brought on by the stress of discovering Chris and Carl? Perhaps she should have told him about Chris, but she'd been afraid it would throw him into a negative spiral where he'd declare that they'd messed up as parents, that they should have been stricter, more aware, done things differently, as if he wasn't talking about two kids who'd possessed minds of their own from the time they could stand. He never used to be like this. What a pity you couldn't converse with your fifty-year old spouse before you married them to find out what you were letting yourself in for.

# CHAPTER 71

Dawn took the cafetière though to the dining room.

'We're going to miss this place.' Zoe was saying.

Douglas beamed. 'Please come back!'

'And please write reviews for the website,' Dawn said, handing around cups of coffee.

'I'm going to post it on all my social media sites,' said Rajesh, 'I have loads of followers. It's a great formula, Doug. I'd never have thought you had it in you.'

'Thanks, I think.'

Debbie let out a sob. 'This break has changed my life.' Alice and Zoe hugged Debbie and Rajesh had the humility to look embarrassed.

'We're going to miss you all. You've been wonderful guests. I feel quite nervous about what the next group will be like.'

'Ahh, they'll love it too,' said Alice.

Dawn smiled at her. 'It has been special. You've been our first group. Please tell us anything you think we should change or do differently. It's a learning curve for us.'

'My favourite was the life drawing,' said Zoe. Dawn shot Douglas a warning look.

Dawn felt quite tearful as she stood and waved in the doorway as they left for the station, Douglas at the wheel. They still hadn't heard anything from Becky. She hadn't posted anything online either, according to Chris. Keep busy, she told herself. That wouldn't be hard: they had just two days to clear up and prepare rooms for the next group of seven guests. While Suzy cleared the breakfast things and hoovered, Dawn stripped seven beds and loaded the washing machine.

Chris emerged about ten and she offered to drop him at the pub on her way to the cash and carry.

As they pulled out of the drive she said, 'Are you and Dad OK?'

Chris sighed heavily. 'I should have told him before. It must have been a shock for him. Dad's always put me on a pedestal. I didn't think he'd take it well.'

'And how do you think he took it?'

'OK. Better than I expected. Is he really OK with it or is he just pretending?'

'I think he started off pretending but now he's got used to the idea he's fine with it.' She must push Douglas to talk more with Chris. 'He can see you're the same old Chris. We're both so proud of you.'

'He keeps going on about his gay friends as if he's trying to prove something.'

Dawn thought, it's one thing having gay friends and another entirely having a gay child. She'd tell Douglas to stop mentioning his gay friends. 'Dad was surprised, that's all. He didn't read the signs like the rest of us. Perhaps I should have told him.'

'No, Mum. It was up to me.'

'How are things going with Carl? You know you can bring him round any time. I know the last couple of times haven't been ideal.'

'With Dad bursting in? Not exactly. Yeah, it's fine. Casual. I'll be heading back to London in six weeks anyway.'

'Will you carry on seeing him?'

'Who knows? Maybe. I feel a bit weird being with Carl around Dad.'

'I don't think he's being weird because you're gay. He doesn't like the idea of Becky and Barney either.'

Chris looked happier when she said this and she changed the subject rapidly and asked him for a rundown on the next group of guests. It was a relief to have a conversation that wasn't about sex.

It was still raining when Chris came back from work. Rain slapped against the windows as they ate. Dawn hoped it wasn't pouring through the roof. Jonno had only done a patch-up job. Chris told them that Sam and Suzy were coming over later to listen to rap music in the studio.

'You were right, Mum. He's really into it. He sort of speaks along with it. You know how fast it is. But if he knows the words, he can speak. It's making up words he finds hard.'

Dawn smiled. Sam and Suzy were friends again. Phew. 'Thanks, Chris. Can you remind them that Sam's next speech therapy session is on Monday?' She was excited as Sam had asked her to go in with him and Suzy. Gillian would come in next. Things were really moving forward.

On her way to their bedroom, she noticed water seeping under the front door. Truffle took a while to settle in his basket as the wind rattled the French windows.

Douglas handed her some keys. 'What are these?'

'The keys to the French windows and the bedroom door. Please hide them so if I wake up in the night, I can't go anywhere.'

The rain lashed the windows and the lights flickered.

'Dammit. I meant to check that the spillway is clear of debris, in case we get a lot of rain,' he said.

'Are you worried about it?'

'There's an amber flood warning. The great British summertime, eh? I'll check it tomorrow first thing.'

Dawn woke to a bang. Maybe it was the wind. She expected it to be daylight but it was still pitch black. Truffle was lying across her legs. She picked up her phone. Two o'clock. She heard something apart from the wind, a sort of rushing sound.

'Douglas, wake up!' She shook him and his head jerked off the pillow. 'What's that noise?' she whispered.

'Foxes.' This was his response to all noises at night. He dropped his head back on the pillow.

'No. It's not the foxes. It's something else. A rushing sound.'

'It's just the wind.'

She needed to wee. She stepped out of bed. Her feet splashed into water. Ankle-deep. 'Douglas! The floor's wet! There's water everywhere! Douglas, wake up!' She flicked the switch on the bedside lamp but it didn't light.

He stirred and sat up. 'Christ! We're flooding!' He jumped out of bed.

'What shall we do?' Dawn asked. She was glad of the dark so he couldn't see her wringing her hands and rocking from foot to foot. She sat on the bed and tried to breathe.

## CHAPTER 72

This was the downside of living in a listed stately home, Anastasia thought, as the wind rattled the bedroom windows and the rain slashed the flimsy panes. 'A month's worth of rain in one day,' they'd said on the national news, and cited the West Country as one of the areas to be worst affected. Storm Agatha. Everyone feared a repeat of the Somerset floods. When she'd seen the forecast was for torrential rain, she'd headed home and arrived late last night, too late to see Samuel. She was sure he would have received her message and anyway, she'd see him first thing tomorrow when he came round to do the horses.

The bathroom door was banging in the draught that whooshed up the stairs. Even though she knew full well it was the bathroom door, not the front door, it was disconcerting when you were alone. So far this summer she'd hardly ever been alone; the boys had been home, though now they were at some adventure camp in Scotland for a couple of weeks. Freddie had been coming down every weekend, albeit to see Suzy, the cheating bastard. And to think she'd thought he was coming down more often to see his family! What a naïve bitch. And then recently, Rex had been staying over. Rex in her bed. She savoured the thought and grew agitated at the thought that he was miles away in London.

'Why isn't he here?' she said out loud. If he was, she'd be able to sleep. Nestling beside that big strong body made her calm and secure. She hadn't realised before Rex came along that she was insecure. Years of living with philandering Freddie had sparked that personality defect. She wondered whether she should text him. But they'd only finished having text sex an hour ago and she didn't want to seem too clingy. Clingy! Her, Anastasia, clingy! What a joke.

A loud sound of splashing water added to the cacophony. Great. The gutter above her bedroom was now over-flowing onto the paving below. She wondered whether the Mill was affected. It was vulnerable as it lay in the valley and in heavy rains water ran off the hills in streams. She'd seen it flood twice from natural causes and once from sabotage. She flushed hot with shame when she thought of how she'd contrived the flood at the Mill last year, and only last week had asked Samuel to do it again. Thank God she'd called him off. She'd almost told Dawn the other night, when she was pissed. How would Rex take the news that, like some Victorian villain, her obsession with the Mill had led her to cause criminal damage and blame an innocent mute? It didn't mesh well with the whole damsel in distress thing she had going.

A rumble of thunder. She'd been to check the horses in the stables when she'd arrived home – Samuel must have brought them in earlier that day – but they would be spooked. Hell, she couldn't sleep anyway, she may as well go and see if they were all right; she felt like company. She pulled on a jumper and leggings, grabbed a jacket and slipped on wellies before heading out the back door. Coco, Mocha and Sprinkles wagged their tails and peeked up at her out of the corner of their eyes but didn't move from their cosy basket. 'I know. I'm mad,' she said to them as she pulled up her hood, switched on the outside light and took the torch from the hook by the door.

Rain hit her full in the face, sharp as needles. There must have been a hole in her wellies as one of her feet was soaked after two steps. Clouds raced across the moon and she saw a lake had formed on the fifty metres of paving between the back of the house and the stables. It was worse than she'd thought. She'd never seen water collect there in the forty-six years she'd lived here. Gingerly, she made her way across the lake pulling her legs through the water. She opened the door to the stable block, turned on a light. The horses blinked and flashed the whites of their eyes at a roll of thunder. Symphony whinnied and Swallow spun around in her stable. 'Whoa, steady.' She scooped horse-nuts from a bin, emptied them into two buckets, stroked their necks and soothed them. She inspected the ceiling; no water coming through. She jumped at another crack of thunder. The lights went out, plunging them into darkness.

As she walked out of the stables, the wind whipped off her hood. She shone the torch at the roof and saw the downpipe had come away, and water was pouring from the guttering on to the paving. Underfoot, she felt the crunch of slates. Bother. She'd have to find someone to fix that tomorrow. Searching for more damage, she walked to the front of the house and saw it was clear of water. Luckily, the lawn sloped away from the Manor towards the ha-ha which must be filling up like a moat. She looked down the valley towards Last Chance Mill. When the clouds cleared from the moon she saw a glint in the valley below. Water? Was it flooding? Shit. Don't say Samuel hadn't got her messages and he'd opened the sluice gate. She had to find him. Now. And warn D and D. She felt sick.

She turned and ran back towards the house but skidded on a slate and slammed to the ground. Ow! Her wrist took the force of the fall and pain shot through her ankle. She was struggling to stand when her phone pinged from inside her pocket. She fumbled to retrieve it with her good hand. It was Rex: approaching Exeter. Be with you soon. Can't bear to think of you alone in the storm.

He'd be here in an hour but that wasn't soon enough. She checked her contacts and made a call.

## CHAPTER 73

Sam paced his room, headphones on, saying Eminem's words in his head. It was like the guy really got him. Words will come. He'll ask Suzy out. He's got one shot. She'll be so shocked she might just say, yeah.

Thunder cracked over the music and he yanked off the headphones. Three days ago, the buzzing in his head had signalled a storm. He missed the horses. Because of the rain, he'd hardly been up the Manor at all. All he did was muck out the stables and feed them every morning. He needed to be with them, to smooth his hands over their flanks and down their knobbly legs, to lean against their warm bulk and nuzzle their muzzles, to breathe in the warm, oatey smell of them. He should have called in to see them after he left the Mill, but it was raining hard and he'd wanted to get home.

Rain splattered the window. He threw it open and the wind caught it and slammed it back against the wall. Clouds raced across the sky. He hated the rain but loved the wind. The wind was a wild stallion, rearing and careering. Reaching outside to pull the window shut, rain slapped him in the face. His eyes closed, he let it lash him. Awesome.

He was outside. Walking. His headphones on, his mouth wrapped round Eminem's words. Some of them were rude but his speech therapist didn't mind. The wind buffeted him across the road making him stagger the way Nigel did when he was pissed. He would call in at the stables, then climb the hill to be nearer the flashes and crashes. He threw back his head so the rain lashed his eyes, his cheeks, his useless mouth.

He climbed the wall rather than the spikey metal gate but his usual foot-holes were slippery and he fell the last bit. He crouched on all fours, waiting for the sensor to pick him up, for the lights to flash on but nothing happened. There'd been no lights in the cottages either. He hadn't tried the lights at home in case he woke his mum. Maybe the power was down. He turned right before reaching the house and cut through to the stables. The horses were spooked. He went over to Symphony and stroked her neck, breathed words in her ear. Swallow wasn't so easy but he managed to calm her. He looked up sharply as a torch shone in his face. It was Her. She was leaning on a stick.

'Samuel! Thank God. The Mill is flooding. Did you open the sluice gate?'

Samuel stopped breathing. Flooding? He couldn't look at Her. She would be angry with him now. He had opened it. He'd sneaked into the mill, grabbed the handle and stuffed it inside his jacket. But when he'd got to the gate and started to turn the screw and water had rushed through, he'd known it weren't right and shut it again. He'd left it open a bit. As he'd found it. Don't say he hadn't shut it enough.

'Well? Did you? Tell me!'

He moved his head a little.

'No? You didn't do it?'

He shook his head harder and became aware of a ringing in his ears.

She breathed out heavily and looked relieved. 'Thank God. You got my text then?'

He shook his head again. He hadn't seen his phone for a couple of days. So he'd done the right thing after all. Doing nothing had been the right thing to do.

'I've been trying to reach Dawn and Douglas but the phone line is down. I need you to run down and check they're awake. I think the Mill is flooding. If the sluice gate is closed it must be that the river is swollen and there may be fallen trees and branches caught under the bridge, like er ...before. Also the leat will be overflowing with all the water running off the hills so first check that the little bridge over the spillway isn't blocked with branches. The rope we used last time is in a backpack the garden room. That might be useful.

Can you do that? I'd go myself but I've twisted my ankle and it's swelling up. Rex is on his way but God knows what the roads are like.'

Samuel nodded. She winced and tears streamed down Her cheeks and he had a feeling it wasn't just the pain from her ankle making her cry. Maybe She was remembering the last time too, the wicked thing they done. When he'd opened the sluice gate and together they'd dragged branches to the bridge and dammed the river.

'Thank you, Samuel, for everything. What would I do without you?' They locked eyes. He wanted to whisper in Her ear until She was calm, as if She were a wounded animal. But She wasn't. She was his boss. He stepped away. He set off at a jog towards the Mill.

She was giving him a chance to make things right.

## CHAPTER 74

'Dawn, go and wake Chris. I need him outside. But tell him to be careful.' Douglas stood on the bed and pulled on his jeans. He watched Dawn spinning around looking for her clothes. 'I'll take the torch. Use the torch on your phone.'

He grabbed his waterproof and paddled out to the hallway. The torch beam illuminated reddish-brown water spurting in on either side of the front door. It reached above his ankles and, through the sitting room door, he saw it had covered the pale carpet and stained the bottom of the furniture. He felt sick. Had someone opened the sluice gate? Or had the river risen? He should have bought sandbags. Idiot. He must focus. He knew he had to act fast but he didn't know what to do. Think! Think!

He waded through the kitchen to the utility room where he found his wellies, floating. Water was spurting in the back door too. How deep was it out there? He felt short of breath. Couldn't think straight. He paddled through the dining room, moved a chair to the window, climbed out and splashed down. He shone his torch. The level of the river was so high that little streams were channelling towards the house. Distracted by a loud splashing sound, he waded round to the side of the house. Water was cascading over the millwheel, and the spillway was overflowing and pouring down the slope towards the house. Why wasn't it draining into the river?

His torch picked up a figure at the little bridge across the spillway. Samuel. He was using a spade to drag out twigs and branches that must have been washed down the leat in the storm and had jammed under the bridge and were damming the spillway.

'Good thinking, Sam.' Douglas shouted above the howl of the wind. 'What can I do?'

Samuel picked up a heavy iron bar, handed it to Douglas and motioned him to use it to dislodge the debris from the other side. He pulled out some twigs and small branches and began to attack a large branch with the bar, trying to prise it away from the bridge. The force of the water conspired against him but he kept on battering. It occurred to him that the footbridge across the river might be blocked too. If they cleared this blockage, the water would drain into the river and raise it even higher. He needed to check the footbridge but he also needed to keep clearing this one. They needed another pair of hands. He looked around desperately, willing someone to materialise. What if Dawn was having a panic attack and hadn't been able to wake Chris? He dialled Chris's number even though he knew he had no signal. Then his torch light flickered and died.

# CHAPTER 75

'Chris, wake up. We're flooding. Get dressed and come outside. Chris?' Dawn shook him awake. She wished Carl was there too for another pair of hands.

'What the hell, Mum?'

'Chris, get up. We're flooding.'

'Shit! OK, OK. I'll get dressed. Where's Dad?'

'He's outside. I'm going out now.'

She ran downstairs, shone her phone torch and gasped at the sight of water spurting through the front door. She was afraid to open it. She splashed up the hallway, across the kitchen to the utility room, grabbed her waterproof and fished out her wellies. Chris came in, grabbed his trainers and they climbed through the dining room window which had a chair underneath. Outside, the moon was hidden by clouds and it was pitch black. Rain slapped her face, water sucked her wellies. The first thing that struck her was the furious roar of the wind. She shone her torch towards the river. It was alarmingly high but she couldn't see anyone. She followed Chris round the side of the house. Water was splashing down from the top of the millwheel. Streams ran towards her, pooling around the house. Her torch beam lit up Douglas, Chris and Sam beside the little bridge over the spillway. Someone shouted but the words were lost as a gust of wind almost knocked her off her feet. Douglas's arm landed on her shoulders.

'Dawn, we need to check the bridge across the river in case it's blocked too. Can you carry on clearing this one? Work from this side so when it clears you're not washed down with it. Can you do that? Is your torch working?'

'Yes. Yes. Be careful.'

He handed her an iron bar and she began to bash the branches. The muddy water reached her knees and filled her wellies. The smell was disgusting. She shone her torch and noticed pieces of tissue floating by. Where had they come from? Then it hit her: the septic tank. She was standing in sewage. Dizzying panic stopped her breath and turned her bones to jelly. The bar dropped in the water. The urge to be sick was overwhelming but imagining that pooling around her knees quelled it. Panic fractured her thoughts. The sob that broke from her chest jolted her back to reality. Douglas was relying on her. She couldn't let him down. How would she live with herself if she couldn't do this one thing?

'You can do it,' she said aloud as she plunged her hand into the filth and felt around for the iron bar. Her fingers curled around it and she drew it out. She got into a rhythm, one two three bash, one two three bash, until she had severed the smaller branches anchoring it to the bridge. If she pulled it from the other side, it would surely come free with the force of the water behind it. She reached under the bridge and tugged the branch. At first it didn't shift. Another tug and she felt it move towards her. A sudden rush swept her down the spillway like a stick in a stream. She lost one boot, then another. She clawed at the stone walls, feeling for purchase, fearing she'd end up in the river. Bam! Her chest smacked into something. It knocked the breath from her. She raised her hands. It was a tree; one of the willow saplings had fallen in the storm. She hooked her arms over it, relieved when her feet touched solid ground. Water swirled around her thighs. Her lip stung and she tasted blood. She tried to haul herself out but feared letting go of the tree. How long could she hang on here?

# CHAPTER 76

Stood on top of the bridge, Douglas could see that downstream, the level of the river was lower than upstream where the water was almost level with the top of the stone arches. There must be a blockage. He shone his phone torch and saw branches and twigs sticking out. His hunch had been right. Little streams were veering off the river and coursing down the slope towards the Mill. Douglas looked around hopelessly. How could they clear a tree that was submerged?

Sam was scrabbling around in his backpack and pulled out a coiled rope. Of course, he'd dammed this bridge with branches before. Hopefully, he knew what he was doing. Douglas and Chris exchanged looks as Sam tied a rope around his waist and handed them the end. Then he took another coil of rope and hooked it over his shoulder.

'Is this safe, Sam?' Douglas yelled above the racket of the river. Sam nodded and they followed him down the bank. They held onto the rope as Sam edged along the side of the bridge, the water up to his chest. Douglas gripped the rope and gave Chris a worried glance.

'He can prop himself against the stone supports, Dad. The force of the water is virtually pinning him to the side.'

Sam took the rope from his shoulder and ventured out towards the arch. He passed the end of the rope around something below the surface, appeared to have secured it, then edged back towards them, struggling against the current. Douglas heaved a sigh of relief when he made it to knee high water. Sam handed him the rope and he passed it around a hefty tree trunk.

'OKK?' Sam stammered, his hair plastered to his head.

'OK,' Douglas yelled. 'You want us to heave yes?'

Sam nodded furiously.

'Ready?' They all grabbed a section of rope as if it were a tug o' war. 'One two three, heave.' The tree didn't budge. Douglas had no idea how big it was but they were pulling not just the weight of the tree but also the force of the water. They tried again. It didn't budge. The enormity of their task hit him. His chest was aching. His boots were full of water and his clothes heavy and sodden.

'One final effort,' he shouted. Thank God he had two fit young men with him. 'One, two, three, heave...' The rope moved. Had the tree shifted a little? Or had the rope just slipped through his fingers? His knees felt weak and his arms ached. He felt a hand on his shoulder, turned and there stood Rex. What the hell was he doing here? A new wave of energy rushed through him. Then other figures slid down the bank towards them, shouting and joshing. The Pooks brothers. Douglas almost teared up. They seized the rope and all of them began to haul. With seven of them pulling, the tree inched away from the bridge towards them. The smaller branches that had been trapped in the tree were now swept downstream as the water coursed under the bridge. The river sucked at his legs and he feared losing his footing and scrambled up the bank. The level began to subside. They all bent over, panting.

'Well done, everyone,' Douglas spluttered between gasps of breath 'Thank you!'

The clouds cleared and moonlight shone on the river and everyone stared at it transfixed. 'We left Dawn clearing the bridge over the spillway. I'd better go find her.'

He and Chris crossed the footbridge and splashed towards the house, relieved to see that there were now fewer streams running off the river. As they approached the spillway, he noticed that it was no longer overflowing but channelling down to the river. Dawn must have cleared the blockage. There was no sign of her at the bridge.

'Maybe she's back inside the house,' Douglas said to Chris.

They met everyone in the kitchen where someone had lit candles. Sam was sweeping mud out the back door, Rex was filling the kettle, and Tony and his brothers were examining the damage.

'Anyone seen Dawn?' Douglas asked. They shook their heads.

He walked through the house throwing open doors and calling her name. She had to be here somewhere. He stood in the kitchen doorway, shaking or shivering, he couldn't tell which, 'I can't find her.'

No one spoke. They rushed for the door and Douglas shone the torch.

'Let's spread out. But be careful.'

'Dawn!' he yelled into the dark but the wind whipped away his words. 'Where are you?'

'Mum!' Chris called, his cries growing fainter as he disappeared into the dark. The rain had turned to drizzle but the wind was bending the trees. Clouds covered the moon and Douglas scanned the blackness, refusing to give in to his mounting fears. What if she'd been swept down the spillway into the river? He blinked back tears. He should never have asked her to take over. If anything had happened to her, he was to blame. Above the sound of rushing water he heard a voice.

'O...over here!'

It was coming from further down the spillway. Douglas shone the torch and picked out Sam and next to him, clinging to a fallen tree, was Dawn.

'Thank God!' He rushed over, bent down and hooked his arm around her shoulders. 'Let's get you back to the house.' She clung on to the tree.

Rex and Chris appeared. 'Mum! Are you alright?'

'I can't feel my legs...can't move them...so cold,' she said.

'Let go of the tree with one arm and hold on around my shoulders.'

She gripped him round his neck, then released her other arm and he and Chris hauled her out. She could hardly stand, let alone walk.

Sam bent over and raised his arms away from his sides. 'P p…piggy back?' They all stared at him in amazement. It was Sam's voice they'd heard calling earlier. Douglas started to laugh, so did Sam and then they all were laughing.

# CHAPTER 77

'Thanks, Chris,' said Dawn as he put a plate of sausage, bacon and eggs in front of her. Truffle trotted over and sat on her feet. He seemed the only one unscathed by the flood. That morning, after Douglas had left, she'd wandered from room to room, numbed by the extent of the damage. A house without people was a shell of bricks and mortar, or so she'd thought. But this one seemed to have a will of its own, a resistance to civilisation. They'd made the Mill habitable and filled it with people: first her and Douglas, then the Pooks, then the kids, then the guests. But now the house had reverted to its previous derelict state, as if that were its true, untameable nature. It had existed long before them and would exist long after. It knew how to survive. It chewed people up and spat them out.

'I thought it was a good idea to eat what's in the fridge before it goes off. I'll leave Dad's in the Aga.'

Dawn winced as she cut the bacon. Who'd have thought you used chest muscles for so many actions? There was a huge bruise where she'd smacked into the tree. Chris had already placed painkillers on the table and she swallowed two. The heating was on full blast and sodden, muddy clothes steamed on the radiators making the kitchen smell of wet dog.

Chris sat down opposite her. 'So what time did the fire brigade go?'

'About four. They were brilliant. Pumped out all the water. They were hunky guys. Shame I wasn't looking my best.'

'Yeah, they were quite fit,' said Chris.

How odd, talking about fit guys with her son.

Dawn heard the front door open and Chris pulled another plate out of the Aga as Douglas walked in. 'Full English?'

321

'Chris, you are a life saver.' Douglas sat down and poured himself a cup of tea. They looked at him expectantly. 'Well, the news from the outside world is that Luke and Tony will be over this afternoon to test the electrics and try and get the electricity back on. But, in the meantime, Anastasia says to take our frozen food round to hers. The Manor roof is damaged. She's sprained her ankle but she's OK. She's got Rex running around after her. And Sam turned up early to do the horses.'

'Did you see John and Andy?' Chris asked.

'Yes. They said there was no need to go in until we've got things sorted here.'

'But can we get things sorted?' Dawn asked. 'By tomorrow? That's when the guests arrive. I mean just look at the place!' She gestured at the brown tidemarks on the walls and the muddy flagstones. The carpet in their sitting room was ruined and the laminate floor in their bedroom was lifting. Not to mention the smell.

'We could email them, explain what's happened. Cancel or postpone,' Chris said. 'It's three couples and a single, isn't it?'

'We could cancel, but we'll lose two and a half grand. What do you both think?' Douglas looked at Dawn as if he were really asking what she thought.

Chris broke the silence. 'Well, I think we should, like try and get it sorted. We only need to clean up the areas the guests use. And the studio's fine, the upstairs is fine.'

'Dawn?' Douglas reached across the table and took her hand.

Two pairs of eyes looked at her expectantly. She'd been prepared to accept that it was all over, that to clear up in a day was an impossible task and they were too exhausted to do it anyway. But here were Chris and Douglas with their positive energy. A sob rose in her throat but she swallowed it. 'I say, I say let's go for it!'

'Yay!' they exclaimed, but heir smiles faded as they looked around the kitchen. Douglas reached for the pain killers.

Dawn left them cleaning up and squelched back and forth over the footbridge to the parking area with bags of frozen food. The river was red with soil, the same colour that stained the lower walls and floor of the house. She admired Chris and Douglas's positive attitude but who knew what damage they couldn't see? Under the floor, the replaced joists in the cottage would be soaked again, the wiring would have to be checked and possibly re-done and the plumbing needed attention by the smell of it. A fluttering started in her chest and moved to her throat and spilled out in a low-pitched wail she hardly recognised as hers. All their hard work and all their money spent. She thought of Douglas's sad expression as he'd moved furniture out of the rooms, and wailed some more. She might be keeping a brave face in front of Douglas and Chris but it was a relief to let out what she was really feeling.

The electronic gates of Dartcoombe Manor stood open. Dawn noticed debris on the ground and looked up at a hole about three metres across in the roof. At least the Mill's roof had stood up to the winds; that was one advantage of being in a valley, they weren't so exposed. Mary came out, led her to a chest freezer in the garage and helped her unload. Dawn made a fuss of Truffle's mum, his sister and brother.

'Come on through,' she heard Anastasia call as she walked in the back door. She looked around the pristine kitchen as she slipped off her boots and coat, absorbed the heat of the Aga. Anastasia lay on the damask settee, her foot resting on a cushion and covered in an ice pack, an arm in a sling. She flung aside a glossy magazine. 'Is it too early to start drinking? I've never been so bored. Rex is exercising the horses. I can't even ride.'

Dawn looked at her watch. It was eleven.

'You poor thing. Douglas told me about your ankle. Are you in pain?'

'I'm on pain-killers. Be a dear and check the info inside the box and see if I can drink with them? If not, I'll take an overdose.'

'The roof looks bad,' Dawn said.

'The insurance assessor is coming tomorrow. Rex has filled me in about your place. I was out checking the horses when I saw water lying around the Mill. Luckily, the moon was bright, otherwise I'd never have seen it. Were you all asleep?'

'Yes. I woke up to a bang. Sam told me he'd knocked on our windows so that must have been what I heard. If he hadn't woken us up, I dread to think what would have happened. Thanks for sending everyone over to help. Sam, Rex and the Pooks. Douglas said they couldn't have shifted that tree without them. You've been a great friend.'

Anastasia looked at the floor.

'What is it?'

'It's just I haven't been a good friend.' Anastasia wouldn't make eye contact. Why would she say she wasn't a good friend? Obviously, she couldn't have come herself, not with the sprained ankle. She read the information on the box of pills.

'Alcohol is permitted,' she said.

'Thank God. Anyway, enough of the moaning...'

Dawn bristled. It was all very well for her to say, enough of the moaning when she had insurance and was loaded. 'You know we don't have insurance,' Dawn reminded her as she poured two shots of vodka. 'We couldn't afford it, not with the history of flooding.'

Anastasia's eyes flashed wide. She sniffed and downed her shot. 'It was an awful storm. Look at that.' Anastasia held out a newspaper.

On the front page was a photo of the railway line at Dawlish. Massive waves had undermined the track and swept it away. Then she saw the date at the top of the page. 'Oh my God. Today is our wedding anniversary. I'd completely forgotten.'

'Really? Congratulations. How many years?'

'Twenty-five.' Dawn handed Anastasia the pain killers.

'That's quite an achievement.'

'Achievement? It's a bloody miracle!'

'Anyway,' said Anastasia washing down the pills with another shot. 'I've had an idea. Your guests arrive tomorrow, yes?'

Dawn downed her shot. It was madness to think they could cope with seven guests. They might not even have electricity.

'I know how hard this must be for you with your CND.'

'OCD,' Dawn corrected with a half-laugh despite her misery.

'Whatever. Well, I'm suggesting that they stay here until you get your place ship-shape.'

Dawn looked up, confused.

'We have enough beds and bathrooms. You and Mary can cook their meals here and Douglas can take them out on excursions, or over to the studio if it's still sodding raining. All I ask is that you help Mary make up the beds as I can't do a thing.'

'I don't know what to say. Are you sure?'

'Very sure. You need the business and I get the company, so we all win.'

'Thank you,' Dawn said, wiping away a tear. 'I left the others trying to make the Mill habitable. But if the electricity isn't fixable we might have to take up your offer.'

'Excellent. Now stop snivelling and pour us another shot. That last one didn't hit the spot at all.'

She thought of them slaving away at the Mill and suddenly needed to be with them. 'I'd better not. I should get back.' Then she remembered Anastasia's comment. 'What did you mean? What you said earlier? About not being a good friend?'

Anastasia rubbed her forehead and still wouldn't meet Dawn's eyes. 'I did something.' She screwed up her face. 'I regret it so much.'

Dawn shifted uneasily. Not more bad news. If she were about to say that something had happened between her and Douglas, she didn't want to hear it.

'If I don't tell you when I'm on the truth formula of vodka and codeine, I fear I never will so here goes. I … it was me that caused the flood last year… not Samuel … I mean … he did it, but he was only doing what I asked.'

Dawn perked up. 'You mean the flood before we moved in? Why?'

'I wanted to put off buyers. Force the Pooks to sell to me. Bring Last Chance Mill back on to the estate. My father sold it to cover death duties and I always wanted to get it back.'

'Why didn't you just buy it when it was up for sale?'

'They wouldn't sell it to me. Because of the dispute between our two families.'

'What dispute?'

'My father sold the Mill to Edward Pooks, father of the brothers you know. The property had a considerable orchard back then and Eddie took out a share in the local cider press with a view to bottling and selling it but drank most of it himself. Things went from bad to worse and he lost his job as a postman. My father took pity on the family and employed him. Well, one evening he was driving the tractor, shifting hay bales, when the tractor tipped over. He was killed instantly. We had insurance, but following a medical report, it wouldn't pay up. There was an unacceptable amount of alcohol in his bloodstream. The Pooks blamed my father, claimed the job was too dangerous and the tractor was faulty. It wasn't of course but they still blame us for his death.'

'Poor Edward Pooks. What a tragedy. So if the Pooks had sold to you, there would have been no need to flood the place.'

'That's right.'

'Everyone thinks Sam is responsible for that flood. The poor lad has been maligned.'

'I've been trying to make it up to him ever since. If the Pooks had known it was me who did it, they would have prosecuted. I'd have ended up in jail. I still could, if you decide to tell them the truth. I wouldn't blame you. But the Pooks believed it was Samuel. And when I threatened to tell the authorities about them smoking out the bats, they backed off.'

Dawn's head was spinning. She wanted to hate Anastasia, but looking at the injured woman on the settee, she couldn't. 'You did that before you met us. I feel bad for Sam, but I don't feel betrayed by you.'

'And I objected to your application for commercial use.'

'But they let us have it anyway.'

'Yes, but I appealed though I did withdraw it. Later.'

Dawn's head was reeling. Anastasia had known them by then. 'We heard it had been withdrawn…'

'There's one other thing.'

Dawn was on the edge of her seat. This was it. The confession she'd been expecting.

Anastasia swallowed and met Dawn's eyes. 'I called in the hygiene inspector.'

'Oh!' Dawn couldn't help the note of pleasant surprise in her voice. 'Anything else?'

'No. That's it.' A puzzled look crossed Anastasia's face. 'I'm so sorry. I'll make it up to you. Truly.'

'Do you still want the Mill? We'll probably have to sell. Tony's giving us an estimate for the damage later and I doubt we'll be able to afford the repairs.'

'No, I don't want it. Since the business with Freddie, I've realised there are more important things in life. If Douglas hadn't tipped me off about those Picassos I might have lost the entire estate. I want you to stay. I like having you as friends, as neighbours and you've made such a success of the business. Can you ever forgive me?'

She suspected Anastasia's lawyer would have warned her not to accept Freddie's valuation and demand her own. But now she understood Anastasia's offer to put up their guests. She didn't have to feel so grateful. Anastasia owed her, and that was not a bad feeling.

'I forgive you. I had a feeling you were up to something. But I don't know if…if we can still be friends.'

Anastasia looked at the floor. 'I understand. I took a risk in telling you. I valued our friendship too much to lie to you. And I haven't told Rex. It's a bit early in the relationship to reveal major personality defects.'

Poor Rex. Anastasia should come with a health warning. 'Dishonesty is not a good basis for any relationship,' Dawn said. She remembered how she'd felt when Douglas had kept things from her.

'Does it count if I did all those things before I knew Rex?'

Dawn raised her eyebrows.

'OK. I'll tell him soon. I promise.' She took a large slug of vodka.

Something Anastasia had said had plunged Dawn into gloom. 'But we haven't made a success of it,' she uttered.

'Ah,' said Anastasia, 'But it's not over yet.'

# CHAPTER 78

A beaten up pickup and a dented white van were parked at the Mill. Out front, their sitting room carpet, only three weeks old, lay in the mud, sodden and stained. A dark mist of pessimism hung over her. She pushed the front door, preparing for the worst, and stopped dead.

Sam and his brother Josh, the one who'd given them the lift to A and E that night, were on their hands and knees in the hallway, soaking up water with towels and squeezing them into a bowl. In the cottage sitting room, Chris was mopping the floorboards using a giant metal bucket. Luke Pooks crossed the hall and poked around in the fuse box. 'Morning, Dawn,' he said, taking off his baseball cap, scratching his head and pausing to stare at Suzy as she came down the stairs looking flushed.

'Hi Dawn. I've made up the beds. One single and three doubles like Chris said.' She shot Luke a disparaging look.

'That's marvellous, thank you, Suzy.' Dawn followed her along the hallway, smiling as Suzy patted Sam on the head and he grinned up at her.

'Hi Sam, Josh. Thank you so much for helping out,' Dawn said, edging around them. 'Sam, you were great last night. We couldn't have managed without you.'

'Nnno ppproblem,' Sam said. Josh grinned at him.

'Oh, there you are Dawn!' said Gillian Grimes as Dawn walked into the kitchen. She was filling up the Aga kettle at the sink. 'I brought the lads round to help. Josh and Sam are cleaning the flags. They'll come up lovely, best flooring in a flood. Nigel and Dan are outside clearing the branches and muck.' Gillian's face gleamed with sweat, the radiators were on full blast.

'I don't know what to say,' Dawn said.

'You don't need to say nothing,' Gillian said placing the kettle on the hot plate. She grasped Dawn's wrist, her eyes round with surprise and spoke in a whisper. 'You've done wonders for that boy, Dawn. He's speaking! Only words, but it's a start. Our Sam!'

Dawn beamed. She loved Gillian more than anyone else in the world at that moment. 'What can I do to help?'

'See that tin of paint over there? Mat Pooks dropped it off. It'll cover them brown tide marks on the walls. You could make a start. How does that sound?'

Dawn thought it sounded better than anything she'd ever heard.

'I'm going to make tea and sandwiches for everyone. Chris said it was all right to use food from the fridge?'

'Yes, of course. Gillian. Thank you. I never expected…'

Gillian waved her hand dismissively 'What? That country folk wouldn't rally round? You may be blow-ins, Dawn, but you belong here now.' She walked to the doorway, drying her hands on her apron. 'Suzy!' she yelled down the corridor. 'Stop distracting my boys and come 'ere and help Dawn with the painting.'

Chris walked in carrying the bucket and mop. 'Hiya, Mum. Great isn't it? It's like some crazy make-over show. Dad's outside with Tony Pooks. He's been there ages.'

Dawn felt sick at the mention of Tony's name. They might be able to manage a cosmetic job in time for the arrival of their next guests but there was serious damage to be fixed.

Dawn was crouching down, painting the wall in the dining room when Douglas walked in. She saw immediately that it was bad news. He hadn't shaved yet and purple shadows circled his eyes. She hugged him. The way he clung to her she knew it was even worse than they'd expected. He was shaking and she realised he was sobbing. He was the strong one; she'd never thought he'd be the one to break down but the Mill meant so much to him. 'There, there,' she said. 'We'll manage. Don't get upset. It looks as if we'll be ready in time for the next guests anyway.'

'Even with the money we'll have coming in this summer, we'll still fall way short. It's not just the repairs inside. We need to desilt the leat to make it deeper. And raise the bridges so trees and branches can't get stuck again. It was the storm that caused the flood this time. The sluice gates were closed and doing their job.'

'Do you think we'd get a bank loan?'

'No. I tried a few banks when we were running out of cash before. So we wouldn't have to max our credit cards.'

Dawn held him tighter and he winced. 'Ouch! My ribs are killing me. I'm too old for all this physical stuff, Dawn.'

'I know. I could hardly walk this morning. Thank God, the youth are rallying round. We have to put on a brave face, Douglas. They think everything's going to be OK. Let's keep up the pretence for a bit at least.'

'Keep up morale, you mean.'

'Exactly. It breaks my heart to see everyone beavering away when I know it's all for nothing.' She stroked his hair. 'Happy Anniversary, by the way.'

'You too. I have a painting for you but God knows where it is.'

'And I have a gift for you too.'

'I doubt that very much.'

'OK, you're right. I don't. I completely forgot. I give you the gift of honesty.'

They worked until it grew too dark to see. Suzy had a pub shift and the Grimes left with their buckets, mops and towels. After she'd waved them goodbye, Dawn flicked the hall light switch out of habit before she remembered. Luke was still scurrying around the house testing fuses and sockets.

She lit candles. In the fading light, shadows loomed from every corner and lurked down every passageway. Someone had mopped the floor in their bedroom and dried off Truffle's bed. She lay down for a moment and fell asleep.

She awoke to the aroma of pizza. Chris was in the kitchen drinking beer and making salad. After pouring herself a glass of red wine, she laid the table for three.

'Any news from Becky and Barney?' She asked Chris. It seemed an age since they'd gone but it was only two days ago.

'Nothing yet,' said Chris. 'She's not posted anything on the internet yet but maybe there isn't any where she is. The hostels are pretty basic.'

Douglas stumbled into the kitchen. 'So sorry. I fell asleep on the settee. When I woke, it was pitch black and I couldn't think where the hell I was.'

'Here, have some pain killer,' Dawn said handing him a glass of wine. She caught his eye and gave him an over-bright smile. He understood immediately.

'Well, isn't this splendid,' he said, sitting down as Chris sliced pizza and doled salad.

'Indeed,' agreed Dawn, loving their new in-denial personas. 'Can you cut a piece for Luke? He's been here hours. And take him a beer.'

'I enjoyed today,' said Chris. 'Good teamwork. It reminded me of school, but with Sam's mum playing the head teacher. She's even bossier than you, Mum. I wish Becky and Barney had been here. They won't believe what's happened.'

Dawn tried not to think about Becky. Why had she still not texted?

## CHAPTER 79

As they were clearing away the plates they heard a knock at the door. Dawn took a candle and went to open it.

'Surprise!' Anastasia and Rex stood on the doorstep, she leaning on a crutch and Rex holding a dark mess of something sliding off a plate.

'What's that? Dawn asked.

'What do you mean, what's that? It's an anniversary cake,' said Anastasia. 'My first. Well, actually it's my second. I dropped the first one on the floor and the dogs ate it.'

Rex handed it to her with an apologetic smile.

'Look what Anastasia's made,' Dawn said placing it on the table. It was much higher on one side than the other and a gooey mess was leaking off the plate. Chris found a knife and started cutting it. Douglas found a bottle of Prosecco and brought over glasses.

'Hmm. It's a bit sloppy. I may have added a tad too much whisky,' Anastasia said as Chris swapped the knife for a spoon.

'I didn't think whisky was a cake ingredient,' Douglas observed.

'Freddie left bottles of the stuff and no one drinks it so I've got to use it for something,' Anastasia retorted. She raised her glass, 'Happy Anniversary!'

There followed a silence while everyone ate the whisky-chocolatey mess and made polite noises.

'So did the Pooks give you an estimate?' Anastasia asked licking her fingers. Trust her to break the spell, thought Dawn. 'I must say it doesn't look too bad. Rex, you must have been exaggerating.'

'We've had massive help today,' said Chris. 'From Samuel's family and–'

'We've managed to patch the place up,' Dawn cut in quickly, afraid Chris might mention Suzy. 'But thanks for your offer to house our guests.'

'Not at all. What about long-term repairs?'

Dawn looked across at Douglas.

'It's not good news,' he told them. 'Tony's estimate is more than we can afford. We'll have to sell.'

The words cut through Dawn like a knife. Even though she'd known, it sounded brutal. Chris shifted uncomfortably. She looked at her lap.

Rex raised his hand. 'Hold your horses, there. We came over not just to bring cake, though it was delicious, we came over to make you a business proposition.'

Dawn's head jerked up.

'While we were in London, Anastasia had an idea. She suggested my employees could benefit from team-building art-breaks. The Company directors have agreed that, from September to December, we could bring groups of up to ten down for long weekends. They're happy to pay five thousand sterling a pop. And here's the good part. As soon as you invoice the Company, they'll pay some of the cash up front to seal the deal.'

Figures whirred around her head. 'But Rex, after all the chaos of Last Chance Mill, are you sure you want more?'

'Well, for you, with the flood and all, it's been a nightmare. But I've had a great time here. And I don't need to tell you that I love coming down to Dartcoombe.' He smiled at Anastasia who actually simpered. Dawn suspected she hadn't yet told Rex about her scheming. 'You take the time you need to get the work done, then we'll start the trips. Even if it's not finished. I don't give a monkey's.'

Douglas burst out laughing. 'I don't know what to say.'

'I think what he means is, thank you,' said Dawn. She looked over at Anastasia. Were those tears glistening in her eyes? 'And thank you,' she said to Anastasia. 'You are a great friend.'

'It's marvellous news. Marvellous,' Douglas was saying. He turned to Dawn. 'We can ask Tony to start work on the house at the end of August when our bookings finish. They can work Mondays to Thursdays. Rex's teams can come on Thursday nights and stay until Sunday.'

The lights flashed on to a triumphant cry from Luke. Everyone cheered and blinked. In the light, Dawn could see her painting hadn't quite covered the brown marks on the walls. But now it didn't matter. They could get through the next weeks and then do it properly. Chris plugged in his phone. Bye-bye conversation, she thought.

Luke appeared in the doorway. 'All fixed. But don't use any low sockets until Tony's hacked off the plaster and dried out the walls. I've started the de-humidifiers.'

Dawn walked over and planted a kiss on Luke's cheek. 'Reckon it's my lucky night,' he said as Anastasia limped over and handed him a plate of cake.

'You haven't tried it yet,' murmured Douglas.

Luke took a mouthful. 'Blimey. I won't be able to get behind the wheel after this.'

'Becky's calling!' Chris cried.

Relief washed over Dawn. Becky was alive and well, Last Chance Mill was saved, Chris was thriving, Douglas was happy and she was feeling pretty good about the world. As Douglas and Chris positioned themselves in front of the screen she heard her daughter say, 'I'm missing you all so much. Where's Mum?'

'I'm here, sweetheart.' She leant across so Becky could see her face.

'Ahh, you're all there. How are you coping without me? I bet the place has completely fallen apart.'

'Of course it has!' said Douglas and everyone laughed.

'It's awesome here. I love it. But we'll be home for Christmas. We can't think of anywhere we'd rather spend it than Last Chance.'

'That's good to hear,' Dawn said as Douglas leant into her and rested his head against hers. 'We're not going anywhere.'

## Acknowledgements

Thanks to my friend Deborah Kidd-Marks for advising me on the technical details of mill workings. I hope your Mill never floods again, but if it does, I'll be there.

Thanks also to my brilliant CBC alumni group: Clare, Emily, Kate and Mary for all your insights and encouragement. And to Sue for inspiring me with her journey to publication.

# Last Chance Mill

Printed in Great Britain
by Amazon